CRACKERS

You can run, but you can't hide

Beth Woffenden

Beth Woffenden
July 2019

Visit me on t'internet at:

https://www.facebook.com/WofferBooks/
https://twitter.com/WofferBooks

Acknowledgements and author's note

The time has come, once again, to start by offering my thanks to a motley (and not-so-motley) selection of individuals who have helped me to draw this trilogy to its conclusion.

My Olds for cat-sitting during my transatlantic reconnaissance missions, sounding out various ideas and fine-tuning them; Victoria Melia at Hawkeye Proofreading for beating those hyphens into the correct places; The FBI's SSA Joseph Lewis and Linda Watkins for helping me get the Tahoe-Reno procedure correct – and the very helpful lady on reception at Reno's Resident Agency who cleared up its 2009 location for me!

To the three amigos at Lancashire Police's Preston-based Cold Case Unit – Dave Meadows, Lisa Baxter and Ian "Jaffa" McVittie – thanks for all those little snippets which continued to make my fictitious work a little more accurate. I also still owe my Mexican expert in all things Mexican, Claudia Tejeda, a flagon of tequila, although it seems these days she prefers the delights of a chippy tea.

As ever, Absolute Write Water Cooler's plethora of patient experts on all things weird and wonderful never failed to answer my often bizarre queries; it's thanks to them I've come to the conclusion I know nothing about everything (probably the safest thing). And, lastly, anyone else I've shamefully omitted.

As in Nutjob and Fruitcake, there are many instances in the storyline of combining fact and fiction; for example, certain FBI departments and where specific teams of detectives work from. Most of the locations mentioned do actually exist, although I may have fictionalised the finer details of some settings and, to varying degrees, fabricated the interior of almost every building that isn't fictitious. Names, characters, events and incidents are either the products of my imagination or used in a fictitious manner. Any resemblance to actual persons, living or dead, or actual events is purely coincidental.

And with *that* all done and dusted (yet again), all I now can ask is that you please enjoy this final instalment of the Unholy Trilogy (its unofficial name shall no doubt stick until time draws to a close)…

Prologue – Friday 4th September 2009

5.31pm – PDT
Greta's Café, South Lake Tahoe, California

'Two pancakes please, Daddy,' the young girl said, her eyes widening when she spotted an older boy at the adjacent table eagerly tuck into his stacked plate. 'And bananas, and chocolate sauce.'

'You'll have to share with your brother,' her father replied. 'And, I think your eyes are bigger than your tummy.'

'But he always wants to eat my food,' she countered.

Sam Bury fixed his scowling three-year-old daughter in a baleful stare. 'You should share nicely, Angela.' He noticed a server weaving towards them through the closely arranged tables. 'It's only because John wants to copy you.'

The scowl morphed into confusion. 'Why?'

'Because,' he said slowly, mindful to build her curiosity, 'little brothers want to do the same things as their clever big sisters.' Sam turned his attention to the teenage girl in a blue striped dress who now waited uncertainly near their table, hoping her arrival would put an end to Angela's questions.

'Hi,' he said, his smile a fraction wider than necessary. 'I'd like a large filter coffee for myself, please. Then there's an apple juice and the double pancake stack with sliced bananas *and* chocolate sauce for the bottomless pit here, and perhaps we'd better have a separate plate so this little man doesn't rupture the entire café's eardrums.'

Sam thanked her as she scribbled on a pad. A few seconds passed before she smiled at the baby and tucked the pen into her top pocket. 'Mr Cutie-Pie here likes pancakes, huh?'

'He likes whatever we're eating, regardless of whether or not he's already been fed.'

'He steals my food,' Angela announced. 'Daddy says you go to prison if you steal.'

'That doesn't include babies,' Sam clarified for the second time that day. 'He's rather a messy eater, so a couple of extra napkins wouldn't go amiss.'

'You got it!' she replied cheerfully and winked at Angela. 'We make everything fresh, so the pancakes will take around five minutes.'

Sam patted Angela's arm. 'No problem, we always tell her it tastes better if you wait.'

She looked across to where the young woman had begun to prepare their drinks. 'Why aren't you hungry, Daddy?'

'I'm *really* hungry, Angela. Remember how Mommy said she's making something special for me to eat when we get... home.' He was loathe to use that word to describe the cabin where they'd lived for the past three weeks, but maybe he should start to accept that a return to Colorado might never happen. At least the children appeared settled, even if he and Anna still found it difficult to adapt to the change and the circumstances behind it.

'What's she making?'

Sam shrugged, genuinely unable to answer. 'I don't know; she said it's a surprise.'

Angela carefully considered his reply. 'Is it your birthday?'

'No, sweetheart,' he replied, chuckling. 'Mommy said she wanted to make something extra special for me once you two are in bed.'

She huffed her indignation. 'I'm going to bed when we get home?'

'That's the deal. We all agreed on going to the beach, having pancakes and then it's your bedtime.'

Their conversation lulled and allowed a relieved Sam to thank the server as she set down their drinks. John saw Angela pull the juice closer and the quiver in his bottom lip grew until Sam swiftly distracted him with a bottle of water he'd pulled from his backpack.

'Just in time, Daddy.'

'Like I said, he wants to be just like you.'

'What do you and Mommy do when we're asleep?' Angela twirled her pink plastic straw in the clear amber liquid and fixed him in an iron stare.

Sam grinned and felt a tingle of anticipation at the thought of an evening he suspected Anna had been planning for a week or so. 'We have something to eat, tidy up, maybe watch some TV and then go to bed. Nothing exciting, you're not missing much.'

An unexpected shrill ringing curtailed Angela's next question. She watched her father pull a cell phone from his pocket and frown at its illuminated display before answering. Sam repeatedly scanned the café's interior during the hurried conversation, his hushed voice and obvious tension unnerving his daughter.

'What's the matter, Daddy? Was it Mommy?' she asked, her tone wary even though he'd forced a tight smile.

He shook his head, unable to formulate a plausible explanation. 'Not this time,' was all he could manage.

'The police?'

'Yeah,' Sam replied, his smile enough to reassure her. 'Something like that.'

Chapter 1 - Friday 28th August 2009

3.28pm – BST
Hutton, near Preston, England

Martin Boothroyd reclined in his seat and stretched his arms towards the ceiling. 'Any update on how much longer it'll take for the Umpleby DNA to come back?' he asked. 'I know it only went in on Tuesday, but we've paid through the nose for that priority service.'

Fellow Lancashire Constabulary Cold Case Unit detectives Paula Phelan and Dave Sanderson both shrugged in unison at Boothroyd from behind their desks. Since being brought together in 2005, the HQ-based team's remit to reinvestigate and bring closure to unsolved cases stretching back years – if not decades – meant their analysis of two suspicious deaths from 1986 and 1990 had consumed much of the past month's workload. A direct approach from a taskforce comprised of LAPD homicide detectives and FBI agents soon led to their decision to reopen these cold cases, the aim being to identify other possible victims of the internationally famous television and movie star Konrad Kratz.

Boothroyd's initial cynicism surrounding why an American media darling warranted police attention in a mundane town in north-west England lingered, until he learned Konrad Kratz was really Preston-born *Peter Konrad Umpleby*. The Umpleby family's August 1990 relocation from Preston to Colorado was driven by Chris Umpleby's transfer to the Denver branch of the printing company he worked for, accompanied by his Bavarian wife, Liesel, and their only child. Since then, Peter had brought a whole new meaning to living the American Dream.

Days of sifting through old crime records flagged up two cases showing distinct similarities to Kratz's earliest favoured modus operandi. In February 1986, a supply teacher at Crettington County Primary School met an unpleasant and untimely demise when her car ploughed into the back of a lorry on the M6. The resulting investigation revealed the VW Golf's brake lines were sabotaged in a manner identical to those of kebab shop owner Stavros Pallis' Ford Escort in August 1990. Neither he nor Grace Winterburn had stood a chance.

During the previous week, Boothroyd had travelled to the small North Yorkshire village of Nidd to obtain a DNA sample from Chris Umpleby's only brother, hoping to confirm a third DNA profile found at Kratz's properties in California and Colorado belonged to their owner. Two separate forensic teams had earlier recovered the same three distinct hair samples from each house, delaying the investigation until two were eventually matched to a pair of Austrian backpackers missing since June.

Meanwhile, in Los Angeles, detectives eagerly awaited the outcome of another DNA test, this time from a six-month-old baby girl allegedly fathered by Kratz. They also hoped both sets of test results would confirm the origin of the blood pool found in a Mercedes abandoned in Las Vegas. The car's owner, one Carlito Read of Atwater Village, had been found riddled with gunshot wounds in Death Valley in an apparent attempt by Kratz to fake his own death.

The investigation's complexities held law enforcement teams on both sides of the Atlantic in an iron grip, and long hours and minimal sleep soon began to take a physical and mental toll on all involved. In Preston, Boothroyd quickly decided his team had escaped relatively lightly, especially after reading regular updates emailed by his American counterparts.

Sanderson sipped his tepid coffee and skimmed through the information he'd recently printed out. 'The lab said they should be able to get the DNA results to us later this afternoon. I've also heard back from long-term storage. They've finally found the brake lines taken from both vehicles. Apparently there was some location mix-up.'

'Bloody typical,' Phelan muttered.

'I'll also get on to Linda Neville,' Sanderson continued, referring to the FBI's London-based legal attaché with whom they'd liaised since uncovering Kratz's Preston connection. 'See if she wants the evidence analysed here or in the states. They've located the brake lines from some cases in Los Angeles and from Sam Bury's car crash in New York last summer, all of which have already been linked to Kratz.'

'He's a decent bloke, that Sam,' Phelan said. 'I've known one of his sisters since we were at school together.' She turned to Sanderson. 'How did it go at the neighbours' place?'

'Ex-neighbours,' Sanderson replied. 'Hence how long it took to track down the ones who hadn't kicked the bucket. I've just visited an elderly couple who lived opposite the Umplebys back in the day and have since retired out to Broughton. They told me Peter was an *awkward little devil*. Unpleasant to the other kids on the street, rude to the adults and there was quite a celebration after the family moved away. They also said his parents tried their best to discipline him, which isn't what you usually hear if some little shit's causing problems.'

Boothroyd ran a hand through his greying hair. 'Did he show any interest in cars?'

'They said he sometimes helped his dad do general maintenance but, other than that, they didn't recall any sort of car fixation. Sounds like any other–' Sanderson heard a new email ping into his inbox and glanced at his computer. 'It's from the lab!' He deftly moved the mouse on his unnaturally tidy desk and double-clicked. 'Let's hope *this* gets the ball rolling.'

****

7.43am – PDT
Kingsbury, Nevada

Supervisory Special Agent Sam Bury glared at the half-eaten slice of toast, his usually healthy appetite decimated by the news he'd heard the previous afternoon.

His wife looked at him and frowned. 'You're not hungry?' she asked, her concern audible. 'You should eat something, especially if you intend cycling back later.'

'About that.' He dropped the crust onto his plate. 'Perhaps you can pick me up today?'

'What time?' 'Anna asked, surprised by his apparent lack of enthusiasm for the fitness regimen he'd recently devised.

'The car place closes at half past five, so at least half an hour before.'

She frowned again. 'Car place?'

He nodded. 'I think we should lease that runabout we discussed, before the weather starts to turn bad.'

'I thought we were going to wait for October, in case they find Kratz?'

Their daughter Angela lifted her blonde head expectantly. 'We're getting a *cat*?'

'No, sweetheart,' he replied. 'Just some of Daddy's work stuff.'

Anna set down her empty glass. 'Do we really need one?'

'This cabin is pretty remote. I don't think it's a good idea how sometimes one of us is here without a car,' Sam said. 'There's the kids to consider.'

She sighed and narrowed her eyes. 'Sam, he's in England, not here.'

'Really?' Sam shot back, his tone sharper than intended. 'They're days, if not weeks, behind him. He could've left the UK already.'

'And if he has, do you seriously think he'd come here?'

'Tahoe, or the US?'

'Either, although the odds of him ending up in Tahoe are pretty slim,' Anna said. She handed a thin slice of waffle to their almost seven-month-old son. 'It's not like he has any connection to this area.'

'That we know of.'

She smiled when John immediately rammed the entire piece of waffle into his mouth. 'The Bureau will have checked; they're hardly going to relocate us anywhere they've linked him to, don't you think?'

'I suppose,' Sam relented. He picked up his discarded toast and spread honey across it. 'I'm sorry. The whole thing has me on edge, especially now he appears to be following Joe Studdert's profile. He said Kratz would stick to places he has a connection to. Switzerland: he visited family there during his childhood. Augsburg: his mum's Bavarian. England: where he's originally from–'

Anna held up her hand to interrupt. 'He might stay there.'

'Too small a place and too densely populated.' Sam gave his head an emphatic shake. 'There's nowhere remote enough to lay low. Even if he crossed the border and headed as far north as the Scottish Highlands, he'd still stand out as either a newcomer or a Sassenach.'

'Sassa-what?'

'English.'

Anna laughed, amused to learn another new slang word over five years since their chance meeting at Boulder's central police station. 'Have you heard any more?'

'Not really,' he replied. 'We try to go on like normal and remember everyone involved is working flat out to catch him.'

Anna poured the last of the coffee into Sam's empty cup. 'You'd better hurry. I need to style my hair and all this mess isn't going to take itself to the dishwasher.'

'Yes, dear,' he said, the underlying affection in his tone not lost on Anna. He watched her load the dishwasher and, not for the first time, wondered how his life might have panned out if he hadn't been summoned to that hostage situation back in spring 2004.

****

8.42am – PDT
San Fernando Road, Los Angeles, California

Unusually for the start of a working day, a jovial mood filled the LAPD's Northeast homicide incident room; the rare treat of bought-in coffee appearing to be a significant factor in the light-hearted atmosphere. Long-serving detective Ronnie Mosley loosened his tie and took a long swallow of smooth Columbian roast whilst perusing the area's latest crime reports. Mosley was well-known throughout the district for his refusal to retire, and only months earlier had celebrated thirty years with the department. Much to his amusement, the other three members of his team attributed his continued success to *'having the memory of an elephant, the heart of a lion – and being a cynical son of a bitch.'*

For the past two months the quartet had devoted excessive hours and an almost obsessive approach to the hunt for fallen Hollywood idol Konrad Kratz, and the case's slow progress meant at some point each detective felt ready to throw in the towel. A tentative new ray of hope would then emerge: a tiny slither of optimism that Kratz's capture would come soon and their lives regain some semblance of normality.

Until the next gang-related feud kicked off.

The team's most recent addition had arrived thirteen years earlier, when Alex Gibson joined Dave Hallberg and Emilio Muñoz, both of whom held an additional four years' service on the Atwater Village native. Since then, they'd consistently boasted one of the best detection rates in the city, leading to their Captain's reluctance to reassign them – a decision welcomed by the four men who, over the years, had become the firmest of friends as well as co-workers.

Hallberg was first to check his email that morning, and his freckled fist shooting into the air to punch an invisible target earned bemused stares from the others. Mosley's delight in learning the DNA sample from Peter Umpleby's paternal uncle proved a partial match to the sample obtained from Kratz's two homes meant he'd wasted no time in forwarding the email to Paul Whitehead, a fellow detective based in nearby Glendale – close to Kratz's home in the affluent Brockmont area of town.

Whitehead had his own impatience to reign in whilst he awaited DNA results from Anya di Marco, the baby reputed to be the result of Kratz's illicit affair with the then nineteen-year-old daughter of his next-door neighbours. If the child and her alleged great-uncle shared DNA, speculation over her paternity would end *and* strengthen the evidence Kratz did indeed murder Carlito Read in Death Valley as a decoy. In addition, assuming Anya proved to be Kratz's child, a half-match to the third unidentified DNA profile at both her father's homes would cement the theory that he'd lured two Austrian backpackers to their deaths in Solvang, then stolen samples of their hair to use as an additional forensic countermeasure.

Muñoz eyed his empty coffee cup and, not for the first time, wished their station house drinks machine met the same standard. 'How long until we hear whether there's a match?' he asked.

'When the DNA lab gets off its ass,' Mosley replied. 'I just sent it to them; figured they could quickly run it against the profiles from his home. There might be a backlog, but it's not like they need to do all their sciencey extraction stuff first, right?'

'And you've sent it to Glendale?' Muñoz grinned in anticipation of Mosley's response.

'What do you take me for? Soon as they get the baby's results, they'll be able to do the comparison.'

Hallberg chuckled. 'I hope the kid doesn't turn into her pop and start generating work for us in twenty years.'

'Hopefully she'll take after her mom's side of the family,' Mosley replied. 'They seem a decent bunch of folks.'

Muñoz nodded. 'Anything new from our buddy Harry Lee?'

Mosley narrowed his eyes and turned his thoughts to the skinny little guy they'd recently brought in. 'He claims he's given us all the names he used to make Kratz's fake passports. I've forwarded them to Niall Demaine at the Denver field office, so hopefully he can use at least some of them to track Kratz's movements.'

Hallberg frowned at Mosley. 'How can we be sure Lee's given us all the names, or that he's telling us the truth?'

'Because he's a piece of chicken shit and he knows he'll get eaten alive in jail. I told him he'd get a reduced sentence if the information he supplies means Kratz is successfully convicted when he gets caught. He damn near snapped my hands off.'

Gibson looked up from his laptop. 'You sound very optimistic.'

Mosley grinned and patted Gibson on the back. 'That's because I'm a *the-glass-is-always-half-full* kind of guy, in case you hadn't noticed.'

****

10.54am – EDT
Port Authority Technical Center, Jersey City, New Jersey

Port Authority Police Department detectives Jim Meaker and Marie Goldstein arrived at the PAPD's headquarters nearly two hours later than usual; the tortuous commute from their respective Hoboken homes caused by a driver who'd apparently mistaken a busy intersection for a racetrack. They'd cursed the man's stupidity during the short elevator ride to their shared open-plan office, where Goldstein wasted no time in booting up her laptop and accessing the emails that had landed in her inbox since she'd last left the office.

One caught her eye ahead of the rest, a more local follow-up to the original request from a team of England-based detectives who'd located a fugitive using the name Anthony Collins on a flight from London to New York. She opened the attachment containing surveillance camera footage isolated by JFK's Head of Security, then skimmed through the first series of images of their person of interest at the airport six days ago.

'You owe me.'

Meaker glanced up from his own computer. 'I owe you what, exactly?'

'Whatever you think I deserve for saving you a trip out to JFK.'

'Jeez, you must really need some more coffee.'

'Remember that quick email I fired off yesterday afternoon containing names and time parameters?' Goldstein rubbed her hands together. 'Look what I got back!'

The first vending machine coffee of the day began to seep into their bloodstreams within minutes of their methodical trawl through the footage. Few words were spoken, aside from occasional comments during pauses to isolate the clearest images for enhancement before running them through the facial recognition software.

Goldstein next suggested publishing the newly-enhanced images in the *New York Times*, irrespective of the results returned by facial recognition. She allayed Meaker's initial scepticism by reminding him of a recent homicide where members of the public helped the police locate the criminals responsible after their photos appeared in the newspaper.

By the time they returned from a second coffee run, Goldstein's telephone call to the newspaper had successfully secured a prominent position for their appeal and a guarantee to run the story in full for the next two days. She subconsciously remembered a favourite childhood superstition and crossed her fingers, hoping to receive the one vital tip-off to change the whole course of their investigation.

****

5.15pm – BST
Blackpool, England

'About bloody time too!' the grey-haired man muttered. He cracked his knuckles and cleared his desk by dropping a pile of half-finished reports onto the floor. 'I've been waiting for those buggers to email me all afternoon.'

Eddie Pell watched fellow detective Harry Irwin move the computer's mouse over the empty surface he'd created. 'The bank finally coughed up then?' he asked.

'Not on my bastard PPI, they haven't,' Irwin grumbled. 'I've just received Roger Mortimer's bank account details going back to 1991. I'll start working through and see if there's any unusual transactions.'

'Not what you need on a Friday night.'

'I'll log in at home, actually. The missus and her sisters are off to bingo, meaning I've got the place to myself.'

Irwin, a Fylde coast native, had landed the role of lead investigator into Roger Mortimer's recent death after the local businessman was found handcuffed to his marital bed, his head cocooned in five layers of cling film. Inquiries had ruled out any extra-marital hanky-panky, and the revelation of a recently returned American business associate now led detectives to believe a business deal had turned particularly sour.

Preston-born brothers Steve and Mikey Garner, the proud owners of a winning lottery ticket nearly fifteen years earlier, had founded the popular Friargate-based Edward II and soon invited Mortimer's brewery to supply their pub with its hugely popular *Isabella's Revenge* ale. Mortimer's heavy investment over the next decade allowed the already profitable business to expand further; with a recently-opened town centre restaurant, the Son of Edward, comfortably emulating their original venture's success.

Within hours of Roger Mortimer's untimely end, Eddie Pell headed west to Blackpool's Central Police Station from his usual Preston base, briefed and ready to liaise between the two towns' police forces. Three decades of detective work in his hometown and his son Tony's long-standing friendship with Mortimer's son-in-law Steve Garner meant Pell was considered an asset to a Blackpool team anxious to solve the crime and bring the presently unknown killer to justice.

Irwin dropped the file into his briefcase. 'See you tomorrow morning then?'

'Yeah, I'll be in by half eight,' Pell confirmed. 'Should be done by noon if we start then.'

'You sound worryingly optimistic.'

'That's because I haven't had a day off since this case started, and it's my niece's engagement do tomorrow night. If I don't show, my wife will make sure I join poor old Roger in the mortuary.'

'That might be useful,' Irwin said. He smirked, fully aware of the likely magnitude of Sara Pell's anger if he missed a party six months in its planning.

Pell rolled his eyes. 'You reckon?'

'Yeah, you stiffs can have a little chat.' He gave a snort of laughter. 'We cancel the séance and put away that Ouija board.'

****

4.44pm – PDT
FBI Resident Agency, Stateline, Nevada

Situated a short distance from an invisible line marking the boundary between Nevada and California, the small resident agency could be considered somewhat of an anomaly by those more familiar with the FBI's big city operations. Each day, a Reno-based agent worked alongside two Sacramento-based agents at a leased suite, located up a sleepy side street five minutes' drive from the lake shore. From here they'd investigate an often-surprising range of crimes, all offered up by the popular tourist destination and its not-so-sleepy surroundings.

Sam regularly joined the trio for an afternoon briefing in a larger office that also doubled as a conference room. In recent weeks, the team's main focus centred on a group of twenty-something men and women who'd set up camp in the woods east of Lake Tahoe. Rumours of a religious cult actively trying to recruit vulnerable locals began to circulate, leading to the FBI's involvement. Their discrete local enquiries quickly identified its leader as Dirk Tyler, an older ex-felon who'd apparently experienced a spiritual revelation during his last prison stretch. Tyler's attempt to befriend two college students home for the summer break backfired when the eldest mentioned it to her father, a member of the Douglas County Sheriff's Office. Naturally concerned, he'd contacted his old buddy Jed Masters, whose preliminary research generated sufficient evidence to start a full-scale investigation.

Sam half-listened to fellow agent Matt Jessop recap the case and the latest plan to bring in undercover agents to infiltrate the group. He gripped the pencil ever-tighter and his knuckles whitened until the wood splintered. Colleen Dexter raised her eyebrows and silently observed Sam continue to make notes with the stub. Feelings which had festered over the past year grew, a malignant rage feeding from his increasingly intense hatred for Konrad Kratz. It now infiltrated his thoughts almost constantly, fuelled by images of the man who'd twice tried to kill him.

Maybe one day, he mused, the boot would be on the other foot.

****

'It's been a while, Dale.' Mike Saunders passed a bottle of beer to Konrad. 'How long are you staying this time? Long weekend?'

Konrad shook his head at his neighbour, a middle-aged man who lived there permanently with his wife of fifteen years. 'Not this time, Mike. Maybe just a couple of months.'

'How'd you wangle that much time off?' Irena asked from beside the barbecue.

'I'm working.'

'From the cabin?' Her gaze flicked over to the compact wooden structure partially visible through a line of sweetly-scented ponderosa pines. 'Doing what?'

'I've gone part-time at the firm,' Konrad replied. He chuckled at how the couple's greyhound sniffed the air whenever any of the three large steaks on the grill emitted an appetising sizzle. 'Looks like fat boy here wants to share. Anyway, the boss sends me the stuff, I write it up and email it back. I've also gotten signed by a publishing company specialising in travel books, who want me to produce a guide to the Tahoe area. I come up here regularly, so I'm pretty familiar with the area already. I do my research, type it up, organise it and it'll hopefully hit the shelves within a year.'

Mike took a long swallow of his beer. 'Free copies for us?'

'You betcha!' Konrad replied. 'Just as long as I can raid your thoughts on the area.'

Irena tipped her blonde head to one side and looked Konrad up and down. 'Why the change of image, Dale?'

'What do you mean?'

'Short hair… new glasses.'

Konrad rubbed a hand over what little remained of his hair. 'Yeah, I've decided to keep it low maintenance, especially now I think it's starting to get thinner. I guess age is catching up with me and it's the same logic behind the lenses – the ol' eyeballs are also letting me down.'

'You're doing fine, Dale.' She set down the metal tongs and picked up a half-full glass of red wine. 'Must be good to be back in Tahoe; it has to be better than the city?'

'I guess so. San Francisco's pretty cool for an urban area, but there's nothing like fresh mountain air and the great outdoors, right?'

'You never said a truer word,' Mike agreed. He deftly flicked the metal top off a new bottle of beer. 'Anyway, 'bout time you got you a lady friend. Cute little cabin in the woods, steady job – the chicks should be lining up!'

Irena leaned over and playfully cuffed the top of her husband's head. 'Like I was?'

He smoothed down imaginary lapels. 'What more can I say?'

Konrad smiled and raised the almost empty beer bottle to his lips. Over the past seven years, the couple had never once doubted his cover story, nor seen through his disguise.

Perhaps I'm a better actor than anyone previously thought?

Chapter 2 – Saturday 29th August 2009

8.48am – BST
Blackpool, England

Eddie Pell pushed open the door, let his briefcase fall to the floor and glanced around the small incident room, surprised to find Harry Irwin absent from his desk. 'Harry?'

'That you, Eddie?' Irwin called through from the adjacent office. 'Printer's been pissing around again, just give me a sec. Help yourself to a brew if you want one.'

Pell strolled through to the narrow kitchenette, where he flicked the coffee maker's switch and lifted two large cups from a faded pine mug tree. 'Did you get anything useful from Mortimer's bank statements?' he asked. 'You know, like any shady-looking transactions?'

'I'll bloody say!' Irwin replied from the doorway. 'Our old pal Roger may have bitten off more than he could chew.' He saw Pell raise his eyebrows. 'In summer 2003 half a million quid landed in his account.'

'Half a million?'

'That's right. The actual transaction was done in American dollars, so I checked the exchange rate back then and that's what $800,000 is.'

Pell struggled to picture that amount of cash. 'Who sent him that amount of money?'

'It came from an online account in the name of Oliver Stamford.'

'Who's he?'

Irwin shrugged. 'Your guess is as good as mine. Soon after, Roger purchased two homes on the south side of town. I got here an hour ago and verified who he paid the money to.'

'Is one where Clive Porter and his family lived before Mortimer served an eviction notice on them?' Pell raised his voice so it carried over the gurgles coming from the coffee maker.

'Yeah, and a local estate agent recently listed both properties.'

'Bit of a coincidence, isn't it?'

'My guess is that Stamford, whether or not it's his real name, is the American businessman,' Irwin said. He passed an almost full pint of milk to Pell. 'To start with, I don't get why a Yank wanted to invest money round here. But, for whatever reason, he wanted his investment back, and when Mortimer didn't immediately cough up he bumped him off.'

Pell picked up the last clean teaspoon. 'Mortimer must've been trying to recoup the money. Serving notice on the Porters certainly suggests this.'

'Clive Porter went mental, but is being asked to leave the home you're renting enough to drive a man to murder?' Irwin patted a copy of last night's *Blackpool Gazette* he'd found on his desk. 'It's not like there's nowhere else to rent in town; the local rag has pages of houses.'

'Porter's an arse, but he doesn't strike me as a murderer.' Pell commented. He poured coffee into the two mugs and gave each one a stir. 'He's thicker than pig shit for a start. Whoever broke into the Mortimer house has the intelligence not to leave any fingerprints, fibres or hairs. They also planned the crime meticulously and it's likely the killer brought the clingfilm to the property. The unopened roll in the kitchen only carried fingerprints from Mortimer's missus, who was visiting family down south that night, and five unknowns who might be anyone from the factory through to the supermarket. Porter just doesn't have enough grey matter between his ears to carry this off.'

'So we focus on this Stamford bloke?'

'Yeah, unless someone else comes into the picture.'

'Why kill him?' Irwin countered. 'He'll never get his money back. Surely waiting for six or so months is better than getting no money at all?'

'You'd think. If Stamford's the culprit, he must've had an additional reason for killing Mortimer.'

'Mortimer found out some dirt on him?'

'Maybe, and then called his bluff.' Pell sipped his drink warily through wisps of steam. 'Have we traced the exact origin of the money yet?'

'I don't have access to that kind of information; I'll have to pass it up the food chain.'

'Who's that?'

Irwin winked and lifted his mug. 'I'll get back to you on that front, I've got an idea.'

****

8.21am – PDT

Mattole Road, South Lake Tahoe, California

An intensely blue sky and bright morning sun maintained their allegiance, ready to deceive those who looked outside and believed the comfortable temperatures inside their home would be matched outside. Although technically still summer, temperatures struggled to stay in the forties overnight and had only now started to creep upwards, adding warmth to what promised to be another beautiful Tahoe weekend.

Since purchasing the semi-isolated cabin, Konrad had become used to this phenomenon and knew he'd catch his breath and shiver when cold air nipped the skin exposed by his shorts and t-shirt. He'd deliberately chosen his attire, safe in the knowledge that the jogger masquerade allowed him to maintain his physical fitness *and* blend into the area unnoticed.

After locking the door and working through a routine of stretches, he left the cabin behind and set a steady pace. During his first visit to the property he'd been surprised to find a single paved width rather than a dirt road, an arrangement offering a combination of advantages and disadvantages. Sure, it would be easier to escape by vehicle if necessary, but this could also work conversely if his cover was blown and the Feds came steaming in to take him away.

Konrad quickened his pace and turned left where the road met another and widened. A quickening series of chemical reactions in his muscles released additional body heat and he inhaled deeply, enjoying the scent of pine in the chilly damp air. Konrad's thoughts flitted between scenarios of how the whole thing might end. If things went in his favour, he'd use the next two months to get his affairs in order and accumulate the resources he'd dispersed, ready to leave the area for good. Beneath the cabin's floorboards, a safe secretly installed during his neighbours' vacation a couple of months after he'd taken ownership was ready and waiting to store the cash he'd soon accrue.

He'd already half-filled it over the years.

And then there was also the Rolex costing more than many families paid for their homes. He'd been careful to obscure his identity during its purchase in Phoenix seven weeks earlier, knowing that even if *they* ever traced the sale to a Mr Chamberlain nothing existed to connect that fictitious identity to Konrad Kratz. He now planned to sell it in Reno, where a rarely used fake passport and matching driver's licence would also enable him to empty a safe deposit box containing close to a quarter of a million dollars.

His breaths came in rapid bursts, drowning the hum of passing traffic where the road widened further to bring Emerald Bay Road into view. A steady stream of vehicles travelled in both directions, their occupants ready to enjoy a long weekend away from the daily grind. For Konrad, there'd be neither rest nor relaxation, his intention being to meticulously plan the final stage in his bid for freedom: going off the grid in Montana's wilderness.

He maintained a stationary jog and repeatedly looked both ways whilst waiting for a break in the traffic. The last vehicle disappeared into the distance and Konrad ran across both lanes of blacktop. He checked his future time to beat, regained his pace and followed the road east towards the beach.

****

4.36pm – BST
Hutton, Preston, England

Dave Sanderson carefully placed a file of paperwork into his briefcase, ready to peruse later once his two young children were tucked up in bed. 'Assuming they compare the brake lines, will it really be enough to link the two incidents over here to those in the US?' he asked. 'I mean, it's a couple of decades since he lived here, so surely he could've refined his methods, so to speak? What if he's used a different tool or technique in more recent years?'

Phelan cleared her throat and nodded. 'Then there's the issue of him sometimes using his non-dominant hand, according to the preliminary analysis report. Remember those stabbings in Chorley we investigated last year? That's what that guy did.'

'Forensics should be able to answer that properly,' Boothroyd said. 'As for the handedness thing, he'd have to be truly ambidextrous for something requiring such precision. I suppose an approach from a different angle and hesitation marks or some other marks to suggest he'd found the action difficult may trigger alarm bells. And, bear in mind the comparison is being done in an FBI lab. They're hardly likely to employ muppets, are they?'

Sanderson snapped the worn briefcase's locks shut. 'Any idea how much longer it'll be?'

'That FBI legat type down in the Smoke reckoned a few days,' Boothroyd replied.

'Will this actually advance the investigation any further?'

Boothroyd shrugged at him. 'Not necessarily, but it'll give closure to the families of Grace Winterburn and Stavros Pallis.'

Sanderson's gaze drifted to the floor and a short silence filled the air until Phelan spoke.

'Seriously though, do you think a ten-year-old is capable of such an act?' she asked, not for the first time wondering whether the investigation had followed the correct course.

'There's been cases of kids that age killing and, as an adult, he's shown no regard for human life.' Boothroyd paused to consider his next words carefully. 'Everyone we've spoken to has said what nice people his parents were, so perhaps in some ways it's a blessing they're not alive to see this. And, *they* also deserve justice, so we know what we need to do.'

****

10.15am – PDT
Sly Park, near Pollock Pines, California

Located little more than an hour east of Sacramento, Sly Park Recreation Area had always been a popular destination for those seeking rest and relaxation away from its urban sprawl. Campsites dotted the area beside Jenkinson Lake, these small havens interspersed between the picnic areas commandeered by other groups who'd chosen to make a day of their visit.

Although the Tahoe area boasted plenty of attractions and leisure opportunities, Sly Park fast topped the Bury family's favourite day out list. The ninety-minute journey traversed a rich variety of landscapes, commencing with a steep climb away from Tahoe which, at its highest point, rewarded them with breath-taking views of their ascent. More rapid progress occurred after the road's altitude decreased and one lane each way widened into two, able to serve a greater concentration of residents. By the time the children became restless they were usually on the journey's last leg through the thickened pine forest, passing widely-spaced homes that blurred to each side of the winding road. One last left turn brought them to a wooden payment booth, where Sam handed over a ten-dollar bill and slowly drove past the main parking area to a small pull-out beside the lake.

Miwok Trail's gently undulating path and varied foliage had readily captured Angela Bury's young imagination, and the family always took an unlimited amount of time to follow the nature trail and answer the little girl's questions. During each visit they'd pause at a tepee; its entrance large enough for Angela to enter a cool, damp interior and inhale the area's earthy scents, which concentrated themselves deep inside the magical hideaway.

John's high-pitched announcement that he'd lost interest encouraged the family to return to the shaded picnic tables near a disused well at the trail's starting point. Sam retrieved a cooler from the car as John gazed at the shadows dancing on the clearing's floor, created whenever sunbeams edged past the overhead leaves constantly swaying in a gentle breeze.

'Apple or orange juice?' he called over to them before checking the narrow road was clear both ways. Angela mulled over the offer as he darted across, the time before her reply filled by the faint sounds of nearby campers and a more distant jet ski.

'Apple, please.' Her reply coincided with the cooler's arrival on the table's faded wooden surface. 'And,' she continued, conviction evident in her tone, 'Mommy also wants apple.'

Anna ruffled her daughter's hair. 'Whatever's left is good for me.'

They watched Angela gulp the sweet juice, then slide down from the bench. She approached a pile of pine cones and crouched to examine the largest. 'I'm gonna make a squirrel house so they can sleep inside in the warm,' she stated.

'Budding architect, I reckon,' Sam commented.

Anna grinned. 'She wanted to be an artist a couple of weeks ago.'

Sam screwed the top back on his water bottle and surveyed the clearing. An oblivious Angela selected cones from the random assortment on the ground, intense concentration never leaving her face. 'You get exactly the same expression if you're switched into something,' he said.

'Yeah, my mom says that,' Anna replied. She swallowed the last of her juice and gave a whoop after successfully aiming her empty carton at a nearby trash can on a wooden pole. 'Dad's the same, so I guess it runs in the family.'

She fell silent and Sam glanced in her direction. 'You okay?'

'I worry about them worrying,' she admitted.

'They know we're safe, and hopefully this'll only be for a short time.'

She stared into the distance and sensed an arm reaching around her shoulders. 'You sound like me. Perhaps I've been trying to convince myself, rather than you?'

'We're more similar than we admit.' Sam gave her a light squeeze. 'Perhaps we haven't always acknowledged that side of our relationship?'

Anna twisted the top off a jar of baby food and lifted a chuckling John from his stroller. Sam cast his mind back to that first Sunday in April, a little over five years earlier. Their first date almost didn't happen, until a couple of bottles of beer bolstered his courage sufficiently to pick up the phone – a small action that would ultimately change the course of his life.

On that fateful day back in 2004, Sam was rendered mortified within seconds of leaving Boulder PD's staff restroom. Not concentrating, he'd rounded the corridor's sharp corner and collided with a young detective. Sheets of paper showered the floor, causing the woman to drop to her knees and hastily gather the scattered evidence she needed for a big case.

He quickly followed her lead, apologising profusely in spite of her assurances it wasn't a big deal – not to mention him blathering on like a bumbling idiot. Sam's embarrassment turned into confusion when she'd passed her business card to him, and added a loaded comment that she could always be reached on the cell phone number printed at the bottom.

For the next two days, Sam repeatedly stared at the card he'd carefully placed in his wallet, wondering whether to call. She'd seemed nice enough and he couldn't deny the lingering attraction. Admittedly, being single for longer than he'd want to admit could be clouding his judgment, but perhaps the time had come to take a risk?

He'd later discovered Anna had been delighted to hear from him. Their first brief conversation centred on the case she'd been working on during the evening they'd fleetingly met. He'd reluctantly ended the call, grabbed a can of beer from the refrigerator and silently cursed his ineptitude in bottling his plans to suggest they meet up.

Sam sipped the cool liquid and allowed his mind to drift back three years, how since then he assumed he'd never find anyone he'd want to be with. Surely he deserved a chance of happiness and the possibility of having someone with whom to share his life? He eyed the phone's defiant blink from the table beside him.

Fuck it.

He pressed the redial button, listened to it ring and ignored the sudden chill passing through him. A crackle told him Anna had answered, followed by a cautious 'Hello?'

'Anna, it's Sam again. I've got the day off on Sunday... Yeah, I... uh... wondered if you wanted to go out for something to eat? I really feel I need to apologise properly for rearranging your evidence.'

He listened carefully to Anna's enthusiastic response and felt his smile grow when she accepted his invitation and suggested a small Italian place in central Boulder, followed by the promise to return his call after she'd made the arrangements. They indulged in a few more minutes of small talk, during which Anna provided directions to her apartment and a suggestion of how to avoid a stretch of construction work nearby.

Sam's mood was considerably brighter by the time the call ended, and a combination of relief and anticipation led to the uncharacteristic opening of a second bottle of beer on a work night. He'd definitely been out of the dating game for too long, he mused, aware of the alcohol's effects on an empty stomach as he reheated a portion of spaghetti bolognaise left over from the previous night. At that–

'You like that, huh?' Anna said, angling the last spoonful of fruit purée into John's mouth. A shudder of delight passed through the baby and he turned his head away from where Angela arranged some of the smaller pine cones she'd collected. Anna set down the spoon and patted Sam's knee. 'I'll give you two cents for your thoughts.'

Sam frowned at a brightly painted red fire hydrant on the clearing's opposite side. 'You don't want to know.'

'Sam?'

'I've had enough of this whole situation,' he muttered, the words forced through gritted teeth.

She squeezed his hand and pressed a kiss to his cheek. 'It's difficult, but it's for the best.'

'Can we really live like this forever?' He stared at her, his gaze so intense she looked away. 'In a strange place with no family nearby, living a lie?'

'They'll catch him,' Anna whispered. 'He'll slip up, and then he'll get himself caught.'

Sam flicked away a piece of dried grass attached to his shorts. 'He'd better bloody well hope so.'

She frowned. 'I don't follow.'

He narrowed his eyes. 'Because if I ever cross paths with the bastard, I'll kill him.'

****

11.33am – PDT
Glendale, California

As had become an increasingly common occurrence since the Kratz case broke, Ronnie Mosley found himself at his desk on a Saturday morning, hoping to catch up on some of the paperwork generated by other Northeast cases. Today had started differently though, thanks to a telephone call from Glendale-based detective Paul Whitehead. An uncharacteristically cheerful Whitehead refused to elaborate on his reason for calling, and ended the conversation by suggesting Mosley detour via North Isabel Street on his way home.

The short and surprisingly quiet journey passed quickly, with little traffic on the roads to darken his mood. Mosley left his car on the third floor of a parking garage behind the main building, made his way to the lobby and signed in. Within minutes, Whitehead emerged from a nearby elevator and waved enthusiastically to Mosley.

'What's gotten you so damn cheerful on the weekend?' Mosley asked, deliberately injecting a healthy dose of cynicism into his tone before the two men shook hands. 'Your state lottery numbers came up at last?'

'We've cracked the Kratz DNA profile!' Whitehead replied. 'Cracked it wide open.'

Mosley's eyes widened. 'For real? He's Anya di Marco's baby daddy?'

30

'Sure is. The third DNA sample recovered from Kratz's homes is a perfect fifty-fifty match to the baby's.'

'Have you informed the di Marco family?'

'They're expecting me at noon.' Whitehead's eyes narrowed and his beaming smile reappeared. 'Do you want to come help me break the news?'

'Will our good friend Bruno be present?' Mosley remembered both occasions when he'd met Galina's father, a high-powered attorney popular amongst Hollywood's celebrities thanks to his no-nonsense approach and an encyclopaedic knowledge of all manner of legal loopholes.

Whitehead's smile faded. 'Yeah, he insisted.'

'Okay, I'll protect your sorry ass,' Mosley said. He patted Whitehead on the back. 'And, don't forget you're doing all the talking.'

****

4.45pm – PDT
Central Park, Manhattan, New York

Bruce Kennedy, a lifelong resident of Melbourne, reclined on the park bench and watched two joggers pass by. 'They're either mad or dedicated,' he muttered, stretching out his legs to relieve the ache generated by a full day of exploring some of Manhattan's most famous sights. There'd be more of the same tomorrow, he realised, and immediately winced thanks to his wife's insistence on an impending day of retail therapy. He stretched out the tension in one hamstring and picked up the copy of the *New York Times* he'd bought minutes earlier from a kerbside vendor.

'Cheers, love.' He smiled at the woman to whom he'd been married for a shade over thirty years. The ten-day trip on which they'd embarked celebrated that milestone anniversary, an occasion they hadn't expected to reach due to Stella's heart attack the previous December. 'Let's see what's on,' he continued, 'and, you'd better keep that newspaper, Mandy will want to read it when we get home.'

Stella nodded and thought of their eldest daughter, who harboured a long-time ambition to live and work in the Big Apple. 'We'll put it straight in my case back at the hotel.' She saw his eyes rove over the third page. 'Anything interesting?'

'Just some police appeal for information,' Bruce replied. His deep brown eyes continued to scan the article. 'They want to identify some bloke who landed at JFK a week ago.'

She brushed strands of silvery hair from her eyes. 'What's he done?'

'Flew in from London and rented a car. He's apparently wanted in connection with a murder over there.'

'It says his name is Anthony Collins.'

Bruce shrugged and chewed his bottom lip. 'That's the name on his fake ID.'

Stella scrutinised the photo covering nearly a quarter of the page. 'The picture quality's pretty good.'

He pointed at the NYPD logo at the top of the article. 'As you'd expect.'

'Don't tell me you recognise him?' she said through a snort of laughter.

'Like I'm going to know a murderous bloody Pom!' Bruce replied with a good-natured roll of his eyes.

'Stranger things have happened,' Stella said. She cast her mind forward to the Broadway show they'd unexpectedly managed to obtain tickets for that evening. 'Come on, my love. Let's go back to the hotel and freshen up.'

Chapter 3 – Sunday 30th August 2009

10.05am – BST
Preston, England

Despite not crawling into bed until the first stealthy shimmer of dawn had crept above the horizon, Eddie Pell forced himself out of its comfortable warmth less than an hour before arriving at the office he and two other detectives shared. Armed with a large cup of sweet tea, Pell returned to where he'd left his laptop on Friday, opened the lid and noticed he'd left it hibernating since its last use – something he'd be more than happy to do on this overcast Sabbath morning.

One sip told him his eagerly anticipated brew remained too hot to drink and, keen to return home in time for lunch, Pell logged on to the laptop and opened a message emailed from Avis' central London location late the previous afternoon. The company had been surprisingly swift in obtaining tracker data from the hire car they'd leased to Anthony Collins, the man now believed to be an American businessman using the alias Oliver Stamford, wanted in connection to Roger Mortimer's recent murder.

Pell read the email's first paragraph and his frown deepened; surprised to learn Anthony Collins had used a UK passport and driving licence to hire the car. He rifled through a file retrieved from his desk's middle drawer and located the details of the identically-named man who'd flown from Heathrow to New York on an American passport. The photographs and personal details of each man were an exact match, leaving Pell in no doubt that Anthony Collins and Oliver Stamford were one and the same.

He leaned back in his seat and contemplated Stamford's real identity: Yank or Brit being the first contentious point. The man apparently imitated both accents sufficiently well not to arouse suspicion. Did he have a parent from each country, or maybe he was a good mimic? Some people possessed such a talent, whereas Pell's continued struggle to imitate his wife Sara's now-deceased Mexican parents was all too real.

Stamford's obvious familiarity with the customs and lifestyle of each country suggested he'd spent significant amounts of time living in or visiting both. Pell pushed himself closer to the screen and read the second part of the email detailing the route and locations visited by Anthony Collins during his time in England. Collins had taken a direct route north from London to Lancashire, spending his days at various locations between and including Preston and Blackpool. The former's Great Shaw Street and, closer to the coast, Keys Drive immediately stood out as locations pertinent to the Mortimer investigation, and confirmed the team were almost certainly heading in the right direction.

Thanks to Harry Irwin, Pell already knew that Port Authority detectives in New Jersey were actively investigating Collins' movements in the US. He forwarded the email to Meaker and Goldstein in the hope it may aid their investigation. Now he knew little more could be done without the PAPD's assistance, Eddie returned the file to his desk and gathered his belongings.

****

9.16am – PDT
Kingsbury, Nevada

In addition to their regular Sly Park visits further afield, spending Sunday morning locally at Kiva Beach had also eased its way into the Bury family's routine. Sam would load up the car within minutes of them finishing breakfast, ensuring their arrival at the lake's sandy shore corresponded with the rise in temperature after another chilly night in the mountains.

Whilst Anna remained inside to corral the children, Sam pushed a large cooler to the back of the trunk and rearranged their belongings to make room for an assortment of beach toys. His thoughts wandered to the next day, focussing on their plan to collect the small all-wheel drive car Anna now insisted the family needed, *if* they were to remain in Tahoe for winter. She'd been pickier than he expected, even though he'd be the one driving the thing to work. However, he had to admit to that the Saab's all-weather design was definitely better suited for Anna and the kids when the snow lay

34

thick on the ground, not to mention the mounds of *stuff* small children generated.

A large inflatable ball rebounded off his arm and he grinned at how quickly Angela repeatedly jumped up and down, her face flushed and eyes gleaming. 'Looks like someone's ready to go to the beach.' He pushed the ball into a small space between the cooler and a bag that contained spare clothing. 'Did you forget anything?'

She stared back at the house. 'Where's Mommy?'

'Probably making sure John's got all his things.'

She frowned at him. 'Why do babies need so much stuff?'

'Says you,' he replied, pretending to pinch her nose. 'Have you seen all the toys in here which don't belong to John?'

'Sorry, you two,' Anna called from the front step. 'This little guy,' she continued, pausing to pull the front door shut and narrow her eyes, 'deployed a particularly unpleasant last-minute delaying tactic.'

Angela pointed at the car. 'Are we going now?'

'We certainly are.' Sam tried not to catch Anna's eye. 'John's such a clever boy,' he added as he bent down to lift Angela into the car. 'Isn't he, Mommy?'

'You'll get what you deserve,' Anna said. She leaned into the car from the opposite side and expertly clipped John into his safety seat. 'He's gotten his orders and he's cutting another tooth, so it looks like *you'll* be in for a fun night.'

****

10.04am – PDT
Mattole Road, South Lake Tahoe, California

Konrad's morning began much like any other. He'd awoken a couple of hours earlier, brewed a large pot of coffee and scanned the most popular news websites over a bowl of oatmeal. The absence of updates on his disappearance sent his mind into overdrive. Had the Feds hit a brick wall in their investigation or, more worryingly, did this uncharacteristic silence suggest swift progress in locating him was happening behind the scenes?

Perhaps he'd have to bring forward his long-time plan to disappear into Montana's wilderness? He pulled on shorts and a tank top in readiness for a run to the beach and back, intending to clear his head and formulate his escape plans without distraction – although today he'd have the company of Mike and Irena's beloved greyhound. The frantic couple had arrived at his cabin late the previous evening, urgently summoned to Roseville after Irena's mother was rushed to the local hospital suffering from a suspected perforated appendix. Konrad readily agreed to *dog sit* for however long they needed him to – he'd quickly found that having a banked favour to call in always came in useful.

Little more than a pup, Stan's tail wagged enthusiastically at the sight of his guardian brandishing the harness and leash. 'Walkies, fella. Or, should we say runnies?' Stan barked twice and bounded across the kitchen's limited floor space. 'We're going on a nice, long round trip to the beach. That should tire you out, right?' The dog's tongue lolled aimlessly from one side of his mouth. He watched Konrad tie his running shoes and listened intently to the monologue about his plans for the next few days, and how he hoped Stan's owners returned before he needed to make good on his escape. 'If not, it'll have to be the Pound for you, pooch,' he concluded, amused that Stan's tail continued to wag after this promise.

The duo retraced Konrad's steps from other mornings, their arrival at the main road coinciding with a large break in the traffic. He knew Sunday mornings tended to be quieter due to both locals and vacationers alike making the most of the weekend's last hours. Now every day mimicked the weekend, even if the pressure of evading capture meant he could never truly relax and enjoy his surroundings.

Konrad knew he should be able to live comfortably for the foreseeable future, on the assumption he budgeted carefully for all eventualities. Maybe once settled in Montana with a new identity and a new life story he'd consider taking on some casual work. He wondered which type of embittered soul he'd become – perhaps one who'd escaped all that reminded him of an acrimonious divorce, or a city executive recovering from a nervous breakdown? He'd have plenty of time to refine the details over the next month. Nevertheless, he fully intended to leave Tahoe for good within the next week or two.

His deep inhalations and exhalations echoed his footfalls and he savoured the pine-scented air he'd grown increasingly fond of since his return from England. That would remain a constant in Montana if he settled in one of its mountainous areas. The road started to climb and he noticed his breaths quicken. At least he wasn't too far his destination, and managing three miles without a rest stop was definitely an accomplishment so soon after his European travels. Past experience told him it wouldn't take too long to reacclimatise to an altitude similar to that found in his former Coloradan patch of so-called Paradise.

Konrad quickened his pace when he spotted the turn for Lake Tahoe's Visitor Center. He approached an invisible finish line and felt the power course through him, as if he'd continue to emerge victorious from every challenge thrown into his path. A tug on the leash directed Stan across the road to Kiva Beach, chosen today for its dog friendly status and a tendency to be quieter than many other local beaches. Once there, he'd be able to catch his breath and throw sticks for Stan before making the return journey. He expected the dog to sleep for a couple of hours that afternoon, which would give him plenty of time to stock up on provisions in the nearby town that willingly catered for its tourists' everyday retail needs.

Relief and a sense of accomplishment combined as Konrad collapsed onto the beach's clean pale yellow sand, closely followed by a panting Stan. He admired the steep mountains ringing the lake's gently lapping waters, its calm surface a mirror image of the sky's vivid blue hue. Behind him, aged pine trees reached into the sky to provide shade for those who'd walked a dusty path between the beach and the parking lot. He knew the lot usually filled by lunchtime, but for now plenty of room remained for more people to enjoy the secluded shoreline.

Nearby, a middle-aged couple propelled balls into the lake for two excited Labradors, who jumped around in eager anticipation of chasing their toys out into the water, apparently immune to the chill. Years earlier, Konrad had chosen to go for an evening swim soon after taking ownership of the cabin, and immediately learned the hard way that the lake was colder than it appeared. He'd never repeated his mistake.

His gaze travelled to the other end of the beach, where a family of four appeared to be enjoying a day out. The couple were of a similar age to him, and their frequently mirrored body language suggested a close and happy marriage. Not for the first time he wondered what it was like to be able to experience such a relationship; where more than physical desire for another person existed. A small, blonde-haired girl watched the man inflate a second beach ball and excitedly clapped her hands now he'd blocked the air valve. He gently placed the ball into her arms, oblivious to Konrad's interest from behind his mirrored sunglasses.

Konrad's thoughts drifted to the child he'd never know, the baby he conceived with the girl – for she wasn't much more than a girl – next door. Would his daughter ever ask who her father was, or would her mother ever tell her? Perhaps she'd stick to the drunken one-night stand tale the parents-to-be devised between them, rather than admit being naïve enough to get herself knocked up by a guy probably soon to feature on *America's Most Wanted*.

The baby, whom Konrad assumed to be the little girl's brother, squealed in delight when his mother handed something to him from the cooler; the item immediately finding its way into his mouth. The perfect family outing, he mused, and took a few seconds to contemplate whether they lived locally or were vacationers. A sudden scowl furrowed his brow and he wondered where all this sentimental bullshit had appeared from. He needed to keep his wits sharpened and hone his plans to go off the grid forever, to never let down his guard and–

'Is that your dog?' a child asked. Her sing-song voice caused Konrad to startle and he pushed himself into a seated position. He noticed the large, red beach ball and forced a smile and a nod upon recognising the girl from the family he'd been watching.

'He sure is! His name is Stan.'

She tilted her head and crouched close to where Stan's long, thin tail repeatedly thumped the sand. 'He's cute.'

'He likes you.'

'I wish we had a cat or a dog,' Angela said wistfully.

Konrad scratched Stan's head. 'You could ask Mommy and Daddy for one.'

She nodded. 'Mommy said we can get a cat when we go home.'

'That sounds neat,' he agreed, impressed he hadn't lost his acting skills. 'Is that soon?'

'I don't know. She said I'm not allowed a cat in this house.'

'You're on vacation?'

Angela frowned, not sure how to respond. 'Daddy has a new job here,' she finally replied.

Konrad smiled again, grateful she couldn't see the indifference in his eyes. 'Cool.'

'He chases bad guys,' she clarified. 'They go to prison.'

'That sounds–'

'Angela! What did we tell you about wandering off?' her father shouted, his English accent surprising Konrad. 'I'm sorry,' he called, swiftly closing the distance between them, 'she's currently obsessed by all things animal.'

Behind the lenses, Konrad's eyes narrowed and a rarely-felt sensation of heavy unease settled in his gut.

No fucking way…

'That's okay,' he managed to reply in a relatively smooth voice, quickly thinking to add a hint of Texan drawl.

'Sorry, Daddy,' she said, then reluctantly accepted his hand as she looked back at Stan.

What the fuck is he doing here?

'Don't ever do that again, Angela.' Sam turned to Konrad. 'Thanks for your patience; she really wants a pet of her own.'

A wide grin spread across Konrad's face. 'Kids, right?'

'I'll say,' Sam replied, although his attention remained firmly focussed on his daughter. 'Have a good one!'

'Yeah. You too, buddy.'

They returned to the woman and baby, their conversation inaudible. Konrad hazarded a guess the child would receive some kind of *stranger danger* lecture. Quite apt, especially since he'd tried to kill her father twice and wouldn't hesitate to make it third time lucky – if the opportunity ever presented itself. He threw a nearby stick into the lake and contemplated Angela's words as Stan launched his retrieval mission. New job? Here? Or back in Denver? Perhaps they were on vacation prior to him starting it? He could imagine Sam quitting the New York role, especially after what he'd learned about how long it had taken him to fully recover from what should have been a fatal MVA. Perhaps he'd jacked in the FBI? And there'd been his daughter's mention of catching bad guys.

If only she knew.

The chance meeting had thrown a proverbial spanner in the works. Kiva Beach's newly-acquired status of *no-go area* posed nothing more than a short-term problem; the pressing issue was now to get his local affairs in order and leave California within a matter of days. He noticed Sam had donned a pair of sunglasses since leading his subdued daughter back to their family picnic; were these to aid his covert observations?

Konrad clipped the leash to the wet dog's harness, ignored Stan's pleading brown eyes and jumped to his feet. They'd be back at the cabin for an early lunch, giving him enough time to complete his errands and devote the remainder of the afternoon to his escape plan. He slowed to a walk in the parking lot and wondered which vehicle belonged to the Bury family. A total absence of the Colorado licence plate's familiar snowy mountains suggested they'd either rented a car or purchased one since moving to the area.

Can lightning really strike thrice?

****

8.31pm EDT
Brooklyn, New York

Maria Volonte let out a tired sigh, placed the last clean side plate on the drainer and looked around her cosy kitchen, the heart of the home she'd shared with her husband for forty years of marriage. 'You want me to make coffee, Vincenzo?' she shouted, hoping he hadn't once again fallen asleep on the couch.

'Sounds great,' he replied from the adjacent family room.

Maria picked up on the distraction in his tone, frowned and lifted a packet of ground coffee down from a nearby wall cupboard. Theirs was a comfortable routine, evolved from the coupledom reluctantly forced upon them when their two sons and one daughter reached adulthood. All three had easily secured employment after graduating college, their eldest son in Chicago now the closest to home. She spooned the rich dark Italian roast into the coffee maker, ensuring she added double the quantity she usually served to their guests.

For the past week, their nephew Giuseppe and his fiancée Carmela had provided the opportunity for Maria to revisit her old family routine from years ago. The soon-to-be-marrieds returned to the brownstone minutes earlier, aching from the day they'd spent in Manhattan shopping for wedding accessories. Maria sighed again and arranged four large cups on a tray, sad the couple were due to return home to England at the end of the week.

Carmela walked into the kitchen, smoothed down her loose-fitting t-shirt and planted a kiss on the older woman's wrinkled cheek. 'That smells wonderful, Maria' she said. 'I need a pick-me-up after a hard day's shopping.'

Maria smiled and placed a plate of homemade biscotti on the tray. 'You had a successful day in the city?'

'Certainly did. I bought some gorgeous jewellery in Bloomingdale's to wear on the big day, and it was marked down in the sale too. I sent Giuseppe to the men's floor and told him I'd meet him in the café, so he won't see it before we meet at the altar.'

'It's all so romantic,' Maria said longingly. 'I do hope we can be there.'

'You told me Vinnie's doing well since that triple bypass,' Carmela said. She put an arm around Maria's shoulders. 'There's nearly six months to go, so he'll be fine.'

'I hope you're right. Anyway, listen to me, silly old woman,' she muttered in annoyance. 'You're such a sweet girl. If you help me carry these, it would be a big help.'

Carmela lifted the heavily-laden tray. 'Consider it done.'

They walked through to the family room; a welcoming space filled by dozens of photographs, three overstuffed leather couches and a large, old-fashioned television set. The couches bordered a low-set coffee table, its countless cup rings telling of years of familial conversations that had eluded a pile of drink coasters in the middle. Maria frowned when she noticed Vinnie's nose buried in that day's edition of the *New York Times*, and set down his cup with a loud clatter.

'Jesus Christ, Maria!' he exclaimed. 'You trying to land me back in the hospital?'

'We have guests staying, in case you'd forgotten,' she shot back. 'Poor Giuseppe left to watch TV while you read that rag. You didn't think to ask him how his day went?'

'I did, for Christ's sake. He said he's all shopped out and gave me this.' Vinnie held up the newspaper. 'There's a half page feature on some shady-looking guy who came in on the same flight from London.'

She scanned its front page and her eyes widened. 'Is he a movie star?'

'Not this time,' Vinnie replied. He reached for the biscotti and licked his lips. 'This guy's wanted in connection with a homicide back in England. Some old guy got himself killed only a half hour from their hometown.'

'For real?' Maria's eyes widened as she glanced at her nephew. 'You know him?'

Giuseppe poured milk into his drink and shook his head. 'Never seen him before in my life, Aunt Maria.' He waited for Vinnie to glance up and raised thick dark brows for added effect. 'Franco said he knows the dead guy.'

'Let me see him properly,' Maria said, more than a hint of impatience detectable in her voice. She grabbed the newspaper from beside Vinnie, carefully lowered herself onto the couch and leafed through the crumpled pages. 'Where is it?'

'A few pages in.' Giuseppe tried to hide his amusement through a mouthful of crumbs. 'There's some photos from JFK's security footage.'

She nodded. 'Found it,' she said. A frown appeared seconds later. 'I know him. He–'

'For real?' Vinnie interrupted. 'How are *you* going to know some Limey murderer?'

'No, I mean I saw him,' she snapped back. 'You know that man I thought was Giuseppe? He had the exact same hair and eyes and I went to go hug him. You put me straight.'

'Is that the one you told me about, Maria?' Carmela remembered their first prolonged conversation. 'You know, when we were talking in the kitchen on the night we arrived.'

She gave an emphatic nod which caused a lock of grey hair to fall across her forehead. 'Yes, yes, that's him!'

Carmela smiled her encouragement, knowing of Maria's recent worry that her lack of specific recall pointed to something more sinister than the occasional amnesia everyone experienced at one time or another. 'You said he seemed familiar,' she pressed gently.

'Other than the hair and eyes, he don't look much like Giuseppe,' Vinnie said, his tone sullen. 'You're not as young as you once were, Bella.'

'Yes, but she said it's *like* she's seen him before,' Carmela said. The firmness in her voice caused Vinnie to remain silent. 'I compared it to seeing some TV soap star in Manchester a few months back, then not realising exactly who he was 'til I next saw him on TV.'

Maria cast another glance at the photos. 'You think he's been on TV?'

'Not necessarily,' Vinnie replied. 'She might have seen him in the city before. Perhaps he works somewhere we visit regularly?'

'What should I do?'

Vinnie shrugged at Maria. 'About this guy?'

'Should I call the cops?' she asked, conscious the idea sounded somewhat melodramatic when spoken aloud.

'And say what?' he replied through a hint of a smile. 'You went to hug him at the airport?'

'I'd just tell them what I know.'

He sighed dismissively. 'Which is?'

'I saw him,' she repeated, nodding her head. 'He headed straight out to the cabs.'

Giuseppe looked up from channel hopping and rolled his eyes. 'They'll have already found any footage of that.'

Carmela nodded at her husband-to-be. 'What if he does work in a public place, or maybe he's been on TV or in the paper before?'

'Christ! What is it with you women?' Vinnie snapped. He shook his head and jabbed a stubby finger at his nephew. 'He's just some guy who looks like *that* guy.'

Maria pointed to the floor. 'What you trying to hide, Vincenzo?'

'Nothing,' Vinnie retorted. He pictured the wine in the cellar he'd taken *delivery* of the previous week. 'Call them if you want, but you ain't involving me.'

Carmela picked up a cordless telephone from a nearby side table. 'If you want, I'll call them on your behalf.'

'Bless you, my darling girl.' Maria smiled gratefully and patted her arm. 'Such a kind heart. You and Giuseppe may not be married yet but, from this moment, I consider you part of this family.' She narrowed her eyes and stared across the room. 'Ain't that so, Vincenzo?'

Chapter 4 – Monday 31st August 2009

2.05am – PDT
South Lake Tahoe, California

Konrad had no prior experience of insomnia: his descent into deep and satisfying sleep guaranteed, untroubled by his conscience and anything else the day threw at him. Tonight appeared to be an anomaly, despite the digital alarm clock's glaring blood red numbers continuing to reprimand his paranoia. Surely it was purely coincidence that he'd seen the family at the beach, and then a couple of hours later at the local Safeway?

The logical part of Konrad's mind stepped in and told himself it was impossible for the Feds to definitely know his exact location. There wasn't a cat in hell's chance they'd provide any opportunity for him to escape if they did and, if they'd harboured the slightest suspicion about his whereabouts, a posse of SWAT agents would have already kicked the cabin's door to smithereens.

So why's that prick Sam Bury in town?

That was the million dollar question he couldn't answer. Konrad flopped onto his back and stared at the ceiling. The usually comfortable mattress had turned into a topographic map of the Rockies and, for a fleeting second, he considered buying one of those memory foam versions. It would be a futile purchase though. He'd done the calculations: it would take around a week to gather his assets and eradicate almost all traces of him being in the area.

The trickiest part would be reaching Montana without leaving a paper trail. He'd accrued too much stuff to make public transport an easy option, to steal a car carried numerous risks and hitch-hiking left him open to recognition – although he'd take whatever steps necessary to protect his anonymity. Whilst the antics of his young daughter distracted Sam, this current disguise hadn't been rumbled by Mr Super-Fed – either at the beach or at the supermarket.

Therefore, he'd maintain it until he was almost ready to disappear…

/////

Konrad initially thought he'd hallucinated the quartet entering Safeway the previous afternoon, the picture of a happy, contented family. From his position waiting in line to pay he saw Sam grab a cart and pretend to dive-bomb his son into the child seat, then lift the giggling baby back into the air at the last moment and set him down in a controlled manner. They'd passed within feet of him; an oblivious Sam's concentration centred on steering the cart and his wife too busy locating her shopping list to notice. Only Angela, for he knew that to be her name, paid him any heed and a shy smile appeared the moment she recognised him from their short conversation at the beach. She glanced at his feet, as if looking for Stan.

The line advanced at a snail's pace and, having time to kill, Konrad contemplated the name the couple had chosen for their daughter. Maybe it was a family name, or a tribute to that guy Sam worked with who'd met an untimely end in Golden eight years ago. Angelo Garcia's death received plenty of media coverage at the time, and the *Denver Post* recently ran an article discussing the possibility of Konrad's role in the crime. He stifled a grin and realised he'd once again become the talk of the nation – this time for markedly different reasons.

Konrad completed the purchase of his groceries and returned to the parking lot to wait for the family to reappear. He idly reached into one of the bags on the back seat and broke off a green-tinted banana from a large bunch, conscious not to arouse suspicion by sitting in his car apparently doing nothing. He chewed slowly, mindful that the under-ripe fruit would take more effort to digest, and hoped the family wasn't there to do a full grocery shop.

The woman emerged fifteen minutes later, balancing the baby in one arm and Angela's hand grasping the other. Sam followed, dividing a quartet of carrier bags between each hand until they stopped beside a large blue SUV, where he pressed a key fob to open its trunk. The vehicle's Nevadan plates suggested they'd either rented it on the other side of the state line or were actually staying there. He watched Sam's wife help buckle the children into their safety seats, then wrap her arms around Sam's waist and invite him to lower his head for a kiss. Konrad couldn't help rolling his eyes and wondered what the hell she saw in a guy who was definitely punching above his weight. Maybe she wasn't quite in the league Konrad had grown accustomed to over the years, but she was certainly attractive enough to make him visualise her doing things to him Sam probably only dreamed of.

Konrad turned the ignition key seconds after Sam reversed the Saab out of its parking space. It headed for Tahoe Boulevard and he flashed two cars to follow before falling into line behind. Thanks to a red light at a nearby crosswalk all four vehicles successfully turned right in quick succession, the gap becoming smaller due to one of the cars moving into the left lane to make a turn into a shoreline motel's parking lot. For the next five minutes he passed regularly spaced hotels and restaurants, aware of the need to maintain sufficient distance, but not so much he risked getting stranded if the lights at one of the many intersections flipped to red.

Taller buildings loomed in the near distance to indicate he'd soon cross into Nevada, where the state's more liberal gambling laws supported a varied selection of casinos – most of which seemed to have been built as close to California as possible, tempting the Golden State's residents and vacationers alike. He swore loudly and swerved around a pedestrian who'd made a last-second decision to step off the sidewalk, the fool apparently eager to lose their money at the gambling tables if they didn't lose their life on the highway first.

The silver Camry enforcing the distance between him and his quarry unexpectedly veered into Harrah's parking lot to leave Konrad with a clear view of the Saab. It continued in an easterly direction, never straying more than a mile or two above the speed limit until Sam slowed and signalled right to join the exit lane for Kingsbury Grade Road.

Konrad followed Sam's ascent away from the lake to where a denser concentration of pine trees enticed him to roll down the window and inhale their sweet, heady scent. The vehicles passed wooden buildings of all sizes, their varied styles mostly able to blend into their picturesque surroundings. He noticed the snow poles had started to steadily increase in height, now he'd reached the mountains separating Tahoe from the hotter, lower area of the Sierra Nevada range to the east. Konrad's familiarity with Kingsbury Grade Road came from his excursions to Reno many times over the years.

Perhaps he'd take a different road tomorrow, *if* the family proved to be staying in this neck of the woods.

The road continued to climb, narrowing a fraction as they negotiated a series of curves flanked by pale rocky outcrops. Konrad hung back, secure in the knowledge Sam would signal his next manoeuvre with plenty of time to spare. The road looped to the right and he passed a small green sign announcing they'd passed seven thousand feet in elevation, making him wonder if Sam had chosen the area for its many similarities to Colorado.

That must be the weirdest of coincidences: both of them living a matter of miles apart today, and all those years earlier. If he was a paranoid man, he'd think Sam had intentionally tracked him down – patiently waiting for the perfect moment to take him out. Konrad noticed the Saab decelerate and its left turn signal start to blink as they approached a wooden cabin-like building that housed a real estate agency, if he recalled correctly. The vehicle made a smooth turn off the main road and continued its journey.

Konrad drove onwards, already nurturing a new idea.

/////

Konrad's thoughts returned to the present and jostled for room amongst the myriad of ideas presently occupying his mind. The most obvious was Sam being on a temporary assignment – maybe a case spanning the distance between Colorado and this small corner of Nevada. He wondered what this could be. His current fugitive situation was the first thing that sprung to mind – even if Konrad still thought it unlikely the FBI had intentionally placed one of their brightest stars in the firing line.

The final option was a permanent or semi-permanent relocation due to a perceived or real threat. He recalled a television documentary about Witness Protection, featuring a DEA agent moved halfway across the country after his identity was compromised during an undercover operation. The same provision must surely be in place for FBI agents? Of all the places, Konrad thought, realising this probably meant the Feds had no inkling of his connection to the Tahoe area – if his theory held true.

Whatever the reason, Konrad intended to make a swift return to the Kingsbury area. Next time, he'd pose as a jogger on an early morning run and attempt to locate the distinctive blue Saab. Only then he'd sleep easy once again, safe in the knowledge his new life could soon commence, unhindered by those who'd always sought to belittle him and bring him down.

What a shame Sam would be unable to rue the day their paths crossed again.

****

11.11am – BST
Hutton, Preston, England

Martin Boothroyd twisted his aching neck sharply to one side, the resulting crunch causing Paula Phelan to wince and punch him in the bicep.

'That's disgusting,' she grumbled. 'You do realise you're probably setting yourself up for problems in later life?'

'It's already been a problem for donkey's years,' he retorted. The ache never failed to transport Boothroyd back to the fracas he'd been caught up in outside a seedy Huddersfield nightspot during his first year on the beat. A small group of visiting Bradford City fans had taken umbrage at their team's heavy defeat by the home team, leading to the consumption of copious quantities of strong Yorkshire bitter. This local brew had fuelled a vicious altercation between them and a larger group of Huddersfield lads, the outcome being that one fellow police officer ended up in traction for a fortnight – and over two decades of enduring neck problems for Boothroyd.

Dave Sanderson looked up from a victim statement he'd recently received and narrowed his eyes. 'Isn't there anything they can do?'

'Not really,' Boothroyd replied. 'If it starts getting crunchy, I remortgage the house and book myself a series of sessions with that chiropractor. She tries to strangle me, I pay her shitloads for the privilege and then I go home to the wife.'

Sanderson stared at the family photo Boothroyd kept on his desk. 'Isn't that a little kinky for your tastes, not to mention illegal?'

'My wallet bloody well thinks so. Anyway, give me some good news on the Umpleby case.'

'The FBI emailed the preliminary results of brake line analysis,' Phelan began, now she'd familiarised herself with this side of the investigation. 'One of their fancy forensics labs identified many similarities between the punctured brake lines from 1986 and 1990, and Kratz's more recent work.

They can't be absolutely certain 'til they've completed all the tests, but, based on the physical evidence *and* the circumstantial evidence, they reckon Winterburn's and Pallis' cars were most likely sabotaged by Peter Umpleby.'

Boothroyd scribbled notes on a pad he always kept within arm's reach. 'Unless new evidence appears to contradict this, we'll go with it. However, a legal shark could throw enough doubts into a jury's mind so, unless he's found, we continue digging. Irrespective that he was supposed to be in America from 1990, I want all unsolved murders between 1986 and 2009 examined and their victimology reviewed. See if any of the deaths have any link to the Umpleby family, however tenuous. We're going to nail this arsehole once and for all.'

****

10.39am – EDT
Brooklyn, New York

Maria Volonte's gaze hovered around the doorway before returning to a carriage clock on the nearby gothic-style mantelpiece. She swallowed away the worst of her nerves, noticing minutes remained until she'd hear *them* arrive at her home's imposing wooden front door.

Carmela patted the older woman's hand and gave her what she hoped was a reassuring smile. 'You'll be fine, Maria,' she whispered. 'They're only interested in what you can recall, and maybe they'll then jog your memory a little.'

'Vinnie don't like the cops in his home,' Maria replied. Her large deep brown eyes darted back and forth. 'He thinks I'm a silly old woman.'

'Who he loves more than life itself. The police aren't bothered about anything else, they just want to catch this guy.'

Maria nodded. 'Yeah, I guess. I don't really see how I can be much help.'

They both startled at the doorbell's chime and Carmela jumped to her feet. 'You let them be the judge of that,' she said firmly. Seconds later she twisted the key in the lock, pulled the heavy wooden front door open and raised her neat brows at a middle-aged man standing on the second to uppermost step.

'Mrs Volonte?'

'Not for a few more months.' She managed to hide her amusement when he narrowed his eyes and offered his credentials for Carmela to inspect. 'I'm visiting from England,' she added. 'You'll want my fiancé's Aunt Maria instead.'

His tense smile struggled to reach his eyes. 'Can I come in?'

'Yeah, she's in the day room.' Carmela pointed to the partially closed door to her right. 'Go on in. Can I make you a coffee?'

'That's great, thanks. Black, one sugar.'

Carmela opened the door and smiled at Maria. 'This is Detective Lopez from the Port Authority police. I'll be back in a minute as soon as I've made us all some drinks.'

Maria watched her disappear into the kitchen. 'She's such a lovely girl. If it hadn't been for her, I doubt I'd have called you.'

Lopez nodded at the woman, who reminded him of the grandmother he'd adored until her sudden death shortly after his sixth birthday. 'We're grateful you did, Mrs Volonte.'

'Maria,' she said sternly. 'I'm not so old you need to be so formal.'

'Maria,' he repeated. 'Tell me about the guy you saw at the airport.'

Her shoulders slumped and she shook her head. 'I'm not sure how much use I'll be.'

'Everything helps,' Lopez said in a non-committal tone. 'We're constructing a timeline of his movements since he arrived in the country. Our counterparts in England have undertaken a similar task and made a great deal of progress. We hope what you reveal may go some way to identifying him.'

Maria nodded and studied the man's lined face, her expression earnest. 'I'll try.'

'Talk me through what happened before you met your nephew at the airport,' he asked, his pencil scratching across a notepad as Maria explained how the tall stranger's colouring and posture reminded her of Giuseppe. He managed to partially suppress a smile at her coy admission that, if hadn't been for the intervention of her sharper-eyed husband, she'd have launched herself at the young man and subjected him to the kind of greeting he'd have been unlikely to forget in a hurry.

'That's great,' Lopez said when Maria's words tailed off. She glanced at the door and wondered what Carmela was doing in the kitchen, besides making coffee. 'Does the name Anthony Collins mean anything to you?' he asked.

'Anthony… Collins…' Maria frowned and rolled the words around her mouth like someone tasting a cheap bottle of wine. 'Can't say it does. What if that isn't his real name?'

'That's almost certain, based on a number of findings I'm sure you'll understand I can't disclose. For now, we're unsure whether he's British or American, if he has any ties to this city or if he's still *in* this city. He could be anywhere by now.'

Maria nodded and considered the small amount of information she'd gleaned from the detective. 'He looked familiar,' she said. 'You know, like I'd seen him someplace else.'

'Please don't think I'm pressurising you, ma'am; if you have a vague idea where you previously saw him, it could really help us narrow down our search parameters.'

'I did have a theory,' Carmela added, surprising them as they hadn't heard her bring the tray of drinks into the room. 'He's got a job which puts him in the public eye. Maybe he works in retail, or his photo has been in the newspaper regularly.'

Maria nodded enthusiastically, much to Lopez's surprise. 'There's that television idea too!' she exclaimed.

'Television idea?' Lopez echoed. He licked his dry lips and realised his busy schedule meant he hadn't had anything to drink since leaving his apartment early that morning.

'Sorry about the stereotyping.' Carmela set down the tray upon which she'd arranged three large doughnuts on a brightly painted plate. 'I'm a sucker for anything from Holey Heaven; I wish we had it in the UK.' She relaxed when he gave a snort of muffled laughter. 'Anyway, the TV thing. It's like the time I spotted a British actor in Manchester. I was sure I'd recognised him. It wasn't 'til I saw him on TV a couple of weeks later I realised who he was. Could've been embarrassing, I was going to go up to him and say hello.'

Lopez reached for a Bavarian cream and heard his stomach rumble. 'You think this guy has been on TV?' he asked, watching Maria's cheeks redden.

'Sounds dumb, right?'

'Not necessarily,' he replied, having heard more outlandish theories over the years than he cared to remember. 'Let's go with the idea you've seen him on TV, however dumb you think it sounds. How long ago do you think you saw him?'

'Can't be too far back,' she said. 'Got a memory like a strainer these days.'

'Which shows do you watch regularly?' Lopez asked. Maria closed her eyes and concentrated hard, then shook her head. 'Would looking through the TV guide help?' he suggested when she didn't speak.

'Here you are, Maria.' Carmela passed the previous week's listings magazine across the coffee table. 'Take your time.'

She picked up the tattered weekly. 'You really will think I've gotten senile in my old age.'

Lopez set down his empty cup. 'Ma'am, I've been doing this job for over a decade. You'd be surprised where the most preposterous-sounding ideas can lead.'

****

7.12pm – BST
Blackpool, England

Long-serving detective Harry Irwin wiped tears of mirth from his ruddy cheeks, slumped into the chair closest to his desk and attempted to regain full control of his breathing. 'Did you see that couple the uniforms brought in an hour ago?' he spluttered.

'A right bloody pair,' Eddie Pell replied, unsure whether to be amused or shocked at the welcome he'd received in the police station's reception area.

'You'd think it wouldn't be such a surprise,' Irwin continued. 'I mean, I was brought up in Fleetwood, I've worked in this town for well over twenty years and we're only a couple of minutes' walk from the Prom. They were proper pissed up though.'

Pell watched Irwin rummage through an assortment of case files on his desk. 'How old do you reckon they are?' he asked.

'At least eighty,' Irwin replied, making a mental note to tell his wife to lay off the sherry during the week. 'Anyway, how's tricks?'

'Fair to middling, I suppose. You?'

'Mustn't grumble.' Irwin located the information he'd been looking for and pushed a copy across the desk. 'Roger Mortimer's bank account is causing us a fair bit of brain ache. A mere northern pleb like me doesn't have access to the account that provided Roger's six-figure dollar injection, so I'll have to put some feelers out.'

Pell nodded and relayed the details of a conversation he'd had earlier that day, during Cold Case Unit detective Paula Phelan's visit to Preston's main police station. After a tense half hour interviewing a newly-emerged witness for another case, Phelan spent a little over twenty minutes catching up with her old mentor. She'd mentioned the recent contact between her team and an FBI legal attaché in London, and theatrically pointed at a discrete CCTV camera to remind him of the Bureau's reputation for having eyes everywhere.

Irwin didn't try to hide his admiration. 'That's a nice little Brucie bonus,' he said, rubbing his hands together. 'You reckon this woman can help?'

'Well, even if she can't she'll contact someone who can,' Pell replied, confident Linda Neville would at least know which government department could action Irwin's request. 'Leave it with me and I'll pass on your details, and those of the Mortimer case. Anyway, how far have you got tracing Anthony Collins?'

'As you know, Avis sent tracking details for the car Collins hired,' Irwin replied as he handed a copy of the data to Pell. 'There's not many places he visited which don't immediately ring any bells, both here and in Preston. That's why I asked you to come over. I wondered if between us we can make some headway.'

Pell nodded, imbued with an unexpected sense of optimism. 'Let's get those garibaldis out of the brew room and dig out a couple of street maps,' he said. 'I'll phone Sara in a bit to tell her I'll be late in and not to make me anything to eat.' He noticed Irwin's raised eyebrows. 'She's got used to it over the years. I'll grab summat from the chippy on the way home.'

'Here's one for Preston, and this is Blackpool's.' Irwin spread the maps over his desk. 'And here's some of those sticky coloured dots to mark where he's been. They don't shit where they eat, so any blatantly clear areas may suggest a location for Collins' base.' He pulled a red marker pen out of the desk drawer. 'But, he's a transient resident, so to speak. Do the same rules apply for fly-by-night killers?'

Pell rubbed his chin and considered his reply. 'That I'm not sure of, but we can certainly make a start.' He picked up a printed copy of the information from Avis. 'Here it is in its full glory: The magical adventures of Anthony Collins.'

'Those maps pretty much meet in the middle, so let's clear all the crap off that desk and lay them out flat next to each other,' Irwin said, surprised by his enthusiasm after a long day shift. 'If we plot the routes he took and then add a date to each move, it may give us some sort of pattern.'

'He arrived in Preston on Monday 3rd August and checked into that Holiday Inn Express near the bus station.' Pell pressed a red circle on to the map and annotated Collins' arrival date. 'It's a convenient location for getting in and out of town, and from what I've heard it's not bad in there. We'll ask the CCTV control room to check town centre footage from the times he's parked up at the hotel. It's a few minutes' walk into town from there and everyone knows parking's always a bastard inside Ringway.'

For the next hour, the duo worked methodically to identify locations where Collins had stopped for more than five minutes and draw the interconnecting routes. A cursory analysis failed to yield any discernible clue, yet they remained hopeful; determined to read between the lines if it led to the capture of Roger Mortimer's killer.

'I suppose it shows where he went, but have we really gleaned anything new?' Irwin asked, his enthusiasm fading in tandem with the light outside.

'Let's discount the places we know he'd got a definite reason for visiting,' Pell said, still confident this wouldn't be a wasted exercise. 'There's the Edward II, Mortimer's house and a pub not too far from the house, where I'd guarantee some sort of business meeting occurred. He's been to B&Q and you can bet your arse he wasn't shopping for a new bathroom suite. Analysis of the clingfilm used to smother Mortimer came back as supermarket own brand type, and on the afternoon he went to B&Q he visited the Sainsbury's near West Side's ground. I'll get on to them with the time parameters in case they can isolate CCTV from that Friday afternoon. If we get an image of someone buying clingfilm matching the guy who flew to New York we've got our proof.'

Irwin nodded and leaned over the nearest map. 'Where else in Preston did he go that day?'

'Before Sainsbury's he stopped in Ashton,' Pell replied. 'The car stayed put for around ten or so minutes, and constantly running the engine suggests he stayed in the vehicle.'

'Maybe he was checking a map?' Irwin couldn't count the number of occasions he'd found himself lost in Preston. 'You know, if he's unfamiliar with the area.'

'Possibly, though there's usually a fairly decent amount of parking on that stretch of Blackpool Road.' Pell closed his eyes to picture the area. 'He wouldn't have needed to turn onto any side streets, let alone go down to the end.'

'You think he had a reason for being there? And, just because the engine was running, it doesn't mean he stayed in the car. Anyway, what's Middleton Avenue like? Perhaps he knows someone who lives there?'

'It's a respectable street if my memory serves me correctly,' Pell replied. A life-long resident of the town, his familiarity with the area frequently served him well during Preston-based cases. 'Mostly three-bed semis popular with young families.' He paused and frowned.

Irwin mirrored the expression. 'What's wrong?' he asked through a mouthful of biscuit.

'There was an altercation there last week. Some Aussie journalist kept hassling one of the families because Konrad Kratz lived in their house twenty years ago. The husband lost his rag and planted one on the hack. Said they were upsetting his wife and young son.'

'Kratz lived there?'

'Down that same far end,' Pell confirmed. 'Why did Collins visit that house?'

'Who said he did?' Irwin scrutinised a printed CCTV image of Anthony Collins at Heathrow Airport.

'I don't follow.'

Irwin typed a well-known name into Google's image search and held the sheet of glossy paper beside the computer's screen.

'You're fucking kidding me?' Pell spluttered incredulously. 'You seriously think they're the same guy?'

'Not for me to say. That Detective Goldstein at the Port Authority police in Jersey City said to get back to her with any developments, even if they didn't seem to amount to much. They've got state-of -the-art facial recognition software over there.'

'You sound bloody ridiculous!'

Irwin patted Pell on the back. 'Let our American cousins be the judge of that.'

****

Maria Goldstein adjusted her glasses and stared over their rims at an assortment of security camera stills taken from locations on both sides of the Atlantic.

Could it really be him?

She narrowed her eyes and wondered if the unexpected phone call from an English detective she had, until then, only communicated with via email actually held any truth. Additional images needed to be obtained and analysed, before they released further information to a public whose imaginations were already gripped by the anonymous fugitive who'd arrived in their city.

JFK Airport's cutting-edge surveillance system made it easy to follow the man out of the Arrivals area to a line of yellow cabs; the identification number of their fugitive's vehicle visible with minimal enhancement. Its driver had checked his records and returned Meaker's call that morning, his scant memories of the passenger he'd dropped off in Chinatown of little help. A team of analysts now sifted through additional footage from around the time the cab reached its destination, eager to trace Anthony Collins' later movements.

Goldstein made a supreme effort to push what she viewed to be random speculation out of her mind and opened a paper copy of the case file they'd built so far. Years of experience told her that the man's frequent change from one mode of transportation to another was a decoy, designed to throw any pursuing law enforcement off the scent. From Chinatown, a succession of cameras recorded Collins hailing a dollar van. She'd have to wait until tomorrow for further details, assuming the van could be electronically followed.

Konrad Kratz? They'll think you've gone goddamn nuts.

But, there'd been that weird coincidence of an old lady in Brooklyn convinced she'd previously seen Collins, and television had been suggested as one of many possible explanations. Goldstein twisted back and forth in her seat to relieve a sudden cramp in her side and wondered whether the woman's viewing habits included anything starring Kratz, then closed her eyes and attempted to massage away the growing tension around her temples.

****

4.22pm – PDT
Rimcrest Drive, Brockmont, California

Detective Paul Whitehead put the sedan in park and stared around the street. 'I always said this is one sweet, sweet neighbourhood,' he commented, his admiration obvious. 'Kind of wish we had more call-outs up here, rather than our usual spots.'

Ronnie Mosley winked at his Glendale PD equivalent. 'Yeah, I don't see it giving South Central much of a challenge.'

'Can't think I've ever been up here other than on this case,' Whitehead replied after they'd left the unmarked vehicle. 'The worst you get in this kind of suburb is the occasional home being burglarised or a domestic dispute. It's not the usual serial killer's playground.'

'Kratz evidently thought so too.' Mosley scanned the immediate area and was relieved to see no evidence of the paparazzi. The last thing he needed was a trashy magazine article focussing on the di Marco family's possible involvement in the case. 'From what her mom said over the phone yesterday, it seems Galina's gotten angry about the situation. Can't say I blame her, she must be feeling mighty shit about the whole thing.'

'Understandable, given the circumstances,' Whitehead agreed, enjoying the warm breeze that gently brushed the hillside. 'She gets emotionally taken in and ends up getting an eighteen year sentence in exchange. I get that she's trying to have as normal a life as possible, but it can't be easy studying, raising a child and trying to make a little free time for yourself.'

The duo walked the short distance across the baked road surface to the di Marco home and stared past its wrought iron gates, the expansive property still able to impress them. 'While it's nice to experience the high life, I sure hope Pops ain't home,' Whitehead added. 'He don't let up when he's angry.'

'I've seen his type before,' Mosley said. 'All talk, although he puts on a damn good show. Explains why he's one of the best in the business.' He pressed the intercom and fell silent during the short wait, listening to the faint hum of traffic rise up from the urban sprawl beneath them.

'Yes?'

The monosyllabic reply left Whitehead unable to identify the tinny voice's owner. 'Galina?' he queried. 'It's detectives Whitehead and Mosley. We're a little early for our appointment.'

'Sure thing.' A loud click sounded as the lock was released remotely and the gates swung open. A large stone-paved driveway stretched ahead of them, encircling an ornate marble statue bathed by its own fountain.

Not for the first time, Mosley eyed the Roman soldier disdainfully. 'That's got to be some kind of weird Italian fetish, right?'

'It's how the other half live, I guess. Mom raised me in a Pasadena high-rise, so I can't get my head around this being normality for some people.' Whitehead whispered, feeling more and more like a fish out of water.

'And it's all funded by the naughty boys and girls of Tinseltown,' Mosley countered. 'Kind of makes me wish I'd pulled my lazy finger out of my lazy ass at high school and gotten myself some better grades.'

The front door opened to reveal an attractive brunette balancing a gurgling, blonde-haired baby on one hip. 'Who are these nice gentlemen?' Galina cooed to her daughter, smiling when the little girl pointed a pudgy finger at the two detectives and giggled in delight.

Mosley raised an eyebrow and stared at Anya. For the first time he saw the daughter of one of the worst serial killers in America's recent history. Would she end up like her father, or inherit the values and work ethic of the maternal side of her family?

The old Nature vs. Nurture debate.

'Hello, beautiful girl,' he said jovially and passed his detectives' shield to her for inspection. Anya's plump hands grasped the gold-coloured metal and her large blue eyes stared intently at the object. 'We're here to speak with your mommy, if that's okay?' The baby chuckled and lifted the shield towards her new teeth, causing Mosley to whisk the item away before it could reach its intended destination.

'So, Galina, how you doing?' Mosley asked.

She led them into the pristine modern kitchen, smiled sadly and strapped Anya into a sturdy oak high chair. 'Okay, I guess. Would you guys like something to drink?'

'Thank you,' he replied. 'Anything cold would hit the spot.'

'My mom left a huge jug of coffee in the refrigerator before heading out to work this morning. Is that okay for both of you?' She smiled at their enthusiastic nods. 'She also baked a zucchini cake yesterday afternoon. It's surprisingly good,' she added hurriedly as she lifted the lid from a large metal cake tin and noticed their dubious expressions.

'If you insist,' Whitehead replied. He watched her pick up a serrated knife and carve three slices. 'It sure looks good. We appreciate your time in this matter; it can't be easy juggling everything.'

'I manage. Life would be very different if I didn't have the support of my family. There's enough money in Anya's account to pay her through college if she ever decides to go, and once I start practising law I'll earn enough to support us both.'

Mosley eyed the cake Galina placed in front of him. 'You haven't received any more money from Kratz?' he asked.

She snorted her indignation, lifted three large glasses from a nearby wall cupboard and then reached into the fridge for the jug of iced coffee. 'Haven't heard from him since June. I don't care about myself, but he provided fifty percent of my gorgeous girl's DNA.' She paused to pass a large strawberry to Anya, who examined it in the same manner as she had Mosley's detective shield. 'Yeah, it helps to think of the asshole as a sperm donor.'

'We have a theory Kratz has at least one more home in an unknown location, probably within a twelve-hour drive or six hundred miles from here, or maybe from Denver.' Whitehead eyed the plate and resisted the urge to immediately tuck into his cake. 'Obviously our counterparts in Colorado are on the case, so meanwhile we need to work out if his hidey-hole is nearer to this place. We–'

'Have you investigated in New York?' Galina interrupted. Her glass clattered when she abruptly set it down on the countertop. 'He filmed *H.O.S.T.A.G.E.* there much of the time.'

'It hasn't been ruled out.' Whitehead nodded his thanks when she pushed two full glasses across to him and Mosley. 'We think within the radius I mentioned of either here or Denver, or what's not to say both, is the most likely. His link to New York is more recent, but he's had ties to this area and Colorado since the nineties.'

She swallowed the last of her drink and picked up the jug to refill her glass. 'I'm always happy to help, but I really have told you everything I can remember.'

'Did you ever notice Kratz come back here after going away for anything up to a week?' Mosley asked. 'I mean whenever he was meant to be staying here, rather than returning from filming in New York.'

'I'm sorry, I can't think.'

Mosley smiled. 'We'd like to try something a little different, which may help you to remember something you hadn't previously.'

Galina nodded. 'It's worth a try, I guess.'

'Is your brother around?'

'Yeah, he's in his room,' she replied, puzzled. 'Why?'

'He'll need to mind the baby,' Mosley said. 'There's nothing to worry about. You'll need as few distractions as possible.'

'Sure thing, he owes me for covering his skinny ass when he stayed out past curfew last weekend.' She scooped her daughter from the highchair. 'Come on, pumpkin. Let's go play with Uncle Mikhail.'

They listened to her slow steps climb the wide sweeping staircase they'd seen earlier.

'You think she knows more than she's letting on?' Whitehead asked. He picked up the cake, took a small bite and cautiously chewed. 'Hey, this is pretty good. My wife would probably want the recipe.'

'It'll be on Google,' Mosley said and sniffed his slice. 'It smells okay, I guess. Galina has more to tell us, but I don't think she realises. She's pissed at him and she's trying to remain impartial.' He took a small bite of his own cake and nodded his agreement. 'That'll make her a decent lawyer one day.'

The sound of footfalls gained their attention, their rapid-fire nature a sign that Galina no longer carried her precious daughter in her arms. 'Told you guys you'd like it,' she said and effortlessly lifted herself onto a bar-style stool. 'Okay, fire away!'

Mosley noticed her subconscious choice to put a protective granite barrier between them. 'This is routine, and can help you recall little things you may have dismissed at the time. It's totally safe and non-invasive. I'd now like you to close your eyes and block out any visual stimuli which may distract you.' She followed his instruction. 'Now, picture yourself near the boundary with Kratz's home. He's been away from home for a couple of days, but his car has just pulled onto the driveway and he's getting out...'

She nodded and scrunched her eyes tightly shut. 'Yeah, I'm seeing it.'

'What are you doing?'

'Watering my new orange tree and waiting for the rest of the family to come back from the hospital. Mom thought Mikhail might have broken his wrist playing soccer with his friends.'

'So we're talking which season?'

'Summertime, quite early on. Konrad was on hiatus from filming in New York and I'd just finished for the summer break.'

'Who acknowledged the other first?'

'He called out to me.'

'Were you sleeping together at this stage?'

She opened an eye for a split-second and fell silent. 'I think so,' she said, and both men detected a degree of caginess in her voice.

'What did you do next?' Mosley pressed.

'Went over to his car. He was getting stuff out of the trunk. A large overnight-type bag and some bags from the grocery store, which I helped carry into the house.'

'Did you stay in the house?'

'He told me to go get something from the car. He said it was a little something he'd seen in San Diego and thought of me.'

'So you went back to the car? Was it the Beemer or the Honda?'

'The Honda, that's the one he always used if he went out of town. I went back out front when he was putting the groceries away and looked in the trunk, but wasn't really sure what I was looking for. There was a cooler he kept water bottles in during the summer.'

'Did you think he wanted to hide something, so he'd sent you to the car to get you out of the house for a minute or two?'

'I guess that's possible. The only other thing in the trunk was lots of pine needles. I remember thinking that was strange when he was supposed to be in San Diego.'

'How long had he been gone for?'

'He'd usually go for a couple of nights, maybe three at the most.'

'Was there anything in the car for you?'

'Yeah…' She bit her bottom lip to stop it quivering. 'I found a little bag on the passenger seat. He'd bought me the most gorgeous pink cashmere sweater; said I'd always feel him close to me when he was away filming in the winter.'

'Did he buy you gifts regularly?'

'Not really. Once I learned I was pregnant we mostly spoke only to get the cover story straight.' She leaned against the stool's backrest and moistened her parched mouth with a large gulp of coffee. 'I'm sorry I can't help you more, detectives.'

'That's okay, Galina.' Mosley replied. 'You've been more helpful than you realise. We should get back to the station now; see if there's been any more developments.'

'You'll keep me updated?' she asked. 'I need to know he's locked up. I never want my daughter to learn who her real father is, I'd rather she think of me as a whore.'

'Sure we'll let you know.' He registered the sudden change in her demeanour on their return to the front door. 'You have both our contact details if you remember anything else, or call me if you ever need to talk.'

'Thank you,' Galina said, struggling to stop the tears from falling. 'Have a safe journey,' she added, before closing the door.

They walked back to the car deep in thought and seemingly oblivious to the relentless heat. Whitehead finally broke the silence. 'Pine needles in San Diego?'

'Looks like someone's not being entirely honest,' Mosley agreed. He opened the driver's side door and winced. 'Jeez, it's like a volcano in there,' he muttered and tapped his foot in irritation during their wait for the air conditioning to do its job.

'Big Bear is only a couple of hours away if you get a decent run though,' Whitehead said. 'It's always been popular with Angelinos and there's plenty pine trees up there.'

Mosley lowered himself into his seat and left the door wide open. 'You think he maintains a secret home so close to the city? My guess is it's further afield, but within our parameters.'

'She said he'd usually be away for a couple nights at a time when he wasn't away for weeks filming. Makes me agree it likely ties in to his little hidey-hole being somewhere within the geographic area we identified.'

'I figure he'd stay within the state.'

'Why's that?' Whitehead narrowed his eyes to watch Mosley pull his door closed now the air conditioning had taken effect.

The other man winked and tapped the side of his forehead knowingly. 'A Cali plate's going to blend in better within state lines than say in Nevada, Utah, or Arizona. Seen it all before. Perps crossing state lines and using fake plates.'

'Good point.' Whitehead agreed. 'Let's go research us some Californian woodland real estate.'

****

11.55pm – PDT
Kingsbury, Nevada

The sound of slow regular breathing filled the room and exacerbated Sam's irritation at remaining awake almost an hour after Anna drifted into sleep. He stared into the surrounding blackness, pictured the ceiling he couldn't see and wondered why his eyes resolutely refused to close. He knew the gradual accumulation of sleep deprivation would soon erode his performance at work, yet another facet of his life Kratz appeared intent on destroying. He'd become aware of how his temper frayed more readily these days, the way he'd berated Angela when she'd begged for a minute to search for her beloved *Teddy* also noticed by Anna. He'd claimed his frustration was due to the car dealership closing for the night less than an hour later, but both of them knew the real reasons were buried much deeper than this.

He sensed Anna moving beside him and imagined her tranquil expression as she slept peacefully in their new surroundings. He wondered what really went through her mind at this time of uncertainty; whether Kratz found his way into her thoughts more or less frequently than the man invaded his. Guilt bubbled to the surface, the unwelcome emotion not having far to travel these days. She'd stuck by him throughout the most traumatic year of his life, and yet he had the potential to destroy the person he held most dear.

From what Sam later learned, signs of his struggle to cope in the crash's aftermath appeared before his transfer from Bellevue's High Dependency Unit to Denver's St Anthony Hospital, where newly-formed memories became more static. Recollection of his time in Bellevue remained sketchy; a complex combination of drugs, not to mention the severe concussion he'd sustained, leaving his memory full of holes. Images swam in and out of focus: some regained their clarity whilst others fell into gaping chasms, consumed until the next trigger.

Since the accident, every awakening felt like he'd been submerged into a viscous liquid from which his body struggled to free itself. Familiar sounds seeped into his aching head and distorted images danced mockingly on the back of his eyelids, cavorting too quickly for him to catch more than a glimpse.

His eyes squeezed tightly closed in one last attempt to rid himself of the horror he knew the images would contain if he could piece them together.

It never worked.

Sam opened his eyes, a brief action he quickly reversed when bright light from above hit his retinas. He swallowed and was surprised to find his throat felt dry and prickly. Something clamped to his face was trying to suffocate him and an attempt to move his head resulted in a faint groan, his sense of detachment from the sound adding to his unease.

'Sam?' A short silence passed and the voice became fainter. 'I think it's wearing off.'

Who was it talking to?

An alarm sounded, another familiar sound reorienting him to the present, and he opened his eyes again. Anna's concerned face hovered a couple of feet away and relief rushed through him at the sight of the tentative smile spreading across her cheeks.

'I have some good news for you,' she said. 'Actually, I have lots of good news for you.'

Sam frowned and lifted his hand to his face. 'What's this?' he mumbled.

'They've put the mask back on until you're fully awake. It's nothing to worry about, you'll have the prongs back in later. Your tests came back fine and you're making good progress.'

His eyes darted around his surroundings when a different monitor bleeped nearby.

'Tests?'

Anna leaned over him and pressed a hand against his shoulder. 'Sam, you're okay. You're still in the hospital and they took some x-rays and scans this morning, so they needed to make you sleepy.' She noticed a fresh sheen of perspiration on his forehead. 'Did you have another bad dream?'

He swallowed again. 'I don't know,' he replied and closed his eyes, wishing more than ever for the empty sleep that continued to elude him.

'You're safe here,' Anna continued, her voice soft. She stroked Sam's tussled hair. 'And you'll be safe in Denver too. The doctors decided you're well enough to be transferred and you'll be there by this time tomorrow. Isn't that amazing?'

His eyes reopened, glazed due to the residual sedation. 'Denver?' he repeated, then winced as he attempted to stretch a cramping muscle in his back, his ribs still painful even though the fractures had started to knit.

'That's right, the next step to going home. How are you feeling today?' Anna's eyes swept over his face and chest. The vivid purple bruising he'd sustained over a week earlier had faded to a sickly yellow, providing a backdrop for an angry red line where the surgeon had operated. 'You're doing really well; every time I visit I can see you've improved.'

Sam nodded. 'Still hurts,' he whispered, feeling empty at what should have been encouraging news.

Seconds later she saw him eyeing a cup of water on the side table. 'I can get you some Ensure if you want. Dr Bassett said you need to build up your strength.'

Sam stared at the coloured lines tracing a steady path across a monitor beside his bed. 'I'm not hungry,' he replied and tried to shift position, suddenly aware of the casts on his arm and leg. The dream receded and Angelo's bloodied face faded from view behind a shattered windshield. 'Denver… how?'

'Dr Bassett arranged a flight for tomorrow afternoon. You'll be at St Anthony until they're satisfied you're ready to come home.'

Sam struggled to process the information. 'On a plane?'

'It's a special medevac plane where you'll be cared for by at least two members of staff. I'll bet you're pleased, right?'

'Have they caught him?' His lips pursed at the sight of her deep frown. She surely knew he was frantic for information and he couldn't help feeling confused about why she'd withhold it. 'The guy who tried to murder me.'

Anna rearranged the thin blanket covering his lower body in an attempt to displace her fear whenever he broached the subject; an increasingly regular occurrence over the past two days. 'Sam, nobody tried to murder you.'

He stared at the fuzzy white ceiling tiles and considered his reply. 'The police know that for sure, do they?'

'They're still investigating what happened.'

'He'll follow me.' Sam's panic was evident as he raised his head. 'I'll never be safe.'

'You need to relax, Sam,' she said, finding it increasingly difficult to eradicate all traces of fear from her voice. 'There's nothing to suggest you were deliberately targeted.'

'Lightning doesn't–' A sudden bout of coughing wracked his chest and he pressed his uninjured arm against the fresh pain from his damaged ribs.

Anna leaned over him. 'Take it easy,' she said. 'You want some water?'

He shook his head between gasps and slumped back against the bank of pillows.

'Did you remember something?' she asked once the coughing had eased.

'I don't know.' He looked at Anna through drooping eyelids. 'How much longer do I need to stay here?'

'Just one more day in New York. In Denver it depends on how quickly you recover enough strength to return home.' She wondered if newly revealed memories were responsible for Sam's restlessness. 'Sam, I get that you're tired and sore. We need to know if you remember anything new from the day of the accident.'

He rubbed his pounding head. 'I don't remember anything; I already told you!' he snapped, glaring at his hand.

'Leave the IV alone, Sam!' Anna said more sharply than she'd intended. 'Try to remember anything from before the crash – it may help solve the case. Joe said memories often return.'

Sam's eyes closed against the vice-like headache now squeezing his skull. 'It's all blank,' he slurred, the words barely audible as sleep took over.

He'd been unaware of Bassett monitoring the exchange from the next bay. The doctor nodded to Anna, who followed him into an office used for family consultations. During their meeting, Bassett first explained the encouraging results of the tests Sam had undergone that morning, in addition to the logistics behind his transfer to Denver.

Bassett watched Anna's face pale within seconds of him expressing the medical team's concerns over Sam's recovery, despite the removal of the chest tube and his slowly returning appetite since his transfer to the High Dependency Unit. He'd noticed her eyes glisten when she heard that over the past two days Sam's ability to process information had improved, yet his responses suggested he'd prefer to be oblivious to everything around him, including the regimen of exercise prescribed by his physical therapist.

In a shaky voice she'd asked if this was a temporary setback; a consequence of the physical trauma he'd suffered only days ago. Bassett paused before admitting his uncertainty surrounding the answer. Yes, the concussion had likely exacerbated Sam's reaction, not to mention his gradual realisation of the serious nature of the other injuries he'd sustained.

The developing nightmares caused them the most concern over the past two days. Sam had regularly awoken suddenly, unable to comprehend his surroundings and what had happened to him. Less than twenty-four hours *earlier, Anna witnessed Sam's increased restlessness growing into obvious distress as he muttered and called out in his sleep; the words incomprehensible, the terror blatant. Helplessly, she'd stroked his face; her soft words doing little to soothe away her husband's fear.*

She hadn't realised this was just the beginning.

He thought back to the preliminary hostage negotiation training he'd participated in nearly six years previously: one of its main tactics to appear calm to those around you, even if you were a seething mass of terror inside. Anna was different though. He put her uncanny knack of knowing how he felt down to her years of detective work, always looking for the tiniest details to crack the most difficult of cases, and never reticent to voice an opinion.

There's only so long she'll put up with all your shit. There's another life out there for her.

Deep down, Sam knew he needed to believe this situation was temporary and that the family would eventually return to Denver. He shifted beneath the comforter and the movement caused Anna to roll onto her side and cuddle up to him. She released a deep breath and a cloud of calm settled over Sam, now certain he'd made the correct decision. He carefully stretched his arm across her warm back and closed his eyes.

Chapter 5 – Tuesday 1st September 2009

7.04am – PDT
Mattole Road, near South Lake Tahoe, California

The relentless onslaught of frigid air pinching his skin gave Konrad few options, other than to question the motive behind dragging himself out of bed two hours earlier than usual. He hurriedly changed into the running gear he'd had the presence of mind to drape over a chair the previous night and, as an afterthought, grabbed a nearby sweater. Whilst eating a light breakfast of oatmeal and fruit, he watched the sun's slow ascent commence; its sharp rays powerless to disperse the cold that mounted a second attack during the short jog to his car. Condensation slicked the vehicle's windows, leaving him in no doubt the area would suffer its first frost by the end of the month.

The ageing car revved into life at his first attempt and the dense white plumes it generated maintained their dogged pursuit beyond the turn for Kiva Beach. By then the temperature gauge had crept upwards, even if the car's interior clung on to its uncomfortable chill – *reyt parky*, his grandmother used to call it.

An almost deserted Tahoe Boulevard stretched into the distance, the hour too early for tourists or locals to be awake in any great number. Its successive green lights meant his journey eastward progressed at a faster rate than usual and, if he'd been into all that superstitious crap, Konrad would have attributed some kind of positive omen to the phenomenon. After all, Preston boasted its infamous red runs: a torturous experience whereby every traffic light turned red on any drive from one end of town to another, regardless of the route chosen. That place had never done him any favours; another part of the conspiracy to smother his hopes and ambitions prior to his parentally-enforced move across the Atlantic nineteen years ago.

Konrad took a now-familiar right turn onto Kingsbury Grade Road and followed the five-minute climb he'd made two days earlier. He eased his foot off the accelerator and, without signalling, swung the steering wheel to the left. A cat's cradle of power lines criss-crossed above him, barely skimming a row of chalet-style cabins where this new, narrower road began its meandering route up to the densely wooded mountains. He peered through the windshield and felt his enthusiasm wane when he saw more scattered cabins than he could count nestled amongst the distant trees. To maintain a gentle jog around the area appeared to be an impossible mission, largely due to the terrain's steepness and its gain in altitude. At least it was early, and surely most of the residents would either still be in bed, or too intent on their morning routines to pay his vehicle anything more than momentary attention?

The last vestiges of nocturnal chill retreated and a defiant morning sun rose into the sapphire-tinted sky. Konrad stopped where the road intersected Bradbury Way and, not for the first time, noticed how the area's widely spaced dwellings and scenic overlooks bore more than a passing resemblance to a forested version of Paradise Hills. A delivery truck laboured uphill, its blinking signal confirming the driver's decision to turn right. It continued past a pair of modest properties and then made a left turn onto a smaller road, running parallel to his present location.

A solitary car drove past, its occupant affording him little more than a cursory glance at the start of her morning commute. Konrad followed the truck to the T-junction and instead chose to turn right where the trees thinned. He noticed the cabins had now become more Alpine in style; the entryways of those to his right on the uppermost floor and their bedrooms beneath, nestling against the steep hillside where it fell away from the road. A raised garage door entered his peripheral vision and he slowed to a crawl to peer behind a small red Suzuki hatchback on the driveway.

There it was: the Saab SUV! He'd only gone and found the proverbial needle in a fucking big haystack. Konrad took full advantage of the road's bulbous end, looped through 360 degrees and slowly rolled past as the cabin reappeared. A shadow flashed behind the front window and he depressed the accelerator harder than intended. Grateful not to have met any other traffic, Konrad continued downhill to the intersection with North Benjamin Drive, where he rested his arms over the steering wheel and considered his next move.

Directly opposite, the forest path to the rear of a dusty pull-out gained his attention, and he decided he may as well maintain his cover story and get his morning run over and done with. Stan would have to be content with a leisurely stroll around the local forest that evening, unless Mike and Irena returned. Hopefully Irena's mom would linger for however long it took for him to leave the area.

Konrad zipped the keys into a small compartment in his shorts and spent a couple of minutes working through a well-practised routine of stretches. He ran between the trees, twice following a narrow path that looped back to his starting point. Had it all really been that easy? If he'd believed in fate, Konrad might have sworn his luck was on the change. Some people said you made your own luck, a belief he'd always dismissed as hokum . He'd need to be patient until he was ready to take care of business in this neighbourhood. For now, other more pressing matters required his attention. He finished the bottle of water he'd left in the car's trunk and, still energised, pulled open the driver's door.

****

10.11am – EDT
Port Authority Technical Center, Jersey City, New Jersey

'Do the Brits *really* think this guy is Konrad Kratz? It's kind of a stretch,' Jim Meaker asked, immediately wondering whether he should have stayed home for another day when his stomach twisted and throated tightened.

'Believe it or not, there's more than one piece of evidence pointing to that conclusion.' Maria Goldstein noticed him shake his head and lean forward. 'Hey, you feeling okay?'

Meaker took a deep breath and then exhaled through his mouth. 'I think I'm hungry. I went to see my PCP on the way here and she told me to be careful what I eat for the next day or two.' He inhaled deeply for a second time and tried to relax. 'Seems like I missed out on quite the excitement yesterday, so take my mind off the killer shrimp and fill me in.'

Her narrowed eyes bored into his pallid face. 'You're sure it ain't a bug?'

'My good lady also ate the shrimp, and so did my buddy. We all got ill. His wife went for the vegetarian option, and don't she keep on reminding us.'

'If you're wrong...'

70

'Yeah, yeah.' He swallowed an untrustworthy belch. 'Spill the latest or I'll spill something less pleasant for you.'

Goldstein managed to keep her face straight, 'You're gross!' she replied. 'Our guy went all the way to Brooklyn on a dollar van and from there disappeared into thin air. I went for the easy option and asked all the car rental agencies in the area to cross-check their security footage against their reservations. Surprisingly, they all got back to me super-fast.' She picked up a large choc chunk cookie and licked her lips. 'Nobody matching this guy's appearance or using the name Anthony Collins rented a car in the twenty-four hours after our not-so-mystery man arrived at JFK.'

Meaker raised his eyebrows, surprised and impressed by the progress made in his absence. 'Suggesting if he escaped in a car it was stolen.'

She sniffed the cookie and nodded. 'You got it. First time. Hey, these smell beyond awesome. You want one?'

'You gotta be kidding me, lady!' Meaker grumbled. 'Anyway, have they found the car?'

'Yeah.'

'No shit?'

Goldstein nodded again. 'Some old guy from Sunset Park was reported missing by his son four days after our guy landed. He hadn't been seen since the Saturday before last and when the son called at his dad's house to take him out for their usual Wednesday lunch he got no answer. His 1997 beige Honda Accord is also missing–'

'There's thousands of those on the road. Collins only needs to change the plates and we'd never find it. And, could he have dumped the body after leaving town?'

'Apparently the old man was quite the security freak,' Goldstein continued. 'He'd fitted a LoJack to the vehicle and we tracked it to Akron. I'm not sure if those devices only give the vehicle's current location, or whether we could get his exact route. Either way, I'm on it.'

Meaker's frown deepened. 'Which Akron?'

'Ohio.' She watched him ball his fists into his waist. 'Are you really okay?'

'Yeah, I'll live,' he replied, his teeth clenched against the dissipating spasm.

Not convinced he was being entirely honest about his recovery, Goldstein paused to eyeball Meaker and then resumed her update. 'Akron PD's forensic team processed the Honda and found a couple of partial prints to put through AFIS. These matched prints recovered from Kratz's two homes: one near Los Angeles and the other in a foothills community west of Denver.'

'So he's back on US soil?' Meaker commented. 'Do the FBI know?'

'Looks that way and yes,' Goldstein replied. 'I also got on to an old friend of mine who's high up in Akron PD. She went down to check it out herself and made some door-to-door inquiries while she was there. Says she misses getting out and about. Anyway, the neighbours said the car had been there since Sunday morning. They assumed the divorcée on the corner had gotten herself a piece of fresh meat to devour… you really, really don't look good.'

Meaker closed his eyes, gulped a couple of times and ignored a loud rumble from his stomach. 'I don't know what's worse: the idea of eating meat, or some old has-been getting her kicks on I-76.'

'You know the area?' she asked and attempted to recall whether he'd mentioned that part of the country during a rare investigative lull.

'Louise's folks live around seven miles west of Akron,' he replied. 'We go out there for the weekend every six to eight weeks. What did your friend tell you?'

'There was nothing to suggest where he's heading. She's assigned a detective to go through stolen car reports in the area, but so far she hasn't been able to link any recent car thefts to our case.'

'Konrad goddamn Kratz,' Meaker said. 'Are we seriously treating this as a viable lead?'

Goldstein quickly covered the short distance to the office's water cooler. 'I guess so,' she replied. 'Those English detectives asked if we could run facial recognition on the images from Heathrow and JFK, and compare them to Kratz's not-so-ugly mug. It might just be a formality now, but I set the wheels in motion while you were getting your ass checked out.'

'Wouldn't be the first time a stranger checked out my ass,' he said. 'So, what do we do in the meantime?'

'For real?' She laughed and set down a plastic cup of chilled water on Meaker's desk. 'Have you seen the pile of other cases I put down here yesterday for you?'

****

Hands on hips, Anna Bury glared at her husband. 'Next time, put them in the bowl.'

'I thought I did,' Sam snapped. He looped his tie around his neck and rammed his feet into a new pair of smart black leather brogues. 'Now I'm not going to get to the office on time.'

'We won't be late if we leave right now.' Anna scooped John up from the floor and resisted the urge to respond in a similar manner as she balanced the tearful baby on one hip. 'You found your keys, so don't worry. Like I said, double check you've put them where they're meant to be the night before. It's really not that difficult.' She scanned the cabin's entryway. 'Okay guys, we're about done here.'

Sam grabbed her free arm after she'd ushered Angela through the door. 'I'm sorry, I–'

'Stop being so English and suggest somewhere we can go this weekend,' she replied, double-checking he'd locked the front door.

He increased his pace and pulled open the nearest rear door before Anna and John reached the car. 'What about Reno for a change?'

Her narrowed eyes followed Sam as he lifted Angela and carried her around to the other side of the car. 'Take the kids to Reno for the weekend? Are you serious?'

'Well, where is there other than Sly Park?' he replied, leaning in to take over the task of strapping the children into their safety seats.

She climbed behind the steering wheel. 'Why not Sly Park? The kids like it there, we like it there… and it's convenient.'

'We could stay somewhere on Saturday night,' Sam suggested, unaware Angela clung to every word. 'Go a bit further afield. Give us something to look forward to.'

'Can we go?' the little girl pleaded. 'Please, Mommy.'

'Where do you suggest?' Anna asked.

Sam considered his reply once she'd reversed out of the driveway. 'It's nice around Mono Lake,' he said, encouraged by her brightening expression and a flicker of a smile. 'That's potentially sorted then. I'll do some research into campsites this evening.'

'What time do you want me to come get you?' Anna asked, always mindful to keep the speedometer below twenty miles per hour during the Saab's steep descent.

His joyless eyes stared out of the passenger side window and drank in the pristine blue sky and the freedom which existed beyond it. 'I'll text when I'm nearly ready,' he replied as he turned his attention to the solitary wisp of cloud emerging from behind a wall of pine trees.

Anna detected his change in tone. 'I'll meet you in the new car, though compared to this one it'll be a squash with the kids and all their stuff.' She stopped to wait for a passing Jeep. 'At least it has all-wheel drive.'

'I'll be using it most of the time,' he said, silently relieved the sometimes-chaotic early morning rush would now be a thing of the past. 'Can't really grumble when the Bureau's picking up the tab. And, hopefu–'

'Jesus!' Anna exclaimed. She yanked the steering wheel to the left, her curse partially drowned by the squeal of brakes.

Sam spun around in his seat and stared at a tall man in running gear only a matter of inches from them. 'What sort of idiot jogs across the road without looking?' He continued to eyeball the stranger. 'And he's got bloody ear buds in.'

Angela's widened eyes flitted from one parent to the other. 'Who's that man, Mommy?'

'He'll wind up dead if he keeps pulling that kind of stunt,' Anna replied. She glanced into the rear-view mirror, surprised to shiver when she saw the stationary figure standing in the middle of the road, calmly watching them accelerate away.

****

11.23am – PDT
San Fernando Road, Los Angeles, California

Alex Gibson stretched out a taut muscle in his calf and winced. 'Think I overdid it on the badminton court last night, guys,' he said in answer to his two co-workers' stares. 'Just proves age can creep up on a world-class athlete like me.' He saw Dave Hallberg roll his eyes. 'You want to play it like that, big guy? I'll see you on that court this evening.'

'No chance.' Hallberg blanched at the thought. 'What time is Mosley getting back?'

Emilio Muñoz glanced at his watch. 'Should be soon,' he replied. 'The old man's gotten a taste for the Glendale high life these days. I know he was meeting that Whitehead guy and they planned to put together a timeline of Kratz's movements since he moved to Brockmont.'

Gibson pointed to the laptop. 'Much like this spreadsheet of every homicide he committed in the Greater Los Angeles area and elsewhere in California since he arrived here in 1994.'

'I thought we identified them already?' Hallberg said.

'Yeah, and the net's closing in on him.' Gibson broke into a shark-like grin. 'A lucky break leads to his capture, and before you know it we've reached the courtroom. You remember Niall Demaine, that tech guy at the Denver field office? He produced something similar for the Colorado killings. Soon as I've finished this he's asked me to send him a copy. He's going to combine the two, then pass it on to the Office of Public Affairs.'

Muñoz shot a sideways glance at Gibson. 'It's going public?'

'It's being seriously considered because it's likely some folks will be so horrified they'll spill any info they're withholding. There's also talk of Kratz being put on the FBI's *Top Ten Most Wanted*, so the information has to be totally accurate before its released.'

The spreadsheet was comprehensive yet concise; stating the names of both definite and probable victims of Kratz's murderous exploits, the uncensored details of each death and his likely motive behind it. Kratz had wasted little time settling into the homicidal side of Los Angeles life fifteen years earlier. His first kill occurred within weeks of him arriving in town when, like so many other hopefuls and wannabes, the young man formerly known as Peter Umpleby soon learned the streets were most definitely not paved with gold.

Dreams, dirt and dog shit: welcome to LA.

Jesus 'Baby' Gonzalez, known for being a particularly unpleasant owner of a fast food outlet *and* a part-time drug dealer, was the first person to meet an untimely end. The middle-aged man who'd employed Kratz within a day of his flight from Denver touching down in the city had met a fiery demise; his Chevy colliding with a pick-up truck at a busy Atwater Village intersection seconds after it ran a red light. Forensic analysis soon identified severed brake lines; the case too random and too distant to be linked to SSA

Angelo Garcia's similar fate in Golden seven years later. These were two of a disconcerting litany of victims, both definite and suspected: their main – if not only – crime being to encounter Konrad Kratz.

Hallberg skimmed the document. 'That's quite a haul,' he said, conscious he'd more than stated the obvious. 'And there could be more out there, right?'

'He's one sick son of a bitch, ain't he?' Gibson agreed. He saved the spreadsheet's latest version and flicked over to the online local weather report. 'I guess we'll now be trying to catch up on our other cases until Kratz rears his ugly head.'

'Someone needs to go interview that guy who phoned the tip line about his neighbour.' Muñoz thought back to the irate message he'd listened to minutes after his arrival. 'Boy was that guy raging! Thinks the newest tenant upstairs is selling drugs, due to a sudden influx of regular visitors to the apartment directly above. Last time that happened in their block the dealer ended up suffering a fatal case of acute lead poisoning.'

'Can't see Mosley volunteering for it.' Gibson returned to his spreadsheet now he knew the day's fine weather looked set to continue into that evening. 'I need to finish this, so it looks like it's fallen to one of you guys.'

The other two men locked eyes, neither willing to show their reluctance to visit the run-down apartment block on Stellar Avenue.

'Rock, paper, scissors?' Muñoz drawled, secure in the knowledge either outcome would earn him an extra beer that evening.

Hallberg's firm nod masked the knot that had crash-landed in his stomach. 'Best of three.'

****

11.47am – PDT
Reno, Nevada

From street level the building blended amongst the others occupying the block, its plain glass frontage criss-crossed by painted steel columns masking a surprisingly opulent recently refurbished interior. James Haigh, as he was known at this branch of the Sierra Nevada Bank, had been a semi-regular customer for the past seven years; an enthusiast for the city's casinos, if anyone inquired as to the purpose of his visits.

76

An address in nearby Sparks had sufficed to open an account, and the fake passport and driver's licence obtained in the name of its actual resident also enabled him to rent a safe deposit box. A new email address, a swift move to internet banking and paperless statements, and a change of postal address to a modest townhouse in nearby Sun Valley ensured the real James Haigh remained unaware of his financial double life.

Konrad was usually loathe to involve banks in the safekeeping of his money. His frozen accounts at Glendale's branch of Wells Fargo proved he had too much to lose if he attempted to gain access. Any cash withdrawal, let alone a sum over $10,000, would now raise all manner of flags at the FBI, IRS and Christ only knew how many more of the three-letter organisations currently chasing his ass. He'd resigned himself to the destruction of his bank cards and forfeiting his seven-digit balance, although his attempts to view the loss as a worthwhile investment in his future remained a source of anger.

To his knowledge, the authorities were oblivious to its Nevadan equivalent: the contents of that lone safe deposit box in Reno. Konrad almost always called in at the bank whenever he visited the area, aware all he needed to do was ask a service representative for uninterrupted access. Once alone in the windowless cell, with its large wooden desk and matching chair, he'd add thousands of dollars to the rented container's contents. Konrad had chosen the largest box available, not knowing how many bundles of cash and other items of value could occupy its interior and, until his recent encounter at Kiva Beach, also intended to store the Rolex he'd recently purchased in Phoenix. The watch proved itself too conspicuous soon after its acquisition; its finely crafted gold inset with diamonds certain to raise eyebrows if he actually dared to wear it.

The ninety-minute journey to Reno via the Californian side of Lake Tahoe passed without incident and his thoughts frequently drifted to his early morning visit to Kingsbury. Reno's roads were quieter than expected and he'd managed to park on a central street only four blocks from his destination, where a handful of quarters sated a roadside parking meter and bought more time than he'd need.

You've got to speculate to accumulate...

Reno's air temperature was always noticeably higher than that encountered around Tahoe, the difference caused by the city's lower altitude and an omnipresent uncomfortable hot, dry wind. A damp area under his backpack quickly reached saturation point and he frowned when a rivulet of sweat trickled down his skin and soaked into his waistband, seconds before the bank's large wooden doors swung shut behind him.

Konrad heaved a sigh of relief, silently welcomed a nearby air conditioning unit's cold caress and scanned the spacious lobby, pleased to see only its fixtures and fittings had been modernised and that its previous layout remained intact. A short line of customers waited patiently for a solitary service representative to become available, this apparent lack of staff causing Konrad to wonder how much longer he'd take to gain access to his cash.

An elderly couple occupied the position ahead, their topics of conversation ranging from the sublime to the ridiculous. Konrad stared up at the ceiling's blue and white pattern, assumedly designed to be reminiscent of the summer sky miles above the city. Would the same Big Sky follow him to his remote destination in Montana? The prospect of a long drive to Portland and then boarding the Greyhound to Missoula filled him with dread. The last time he'd travelled on one of those coaches was nothing less than a nightmare, and that fat–

'Sir, can I help you with anything?'

Konrad startled back into the present and smiled at the petite redhead behind the glass. 'Yeah, sorry. I was miles away.'

She nodded and attempted to recall whether she'd previously served him. 'Did you go anywhere nice?'

'Just planning a short vacation for later this year,' he replied, never missing a beat.

'So you'll be needing foreign currency, or maybe some additional insurance?'

'Not yet. What I do need is access to my safe deposit box. Here's my driver's licence…' He pulled it out of his wallet and waved it at her, 'and I guess I need to sign the sheet?'

The young woman turned away to search for Konrad's current Entry Record Card inside a large filing cabinet. She listened to him drum his fingers on the countertop until the slip appeared and wondered why he was in such a rush. 'Will that be all, Mr Haigh?' she asked, satisfied his latest signature matched those from previous visits.

'Sure will, Becky,' he replied. His gaze lingered on her name badge and it took all his willpower not to lick his lips when a warm pink glow spread across her cheeks. 'Thanks for all your help.'

'You're so welcome, sir!' Becky gushed. She pressed a date stamp onto the small space beside his signature and made a note of the time. 'My co-worker is coming back any second, so I'll take you down when he arrives.' She pointed to a pair of deep red armchairs nearby. 'Feel free to take a seat and thank you for your patience, sir.'

'No worries,' Konrad replied. He stretched out against the soft leather and flashed his best Hollywood grin. 'I've got all the time in the world.' He noted her nod and smile, then divert her attention to the middle-aged woman who'd been behind him.

Ten minutes later Konrad found himself inside the vault, encased by solitude. It took less than two minutes to empty the box and arrange its bundles of cash inside a plastic bag lining the backpack. He tied a knot in the polythene and zipped the outer bag shut, intent on an immediate return to the cabin, where he'd store the cash in the subterranean safe.

Becky Weber found it impossible to hide her surprise when her arms unexpectedly moved upwards in anticipation of the box's increased weight. She returned his smile, but this time it didn't reach her eyes as she silently wondered exactly what he'd removed.

****

7.58pm – BST
Son of Edward, Preston, England

The restaurant, an offshoot of one of Preston's most popular pubs, had opened a little over a year ago on a side street near Fishergate. This second string to the Garner brothers' culinary bow abandoned the Edward II's modern yet cosy interior; its black glass dining tables and minimalistic décor the epitome of modern chic. Its continued rise in popularity since opening night meant a constant stream of locals and people from further afield filled the town centre location's dozen tables, keen to consume fine food in a more contemporary setting.

The aforementioned pub's prime location on Friargate had been a Preston staple since brothers Stephen and Michael 'Mikey' Garner pooled their shares of a winning lottery ticket and invested in a derelict former restaurant. Since the mid-nineties, their expanded business had gone from strength to strength under the well-timed investment of recently deceased Blackpool businessman Roger Mortimer. The pub's reputation had also been enhanced by the high-quality fare prepared by chef Franco Volonte, an old school friend of Steve's they'd employed soon after opening. It was one of Franco's culinary creations that prompted one of the Edward II's regulars to suggest they open a restaurant serving more refined versions of the pub's usual fare. Steve and Mikey later discussed the idea with Franco, who readily agreed to train a pair of apprentice chefs for their new venture.

'You know, I actually think I prefer this place to the pub, and having no students around is always a bonus,' Martin Boothroyd commented. The detective set down his pint of *Isabella's Revenge* and surveyed his surroundings. 'The beer speaks for itself, so it's a good job buggerlugs here is giving me a lift home in her chariot.'

Paula Phelan winced at the heartier than intended pat reverberating through her back. 'Anything for you, dear,' she replied through gritted teeth. 'Just means I own you ready for the next awkward witness we need to interview.'

'Give them to Sanderson,' Boothroyd replied, watching the same teenage waitress who'd good humouredly noted their demands now take an order from a middle-aged man and woman across the room. He observed the expensive clothing they'd worn to a mid-priced restaurant and assumed it was a special occasion for them – maybe a birthday or wedding anniversary? He suddenly realised four weeks separated him from the wife's birthday and decided to make a reservation later on his way out. That would definitely earn him a fair few decent Brownie points.

Detectives Eddie Pell and Harry Irwin had arrived at the restaurant shortly before their Cold Case Unit counterparts, the day and time deliberately chosen after Steve Garner informed Pell the place was usually at its quietest on a Tuesday evening. Irwin sipped from a glass of fizzy water and enviously eyed Pell's almost empty pint class. Ever the cynic, he'd already suggested the reason they'd arranged to meet in Preston was so Pell could cadge a lift home, knowing Irwin had little option other than to head north to the M55 on his way back to his Fylde Coast home.

'Penny for them, Harry.' Boothroyd tried his hardest not to smirk at the man's obvious disdain for his glass of water. 'The stuff surely can't be that bad?'

'It's worse. Might have to do the big girl thing and have a J2O instead,' Irwin replied. 'How do you people think we should approach the search for Kratz from this point?'

'I'd be inclined to form a small task force,' Pell said. 'Us five, and maybe get one of those new uniforms at the station doing any additional research we need. We divvy out the tasks because there's always the risks of duplication or omission if we work as separate teams.'

Irwin nodded. 'I'm all for that, so where should our base be?' He gazed around the table. 'Oh, come on!'

Pell swallowed and set down his empty glass. 'Four against one.'

'It does make sense,' Boothroyd added. 'I know Roger was killed on your patch, but this is Kratz's hometown and the vast majority of his criminal activity occurred here.'

'And at least the motorway will lull you to sleep on your way home,' Pell said. 'You're always complaining about what a mundane drive it is.'

'It's worse eastbound,' he countered. 'And I'll still make you drag your sorry arses over to my neck of the woods if I'm busy over there. Anyway, we're pretty much certain Konrad Kratz is both Anthony Collins and Oliver Stamford, so that's the mystery of who killed Roger Mortimer solved. We'll do whatever we can to assist the hunt for Kratz, even though he's buggered off back across the Pond. Something we uncover here may lead to his capture.'

Phelan nodded. 'Like the origin of the money paid into Mortimer's bank account.'

'Exactly,' Irwin replied. 'Shame we don't have the authorisation to find out that kind of information.'

Boothroyd thanked the waitress as she placed a well-stocked bread basket and a selection of butter pots between them. He selected a granary roll and smiled at his companions, 'I know a woman who does, or at least has the contacts.'

Pell frowned and looked around the table, unable to focus his thoughts now his stomach had growled pointed a reminder he'd eaten little since breakfast.

Irwin licked his lips and slathered pesto-infused butter onto his roll. 'That legal attaché from the FBI's London office we've been liaising with has kept us informed about where they're up to over in the states,' he explained. 'She works out of the US Embassy, as I understand it. Anyway, she's our contact. Efficient and polite, although I don't think she fancies a trip to Preston – or Blackpool, for that matter.'

'She's got a fair point, I reckon,' Boothroyd said, his voice muffled by a mouthful of bread. 'That Los Angeles detective I've been emailing also gave us a long list of names Kratz used for fake ID.'

'How did they manage that?' Irwin asked.

Boothroyd swallowed and cracked a smug grin. 'Caught the man who supplies the Hollywood area and threatened him with a long stretch in the worst prison in the whole of California. He sung like a canary, but the name Anthony Collins doesn't feature.'

Irwin set down his knife. 'Are they sure they got the full list?'

Boothroyd broke off another piece of bread roll and lifted it to his mouth. 'That's what this Mosley guy now thinks. Either some information was withheld, or Kratz used another source to supply additional fake ID. Christ only knows how many suppliers he has.'

'Which doesn't really help any of us.'

'I got an email through from Mosley shortly before I left the office,' Boothroyd added. 'He's planning on giving his grass another grilling later today. He also asked an FBI contact to put the name Anthony Collins through various national databases. Nothing pertinent to the Kratz case came up, suggesting he's chosen a new name for this trip.'

Pell spied the waitress approaching their table to take another order of drinks. 'Wherever he is, you can bet your arse he won't be eating any better than we are tonight.'

****

11.57pm – BST
Edward II, Preston, England

Across town, as the detectives bade each other farewell, a different group also relaxed now their respective busy evenings had drawn to an end. Assisted by two extra newly-hired members of bar staff, Steve and Mikey

Garner had overseen another non-stop night in the pub they'd run for the past fourteen years; the latter taking great pleasure at sliding the thick bolts across the main doors minutes earlier.

'She might be a bit of a bitch, but she's more than got her uses at this time of night,' Mikey commented. He poured a pint of Guinness into a large stainless steel bowl and blew a kiss across the bar. 'A bit of growling and a flash of those fangs, and the stragglers move faster than shit off a shovel.'

'Perhaps we should get one?' Steve ruffled a collar of dense fur around the German Shepherd's neck. 'You're a good girl aren't you, Lady Daisy?'

Their head chef, Franco Volonte, dropped three left-over sausages into a second bowl. 'How long have you got her for?' he asked, the food gone before he finished his sentence. Daisy licked her lips and waited expectantly for a second helping, her head tilted to one side.

Mikey looked up from two settling pints of Daisy's preferred tipple. 'Mum and Dad get back from that Caribbean cruise in a fortnight,' he replied as he deftly levered the metal tops off a pair of continental bottled lagers. 'Okay for some, buggering off like that.'

Franco watched Daisy lick her bowl dry of any remaining drops of stout. 'Who's running the Crett Inn?' he asked. The Crettington Arms, a popular local's pub run by the Garners' parents for over thirty-five years, was located a couple of miles out of town. The brothers had been brought up in the spacious flat above the premises, an educational experience in itself.

'A relief landlord,' Steve said. He observed Mikey slowly top up the Guinness he'd been anticipating since sounding the bell for Last Orders. 'He's a decent enough bloke; they got him in last time too.'

Andy Parker doubled up and massaged the cramp making an unwelcome return to his calf muscles. Another long-time former school friend of the Garners, Andy had made West Side FC's first team whilst still in his teens and, over the years, regularly guested at the pub's regular promotional evenings. 'I'll have a whisky to go with that pint, cheers,' he said.

Mikey glared at Andy from behind the bar. 'Says who?'

Andy righted himself, puffed out his chest in an exaggerated manner and reminded them that West Side's football match finished a little over two hours ago. 'Says the knackered old bastard who managed to score tonight,' he added, stretching out his sore legs.

Franco eased himself into a large leather armchair and accepted the pint of thick, dark stout from Mikey, his gratitude echoed seconds later by Andy.

'How's your Vicky doing?' he asked, keen to learn whether Andy had gleaned anything new about the Kratz situation from his older sister. Soon after her graduation in the late nineties, Vicky Parker landed a plum job at a stateside TV company. She'd been distinctly nonplussed by the household names for whom she'd designed sets, until hers and Konrad Kratz's paths crossed at the New York studios where *H.O.S.T.A.G.E.* was filmed.

'All the better for not having to work with Kratz,' Andy replied, directly quoting Vicky's last email. 'The knobhead's officially been sacked and some actor he tried to bump off before the original auditions landed the role of Kratz's now-deceased character's replacement.'

The slender bottle of lager paused on its way up to Mikey's mouth. 'Who's that?'

'Dunno,' Andy replied. 'Vicky says he's the total opposite of Kratz.' He watched Mikey's mouth open again. 'Save it, sunshine. I'll check my email and get back to you. They reckon Kratz chucked him off his apartment's balcony, or something.'

'Martin Crophill?' Mikey applauded and took a bow when Andy confirmed his deduction. 'Wonder if he'll be a better actor? Anyway, speaking of our dear friend *Peter Umpleby*, has anyone heard word from Tony or Sam recently?'

Franco swallowed another mouthful and nodded. 'I heard from Tony a couple of weeks ago,' he said, thinking back to the most recent emails he'd exchanged with their old school friend, who'd also headed stateside to study. 'Said he'd stayed at his in-laws' place for a few days to consult on the Kratz case. Seems quite happy, and him and Susie are both still doing their forensic science thing, though they're now considering moving closer to her family.'

'I never really understood why they moved so far out of the city in the first place,' Andy said. 'He's also got family there, his wife's a local girl and there'll always be a ready supply of dead bodies to keep them in work.'

Franco sipped his drink and shrugged. 'His mum's brother was a bit of a local villain and Susie didn't like the influence he exerted over the family.' He poured the last of his pint into Daisy's empty bowl. 'The uncle died back in July, along with four cousins.'

'Is that the car accident they think Kratz was responsible for?' Andy asked, his unrelenting curiosity a surprise to the others. 'Why would he kill them?'

'Because he's a murdering piece of shit, that's why.'

Andy patted Steve's shoulder. 'Still no arrest for Roger's murder?'

Steve shook his head. 'Absolutely nothing. The police say they may have a possible lead, but now won't tell us anything more. They don't want to get our hopes up.'

'How's Charlotte?' Franco asked. 'Must be terrible for her?'

'She has her good days and bad days. More of the latter, I'd say. I'm worried she's bottling things up and the last thing I need at the moment is for her to be stressed.' He met his brother's eye. 'She's pregnant and it's early days, so don't broadcast it.'

'Congratulations!' Mikey exclaimed, the sentiment similarly echoed by Franco and Andy. 'I'm going to be the best uncle ever, and you can quote me on that.'

'Still no word from Sam?' Franco asked.

'Not for weeks,' Steve replied. 'I've tried phoning, texting, emailing and I even put a letter in the post. Charlotte saw one of his sisters coming out of Sainsbury's a couple of days before Roger died and said she was cagey as hell. Olivia, I think it was. Said she was in a rush to get to the child-minder, but it was only mid-afternoon. Charlotte just assumed one of the twins must be ill.'

Franco headed for the bar. 'Konrad Kratz is all over the news, Sam disappears off the face of the Earth...' He lifted another pair of pint glasses down from above the beer pumps. 'Coincidence?'

Mikey dropped his empty bottle into a recycling trolley and flinched when it shattered. 'No such thing, my good fellow. No such thing.'

Chapter 6 – Wednesday 2nd September 2009

9.06am – BST
Hutton, Preston, England

Harry Irwin's early morning journey inland came as an almost-pleasant surprise. Minimal congestion on Blackpool's roads and the A583's metamorphosis into a prime example of civilised driving made Irwin certain he'd landed in the midst of some sort of conspiracy theory; his conviction apparently fully confirmed when he only encountered one red traffic light between Preston's Docklands...

Marina, my arse!

...and his destination at Lancashire Police's headquarters. The security guard at the main gate appeared to have been primed ready for Irwin's visit and waved him through after casting a cursory glance at his police ID card. Irwin proceeded at a crawl until he spotted Eddie Pell's BMW parked close to the main building's entrance. Pleased to see a solitary parking space to the vehicle's left, he eased his own car to a halt and wondered how much time had passed since Pell's arrival.

The light drizzle of earlier continued to ease; the retreating cloud cover offering a tantalising glimpse of the fine sunny day mentioned on the weather forecast. Irwin grabbed his mobile, slammed the driver's door and pressed the Mondeo's key fob. The central locking clicked and a corresponding flash of the indicators reflected in a nearby windscreen as he set off towards a pair of double glass doors, which slid open seconds before he reached them.

Pell stepped out into the damp air. 'You all right, Harry?' he asked in a cheery tone. 'I've just checked in at reception. Boothroyd's coming over to meet us.' He pointed across a wide stretch of neatly mown grass. 'The cold case office is right over there.'

The area reminded Irwin of the school field on which he and his classmates played lunchtime football more years ago than he cared to recall. 'Bloody hell!' he grumbled. 'Better start walking, or else it'll be evening before we get there.'

Pell jabbed a finger into the other man's gut. 'It'll work off last night.'

'I'll look like a bloody twiglet if we keep on having to walk over there every time we come here,' Irwin continued. 'Might even have to have a lie-down and a cold compress.'

'I don't see why there's any reason we can't park nearer,' Pell said, more to himself than Irwin. He opened his mouth to continue, but an approaching figure caught his eye. 'Looks like Boothroyd. Don't worry, I'll ask him if there's an old folk's parking spot he can spray-paint your name on. I reckon he'll be able to lend you a Zimmer too.'

Irwin shot a dirty look sideways. 'Cheeky bastard.'

'Sorry to disappoint you, but my Olds got married ten months before I appeared' Pell replied as he returned Boothroyd's wave. 'And, it's for the benefit of our investigation. He didn't give much away, though from what this fella's good morning text said there's been a fair few useful emails winging their way across the Atlantic overnight.'

Martin Boothroyd's brightly checked shirt flapped in the light breeze. 'Good to see you, gents,' he called. 'You should've parked over there.' He pointed to a roughly tarmacked area near the scattered identical buildings, whose drab exteriors provided scant clue about the nature of the work carried out within.

Pell shook Boothroyd's hand. 'Told you!' he said, unable to resist.

'Yeah, yeah,' Irwin replied, genuinely tired after a late return home from last night's meal and another early start.

Boothroyd's sharp eyes darted between them on the walk to the nearest building. 'What's up?' he asked.

Pell ignored Irwin's stare. 'Gramps here found the hike a bit too much.'

'A nice big brew will see you right.' Boothroyd held open a partially glazed door and nodded at a narrow staircase. 'We're up here, nicely out of the way. Let's dig out that tin of Fox's to celebrate us being another day closer to Kratz's capture.'

Irwin paused halfway up. 'They're that close?'

'Linda Neville seems to think so,' Boothroyd replied. 'Go through that second door and along to the end. You should see a pair of lazy buggers who probably couldn't be arsed to put the kettle on.'

They passed a researcher reading through a yellowed case file in front of her. The young woman watched the two unfamiliar men exchange greetings with Boothroyd, Sanderson and Phelan, wondering whether they were linked to the current Peter Umpleby investigation. She took a sip of her tepid coffee and returned her attention to the file, almost certain the investigation into Stavros Pallis' death nearly two decades ago would offer no further clues.

The first ten minutes of the meeting revolved around finding enough mugs to avoid the need to rehydrate in shifts. Once their drinks were distributed, the conversation quickly turned to the unit's successful approach to the BBC's *Crimewatch* programme and its agreement to feature the Crettington Park serial rapist case.

'Paula's always fancied giving acting a try,' Boothroyd said, the glint in his eye unmistakable. He pried the lid off a colourful metal biscuit tin and chuckled. 'We reckon she'd be a natural standing on a street corner wearing a skirt barely covering her arse.'

'He's already secured the kerb crawler role,' she retorted, raising a middle finger at Boothroyd. 'Saying that, he'd be ruled out as a suspect immediately – they hadn't invented those nice little blue tablets back in the eighties.'

Pell noticed Irwin grab a pair of chocolate-covered shortcake rounds. 'Don't go nicking all the best ones, you greedy sod,' he said, irritated he'd again lost out on his favourite.

'You snooze, you lose,' Irwin replied. 'Anyway,' he continued, his voice muffled, 'what's been going on with our buddies across the ocean?'

Between sips of tea, Boothroyd shared a summary of the series of forensic reports he'd received via FBI legal attaché Linda Neville. A Virginia-based FBI laboratory had subjected brake lines from Grace Winterburn's and Stavros Pallis' cars to the same intense analysis carried out on those from Lena Hanson's elderly Beetle, the Fernandez family's pick-up truck and the government-issued SUVs driven by Angelo Garcia and Sam Bury. Despite minor differences in striations, the results concluded all seven vehicles underwent a similar manner of sabotage; this signature suggesting the same individual could likely claim responsibility.

A second email from Neville revealed the source of the cash transferred to Roger Mortimer's bank account six years earlier. Until then, all Irwin knew of the money's origins was what its currency suggested. The FBI's Cyber Crime Division soon successfully traced the money back to its starting point in the Nevadan city of Sparks, via half a dozen offshore servers, and Neville concluded her update by offering to liaise between them and the FBI's Reno Resident Agency, where an investigation into the cash's owner was already underway.

'So this Oliver Stamford, who's probably Konrad Kratz, must be some sort of computer genius?' Irwin said, convinced he'd stated the bleeding obvious. 'Does he have any connection to this Sparks place? Never heard of it.'

'I found it online,' Boothroyd replied. 'It's near Reno, which is some sort of mini-Vegas nearly five hundred miles north of the real one. As for Kratz's computer skills, who knows?'

Pell glanced across the table and met Boothroyd's eye. 'Do you think he got someone to do it all for him?'

'I suppose he could've paid a local who'd got the relevant knowhow.'

'Even if he paid them, it's certain they're long dead,' Irwin said.

Boothroyd frowned, his thoughts saturated by their current caseload. 'Why do you think they'd be dead?'

'Because how else could he secure their silence?' Irwin replied. 'The local Feds over there will need to investigate deaths or disappearances of computer experts in 2003.'

'Don't you think they'd think of that?'

'Probably. Won't hurt to run it by that Neville woman down in the Big Smoke though.'

Phelan picked up her mug and wrinkled her nose at the sight of a thick sludge of sodden crumbs coating the bottom. She listened to Boothroyd sum up yet another email, this time from a detective working for Newark's Port Authority Police Department. Maria Goldstein's despondent report stated that no new leads had emerged since the forensic examination of a stolen car discovered abandoned in an Ohio suburb, meaning the Anthony Collins trail was – at least for now – stone cold.

'My geography of over there is shit,' a visibly disappointed Sanderson commented. 'How far is it from Akron to Sparks?'

Sanderson bit his lip in concentration whilst entering the search on his computer's keyboard. He tapped the mouse impatiently and stared at the screen, willing the map to load. 'Poxy internet's been playing up for the past couple of days,' he grumbled. 'It's well over two thousand miles, and that's if he went direct. And, just because he went to Sparks a few years ago, doesn't mean he's there now. If he has half a brain he'd pick a new spot.' His eyes roved over the map, impressed by the country's sheer magnitude. 'It's not like he's got a limited choice over there.'

'Bloody massive, it is,' Pell agreed. 'My youngest lad works out in California. You can drive and drive and see hardly anyone if you're in the right area. The roads are long and empty, the scenery outside the cities is amazing and he never complains about the weather.'

'So it looks like Kratz or Umpleby or whatever the hell he's called is back in the States,' Sanderson said. 'What do we do now?'

'Hope the bastard doesn't come back here,' Boothroyd replied.

****

12.44pm – PDT
San Fernando Road, Los Angeles, California

Nearly twelve hours later and eight time zones to the west, LAPD detective Ronnie Mosley and his team were unintentionally replicating the exchange at Hutton earlier that day. Their English counterparts would, however, have been swift to point out the differences the American detectives took for granted, the most obvious being their clement weather and the movie-propagated cliché of a doughnut shop down the block.

The team's discussion turned to Mosley's most recent interview with Harry Lee, a local man revealed as the city's leading supplier of high quality fake identification. Lee's reluctance to share the full extent of his criminal activities and client list during Mosley's previous interviews had baffled everyone involved, especially when the promise of cutting a deal dangled like a fat, juicy carrot. This latest interview started in an unconventional way by Mosley encouraging Lee to read the details of a particularly unpleasant prison assault, which put the misidentified victim – a Chinese man in his mid-forties – in the facility's hospital for three days. Lee's all-over sheen of perspiration told Mosley all he needed to know, a hunch confirmed during a productive, mostly one-sided conversation observed by Hallberg. Three more names landed on the table, the second none other than the elusive Anthony Collins.

Fat droplets of sweat hit the worn wooden surface when a deflated Lee admitted supplying UK versions of the passports and driver's licences for his client. Lee concluded the interview with a detailed account of how the menacing German-accented man threw an extra ten thousand dollars into the deal, and its attached condition of never revealing this trio of names to anyone else – especially the police. Drained of emotion and suffering the effect of nights of minimal sleep, Lee's hysterical outburst when Mosley left the interview room echoed along the corridors, offering an irresistible invitation for two other detainees to add their own unique brand of backing vocals.

'John Smith? Is this guy for real?' Gibson said, his tone despondent. 'And, if Kratz has used James Goodman since he's gotten back, it'll take one hell of a long time to trace him.'

'You remember Niall Demaine, the computer guy in Denver?' Mosley asked. The others nodded. 'He's already working through the three aliases for the previous ten days to see if he can trace any of them leaving Ohio.'

Gibson stared into his almost empty coffee cup. 'That's still a monumental task.'

'It's a starting point.'

Hallberg looked up from a witness statement he'd taken in the aftermath of an attempted burglary the previous evening. 'Did he give a timescale?'

'No,' Mosley replied, aware he hadn't communicated the confidence he held in Demaine's abilities. 'Said he'd start searching for John Smith and leave Anthony Collins for last.'

Muñoz frowned. 'How did he figure that out? Surely it'll be faster to rule out James Goodman?'

'I doubt he'd use Anthony Collins again,' Mosley said. 'John Smith's sounds too much like a pseudonym, so if anything he'll use it now and save James Goodman for lying low.'

'Unless he's living under a different alias we haven't discovered yet,' Muñoz suggested.

'That's something we'll consider if Demaine comes back empty-handed.'

'It's a long shot,' Gibson said. He silently wondered why everyone seemed so certain Kratz would be caught soon when, in reality, his possible whereabouts covered an area too huge to comprehend.

Mosley offered a familiar shrug. 'For now, it's the best we have.'

****

7.09pm – PDT
Mattole Road, near South Lake Tahoe, California

The swollen evening sun sunk lower in an orange-tinted sky and cast long shadows across the darkened forest floor. A Steller's Jay perched on a nearby branch repeatedly ruffled its sleek, deep blue plumage, the bird's beauty lost on Konrad as its harsh cries scratched deeper into his mind. Stan pricked his ears and idly scanned the forest for the source of the disturbance, his attention unwavering until a new smell invaded the dog's nostrils.

Wherever possible, Konrad chose to walk deeper into the forest, avoiding the vacation homes and permanent residences of varied sizes and designs that dotted the small clearings nearby. Chance identifications had already occurred when Milagros Fernandez and Freya Burdett separately saw through his carefully constructed disguises and web of lies. Milagros' fiery end came in a split-second collision with a flyover pillar, seconds after the brakes failed on the pick-up truck in which she, her father and three brothers were travelling to Mexico. This was the last time he'd used his preferred MO, three days after the siblings had identified him at Caesars Palace. Freya's demise happened days later, the result of a chance conversation at an airport check-in desk and their later encounter in a Zürich restaurant.

To his knowledge, nobody else had rumbled the disguises he'd used since then. Once he reached Montana, the dark and brooding Konrad could emerge; a tube of brown hair dye and similarly coloured contact lenses at the ready to alter his current appearance. Sam's presumed failure to identify the jogger his wife came inches from mowing down must have bought him more time, even if the memory of the man's angry glare and the confusion on his wife and daughter's faces was more than enough to stir Konrad's rage.

Let's see how they like living without you, although they'd probably thank me for doing them a massive favour.

His ultimate act in the days leading up to his departure would be to eliminate the one person who'd persistently conspired to end his dreams. From their first day at Crettington County Primary School nearly thirty years earlier, Sam had always been the teachers' golden boy – that rare breed of swot who also managed to make and keep friends. Peter remained on the periphery; an unpopular kid loathed by staff and pupils alike, the regular recipient of his father's ire and mother's sorrow, the blackest of black sheep.

The Jay's birdsong changed to a malevolent cackle, intensified by the diminished daylight and a lull in traffic on the nearby highway. Stan whined and tugged on his leash, keen to return to the cabin and his soon-to-be replenished food bowl before nightfall. They meandered between the trees until the small cabin came into view against a cooling charcoal-grey backdrop, its lights reminiscent of frantic eyes searching for something that urgently needed to be found.

Except in his case, he was almost home and dry.

****

7.41pm – PDT
Kingsbury, Nevada

Sam watched Anna appear at the top of the staircase and raised his eyebrows at her drawn-out sigh. 'Sound asleep,' she confirmed as she reached for a baggy sweatshirt and pulled it over her head. 'Tiring out our pair of terrors at the beach and then letting them eat their bodyweight at the dinner table is officially the perfect recipe for a quiet evening.'

'Do you reckon Angela is okay?' he asked, his tone serious. 'She usually complains for at least another half hour.'

Anna padded across the open plan living area. 'It's been a busy couple of days. Anyway, stop complaining, else she'll sense it.'

'Yeah, mustn't tempt fate.' He joined her at the sliding glass doors that opened onto the balcony and wrapped his arms around her waist. They stood in silence to watch night regain its grasp on Lake Tahoe, darkening the glassy sheet of water three miles to the west.

Anna reluctantly broke her gaze away from the faded light lining the horizon. 'That view really is something, right?'

'I'd enjoy it more if this was a vacation home.'

She reached for his hand and led him to the large couch opposite a new flat screen television which, to Sam's chagrin, they'd found little time to relax in front of since moving in. 'Perhaps one day we can come back here with that purpose? You know, create some more favourable memories of such a beautiful part of the country.'

'Who's to say this isn't permanent?'

Anna sighed and sunk into the couch's comfortable upholstery. 'Come on, Sam. We've had this discussion more times than I can recall. He'll get caught, they always do.'

'Always?' he shot back, his tone harsher than intended. 'Have you got any idea how many unsolved homicides there are? There's thousands of killers who've literally got away with murder. Why should *he* be any different?'

Anna grabbed Sam's hands and squeezed tightly. Their eyes met; tears shimmering in the corners of hers, his ringed by dark shadows. 'We can't continue like this. Angela knows something's wrong.'

'What do you mean?'

'She's now asked at least three times why Daddy looks so sad,' Anna replied. 'I told her your new job makes you tired, but you know what she's like.' She watched his limp hands fall into his lap. 'And I can see you're trying to maintain a normal front.'

Sam felt a chill pass through him. 'Anna?'

'After your accident you were so...' She paused, unable to locate the correct word. 'I saw you descend into this horrible place and whatever I did I just couldn't reach you and pull you back into happiness. You slipped further and further away from me. I couldn't–'

He stared into a pool of light on the polished floor. 'I won't go that way again, I promise,' he whispered, then reached a hesitant arm around her shoulders. The slight shudder he detected combined a new wave of guilt and the fear he'd gradually become aware of in recent weeks. Deafened by silence, Sam stared into the darkness beyond the balcony doors. Anna's eyes clenched in a futile attempt to stem the tears trickling down her cheeks, neither of them sure what to say next.

Anna managed to compose herself and followed Sam's lead when he leaned against the sofa's plump cushions. 'How can you be sure?'

He took a deep breath and pinched the top of his nose to steady his nerves 'This time last year I wasn't myself,' he replied. 'These days it's not always easy to be the person I was before the accident.'

She grabbed his free hand and squeezed it more firmly this time. 'You must realise how much progress you've made?'

Sam shook his head and listened to a nearby car's engine fade to nothing. 'It's still not the same. Before, someone could ask me anything and I'd know the answer, or where to find it straight away. Now, sometimes my mind goes blank, like there's holes in it. Then I get these headaches, real humdingers. The doctors said I might, but they've got worse recently. I, uh–'

'You're stressed and tired.' She saw his jaw clench. 'It doesn't help.'

He shook his head again and looked Anna directly in the eye. 'I've decided I'm quitting the New York job if we're ever able to return to Colorado. That's final.'

Anna's mouth opened and closed repeatedly for the time it took her to process his words. 'You've worked so hard to build up that department to what it is now,' she eventually said, incredulous to hear Sam make such a statement.

'I don't give a shit anymore.'

'You don't mean that,' she countered, surprised by the hardness in his expression. 'Surely not, Sam. You're so highly regarded by your team.'

'Maybe, maybe not. Either way, it's you and the kids I want to see every day, not some dingy hotel room. I can do something in Denver full-time.'

'Like finally pursuing the hostage negotiation?' she asked, hopeful he'd reconsider.

Sam shrugged and rubbed away an intermittent twitch in his eyelid. 'Who said I'm staying at the Bureau? There's always the School of Mines, it's not like I'd have far to travel.'

'You told me joining the FBI was all you ever wanted to do since you were a little kid!' Anna exclaimed, for a split-second wondering if Sam's words were merely a figment of her imagination. 'You said it was your ambition, ever since your mom told you about the federal agent who lived in the apartment next to hers in Manhattan when she was a girl.'

Sam's love of listening to his mother's stories of her upbringing in the city where he'd almost met his death had endured into his teens and beyond. Childhood had been an exciting time for Sally Murphy, as she was known back then; punctuated by brief returns to England thanks to her British parents' employment at the then recently formed United Nations. She'd secured dual nationality for all three of her children, determined to offer them all the opportunities she could, although Sam was the only one to permanently cross the Atlantic.

'Life doesn't always turn out like we expect it to.'

'*Life* is what you make it.' She turned her head to kiss his cheek. 'I worked my ass off at Boulder to become a detective. Everyone said they were so proud of me and I enjoyed the challenge. I didn't realise how it would destroy my personal life. Many of my so-called friends stopped inviting me out because I'd have to work late on a case and always bailed on them, and meeting guys you'd want to have a relationship with was impossible.'

Sam couldn't help smiling. 'So you were desperate when we met?'

'You have no idea.' She patted his thigh. 'Seriously, I'd resigned myself to being alone.' Sam noticed her cheeks colour and raised an inquisitive eyebrow. 'I've never told you this,' she continued, blushing an intense shade of crimson. 'The night I worked late on that case we took a ten-minute coffee break and watched TV. You were being interviewed on the news channel and I made a passing comment about your accent being sexy. The guys started their usual teasing, telling me I should go on down to the store where that nutjob held those workers hostage and see if I could *negotiate* myself a date with you.'

'You're not just saying this to make me feel better?'

'Asshole,' she replied, delivering a sharp nudge to his ribs. 'You were obviously so passionate, like it's what you were meant to do in life. Once I met you at the stationhouse and you destroyed my carefully organised case file we needed for court the next morning, I decided to live dangerously.'

He let out a long chuckle, a warm sound she'd missed since their recent move. 'You seduced me.'

She snuggled against his chest. 'I didn't hear you complaining,' she retorted. They both closed their eyes and slid further down the couch's soft brown leather. 'And you obviously liked it enough to propose.'

Sam nodded and brushed the tip of his chin against Anna's hair. Some of the tension left his body and he opened his eyes, the lids heavy as if roused from sleep. Anna's breaths soon became deep and regular, and Sam observed how the cosy light emitted by a small lamp reflected off her dark hair, its ever-present gleam something he'd noticed during those early days of their budding relationship.

The growing trepidation he'd experienced on the drive north to Boulder thrived in the seconds of booming silence after he pressed the buzzer for Anna's apartment; the crackle of static and a breathy 'Hello!' enough to send surges of panic along his already-frazzled nerves. A soft bleep announced Anna had unlocked the main door and a metal sign to his right directed Sam to a quartet of second floor apartments. He checked his reflection in a large window and then cautiously ascended the wide stairway to the first landing, where a slim figure appeared from behind the nearest door frame.

'You found the place okay?' Anna laughed and shook her head. 'Well, sure you did, else you wouldn't be here.'

Sam nodded and tried not to stare at the pretty strapless floral dress she wore, its fifties style emphasising her narrow waist and toned arms.

'Yeah, didn't get lost once,' he replied with a shy grin and held out a neatly wrapped parcel. 'This is for you.'

She brought her hands together and mirrored his smile. 'Thank you! You shouldn't have, but I won't complain. Anyway, uh... come in,' she continued, directing him to the neat lounge area; its cream décor warmed by the evening sun that diffused through a large window overlooking the small residents' parking lot. 'Can I get you a drink before we go?'

He nodded, realising his throat had become parched since entering the apartment. 'A small glass of water would be great, please.'

'Sure,' Anna replied. She walked through to the small kitchen and retrieved an almost full jug from the refrigerator. 'I'll have to find my coat and shoes, then I'm ready to go.'

Sam lowered himself onto the couch and ignored the butterflies fluttering in his stomach. 'Thanks,' he said, resisting the urge to gulp the cold liquid. 'You look lovely,' he added, and cringed when a heated blush spread across his cheeks.

The corners of her mouth twitched in amusement. 'Nearly as lovely as that parcel, it seems a real shame to open it.'

'I didn't know what to get, and I thought flowers were too presumptive.' Sam shrugged and took a sip of the water. 'Knowing my luck you'd get hay fever.'

Anna laughed, picked up the gift and eyed the thick gold paper. 'Flowers are fine, I won't turn into a puffy mess of histamine. Now, let me at this beautiful box.'

She gently pulled the silver ribbons to one side to preserve their ornate bows and opened the paper to reveal a box of Godiva truffles.

'Oh yes!' she exclaimed, and the sparkle in her eyes caused a flood of relief. 'These are the perfect antidote for a long day at work. I'll sure enjoy them this week.' She glanced shyly at the couch, unsure whether to sit beside him. 'Our table's reserved for seven. I figured because we're both working tomorrow we better get an early sitting.'

Sam recalled the drugs bust that had taken up most of his time over the preceding four days and rolled his eyes. 'At least we both got the day off today.'

Anna slid her feet into a pair of low-heeled shoes and belted her coat firmly. 'Yeah, my week's been pretty much like yours' she replied. 'Are you sure you don't mind driving?'

Sam shook his head and walked towards the door. 'Your chariot awaits, ma'am.'

They left the apartment and headed into town, where Anna directed Sam to a road located off Pearl Street, a couple of minutes' walk from the cosy Italian place she and some friends had recently visited. Over their meal the conversation flowed easily, both exchanging workplace tales and what drove them to pursue their respective careers. Sam initially relaxed during the two hours they'd spent in the restaurant, even though he couldn't help wondering how he'd managed to secure a date with an attractive woman who genuinely appeared to reciprocate his interest.

His thoughts soon turned to how the evening's end: whether she'd expect nothing more than an escort back to her apartment, or whether she'd expect considerably more. He felt the butterflies return and inwardly cursed himself for shunning female company for much of the time since he'd relocated from the UK. A handful of relatively brief relationships – one of which he still tried not to think about, not that he'd have considered it a relationship – ultimately fizzled to nothing, doing little to bolster his confidence.

He'd decided to play it safe upon their return to Anna's apartment building by thanking her for a wonderful evening and pressing a gentle kiss against her cheek. Filled by an unfamiliar elation, Sam drove south back to Golden along an almost deserted Route 93, already looking forward to his return journey the following Saturday for their second date.

There were many more memories ready to be made, he thought. Nobody would change that.

Chapter 7 – Thursday 3rd September 2009

10.33am – MDT
FBI Field Office, Stout Street, Denver, Colorado

The city appeared deceptively peaceful from eighteen floors up, its elevated vista able to lull new agents into a false sense of security that only a ringing telephone or the ping of a new email could shatter. Special Agent in Charge Colin Milne knew from thirty years of experience that despite the tranquillity blanketing the grid of streets beneath them, the ugly head of serious crime would invariably rear itself within hours. He placed an empty glass on his desk, turned to the office's window and stared beyond its tinted glass and the nearby skyscrapers to where deep blue sky collided against the Rockies' jagged peaks.

The bastard's out there somewhere…

'So, what do we do?'

Jared Pearson, a slightly-built silver-haired man five years Milne's junior and one rank below, blinked a couple of times; surprised to hear confusion in Milne's usually calm and decisive voice. He got up from one of the office's deep leather armchairs and pursed his lips. 'Regarding Kratz, or Sam?' he replied.

'Both, I guess.'

'We keep up the hunt for Kratz. And Sam–' A pair of car horns beeping for supremacy at a nearby intersection startled Pearson. 'Do we really need to worry him?'

Milne's expression hardened as he returned to his desk. 'He's entitled to know.'

'I wish it could be one of us who tells him.'

Milne refilled his glass. 'Unfortunately, that's not possible,' he said, righting the pitcher to prevent a flotilla of ice cubes from escaping. 'I'm sure he'll handle the news appropriately. Jed Masters' feedback has been nothing other than positive about Sam's induction and his work.' Milne paused again and thought back to his first weeks at the FBI Academy, where their friendship of over half a lifetime developed from a training exercise's accidental clash of heads. 'Jed is an exceptionally experienced agent,' he added. 'He'll help Sam rationalise these developments, and the likelihood of Kratz settling in the Tahoe area is negligible.'

Pearson skimmed an email recently received from London-based Legat Linda Neville. 'There's always a chance of Kratz returning to Reno if he thinks nobody knows he's familiar with the area,' he said. 'How likely is it that six years ago he rocked up in a town he'd never visited, found some guy to wire hundreds of thousands of dollars to some other guy in England and then never went back?'

'Anything's possible,' Milne agreed. 'I've already contacted Reno's resident agency and they're now also investigating whether there was any unexplained disappearances or deaths in the area around the time of the bank transfer.'

'Has there been any progress from the Den of Iniquity?' Pearson asked, referring to the office occupied by Niall Demaine and his array of ultra-sophisticated computers.

'He's on it,' Milne replied. 'Niall's one of the best, but he may be looking for a ghost.'

Pearson poured himself another glass of water and took a sip. 'Kratz is all over the media and a nationwide police bulletin has been sent out. Surely someone's going to see through his latest disguise? It's happened before.'

Milne's gaze returned to the distant mountains. 'And look what happened to those people.'

****

5.56pm – BST
Hutton, Preston, England

Sanderson rubbed his concave stomach and tried to wipe the grin off his face. 'Chippy tea for me tonight,' he announced happily. 'Haven't been for at least a fortnight, you know, and I'm wasting away here. Konrad bloody Kratz has a lot to answer for.'

'One day you'll turn into the fattest of fat bastards,' Boothroyd retorted, conscious of the recent snugness around his waistband. 'And I'll gladly allocate extra funding from the budget for a reinforced chair.'

'That'll never be me,' came the ambivalent reply. 'Got a metabolism that destroys whatever I put in its way. Call it a gift, fat lad.'

'Just because you're a skinny bastard on the outside, doesn't mean you're one on the inside,' Boothroyd said, his tone smug as he loosened his belt a notch. 'At least I know I'm doomed. Your level of denial is astounding.'

Sanderson laughed. 'This body can handle anything. You're jealous, just admit it.'

Boothroyd held his breath and turned to Phelan. 'Someone's keen,' he said, embarrassed by being the first to turn off his computer.

Phelan read the end of an email she'd recently opened. 'That Linda Neville seems on the ball. She's already heard from some of her cronies in Reno.'

'What's the latest on the Oliver Stamford bank business?' Boothroyd asked.

The printer beside Phelan's desk ejected a single sheet of A4 paper. She reached across and glanced at its contents.

Boothroyd's fingers drummed on the corner of his desk. 'Well?'

Within a minute, Phelan summarised how a Reno-based agent quickly identified a man likely to have helped Kratz transfer the money. Joel Nattrass, a highly rated forty-year-old software engineer, was reported missing five days after Mortimer's bank account swelled; his fourteen years of exemplary employment at a Sparks-based gaming company meaning that an uncharacteristic no-show at the office rang immediate alarm bells. An extensive search far beyond the Reno-Sparks Metropolitan Area failed to locate the missing man, irrespective of his girlfriend's insistence that there had to be suspicious circumstances.

'So how did Kratz meet Joel Nattrass?' Sanderson asked, the gnaw of his empty stomach temporarily forgotten. 'You don't just roll into a town you've never visited and start randomly asking for the nearest computer geek.'

'Nattrass used to do some freelance computer work on the side. Him and the girlfriend were saving for their wedding,' Phelan explained. 'He had a secure job, no debt and a happy relationship. There's no known reason for him to disappear off the face of the Earth.'

Boothroyd gave a derisive snort. 'Apart from Kratz needing to ensure the poor guy remained silent.'

'And they didn't find a body?' Sanderson asked, his cynicism generating all manner of possible reasons to explain a man of a similar age to him doing an unexpected runner.

'Nope,' she replied. 'The girlfriend learned she was pregnant a month later and allowed the local press to publish an article. She never married in the hope he'd return one day to see their daughter.'

Sanderson paled, unable to imagine never being a part of his own young daughter's life. 'Does she know?'

Phelan shook her head sadly. 'The Reno agents don't want it getting out in case Kratz intends to return to the area. Neville said they've got a team of agents in Reno ready to investigate Nattrass' disappearance, should further evidence appear.'

The office fell silent, the three detectives reticent to engage in their usual brand of dark humour now they'd learned Kratz's list of victims continued to expand; an unofficial tally theoretically including the families of those he'd killed. They traded solemn goodbyes and walked into the muted evening sunlight, grateful for the loved ones to whom they'd return.

****

12.39pm – PDT
Reno, Nevada

Juan Valdez's leer loomed large across the polished melamine. 'We have a deal, right?'

Konrad calmly surveyed the jewellery store's seventies-inspired furnishings and décor, faded by years of sunlight streaming through a pair of triple-glazed windows. The croupier he'd engaged in conversation in a nearby casino had quickly recommended Valdez's small independent store and his willingness to purchase high-class jewellery at a good price – omitting that he'd then supply her with one hundred dollars for her trouble.

'It's kind of less than I'd hoped for,' he eventually replied, keeping his anger buried.

'Hey man, you want to sell it? Seventy-five is my final offer and it'll take me a half hour to go get the green.' A plump finger pointed beyond the window display and its chunky gold ruby-encrusted ring twinkled in the light. 'Don't keep it on-site these days, not since some fucking gang's initiation rite was to rob my store.'

'Did the cops catch them?' Konrad asked, not really caring unless it meant he got a better price for the watch.

Valdez shook his head. 'I built up this place after my uncle died, he didn't have no kids of his own. A few items got recovered, but them sneaky bastards didn't leave enough evidence to pin it on any of the gang members.'

'That's rough.'

'Yeah. Some asshat detective even accused me of setting it up. Can you believe the goddamn nerve of some people?' Valdez warmed to a well-rehearsed diatribe against Reno's police department. 'My uncle always kept some shady deals going down, get what I'm saying, but my life is clean.'

Konrad stepped back from the counter and folded his arms. 'I really don't know.'

'Take it or leave it,' Valdez snapped. He pushed the green box back to Konrad. 'I ain't bothered. I got plenty more where that came from, thanks to Sadie sending them my way. The number of douchebags in this town crazy enough to sell their shit so they can lose it in the casinos...' His anger dissipated and he re-established eye contact. 'Last chance, buddy.'

'I guess–'

'Awesome.' Valdez's demeanour changed faster than Konrad could blink. 'You get your ass back here around one, and I'll go get your money and we'll sit down and do the paperwork. Do we have a deal?'

Konrad shook the other man's hand with considerably less enthusiasm than he'd experienced when buying the Rolex. 'Yeah.'

'Sweet!' Valdez brandished a large bunch of keys he'd pulled out of a drawer hidden beneath the counter. 'Here's ten bucks,' he continued, pressing the bill into Konrad's hand as he ushered him through the door. 'The coffee shop over there makes awesome cakes; that's why these old pants have gotten too tight. When you see me back here, come on over.'

He patted Konrad on the back and lumbered to an immaculately restored DeLorean. Konrad clutched a pristine blue backpack to his chest and watched the guy zoom away in a cloud of dust. His cold blue eyes settled on an old-fashioned café across the street, its promise of coffee too great to ignore after another early morning visit to Kingsbury.

Now he'd converted the watch into cold hard cash, one more plan required Konrad's attention. He checked to see whether the road was clear, waited for a police cruiser to pass and stepped out onto the empty asphalt.

****

Sam cautiously lowered himself into a vacant swivel chair and took a deep breath that failed to dispel his unease. It felt akin to being back at school again; the same trepidation produced by a summons to the headteacher's office. Why did Masters want to see him? Was there a problem with his work, or maybe it was something relating to the Kratz case – something that could end everything he'd ever wanted, once and for all? Within a couple of weeks of meeting Anna, he'd known she was the one he wanted to grow old alongside; how much longer would she endure this new upheaval in her life?

Their second date had commenced in an almost identical manner to that of six days earlier. Sam picked up Anna from her apartment before driving across town to the Chinese restaurant recommended by Anna's elder sister, who'd recently moved into that neighbourhood. This time their conversation centred mainly on their childhoods and families; Anna fascinated to learn how the quiet, unassuming Englishman seated opposite her became a highly regarded federal agent.

They'd taken less time over their meal this time, ensuring they arrived at the movie theatre with enough time to collect the pair of tickets Sam had reserved online and then locate their seats. Anna's fingers gently stroking his meant he'd been unable to allocate his full attention to the images flickering across the screen, and once again he contemplated the various permutations of how this date may end.

Shortly before midnight, Sam parked in one of the visitor spaces in the residents' lot and walked around to open the car's passenger door, certain Anna would be able to hear his heart pounding. They approached the main entrance, where he placed his hand in the small of her back whilst she rummaged through her bag.

'I, uh, had another lovely evening.'

'It's not too late, so why don't you come up for coffee?' she suggested whilst holding up an assortment of keys until the correct one caught the light. 'I bought some of the good stuff in town this morning. My Technivorm turns it into liquid magic.'

His jaw dropped. 'You have a Technivorm?'

'Sure do, and it's the most essential aid to solving crime in this city.' She smiled knowingly at Sam. 'I need at least two cups to set me up for a day at the station.'

'I know the feeling,' he replied, following her up the stairs. 'You'll have to convince me how good this stuff really is.'

Anna pushed the door open and then turned to face him. 'I accept your challenge. Why don't you relax while I cast my spell?'

Sam nodded and watched her disappear into the kitchen. Still feeling pleasantly full, he leaned back against the couch's thick cushions and listened to the sounds travelling through to the lounge.

'You've got a lovely apartment,' he commented when she returned with a large tray. 'It's very calming.'

'It needs to be. I don't seem to spend much time here these days, but whenever I do the place really chills me out.' She set down the tray on a coffee table in front of the couch. 'Having this weekend and next weekend off is a real treat. The big boss insisted because of the extra hours we needed to put in over the past month.'

Sam nodded. 'Yeah, we really appreciate our time off in this game, don't we?'

'Definitely,' she agreed. 'Do you take milk or sugar?'

'Just milk,' he replied.

She placed his drink in front of him and raised her eyebrows. 'I defy you not to like it.'

He picked up the large red mug, sipped the dark liquid and smiled. 'I concede defeat.'

'Told you,' she retorted triumphantly, after taking a long swallow of her own. 'Nectar of the gods, and don't you forget it.'

Sam hesitated and took a deep breath. 'Anna, you said you had next weekend off?' He saw her smile. 'Have you got any plans?'

She laughed and swirled the remaining coffee around her mug. 'Does spring cleaning this place and going to Target count?'

'Would you like to come to Golden next Saturday? There's some great restaurants, and bars. We could...'

'I'd love to,' Anna said, her voice low. She placed her almost empty mug on a coaster and locked eyes with Sam. 'You'll have to pull something really special out of the hat to better these two dates. Are you up to the challenge?'

He nodded and saw her eyes soften as she moved closer. Their heads tilted to allow their lips to meet and a cautious kiss soon increased in confidence, now they realised both of them welcomed this latest development.

'Your coffee,' Sam muttered.

'Coffee?' she echoed.

'Yeah, it must be exquisitely good stuff.'

She arched a single brow. 'How do you figure that?'

'It tastes even more amazing second-hand.'

'Ass,' she said, pulling him closer. Anna sensed his hand tentatively stroking the back of her neck and reciprocated. Their breathing deepened and her hands moved lower, eventually slipping into the back pockets of his new 501s.

'Nice arse,' she whispered, pronouncing the second word in an exaggerated manner. 'You're a man of hidden talents, Sam. How else are you going to surprise me this evening?'

'Anna, wait,' he said and lifted his head, suddenly embarrassed.

Her face fell. 'What's wrong?'

'Nothing's wrong, that's the problem.'

'Problem?'

'Yeah. It's...' He noticed her puzzled expression and hoped he wasn't going to blow his chances of their third date actually happening. 'I don't want to, but I think I should go. It's getting more and more difficult for me to remain a gentleman, as my dad would say. The longer I stay, the more I want to stay.' He sighed. 'I'm sorry, I'm not making much sense.'

Anna pushed herself into an upright position and smoothed the casual black linen dress she'd bought that morning. 'It's fine, and there's not enough gentlemen left in the world,' she said, unable to hide her disappointment as she got to her feet. Seconds later she opened the apartment door and glanced outside to ensure the landing was empty. 'However,' she added, toying with his belt buckle, 'I hope there will be times in the not too distant future when the word 'gentleman' won't exist in your vocabulary.'

He nodded and lowered his head to kiss her cheek. 'Thanks for a wonderful evening.'

'See you next weekend,' she called, watching him from the doorway before she slowly closed the door.

Sam heard the door handle start to turn and pushed himself into a more upright position. His gaze flitted from one framed photo to the next, yet hardly registered the images of the two teenage boys clutching a pair of gleaming trophies and a football, and another picture of Masters himself proudly holding a huge trout aloft.

'Goddamn thing was a pain in the ass to reel in, but I got it in the end,' Masters said from across the table. His strained cheer didn't fool Sam for a moment. 'You'd think I'd have gotten used to that in this line of work, right?'

Sam forced a smile in return. 'I didn't think we were meeting 'til later this afternoon?' he said, almost certain he knew why Masters unexpectedly requested they meet in his office.

'Yeah,' Masters replied. 'There's something I need to tell you, Sam. I want you to listen, process the information and don't go making any rash decisions. You got me?'

'Kratz is back.'

Masters attempted to gauge Sam's real feelings behind the mask he wore. 'I have to admit that this concerns him.'

'What's the latest?'

'He's in the US.'

'Have they found him?'

'Not yet.' Masters inwardly cringed at the banality of his words. He stole a longer glance at Sam, whose lack of emotion had fast become unnerving.

'Not yet?' Sam echoed. 'That means they haven't. Where was he?'

'The last confirmed whereabouts is ten or eleven days ago in Akron, Ohio.'

Sam nodded and the frown crinkling his brow disappeared as quickly as it formed. 'And they're sure it's him?'

'Yeah.' Masters' feelings of unease increased by the second. 'A lot's happened on both sides of the Atlantic since you've been living here.'

'Ten days? Anyone can easily get anywhere in the country within half that time.' Sam stared into the depths of Masters' dark eyes. 'Have they any idea where he could've gone?'

Masters severed their eye contact and turned towards a map of the Tahoe region he'd pinned to the opposite wall. 'They're working on it,' was all he could bring himself to say.

'That's a fat lot of good.'

An ignored opportunity to share Kratz's newly-discovered Reno connection further increased Masters' guilt. 'That's the best I can do at present.'

'So what do I do in the meantime?'

'Live as normal a life as possible, be a husband and father, do your job, try to relax.' He noticed Sam's top lip curl and shook his head, embarrassed. 'Yeah, I know. Easier said than done. Apparently they've stepped up the investigations in both Denver and LA.'

Sam snorted and folded his arms tightly across his chest. 'You seriously think he'd go back to either?'

'Probably not, but hiding in plain sight is the ultimate double bluff.'

'Who says he wants to kill me anyway?' Sam readjusted his collar as he strode to the doorway. 'If he has any sense he'll keep away from me.'

'Sam?'

Masters cradled his head in his hands when, seconds later, Sam's voice echoed along the corridor.

'I've got work to do.'

****

2.42pm – PDT
San Fernando Road, Los Angeles, California

Gibson stared at his laptop's screen and felt his forehead furrow into deep lines. A dull headache increased its tempo, fuelled by a combination of intense concentration and the after-effects of joining his eldest brother and two cousins for what had rapidly devolved into an evening of bar hopping. Gibson eventually made his excuses and departed around the time the party got fully underway. He sighed and wondered whether the time had arrived to acknowledge that more than a couple of beers were enough to wreak havoc on his increasingly intolerant bloodstream these days.

'What gives?' Hallberg asked, his unexpected words and pat on the back startling Gibson.

'Jeez, give a guy a heart attack, why don't you?' he replied. 'Mitch managed to get four goddamn beers down me last night.' He pointed a hesitant finger at the email he'd read three times. 'Read this and tell me I'm not dreaming or drunk or a dumbass.'

'Can't guarantee the last one,' Hallberg said. 'A Rolex? Someone's gotten a taste for the finer things in life. Who gave you a pay rise?'

'Shut up and read,' Gibson grumbled and experienced immediate remorse at Hallberg's surprised expression. After returning from their enforced road trip, Muñoz had immediately contacted the watch manufacturer's New York headquarters, explained the seriousness of their current case and requested that should the item ever be sold, they provide him with a date and location as soon as possible.

Hallberg looked up from the screen, his eyes gleaming. 'It's Chamberlain's watch, the one he bought in Phoenix.'

'Sold to a dealer in Reno a little over an hour ago, who registered it immediately,' Gibson confirmed. 'You think this is it?'

Hallberg's mouth hung open. 'Kratz is definitely in Reno?' he managed to splutter.

'Not necessarily,' Gibson replied, reluctant to burst the glimmer of hope they'd embraced. 'Perhaps Kratz sold it for cash, and whoever bought it from him sold it on. Does he have a Reno connection?'

Hallberg shrugged. 'Not that I know of. What do we do now?'

Gibson thought for a moment and picked up the phone. 'I'll get on to one of my buddies at the LA field office. The guy owes me a couple of favours.' He pictured the Oklahoma native who occasionally picked his brain about growing up in Atwater Village. 'I guess he'll pass it to the Reno agents and tell us if they discover anything.'

'Sweet!' Hallberg's smile grew. 'Perhaps this means his time's nearly up.'

****

6.23pm – PDT
Kingsbury, Nevada

The Bury's evening closely mirrored that of many families across the world: an uneventful, well-rehearsed routine providing a smooth and enjoyable transition from day into night. Sam's return journey to the cabin saw him better his previous best time, the ride easier now his fitness levels were comparable to the months leading up to last summer's accident.

Red-faced and with sweat soaked into his cycling gear, Sam called a hurried greeting and disappeared beneath the power shower's warm water; eager to sooth away the work day and relax his aching muscles. The double cubicle offered enough room to work through a range of stretches, ensuring he'd soon be able to meet the challenge again without too much discomfort. Perhaps alternating cycling and driving would be better for a while, he mused?

He reluctantly turned off the shower, grabbed a large towel from a nearby heated rail and wrapped it around his waist. The warmth it had absorbed felt good against Sam's rapidly cooling skin as he returned to the bedroom, where he stood in front of its full-length mirror in an uncharacteristic display of self-interest. Twenty years ago he'd never expected to end up a little over six feet in height and, due to the physical requirements of the job, with a physique many men would envy. His eyes settled on his abdomen, toned by months of physical therapy and exercise. Eleven months earlier he'd left hospital almost totally reliant on others and even a short trip to the bathroom proved exhaustive in those dark days. Hours of hard work had paid off since then, although the emotional difficulties he'd encountered whilst coming to terms with the ordeal slowed his physical progress by months.

Had he *really* come to terms with it all though? His scrutiny turned to the long, faded scar following a straight path from his sternum to below his belly button. Did the surgeon really mean to give him such an obvious reminder of the day that had changed his life forever? Sam twisted his torso and closed his eyes, nauseated at the sight of where a chest tube was probably the first thing to save his life. At least clothing covered these, and socks masked where an orthopaedic surgeon gained access to plate and pin his ankle. The two scars on his left arm were harder to hide and, on a couple of occasions, he'd half-heartedly joked about having a fight with *Jaws*. A small ragged white mark glared at him from the inside of his right wrist, another constant reminder of something he'd never recollect apparently distressing him to the point he'd torn out an arterial line.

He knew his wish for all visible reminders of that day to be obliterated would, once more, not be granted and he reluctantly reopened his eyes. To all intents and purposes he'd made a full recovery: his cognitive abilities, strength and coordination restored to levels almost commensurate with those before the accident.

But, was he really *fully* recovered? Sam slumped onto the edge of the bed and slowly fell backwards. He lay there for an indeterminate length of time, attempting to fill in the blank spaces which, in spite of a year passing by, consumed his thoughts more and more in recent weeks. Recollections of his time at Bellevue were sketchy at best, although his memories of the three weeks he'd spent at St Anthony following his transfer from New York to Denver held considerably more clarity. These included, surprisingly, the five days he'd spent in the Step Down Unit, three days after his admittance to the Medical-Surgical floor. At first Anna blamed the hospital for her husband's pneumonia, until she'd learned he'd been a prime candidate for a chest infection all along.

He remembered feeling off-colour upon waking that morning and assigning the discomfort in his chest to the rigorous physical therapy regimen since his transfer. Even though Sam had been desperate to accelerate his recovery and leave the hospital, he wondered whether he'd pushed himself too hard and decided to mention his concerns during that afternoon's session. He'd already learned they intended to get him fully out of bed; maybe a couple of days of lighter work would leave him without this feeling of exhaustion, which seemed to be getting worse with every passing minute.

A cheery nurse asked how he'd slept, picked up a checklist and prepared to record the observations she'd made minutes before he woke. Her smile failed to reach her eyes and Sam ignored a pang of guilt telling him he'd lied to her. She didn't need to know about the two occasions he'd woken in a cold sweat, unable to rid himself of the visions plaguing him for the best part of a week. His gaze settled on the blood pressure cuff she wrapped around his arm and this time he decided to give an honest answer when she asked if he was looking forward to breakfast.

The nurse frowned at Sam's reply and reminded him of his eagerness to have a second Jello pot at lunch the previous day – and the medical team's intention to remove his last IV if he could maintain a decent fluid intake. Sam had shaken his head and eyed the drip balefully. He wanted to be rid of it, but the thought of food made his stomach turn. To confess to feeling worse must certainly be a sure-fire way of extending his stay; perhaps she'd fall for a story that he'd overdone the physio the previous afternoon?

Her frown deepened as she moved a stethoscope over his chest and back, and a fearful Sam found himself confirming the discomfort produced by a series of deep breaths. A bout of coughing exploded from nowhere and he'd wrapped his right arm around his chest in an unsuccessful attempt to stop the pain shooting through his ribs. The soothing circular rubbing on Sam's back continued whilst he repeatedly gasped; his hidden fear freeing itself in the time it took for her to elicit how much it hurt to breathe, and to establish that his temperature had risen since the last set of observations four hours ago. Sam looked up her through streaming eyes, barely able to whisper any response to her questions.

He heard her softly-worded instruction to rest, closed his eyes and fell back into a fitful doze where light and sound merged into one confusing mass; unaware of Dr Gilani timing his inhalations and exhalations against a large clock on the wall.

'I understand our patient isn't feeling too good?' The way he phrased the statement made it sound like a question.

The nurse nodded and handed over Sam's chart. 'Fever of one hundred, cough, discomfort upon inspiration and slight nausea,' she confirmed. 'Blood pressure has dropped and his respiratory rate increased since his two o'clock observation.'

'Sam, can you wake up for me?' Dr Gilani asked. He held the metal part of his stethoscope between his hands and observed Sam open his eyes and glance between them. 'That's great. I need to check you over this morning and see how you're doing. Is that okay?' He noted Sam's nod and smiled at his patient. 'How are you feeling this morning?' he added, the softest trace of an accent hinting at a childhood move from the Middle East. 'Tell me what's different today.'

'My chest is sore after the physio and I feel cold.'

'I'm going to listen to your chest, so you need to breathe deeply so I can hear everything's working okay.' Sam closed his eyes again when the warmed metal made contact with his skin. 'That's really good, Sam. Just some more deep breaths... excellent.'

Sam's clouded mind processed the doctor's actions. 'Am I ill?'

'I think you might have developed a slight chest infection, Sam,' he replied, looking guardedly at the nurse. 'We need to run some tests, take an x-ray and keep an eye on you. We'll also start you on some antibiotics, just in case.'

Sam stifled a cough and grimaced. 'Where's Anna?' he asked, suddenly wanting her beside him more than anything else.

A little over an hour later she arrived on the ward, concerned to receive an early morning phone call from the hospital on her way to taking Angela for a play date in Genesee. On her way to Sam's bedside she was updated on the results of a preliminary round of tests, including a chest x-ray that strongly suggested that he'd developed pneumonia; a likely complication from the trauma he'd suffered, and the subsequent life-saving treatment.

Sam remembered the concern on her face and how she'd held his hand and talked quietly to him whilst tests to ascertain the microbe responsible for the infection were carried out. She'd dispelled his worry over being put on intravenous antibiotics and extra oxygen, calmed him when the coughing became more frequent and painful, and wiped a damp cloth over his face as his fever escalated to 104°F.

By lunchtime, Sam's worsening condition meant breathing became more of a struggle and his chest felt ready to ignite at any minute. His exhaustion was evident, but the effort required to keep air moving in and out of his congested lungs made sleep an impossible option. Anna managed to shield him from the worst of the medical team's concern, until they made their decision to transfer him to the hospital's SDU – where closer monitoring and non-invasive ventilation could be provided.

Sam pleaded to remain where he was; certain he'd end up back in ICU, where his limited recollections were confusing at best and terrifying at worst. For the next three days and nights he lost all sense of time; drifting in and out of sleep and resisting the urge to pull the claustrophobic mask off his face. After two more days he returned to the Medical-Surgical Unit, still on IV antibiotics and too weak to resume his physical therapy. A further eleven days passed before he was deemed well enough to leave the hospital, from which point the road to recovery would be a long and complex one.

Footfalls from above jolted him back into the present. The sounds were quieter than those made by an adult and suggested Angela was probably copying some new dance moves she'd seen on television. An unexpected smile edged across Sam's face, only to be doused almost immediately by recollections of his last conversation in Masters' office. Did Anna really need to know Kratz had been traced to Ohio and, since then, apparently given the FBI and every other group of law enforcement the slip? Did she need to become increasingly vigilant; constantly looking over her shoulder and wondering if every tall man with sharp blue eyes was the guy who wanted to kill her husband?

Don't be such a pillock! Is Kratz actually going to turn up on your doorstep? This country is bloody massive. He probably headed south, ready for a lifetime of tacos and tequila.

Maybe he'd keep the news to himself this time, rather than worry Anna? They were making a go of things here and the kids were more settled. Why ruin what had become a tolerable situation? And, there was also the impending weekend camping trip to Mono Lake for them to look forward to. He heard her voice from the top of the stairs informing him only a few minutes remained until she'd dish up.

Sam rearranged both towels on the heated rail and walked through to the bedroom, an action unable to distract him from the dilemma he'd mulled over since lunchtime. 'Two minutes,' he called back, hurriedly pulling clean underwear, shorts and a t-shirt from a nearby chest of drawers. A smirk appeared from nowhere at the thought of Anna's usual reaction to the orange and blue shorts she claimed to regret adding to his stocking a couple of Christmases ago. He smoothed down their creased fabric and winced at a muscle tightening in his lower back. Perhaps there was time to–

'Sam!'

'Coming, dearest!' Sam retorted, unable to suppress a grin on his way to the kitchen. 'Looks good,' he added at the top of the stairs, from where he watched her carry a bowl of salad and a basket of bread rolls to the table.

'Daddy, I got a ballerina dress today,' Angela announced. She smiled at her father and twirled around fast enough to blur its pale pink fabric.

'That's so pretty,' Sam said. He moved across the room in readiness to catch Angela. She dropped to the floor with a bump before he reached her, giggling at how the vortex above distorted the ceiling lights.

Anna narrowed her eyes. 'Shame I can't say the same for your shorts.'

Strong arms clasped around her waist and tightened when she squealed and tried to break free. 'I'm beginning to think this is an act, that you pretend to hate them just so you can order me to take them off,' Sam whispered, his mouth now only a couple of inches from her ear. He saw Anna's reddening face catch sight of Angela's quizzical look. 'In reality, I know they have the opposite effect. Why do you think I keep wearing them?'

Angela climbed to her feet and wobbled to one side. 'What did Daddy say?' she asked, excitement widening her eyes.

'Daddy's being silly,' Anna replied. A sharp nudge in Sam's ribs ensured her release and allowed her to take her seat at the table. John observed from the confines of his highchair, oblivious to the remnants of a slice of buttered bread smeared across his plump cheeks. 'So, he's going to clean up your little brother and then the rest of us can eat.'

Sam lifted Angela onto a chair, where a car booster seat enabled her to comfortably reach her plate. 'Did Mommy take you shopping today?'

'I got my dress and a book, and John got a toy cat. I chose it for him.'

He met Anna's stare. 'What did Mommy buy?'

'She said it's a big secret,' Angela replied, repeating her mother's earlier words.

'Where did you go?'

Anna reached into the bread basket and selected a sourdough roll. 'Reno was the original plan,' she said. 'Then I figured Carson City fitted the bill and it saves an hour in the car. We picked up some groceries on the way back, so stay out of the refrigerator.'

He nodded, lifted a forkful of bolognaise-coated pasta to his mouth and wondered what she'd planned for tomorrow evening. Since their enforced move, the couple's monthly *date night* soon became a faded memory. Anna's parents had always taken great pleasure in having their grandchildren to stay overnight every fourth or fifth weekend. Sam and Anna endeavoured to make the most of their precious alone time, often staying in Golden to visit its eclectic mix of bars and shops. On other occasions Denver was their destination, or they'd head in the opposite direction to grab a last-minute bargain stay at an upscale hotel or cosy guest house high up in the mountains.

Sam's instructions were to return to the cabin by half past three the following afternoon, take the kids to the beach and return home via Angela's favourite local pancake house. He and Anna assumed the combination of fresh air and rich food would be more powerful than any tranquiliser, guaranteeing two exhausted children and a quiet evening to themselves. They ate and listened to an excited Angela telling her baby brother that Daddy was taking them out tomorrow afternoon, and how he needed to be a good boy or else this might the last time they go to the beach and eat pancakes. John's solemn eyes never left her face, his almost empty dish of puréed chicken and vegetables forgotten whilst he hung off every word. Their parents stifled their mirth at his apparent nod of agreement, the illusion dispelled by the time his eyelids drooped and his head tipped forwards.

Angela joined her sleeping brother downstairs shortly after the reddening sun skimmed the mountains, her parents' gentle reminder of being able to choose any pancake silencing her plea to stay up past bedtime. She'd hugged Sam tightly and promised to go straight to sleep and to help her mother around the house in the morning. Meanwhile, Anna stretched out on the sofa to enjoy a few minutes of solitude and half-listen to the dishwasher compete with the washing machine.

'The bribery worked?' she asked when Sam returned. He nodded and casually pulled back the deep red fleecy throw she'd purchased that day. 'You like?'

He dropped down beside her, looped an arm around her shoulders and stroked the throw's softness between his fingers. 'Which bit?' he asked with a wink. 'I like the whole lot, and I especially like this blanket thing.'

'That's what I meant, dumbass,' she replied. 'I figured it'll be nice for those cold winter evenings, here or back home.'

Sam turned to face her and lowered his head. 'There's plenty of other ways to keep warm, you know,' he said, his expression deadpan. He placed his other hand on her hip and eased a thumb beneath her waistband.

Anna pressed a hand against his chest. 'Like wearing sweatpants instead of those shorts.'

'I can always get rid of them,' he suggested, the words punctuated by the row of kisses he planted along her jawline.

'Save it for tomorrow, Romeo,' she drawled in an exaggerated manner and pulled away from him.

He noticed the grin she'd failed to suppress. 'So I'm on a promise?'

'That's classified information for another twenty-four hours.'

Sam flopped back against the cushions and exhaled. They surveyed each other through narrowed eyes until Sam reached across to the nearby coffee table to grab the TV's remote control, unable to stop his laughter as Anna made a futile lunge for it.

'I thought we were going to watch those *Breaking Bad* re-runs?' she said. 'Please don't say you want one of the sport channels.'

'Quite a telly, isn't it?' he commented, avoiding the question. 'We should use it more often.'

Anna aimed a punch at his gut. 'Since when did you become a couch potato kind of guy?'

'Since my normal life was stolen from me and, beyond these four walls, there's very little worth bothering with.'

She detected his change in tone and raised an eyebrow. 'There's plenty to do around here.'

'Maybe during daylight. I'm not happy leaving you and the kids here in the dark while I go off doing whatever.'

'What's brought this on?'

Sam stared across the room to the balcony doors and the impenetrable darkness that lay beyond. 'It's more isolated than we're used to here.'

'There's a whole bunch of other houses nearby.'

'It's also a lot further for the emergency services to get to us.'

Anna grabbed his hand. 'Sam, what's this about?'

'Nothing really, just been thinking about living here over winter I suppose.'

'Sam?' Her voice hardened and left him unable to evade a truthful reply.

'Jed Masters called me in for a little chat this afternoon.' He slowly met her gaze. 'There's pretty conclusive evidence Kratz has been back in the US since the last week of August.'

'What did he say?'

'Just that he'd been traced from England to New York, and then to Akron.'

'As in Ohio?' She watched him nod. 'Does he have any connections in the area?'

'None that anyone's aware of,' Sam replied. He pushed the throw away from his lap and ignored how cool the room's air felt against his bare legs. 'Surely he'd make for Mexico, or beyond. That's always been a popular destination for criminals on the lam.'

'If that's true, why not fly directly to Mexico, or another country?'

'He's always been a devious bastard.'

Anna leaned against Sam and stroked his cheek. 'You've never really said what he was like as a kid.'

His jaw tightened. 'It's not something I like to dwell on.'

'Do you remember much?' she pressed, realising how little her husband had told her about this chapter of his life.

'We started primary school on the same day,' he said. 'He pulled my hair and punched me where it hurts.'

She pulled the fleece across both of them and rested her head on his shoulder. 'Why did he do that?'

'Because he's absolutely crackers, that's why,' Sam replied, his voice flat. 'I probably left myself open to it because I could read and write by the time I started school. I wanted to learn, so Mum taught me. The teachers got work from older classes for me. I never thought much of it and the other kids never seemed bothered – apart from Peter.'

To Anna's surprise, a tear traced its way down her face before soaking into Sam's t-shirt. 'How many years did this last?'

'Pretty much all the way through primary,' he replied, oblivious to her sadness. 'I had an escape route at eleven. This posh private school out of town offered me a scholarship, but I'd made some really good friends at primary school and wanted to go to the same local secondary school.'

'I thought you went to that private school?'

'I did. A couple of weeks into the first term he blackmailed some older boys to start on me, after he'd seen them stealing stuff from the science labs. They beat me up, stole my glasses and then...'

A deep and unwieldy silence filled the room. 'What did they do?' Her voice wavered on the last word.

'Pushed my head down the toilet and pulled the chain,' Sam continued in the same matter-of-fact tone. 'I couldn't hide that, so I walked out and went home. Mum and Dad went into school later that afternoon, had it out with the headteacher and immediately withdrew me.'

'Goddamn piece of shit,' she exclaimed. 'It's like he knew you were better than him, and he wanted to destroy your spirit. Even now, you sometimes let him in.'

'Now and again I think it was him who really gave me a drive to succeed, to prove nobody can hold me back. He might have done well for himself, but he built every last bit of his success on a web of lies.'

'And then he fucked up,' Anna said, her uncharacteristic venom surprising Sam. 'Just like he's going to fuck up this time, once and for all.'

Chapter 8 – Friday 4th September 2009

Over four hundred miles north-west of Las Vegas, the FBI's Reno base occupied an unremarkable second floor location adjacent to the freeway linking Reno to Carson City, and beyond. One of an almost identical quartet and only a ten-minute drive south of the city centre, the building had been divided into suites of various sizes; leased by a diverse selection of local companies and other larger organisations in the twelve years since its construction.

Nearly an hour earlier than their usual arrival time, Raquel Vasquez, Rick Jones and Anahid Avakian occupied a trio of seats around a conference table, sipping from large mugs of coffee as each skimmed a single page of information received on their arrival. Supervisory Senior Resident Agent Denise Grainger, in the sixth year of her role, had summoned the three younger agents to her office shortly before they'd departed for home to request they return to work by seven o'clock the next morning to work on a strictly confidential assignment.

Avakian, a recent graduate of the FBI's Academy, leaned forward in her seat and slid a hairband off her wrist. 'So, let me get this straight...' She deftly twisted her dense mane of black curls into a ponytail. 'Konrad Kratz came to town? I get that Rick here just helped identify Joel Nattrass as a probable victim from six years ago but, while the victimology and circumstances fit, would Kratz really come back?'

'The Rolex he bought in Phoenix this summer was sold in Reno yesterday afternoon,' Grainger said. 'I realise Kratz maybe sold it to someone else who then sold it in Reno but, based on his previous link to Reno, we treat this like he's in town and looking to lay his hands on as much cash as possible, unless we can conclusively prove otherwise.'

'Reno's kind of out on a limb,' Avakian said. 'Unless he passes through on I-80 on the way from one hideout to another?'

Grainger, a tall woman in her late forties, spooned a second hit of sugar into her drink. 'I had a long conversation with the Special Agent in Charge from Denver yesterday,' she said. 'There's a lot of theories surrounding Kratz, from the Bureau and from more detectives than I can keep track of. The general consensus is he's gotten himself some unknown residence away from Denver and Glendale, so why not around Reno? It fits. If he's been banking large sums of cash, what better cover story than getting lucky in one of the casinos?'

Avakian nodded. 'I can buy he'd come here from Glendale. Hell, I drove down there in one day for my grandmother's birthday, and back here a couple of days later.'

Jones' eyes widened in surprise. 'You didn't fly down?'

'Flights were sold out. I didn't know if I'd get the extra leave until four days before and by then it was too late.' She squinted at a map on the opposite wall. 'From Denver it's around one thousand miles, which may be possible in a day *if* there was someone to share the driving. If I was driving solo, I guess I'd need to break for a night around Salt Lake City.'

'Reno serves a pretty big area,' Jones added, warming to the discussion. 'He could have come into town from further afield; it's only a couple of hours drive here from Sacramento. Don't the big guns think he's hiding somewhere in rural Cali?'

'That's the current theory,' Grainger confirmed. 'Californian licence plates wouldn't stand out across the state line like they would in a rural location around here. Like you said, he'd comfortably drive here in one day from Glendale.'

'So me and Annie are heading into town this morning?' Vasquez asked. Although seven years older than the rookie agent she'd been paired alongside, both women bore an uncanny resemblance to each other – leading to a frequently-peddled theory amongst the older agents that they were the product of a top-secret government cloning experiment.

'Start with the banks and see if anyone has attempted to withdraw a large amount of cash over the past twelve days. Ask for their security footage if anything significant flags up.'

Avakian narrowed her eyes and looked at Grainger, 'What if they don't want to hand it over?' she asked and, not for the first time, wondered if she lacked the experienced required for such a high-profile case.

'The banks and casinos in this area are usually cooperative. They keep us sweet in case we're called to any crime committed against them,' Grainger replied. She took a couple of minutes to run through the list of banks and, if necessary, the casinos Avakian and Vasquez were scheduled to visit that day. They listened intently and stared at a series of colour photographs, each showing Kratz in a different disguise.

'Do we show these pictures to the tellers? I mean, this one here makes it obvious who our fugitive is.' Avakian pointed at the image of Kratz on the *H.O.S.T.A.G.E.* set. 'The last thing we need is this to get out around Reno, Kratz hears of it and then disappears into the night.'

'I've printed copies which don't include that photo; you can show these to staff if they need something to jog their memory. If you have *any* suspicions, and I mean about anything – however insignificant it seems – send it through to Jones. He'll stay here to work on tracing Joel Nattrass' email communication in the days and weeks leading up to his disappearance.' She looked around the table and raised an eyebrow. 'Did you guys eat breakfast?'

'No ma'am,' Jones replied, relieved to see the others also shake their heads. A member of Reno's Cyber Crimes Task Force for the past four years, he'd built a double-edged reputation on being completely obsessed by anything computer-orientated at the expense of almost everything else in his life. 'Figured I'd pick something up on the way, but I was running late.'

Grainger placed a notepad and pen on the desk. 'Write down what you all want from that new Holey Heaven down on South Virginia, and I'll head on over before the traffic builds. While I'm gone, give the evidence another once-over and see if something less obvious has gotten missed.' She strode from the room and silence seeped into every corner, amplifying the *drip-drip-drip* of a coffee maker beneath the window.

'Fresh eyes?' Jones queried through a yawn and checked his watch. 'At this hour?'

****

The pull-out opposite Bradbury Way was one of four parking spots inside a ten-minute jog of the Bury family's cabin; each carefully chosen to ensure its location prevented local residents noticing an unfamiliar car on two consecutive mornings. Fitness was the key, Konrad mused; something that could be the difference between escape and capture.

Life and death.

The looped route he'd chosen to run that morning provided another opportunity to survey the cabin. This time he spotted a balcony to its lower floor's rear, presumably where the bedrooms were located. An embankment opposite brought tall pines to within a couple of feet of the roadside, the absence of another cabin there decreasing the likelihood of witnesses.

Reassured by the clarification offered by this latest visit, Konrad returned to the car, leaned against its dulled bodywork and shifted his weight from one foot to another whilst stretching out his hamstrings. The gentle purr of an engine gained his attention, the sound louder now the small car descending towards him had come into view.

The Suzuki appeared familiar, although Konrad was unable to place the vehicle prior to it coming to a halt. A furtive glance through mirrored sunglasses confirmed its ownership; Sam too engrossed by a cyclist speeding down the hill to notice the man observing him from across the intersection. Konrad wondered if Sam had an early morning meeting, his smart shirt and tie and choice of transportation hinting that something differed about today.

Sam eased the car through a left turn and accelerated. Its fresh red paintwork reflected a sharp beam of morning sunlight and the unexpected glare piercing his dark lenses caused Konrad to flinch. Satisfied his lower legs wouldn't cramp during the drive back to his own bolthole, he pulled a small bunch of keys from a zipped pocket in his shorts, deactivated the central locking and lowered himself into the driver's seat.

One more visit should crystallise things.

****

Rick Jones stretched until his fingertips touched the office floor's carpet, exhaled loudly, closed his eyes and felt the tension in his shoulders gradually relinquish its grip. He wondered whether he'd overdone it in the gym the previous evening, and whether this recently-devised plan to add bulk to his admittedly skinny frame was really worth the effort.

Lost in his thoughts of the Kratz case and his new fitness regimen, Jones failed to hear a light knock at the partially open door. He recalled the advice given to him by a yoga-endorsing ex-girlfriend, took a deep breath and held it for a few seconds, oblivious to Denise Grainger's smile as she watched from the doorway.

'Feels good, right?' she commented, after he'd returned to an upright position and opened his eyes.

'Yeah,' he agreed, wondering where the conversation was heading. 'Have you heard anything from the Ugly Sisters?'

'I can't imagine them ever calling you Prince Charming, sweetheart,' she said, enjoying the light-hearted moment. 'Do *you* have anything new?'

'Getting there,' he replied. 'I made a phone call to Joel Nattrass' girlfriend and explained we're investigating a recent death which may be linked to the disappearance of her fiancé. She wasn't happy when I said we couldn't elaborate at the moment, but allowed me to access the Hotmail address Joel used for his freelance work. She keeps it active in case he returns.'

'I hope you got her permission in writing?'

Jones nodded. 'She emailed it through. Saved me asking Judge Schneider for a warrant.'

'Did you find something?'

'Sure did,' he said. 'For the three weeks leading up to Joel Nattrass' disappearance he exchanged regular email correspondence with none other than a certain Oliver Stamford.'

'No shit?' Grainger pushed the door closed behind her and dragged a swivel chair closer to Jones' desk. 'That's the alias Kratz used to transfer money to the UK six years ago.'

'That's right,' he replied. 'The emails were pretty vague. They mentioned transferring money internationally a couple of times.'

Grainger's nails tapped on the desk as she considered their next moves. 'First you'll need to get a warrant so we can check out the origin of these emails.'

'Yeah, I had to ask Schneider for that one. He's sending it to Microsoft later this afternoon. My old college friend Aaron works there, and let's just say I defended his sorry ass on more than one occasion during our first couple of semesters.'

Her neatly curved eyebrows shot upwards. '*You* called in a favour?'

'Of course,' Jones replied, somewhat concerned to hear another comment lending credence to the commonly held idea he was an absolute stickler for protocol. 'Soon as he receives the warrant, Aaron will trace the IP address or addresses Stamford's emails were sent from. Although it's six years ago, I'm confident any information we get back will help to narrow down the search.'

'When did this Aaron guy say he'd get back to you?'

'If he gets the warrant through tomorrow morning and there's no use of multiple servers, either here or internationally...' He noticed Grainger narrow one eye. 'If it's straightforward he may be able to give us the results by the close of business tomorrow.'

She whistled and broke into another smile. 'That's fast.'

'That's Aaron. He knows his stuff.'

'Does Kratz?'

'Pardon me?'

'How computer savvy is he?'

Jones handed a slender file to Grainger. 'From what I can glean he's nothing special. His agent ran his website and Facebook page, although he seemed capable of formulating enough inane drivel for his Twitter feed.'

'Isn't everyone these days?' She wrinkled her nose. 'You'll keep me updated?'

'You'll be the second to hear,' he replied. 'How are Raquel and Annie doing?'

'Slowly working through the list. Raquel texted just before I came in and said they were going to check out one more, then they'd grab some lunch.'

His stomach gurgled, the pair of Bavarian creams he'd devoured at breakfast a distant memory. 'Sounds like a plan.'

****

124

Avakian and Vasquez paused on the sun-drenched sidewalk and took turns to gulp from a bottle of tepid water. The fifth bank on Grainger's printed list was a tall, glass-fronted building stretching skyward over six floors, its exterior broken up by a checkerboard of painted steel columns. At street level, a steady stream of customers entered and exited the building, blissfully unaware of the two federal agents nearby and the reason for their visit.

'Please say we're definitely grabbing lunch after this one,' Avakian pleaded, unable to ignore the feeling that her stomach was ready to devour itself.

'You don't have to convince me, sister,' Vasquez replied. 'There's a large club sandwich at Toni's hollering to me.'

Avakian scrunched the plastic bottle, carefully screwed on the lid and threw it into a nearby trash can. 'Let's do this!' She patted the reassuring outline of her credentials in her trouser pocket and activated the automatic sensor above a pair of glass doors. 'And don't forget you're doing all the talking this time,' she added with a sly grin. 'You owe me after that creepy guy at the last place.'

'That creepy guy could have been the man of your dreams.'

'He's all yours. At your age you can't afford to be so choosy.'

'Focus, woman!' Vasquez whispered. She nodded at four people standing beside a customer service desk directly across the lobby. 'Let's get in line before the lunchtime rush.'

They crossed the atrium's polished floor, noticing how their formal attire and the tap-tap produced by their heeled shoes gathered a number of second glances from a wide-reaching selection of Reno society, all patiently waiting for any one of the tellers. The two women joined a second shorter line where they waited in silence, shuffling ever-closer to the countertop and a small bowl of mint candies Avakian hoped would stave off the worst of her hunger pangs for the duration of their visit.

The line quickly cleared when, by pure luck, a succession of minor queries freed the young man and woman behind the service desk's counter. Avakian's hand returned to her trouser pocket and eased the plain black wallet from its hiding place.

'Agents Avakian and Vasquez from the FBI, can we speak with one of you privately?' she said quietly, unfazed by the identical panicked expressions plastered across the two faces opposite. 'We're just making routine inquiries and I promise it's nothing to worry about.'

The woman looked sideways at her co-worker. 'I'll go first. You keep it moving here until I get back.' She watched him nod hesitantly and then turned back to the agents. 'There's a private office right through there,' she added, pointing to a doorway and the illuminated internal corridor visible beyond its arch. 'Will that be okay?'

'That's great, thank you,' Vasquez replied, silently envious of the representative's glossy auburn waves as she fell into step beside her. 'And you are?'

'Becky Weber.'

'Have you worked here long?' Avakian asked from two paces behind.

'A couple of months,' Becky replied. She paused to tap a security code into a keypad and pushed open the door. 'I'd planned to go out of state for college, but the people here are real friendly, so I figured I'd stay for at least the next year or two and save some money.'

Vasquez smiled her thanks at the younger woman and scanned the empty break room. 'You're from Reno originally?'

'Yeah, pretty much my whole family is here,' Becky said. She pointed to the nearest seats and stole a glance at a digital clock mounted high on the opposite wall. 'We're all close, so I guess that's another thing to keep me in this little city.'

'So you recognise most of the customers?' Avakian asked.

Becky's faster than normal nodding hinted at her enduring nervousness. 'Certainly the regulars, and there's also others you see from time to time. Not that you'd know them well enough to make casual conversation.'

'Do you get many strangers?'

'Sure we do. There's always those who frequent the casinos. Some like to bank their winnings, others like to empty their accounts.' She eyed Vasquez. 'What's this about? I know you guys investigate all the bank robberies and–'

'This is nothing like that,' Vasquez interrupted. She reached into the inside pocket of her jacket and retrieved the folded sheet of photographs. 'I want you to look carefully at these photographs and tell me if you recognise any of these guys. He may have visited in the past week, or maybe you served him on another occasion since you started working here.'

Becky pulled the sheet closer and scanned from one photograph to the next. 'This one here...' She pointed at an image of a dark-haired man wearing a pair of heavy-framed glasses. 'There's a guy who came in two or three days ago who kind of looked like him.'

It took every last reserve of Vasquez's self-control to keep her face straight and voice even. 'Did you serve him?'

'Yeah, he came up to the counter and asked for access to his safe deposit box.'

'Where are they?' Vasquez pressed. She coughed and scratched her right ear to give Avakian the pre-arranged signal that she'd continue with their questioning.

'Downstairs, in the vault,' Becky replied. 'He had to wait around ten minutes before I could take him down, but he was cool about it.'

'Did you notice anything, and I mean *anything*, strange about this man?'

'I remember when I took the box from him after he was done it felt so much lighter.'

'Like he'd emptied it?'

'Maybe.' She thought for a couple of seconds. 'I think he wore a backpack, kind of like the type a hiker would wear.'

'Have you seen him previously?'

'No. When he signed the card I remember seeing entries from other visits.'

'Can you remember the dates?'

'Not without looking. You'd need a warrant for that, right?'

Avakian leaned forward again in a routine they'd choreographed should they appear to hit the Konrad Kratz mother lode. 'We can get one through pretty quickly to gain access to the safe deposit box.' She flipped open her cell phone and headed for the door. 'Excuse me,' Avakian whispered as she stepped out of the room.

'Would security camera footage help?'

'Almost certainly,' Vasquez replied. She smiled at the marginally less nervous bank employee. 'Do you have access?'

'Not personally,' she said. 'The manager will be able to help you out. She's due back from lunch at one.'

Vasquez's empty stomach clenched in silent disapproval. 'Can we wait for her?'

'Sure. Would you like a coffee or something?'

'Black, no sugar. Same for both of us, please.' Her attention turned to Avakian now she'd re-entered the office. 'You got anything?'

'Grainger said she'd get straight on to Judge Schneider once we've gotten the guy's name, and he'll get the warrant signed. It could be around a half hour from then.'

'So you're okay to wait here while I go get your coffees and find my boss?' Becky asked, relieved that at least for the time being the interview appeared to be over.

'Sure we are,' Vasquez agreed, pleased this looked to be their last stop before returning to the office. She watched Becky leave the room and head for a coffee machine along the corridor. 'Food tastes better if you wait,' she continued. 'Mind over matter, as my mom says.'

'That's if I don't begin to digest myself from inside,' the younger woman shot back. 'You think this is him?'

'It's the best lead we've gotten all day and this guy possibly emptying the box is kind of suspicious,' Vasquez said, her hunger forgotten. 'He might have been coming here for years. Paying large sums into an account and making large cash withdrawals flags up, so he'd need to find a way of banking his money without anyone discovering how and where he was doing it. He could hide literally hundreds of thousands of dollars in one of the larger boxes if he used hundred dollar bills.'

Avakian shrugged and wondered how she'd handle the financial side of things if she ever found herself in such a predicament. 'That's risky if he wants to live off the money for the rest of his life. What if the bill designs are changed in the future?'

The tap of low-heeled shoes increased in volume and Vasquez lowered her voice. 'What's he got to lose?'

****

4.03pm – PDT
North Benjamin Road, Kingsbury, Nevada

Beneath the aspens dominating the short stretch of road, the gentle slap of rubber soles on the pavement slowed and then stopped. A pair of tiny stones fell to the ground, tipped free from Konrad's left running shoe whilst he rested against a utility pole and caught his breath.

The blue Saab SUV failed to gain his attention until it had passed him on its way to the nearby main road. Because he'd seen Sam leave that morning, Konrad knew he must still be at work so only one conclusion remained. A frisson of excitement spread throughout his body, sparked by the thought of investigating how best to access the empty cabin.

He twisted his torso from one side to the other, inhaled deeply and resumed his ascent.

****

4.12pm – PDT
Kingsbury, Nevada

Now she had the cabin to herself, Anna couldn't help feeling amused by the interior's unnatural quietness. Her thoughts drifted, never straying too far from the final preparations for an evening she'd been anticipating since before the weekend. She smiled and wondered if they were too old and too married for *date night*; a ritual many of her college friends enthusiastically endorsed, especially once they'd had children. Sam's scepticism endured until a night away in Denver, five months after Angela's birth, allowed him to consume dinner before it went cold and view an un-paused movie. The opportunity to revel in the restorative properties of nine hours of uninterrupted sleep in a luxury hotel fully converted him, and the notion of incorporating some romance evolved over their next few *dates*. To maintain this routine in their current situation would be challenging, although no reason existed to say why the evening shouldn't become a monthly occurrence in this area. Maybe a new dress each time was indulgent but, on this occasion, the effort was sure to be worth it.

The build-up of heat inside the towel wrapped around her damp hair became progressively more uncomfortable and she untangled the thick material, dropped it into a nearby laundry basket. Tousled dark wisps spilled over her shoulders, a style Sam championed despite Anna's resolute attachment to her straightening irons. She reached into the closet to retrieve the dress she'd fallen for in a small Carson City boutique the previous day where, to her delight, its soft fabric and rich crimson hue had skimmed her slight frame and complimented her lightly tanned complexion. The price tag also carried a substantial reduction and enticed her to peruse the sections devoted to shoes and lingerie, much to Angela's interest.

Anna tightened the belt around her robe and carried the dress through to the spare room, where she'd later change. She climbed the stairs to the kitchen and estimated their meal would take around half an hour to prepare, leaving enough time to enjoy a second glass of wine, style her hair and apply make-up ahead of Sam and the children returning. A gentle pull opened the refrigerator, revealing the ground lamb and potatoes ready to be converted into a shepherd's pie. It wasn't haute cuisine, but she knew one of her husband's childhood favourites would be a sure-fire winner, food being one of the few English things Sam admitted he missed. She broke the meat into pieces, placed it in a saucepan and turned her attention to an onion and two large carrots nestling in the vegetable drawer.

Her mind wandered back to the first time Sam cooked the same meal for her at his cosy home in Golden's historic district. Life seemed so simple back then, the demands of their respective careers unable to derail what they'd found together. Theirs was an unspoken pact, based on the premise that so many of their co-workers' relationships had floundered and died: one that vowed to put each other first, to support each other through good times and bad times, to never abandon hope.

The past year proved the ultimate test: the accident, Sam's long road to recovery, the arrival of their second child and an impromptu relocation to this little corner of Nevada. There were times she'd considered giving up; that walking away would be the easiest option.

But, she'd always chosen to stay.

Anna swallowed, surprised to feel a lump in her throat. This wasn't the first time her emotions had unexpectedly sneaked up on her and she wondered why she appeared to have abandoned her compartmentalisation skills. She reached for the radio and frowned. Perhaps silence would be a preferable complement to her current solitude? What had been the norm in her singleton days occurred so infrequently these days she didn't know whether to enjoy it, or to allow her fear of the unknown beyond the cabin's four walls to curtail her enjoyment of its quiet, secluded location.

Dessert would also come from the British cookbook gifted by her mother-in-law four Christmases ago; a simple, old-fashioned recipe requiring minimal preparation before she could change into her new dress. Anna's mood lifted and thoughts of the evening ousted their negative counterparts as she began to whip cream in a large bowl.

****

5.24pm – PDT
Bradbury Way, Kingsbury, Nevada

A small, insignificant road in what many considered a small, insignificant place held an almost magnetic attraction for one man. Apart from those who lived there, Kingsbury was one of those places people usually only passed through: locals on their way to or from Reno, or the occasional vacationer heading north from an overnight stop in the boonies on their way back from the bright lights of Las Vegas to the south.

It was all well and good knowing *what* to do; the pressing issue was *when* to do it. Ideally, he should isolate the target from his family. Saying that, if the wife and kids ended up being collateral damage, so be it. Any attempt to ambush him in a public place carried the risk of witnesses, a risk not worth taking now freedom hovered so close. Besides work, was there any time Sam separated himself from his family? Did he *ever* stay home alone?

Accompanied by a cover story of training for the next Los Angeles marathon a little over six months into the future, should anyone possess the temerity to ask, he'd returned to that small insignificant road minutes away from his target. Nothing remained to hold him back. Ever since news of supply teacher Grace Winterburn's fiery death on the M6 spread throughout the school back in 1986, Konrad realised he did indeed have the power to shape his future and obliterate any barriers conspiring to hold him back. One last gentle climb out of a dip brought him to the modest wooden cabin where, to his surprise, the small Suzuki he'd seen Sam driving earlier occupied the driveway.

A familiar irritation inside his left running shoe confirmed the presence of yet another small stone. Konrad leaned against a walled embankment opposite the trio of cabins, realising he'd found the ideal vantage point. Sharp blue eyes froze behind mirrored sunglasses when he detected movement behind the largest window. The shadow disappeared and a blurred figure morphed into someone he knew, someone he intended to refamiliarise himself at the right moment. He pushed himself away from the embankment and readjusted his backpack.

Maybe that time had come.

****

5.33pm – PDT
FBI Resident Agency, Stateline, Nevada

'Jeez!' Jed Masters stared at his cell phone and shook his head. 'Give me a break, man.'

Special Agent Colleen Dexter shot a wary glance in his direction. 'Is that the Sheriff?' she asked, hoping the call was nothing more than an update which wouldn't delay the two-hour return journey to her home in Sacramento's eastern suburbs.

Masters shook his head. *Grainger*, he mouthed, lifting the handset to his ear. 'Ma'am?'

Dexter noticed deep rifts form across Masters' forehead. Grainger's words were inaudible to her and Jessop, although the two agents were uncomfortably aware of their effect on the usually cool and collected Masters.

Masters slammed the phone's handset into its cradle. 'We've gotten ourselves a problem: a fucking big problem.' He rubbed both hands down the sides of his face. 'Sam left early like he'd arranged. Did he say exactly where he was going?'

'Something about taking the kids out for the afternoon,' Jessop replied. 'He said he'd work at least a couple of extra hours next week to make up the time.'

'He knows that's not important. I need to get a hold of him.'

Dexter swallowed away the constriction in her throat and took a hesitant step closer to Masters' desk. 'What did Grainger have to say?'

'She's gotten three of our Reno agents working together to learn whether or not Kratz has a definite Reno connection.'

Dexter frowned and wondered if she'd misheard Masters. 'Reno? That's…'

Jessop's dark eyes widened. 'Too close for comfort.'

'What evidence is there to suggest he's in Reno?' Dexter asked.

132

Masters paused from picking at a piece of ragged skin he'd found on his wrist and took a long swallow from a bottle of water on his desk. Jessop and Dexter listened to his update on the Joel Nattrass case and the recently sold Rolex, their horror enough to convince Masters his silent panic was justified.

'Is that enough to lead to a full investigation?' Dexter asked.

'It gets better.' Masters sprang out of his seat and repeatedly tossed his car keys from one hand to the other. 'Two of her agents spent the majority of today pounding Reno's sidewalks and quizzing bank employees. Grainger figured if he needed to sell a watch to make some cash, he'd also try to lay his hands on any other money he has in the area.'

Jessop observed Masters drop the keys and pace back and forth behind his desk. 'He's definitely in town?' he asked, detecting a sudden tension wrapping itself around his chest.

Masters nodded and continued. Now they suspected Kratz had accessed a safe deposit box at the Sierra Nevada Bank three days ago, Grainger immediately pulled the strings required to obtain the necessary warrants. Vasquez and Avakian discovered an empty box contradicting its owner's semi-regular visits over the past five years and, on the women's return to the office, Jones ran the bank's security footage through the latest photogrammetry software. He'd matched the suspect's height and build to Kratz and, with this possible identification, Grainger asked Vasquez and Avakian to cross-reference the dates provided by the bank against known breaks in filming schedules of any TV show or movie Kratz had appeared in.

Dexter stepped away from a small window overlooking the almost empty parking lot and stared at Masters. 'Are you going to tell Sam?' she asked, silently thankful such a task was unlikely to fall on her.

He contemplated his response in the same manner as someone in receipt of an ill-chosen gift. 'I'll tell him we've obtained evidence Kratz has conducted business in Reno in the past. Until we have a firmer lead, we tell him only what he needs to know.'

'Which is?' she asked, ignoring a stern look from an apprehensive Jessop.

Masters picked up the phone for a second time. 'What I just said.'

Dexter's jaw dropped. 'You're telling him over the phone?'

'What else do you suggest I do? Rock up at the cabin on my way back to Minden?'

'It might not be a bad idea,' she said, wondering if she should offer. Although she'd only known Sam for a matter of weeks they'd developed a sound working relationship and often shared tales of their respective families and a mutual interest in hiking in the mountains. 'I could swing by. My husband's in San Francisco on business for a couple of nights and the kids are at my sister's place for a sleepover. It's not like I need to be home in a hurry tonight.'

Masters shook his head and passed the phone from one hand to the other. 'I'll tell him about the Reno connection from 2003, then leave the family to their plans and let them have a nice evening. I'll fill in the most recent details tomorrow morning.'

'But...' Jessop caught the brunt of Masters' glare and decided to remain silent.

'But nothing,' Masters snapped. 'If you get gone, you'll both be home before nightfall.'

Dexter scowled in disagreement and jangled her car keys. 'I hope you're right, sir.'

****

6.13pm – PDT
Kingsbury Grade Road, Stateline, Nevada

The Saab idled with a quiet purr, a comforting low frequency that enticed its driver's thoughts to wander whilst waiting for a red light to change. As had become more frequent over the past year, Sam's thoughts wandered to what he'd be doing these days if he hadn't been summoned as a reserve negotiator to that hostage situation in Boulder. Would he have remained in Denver, or made a permanent move to New York? If he hadn't bumped into Anna at the police station, would they ever have met or would he still be alone? He smiled at the children's reflections in the rear-view mirror; Angela flicking through her favourite book and John's eyelids struggling to remain open after he'd eaten more than his fair share of his sister's smothered pancakes in a South Lake Tahoe café.

'Hey, little man! You need to keep awake!' he called, chuckling at the baby's attempt to widen his heavy eyes. 'No napping for you yet.'

Angela carefully placed her book on her lap and clasped her brother's hands in hers. 'I'll keep him awake,' she announced. 'Mommy says if he sleeps too early he won't sleep later.'

'Mommy's absolutely correct.' Sam saw the lights changed to green and moved his foot from the brake to the accelerator. 'Why don't you show him your book?' he added when their climb to the cabin commenced and the car's speedometer nudged past the 35mph speed limit.

'I can tell him all about cats,' she exclaimed and happily clapped John's hands together. 'Then he'll stay awake all the way home and he'll stay asleep later.'

Sam forced a tense smile and wondered whether he should share with Anna the revelation Masters had dropped – by phone, of all ways – at the café. 'And will you stay asleep later?'

'Yes, Daddy,' Angela replied. She opened the book and passed it to John, who cooed happily at the photo of a large blue Persian. Sam glanced at the children again, not wanting to contemplate life without them or their mother: the three people he loved more than anyone or anything else in the world.

They'd spoken on the phone twice during the week leading up to their third date. The first time to confirm their plans for Saturday night; the second because Sam, having debated whether or not to call for nearly twenty minutes, purely wanted to hear Anna's voice. He knew they'd only met twice, if he didn't take their first short encounter into consideration, and he'd started to wonder whether he read too much into how she constantly infiltrated his thoughts. He'd continued to keep a lid on his anticipation of sharing a candlelit meal at the small Chinese restaurant he'd occasionally visited over the past two years, followed by a couple of drinks at a nearby bar. After that... well, he supposed that depended on Anna. Would she want to stay over? Should he suggest it? It seemed pointless to dwell on previous experiences, this was the first time he'd actually thought there was something at stake.

Sam eyed the clock and wondered whether he'd left enough time for a quick drink. The chime of the doorbell answered his question and he took a deep breath and walked purposefully down the stairs, opening the door at the same moment Anna raised her hand towards the bell for a second time.

'Sorry, I'd gone upstairs,' Sam said. He felt his mouth go dry at the sight of her simple black shift dress covered by a fuchsia-coloured pashmina, her attire simultaneously managing to combine alluring and modest. 'Welcome to my humble abode.'

'Well, I guess I'm a little early. I didn't want to get lost and be late,' she replied, following him through to the lounge. 'This is such a cute house,' she added enthusiastically and clasped her hands together as she twirled around to take in the small period townhouse's first floor.

'Yeah, I really like it. The previous owner sorted out the larger renovations, so all I needed to do a couple of years ago was decorate and put my own mark on the place.'

Anna's eyes settled on a pair of large bookcases occupying nearly half of one wall. 'You've done a great job, it looks so cosy.'

Sam smiled and thanked her, enjoying the compliment until he realised her hands remained empty. 'My manners have deserted me again. Would you like a drink before we go? The table's booked for eight and it's only a five-minute walk. We've got...' he looked at the clock on the mantelpiece, '...nearly half an hour before we need to set off, and I have a nice bottle of champagne chilling in the fridge.'

'Champagne?' she echoed in approval. 'Are we celebrating something?'

'Possibly,' he said. The hair on the back of his neck rose when she touched his bare arm. 'I've been saving it for a special occasion.'

'Which is?' She followed Sam into the kitchen, where he opened a window and then removed the bottle from the refrigerator.

'This evening; my third date in as many weekends with a beautiful woman.'

She laughed, the sound turning into a squeal when the cork popped and flew out of the window into a dark corner of his small backyard. 'You're spoiling me.'

'You deserve it.' Sam poured the foaming liquid into a pair of flutes and passed one to Anna. 'To a wonderful evening!' he added quietly.

'A wonderful evening!' she murmured, the glasses clinking in unison. They both took a sip and returned to the lounge, where Anna copied Sam's lead in sitting on the nearest of two couches. He placed the flute on an adjacent side table and took her hand.

'About what happened last weekend,' he began, wanting to get what he assumed would be an uncomfortable conversation out of the way. 'I'm sorry.'

Her neatly sculpted brows rose. 'Whatever for?'

'It was a really big dilemma, I'll say that. By leaving I thought you'd think I didn't find you attractive, but if I'd stayed–'

'I appreciated the gentlemanly gesture,' she interrupted. 'Anyway, we still have a little time now, and the rest of the champagne won't take long to drink.'

'The rest?'

'Oh!' Anna blushed. 'I assumed I didn't need to drive until tomorrow, and that you'd like me to stay over.'

'I'd like that a lot,' he whispered, moving closer as Anna reached for her drink. They'd parted only minutes before eight to reluctantly straighten their clothing and don their coats. Hand-in-hand, Sam and Anna walked the short distance along 12th Street and made a sharp left turn onto Washington Avenue. The food had been excellent, the overall experience enhanced by an endless flow of conversation. Their date continued in a bar a block closer to Sam's home, where being seated in closer proximity and two large glasses of wine ramped up the growing tension between them.

By the time they decided to leave the bar and resume the short walk back, neither Sam nor Anna harboured any illusion over how the evening would end. The snatched kisses of earlier became prolonged, increasingly sensual affairs once they'd turned the corner into 12th Street's tree-lined seclusion. They eventually pulled apart, laughing at Sam's failed attempts to unlock the front door without ending their shared embrace on his doorstep.

Anna kicked off her shoes and hung her coat on a hook whilst Sam switched on a desk lamp near the door, its yellow glow rapidly warming the room. She cautiously approached the larger of the two couches and giggled at the realisation she was responsible for the slight sway she now experienced. 'I guess a nightcap wouldn't go amiss?' she said, draping herself across one half of its leather upholstery.

'I'm thinking exactly the same,' Sam replied. 'Irish coffee?'

'You actually have Baileys?' Her gaze slid over the back of his fitted black trousers in the time it took him to open the drinks cabinet. 'Maybe just the Irish part then.'

'My parents came over via the duty free shop last month. So, it'll be a Bailey's for you, and a fine Scottish single malt for me.' Sam carried two small glasses across the room and passed one containing creamy liquid to Anna. She moved closer as he sat beside her and touched her glass to his.

'Another toast?' he questioned, wondering what was coming next.

Anna nodded. 'To an awesome evening.'

Sam sipped his Laphroaig and placed the half-consumed glass on the side table. 'An awesome evening.'

'Which isn't over yet,' she added after swallowing most of her drink.

Sam took Anna's glass from her and positioned it beside his. 'So tell me, how do you plan to extend it?' he asked when they resumed eye contact.

'I'm sure we can think of something,' Anna replied. She unsteadily got to her feet to hitch up her dress before she climbed onto his lap and rested her hands on his shoulders.

'How's this?' Sam whispered as he pressed light kisses along her exposed wrists.

'A nice way to start.' She lowered her head until their lips met, all traces of hesitancy forgotten. Sam felt her eagerly pull on his shirt buttons and part the fabric. His uncoordinated fingers attempted to unzip the back of her dress, his usual dexterity hindered by more wine than he'd consumed in years.

'Need some help?' she asked, narrowing her eyes in amusement.

Sam shook his head and tensed at the sensation of her hand moving lower across his stomach. 'Men thrive on challenge. It makes the outcome so much more reward–'

Anna cut him off with another kiss. 'Whisky and Irish Cream,' she eventually announced and broke into giggles. 'We made our own cocktail.'

'Is it better than your coffee?'

'That remains to be seen, but there's something else I'm ready to find out.' She pushed herself off his lap and held out her hand. 'Are you?'

A dip in the road returned Sam to the present and informed him they'd almost reached their cabin, beyond which a succession of clouds rolling across the horizon slowly diluted the evening sun's orange hue. He checked the road was clear, pulled onto the driveway beside the Suzuki and turned off the SUV's engine. 'You guys stay here a minute,' he said, lowering the rear windows a couple of inches. 'Daddy's going to call Mommy to help bring you two monsters and all your stuff into the house.'

'Okay, Daddy,' Angela replied, comforted by the familiar routine. She picked up the book she'd been enthralled by for the past couple of days, her baby brother forgotten by the time his heavy eyelids succumbed to the fresh air and food he'd enjoyed that afternoon.

Sam swung himself out of the Saab and stretched away the tension that had diffused through his lower back during the fifteen-minute journey. He scanned the area and inhaled deep lungfuls of pine-infused mountain air, the evening scent more intense than he'd previously noticed. Now satisfied nothing appeared out of place, he looked through a selection of keys to locate the notched one he knew opened the front door.

'Anna?' he called, his feet remaining on the external doormat as he leaned into the cabin. 'We're back. I've got two greedy monsters in the car who've eaten my wallet dry and I can't get them both into the house at once.'

Silence. The type of deafening silence Sam rarely heard since he'd become a family man.

'Anna? You in the bathroom?' he shouted, his voice louder and more insistent this time.

A plaintive voice drifted from inside the car. 'Daddy? Where's Mommy?'

Sam ran back to the car. 'She's probably downstairs. I'll try calling her again.'

'I want Mommy!'

'ANNA!'

Silence.

He returned to the open doorway and hesitated on the doorstep. An unhindered sense of unease dried his mouth and twisted his insides. Should he go in and look for Anna, even though he'd have to leave the kids in the car? It was always quiet around this part of Kingsbury, but that meant nothing. His years at the Bureau had exposed him to a catalogue of horrific acts too vile for most members of the public to comprehend.

She could have fallen and hurt herself, you know.

'Hey, buddy,' said a gruff voice he recognised as their neighbour's. 'You okay?'

'Anna's not answering, Mal. Can you mind the kids while I go in and see where she is?'

'You panic too much, my man,' Mal replied through a crooked grin. 'She's taking a long soak in the tub... chocolates... glass of wine. That's how my first wife liked to spend her evenings,' he added with a wry chuckle and brushed wisps of grey hair away from his face.

'She knew we'd be back by now,' Sam shouted from inside the entryway. The knot in his gut grew large enough to cause physical pain. 'Something's wrong.'

He paused for a split-second and listened for any sound from inside. Sinister thick silence permeated the cabin, drowning the usual birdsong and occasional faint sounds from nearby homes. The living area's normality drew him further into the open-plan space, its pristine appearance evidence that Anna had tidied the area since he'd taken the children out.

'Darling, where are you?' Sam shouted, angry to hear his voice tremble. 'Anna?'

Silence.

An indeterminate memory triggered by a faint savoury aroma led Sam to the kitchen, the bait impossible to ignore. He rounded a countertop, the floor beyond previously obscured by the lower units, and his jaw sagged; immediately followed by a sharp intake of breath as his knees hit the hard slate floor.

'Oh no!' he groaned, oblivious to the cold, sticky liquid coating his skin. Anna's robe lay crumpled beneath her, the macabre contrast between the soft cream and a deep red abstract pattern soaked into its thick fabric rendering Sam speechless. She lay on her back: one blood-stained arm draped across her lower abdomen, her head twisted to one side, eyes sightless behind pallid lids.

Sam leaned over Anna's body and shook her limp shoulder for a second time when she didn't respond. 'Anna? It's me, Sam,' he choked out, at last finding his voice 'Wake up! Please, wake up!' He stared at her previously tanned skin, its colour drained from her body long before he arrived. 'No! You can't do this to me, Anna. Come on, please!'

He heard a faint voice from the doorway. 'Sam, you okay? What the hell is going on?'

'Mal, call 911!' Sam yelled, his eyes never leaving Anna. He pressed two shaking fingers to the side of her neck.

'911?'

'NOW!'

****

7.07pm – PDT
Barton Memorial Hospital, South Lake Tahoe, California

The hand resting on Sam's arm was barely detectable, although its presence was enough to make him flinch. Stark overhead lights scorched the Emergency Registration area and battled the indistinguishable haze drifting

140

in and out of his consciousness. Across the room, a pair of doors swung first towards and then away from each other with an ever-decreasing momentum, each movement a prompt to count the seconds since Anna disappeared behind them. He focussed on the crimson droplets marking the start of her route to the operating room, this regularly spaced trail the only physical reminder Anna had really been there.

'Dr Bury?'

He couldn't blink. The action would surely severe the only connection they shared and allow the last of her blood to leach from her body, to leave him clutching onto fading fond memories and a lifetime of regret.

'Sir?' the voice crept into his thoughts for a second time. 'I know you're worried, but I need to ask you some questions.'

'Sam.'

A nurse stared at him. 'Pardon me, sir?'

He rubbed an unsteady hand over his face. 'My name is Sam.'

'Sam,' she repeated. 'I need to ask you some questions about your wife.'

'I want to be with her.' His eyes never departed from the now-stationary double doors. 'Don't you understand? What if she dies in there?'

'Sam, your wife is being prepped for emergency surgery as we speak. Every single minute counts. What I need is for you to focus on her while I ask some questions about her medical history.' She watched him nod. 'We already have the basics you gave in the ambulance,' she continued and hurriedly confirmed the details Sam had already provided.

He glared at her. 'You should be helping Anna; we've already been through this.'

'Is she currently taking any medication?'

He gave a weary shake of his head.

'Does she have any allergies?'

'Not that she's ever mentioned.'

'Previous surgeries?'

'An appendectomy aged thirteen, I think. She told me she'd been pretty ill at the time.'

'Is your wife pregnant, Sam?'

'No.'

'Is there any chance?'

'I suppose.' He turned to the nurse, her warm brown eyes full of concern. 'Do you think she'll make it?'

She rose from the chair and touched Sam's shoulder. 'I have every confidence in our surgical team. Give me a couple of minutes to put this info on the system and I'll take you to a private waiting area.'

Sam's foot drummed frantically on the vinyl tiles. 'When can I see her?'

'She'll be in surgery and then Recovery for at least two or three hours. Is there anyone who can wait with you?'

'One of my co-workers said he'd be down shortly,' he replied. 'His name's Jed Masters.'

Sam watched her walk away, then surveyed the small waiting area. Nearby, a red-eyed young woman clasped her left arm to her chest, her narrow face pinched in pain. Two rows behind her, a man at least three decades her senior gazed at the stark white ceiling, his calm demeanour a mask for the real reason behind his visit. The tap of his nails on the adjacent low-level table soon ceased and allowed nearby sounds to merge into one that ebbed and flowed with the blood pounding in Sam's ears.

The same nurse he'd spoken to minutes earlier reappeared and lowered herself onto the nearest plastic chair. 'The surgical team are now taking her through to the OR. Are you sure you don't want to go somewhere a little more private? I promise your co-worker can stay and you'll hear immediately if there's news of Anna's condition.'

Sam shook his head and averted his eyes to a large clock above the check-in desk. A long, thin hand jolted around its orbit, each angry movement marking the moment between life and death. He wondered how many might pass before he received the news he hoped for, or if he ever would.

Masters' voice reclaimed his attention. The older man's tanned face came into focus, hooded by an emotion Sam assumed to be worry. 'I drove here as fast as I could, Sam. Is there any news?' He peered around the brightly lit room, its air conditioning too efficient for both the altitude and time of day. Masters noticed the nurse give Sam a final reassuring smile and then approach the young woman who suspected she'd broken her wrist.

'They've just taken her through to surgery and it's likely to be over a couple of hours 'til she comes out. That's if she makes it.'

Masters placed an arm around Sam's shoulders and saw his jaw clench. 'Positive thoughts,' he replied. 'She'll be busting your ass for not doing the dishes before you know it.'

A hint of a smile erased some of the tension from Sam's face for a couple of seconds. 'Yeah, isn't that the truth. So,' he continued, after a short pause enabled him to formulate his reply, 'did you find out who's responsible for trying to murder my wife?'

'The Douglas County Sheriff sent a crew of Evidence Technicians from Minden up to the house to process the place. There's also a specially trained forensic nurse here who'll collect samples from Anna when she's stable.'

Sam nodded. 'I told them to bag her hands, in case she fought back.'

'Good work,' Masters said. He glanced at Sam and wondered whether any skin scrapings obtained would reveal a stranger's DNA, or that of the high-profile fugitive currently giving Reno's FBI agents a huge headache. 'Listen, I understand if you insist on staying here to wait for Anna to get out of surgery, but you also have a local detective waiting to walk the–'

'You can say it.'

'We have to discover the motivation behind this crime. Was it a robbery gone wrong, a crime of opportunity, or something completely different? Although the evidence doesn't point to it, could there have been a sexual component?' He felt Sam tense beside him, the pained expression on his face obscured now he'd moved his head. 'I'm sorry. Discovering the motivation behind the crime could help bring the piece of shit who did this to justice.'

Sam maintained his posture. 'You want me to go back to the house?'

'Only if you want to.' Masters sensed Sam's quandary. 'We need to know if they stole anything, or whether any of your stuff is significantly out of place. I'm insulting your intelligence and experience by telling you the tiniest details can crack a case wide open.'

Sam cast one last look at the clock and its second hand that continued to spasm. 'Thirty minutes. Lights and sirens all the way, then I'm back here,' he replied, reluctantly standing.

Masters placed a hand on Sam's back and guided him to the exit. 'You got it.'

****

7.43pm – PDT
North Benjamin Drive, Kingsbury, Nevada

Darkness had fallen by the time Masters brought his Jeep to a halt down the road from where, only hours earlier, the cabin he'd owned for the past eleven years provided a safe haven for Sam and his displaced family. The road was usually wide enough for two cars to cautiously pass, but now a scattering of police cruisers, a dark-coloured SUV and the Evidence Technicians' minivan formed an almost complete obstruction. A small cluster of residents had gathered further up the road, their intrigue obvious since being questioned during the investigation's preliminary inquiries.

Sam snapped his cell phone shut and stared through tinted windows at the strip of yellow crime scene tape flapping in a gentle breeze. He'd already observed the circus that had descended on the quiet street and wished he didn't have to leave the Jeep's confines.

Masters removed the key from the ignition and the vehicle fell silent. 'Are the kids okay?'

'Yeah, there's a female officer looking after them,' Sam replied. He closed his eyes when the sight of the brightly lit cabin became too much. 'John didn't wake but Angela won't settle. I don't know what to do, Jed. My kids need me and I need to be there for them. But...'

'Anna, right?'

'I should be at the hospital. What if she comes round after surgery and I'm not there?'

'Ten minutes here, Sam, that's all it'll take.' Masters eased his door open with a faint creak. 'That's enough time to check if anything obvious is out of place inside the house.'

'Besides the puddle of my wife's blood on the kitchen floor?' Sam shot back. He climbed down onto the faded blacktop and looked at the cabin again, its entryway visible through the open front door. At least someone had thought to close the front drapes and form a barrier against the prying eyes of those unrelated to the case, he thought.

Masters spotted a pair of young men edging closer and recognised the taller of the two as a Tahoe-based blogger popular for his alternative slant on local news stories. 'Walk with me,' he said quietly. 'We'll go from room to room, you tell the detectives if you see anything different, and then I'll drive you straight back to the hospital. No other stop-offs, I promise.'

'Don't you need to go home?'

Masters slammed the driver's door shut and activated the central locking. 'I don't need to go nowhere,' he replied.

Sam leaned against the bodywork. 'What about Buddy?'

'That crazy mutt is staying at my son's place tonight. I called Dylan earlier and he drove on over to my place to pick him up,' Masters replied. He pulled his credentials out of his pocket on the short walk to the cabin's main entrance, where a uniformed officer Masters recognised from a series of assaults on gamblers last year stood guard.

The young officer stepped aside and nodded at the road. 'Is that the guy who lives here?' he whispered, causing Masters to turn around to face his vehicle.

'Sam?'

'I can't,' he replied, his expression riddled with despair when the Jeep's door handle refused to yield.

Masters didn't relent. 'You're our best hope of finding something to help identify the piece of shit who did this. This is the last place you want to be right now, and I hate to guilt trip you, but Anna's relying on you.'

Sam shook his head and sighed. 'It was supposed to be such a perfect evening.'

'Tell me about it.'

'Here?'

'Let's go inside. What do you say?'

Sam walked towards the doorway. 'Have the neighbours seen anything suspicious?'

Masters gestured to Officer Williams. 'You got anything?'

'There's a pair of uniforms canvassing the area, they went up that way five minutes ago.' Williams pointed at a quintet of houses which fanned around a turning circle at the road's furthermost point. 'The main problem is getting *those* assholes to keep a respectful distance.'

'News travels fast,' Masters remarked dryly, tilting his head in an exaggerated fashion to observe an immaculately attired thirty-something woman alight from a news van. 'Do you want me to move them on?'

'No,' Sam replied, much to the others' surprise. 'They've got nothing to report and we give them the bare minimum. If the bastard who did this thinks we don't have a clue they're more likely to get cocky and slip up.'

'Now you're talking,' Masters said with obvious admiration. He pointed to the area beyond the doorway. 'Ready?'

Sam released a deep breath. 'I guess so.' He passed through a wide entryway, where coats and shoes competed for space alongside a growing collection of beach toys. At first sight the cabin's interior seemed deceptively normal, until a sinister aura seeped from the pale walls and threatened to smother him in its cold embrace.

145

A tall, fair-haired man whom Sam guessed to be in his late thirties appeared from the kitchen and smiled a greeting to Masters. 'I'll need you both to wear these,' he said in an apologetic tone and held out two pairs of disposable blue shoe covers. 'Forensic processing of the house just started and they're beyond pissed we've demanded access already. I'll warn you one of them has insisted on following us around the place.'

'Sure,' Masters replied. 'Sam, this is Detective Jonno Heikkinen from Douglas County Sheriff's Office. We've crossed paths way too many times over the years, since he decided to move out west for some proper snow.'

'Asshat!' Heikkinen retorted, accustomed to this occasional teasing over his Michigan origins. He turned to Sam, who'd resumed an upright stance once he'd covered his canvas deck shoes. 'You okay, man?'

'Let's just get this done,' Sam snapped. He ignored Heikkinen's outstretched palm and glared at the front door. 'I need to get back to Anna.' Masters hung back to allow Sam to walk through the large open-plan living area. Three people in gender-concealing white coveralls congregated in a small recess adjacent to the kitchen, deep in whispered conversation whilst annotating what Sam assumed to be a crime scene sketch. Bright portable lights erected around the room's periphery made the kitchen centre stage in what could soon become a homicide, if Barton's surgical team was unable to work its magic that evening.

A fourth crime scene investigator appeared at the top of the stairs and caused a startled Sam to drag his gaze away from the kitchen. The figure's short stature and petite built hinted at it being female, a fact confirmed when she eventually spoke.

'I guess you're the husband?'

Sam nodded and swallowed hard.

'Carrie Larson, lead CSI on this case,' she added without offering a nitrile-enclosed hand, much to Sam's relief. 'Listen, I'm sorry for what happened to your wife and that we need to follow you guys around. It's nothing personal, okay?' Sam nodded again. 'Please don't touch anything, we'd hate to render any evidence inadmissible in court.'

'How do you think the perp got inside?' Masters asked.

'There's no sign of forced entry,' Heikkinen replied. 'But there's an unlocked door in the master bedroom which opens onto the balcony.'

'Anna likes to leave it open for a couple of hours each day.' He walked around the undisturbed dining area. 'She says it's good to get fresh air into the bedroom. I warned her about leaving doors unlocked when I'm out. She thought I was being neurotic.'

'Based on that, we could assume they gained entry on the lower floor. Before we go downstairs, could you please run through your plans for the evening, Sam?' Masters asked. 'When we were outside a few minutes ago, you said it was supposed to a perfect evening.'

Sam paused by the glass doors leading to the wooden balcony. Masters and Heikkinen noticed his shoulders tense and both wondered whether Sam and Anna regularly enjoyed the lake view; something beautiful in the midst of a terrible situation. 'We used to have a monthly date night back in Denver,' he said, his words slowed as if translating something sacred into meaningless conversation. 'Anna's parents took the kids for a night and part of the next day, and we'd have that time to ourselves. Both of us have seen so many marriages in our line of work end in divorce and we always said it would never happen to us. Although it's not as easy here, we decided to keep up the routine.'

Heikkinen nodded. 'How did you intend to do that?'

Oblivious to Masters' firm hand on his shoulder, Sam told them how he'd taken the children to the beach and then for an afternoon snack, after which he and Anna planned to put them to bed on his return to the cabin. Masters and Heikkinen nodded their simultaneous acknowledgement, both men's marriages the casualties of long hours, bottled-up stress and a mutual lack of open communication.

'It appears the perp came up the stairs, encountered Anna in the kitchen and, like the evidence suggests, there was a struggle during which the intruder stabbed her twice in the lower abdomen,' Heikkinen surmised. Sam fell silent, his thoughts once again consumed by the evening's dramatic change of direction. 'Based on the lack of disturbance elsewhere in the house we assume they came to her, rather than she went to them.'

Masters angled himself through a full turn and looked for an unconventional exit route. 'And how did they leave?'

'Presumably the same way they came in,' Heikkinen replied. 'Sam, we need you to take a look around and see if anything's moved location, or is actually missing.'

Faint hazy lines produced by the intense lighting and Sam's suppressed grief traced their way over the furniture's topography. Laconic steps carried him around the space the family used for eating and relaxation, the table set ready for a meal he and Anna would never consume. Plumped-up cushions adorned both sofas and Sam tore his eyes away from the swinging pendulum of a nearby Swiss-style clock on a bookshelf. He nodded at the detective. 'It's all okay,' he announced and led them to where the staircase descended into semi-darkness. 'Shall we go down here next?'

Heikkinen frowned. 'You sure?'

Sam nodded impatiently.

The three men followed Larson's ghostly white figure down the staircase to where patches of light leached onto the long empty corridor. 'That's the main bedroom.' She pointed to the second partially open door for Heikkinen's benefit. 'There's one more bedroom to its right, the kids' rooms are those two furthest doors and the middle door is the family bathroom.'

'There's also a shower room off our bedroom,' Sam added. He checked his cell phone and shoved it back into his pocket. 'Can we hurry up? I need to get back to the hospital.'

Masters raised a quizzical eyebrow. 'Has there been any news?'

Sam shook his head and followed Larson through the closest door into what fulfilled a dual role as a spare bedroom and luggage dump. A patchwork comforter covered the three-quarter bed and the crimson dress Anna had lovingly chosen for the evening hung from a tall bookcase opposite. They returned to the bed, where a set of carefully laid out similarly coloured underwear and sleek black shoes complimented the outfit. Sam exhaled loudly and sensed the blush flooding through his cheeks.

'She was obviously ready for the evening,' Heikkinen commented, satisfied it was unlikely anyone other than Anna had entered the room that day. 'My ex-wife also used to get changed for a night out at the last minute, ever since she threw an almost full milk carton over herself when she tried to put it back in the refrigerator.'

Masters noticed Sam's fists clench. 'Let's move on,' he suggested, the hint taken by Larson who quickly directed them to the master bedroom. Sam walked towards the open windows where a pair of pine moths had gained entry, the room's heavy silence peppered by their dance around the light fitting.

'I think those were also meant for tonight,' Sam commented when he spotted a pair of smart trousers and tailored shirt hanging from the closet door. 'They look like my size and I've never seen them before. Anna was so cagey last night whenever I asked what she'd planned. It looks like she wanted to make tonight something really special.'

Heikkinen's smile struggled to reach his eyes. 'Have you seen anyone strange hanging around the neighbourhood?'

'It's hard to tell,' Sam replied. He paused to consider how insular the family had become since their move. 'We haven't really met anyone, apart from a couple of the neighbours.'

'Do they know why you're here?'

'Not the truth. We did think about–' Sam dropped to a crouch beside a large chest of drawers. 'Anna never leaves any of the drawers open, and there's absolutely no way she'd ever leave any of my sports gear like this.'

Larson immediately mirrored his stance and her gaze flitted between Sam and the haphazard garments. 'Do you think someone's been in here?' she asked.

'Can I check?'

'Let me get some photos first.' She pulled her camera from a metallic case she'd set down on the fawn-coloured carpet and rapidly captured a quintet of images. 'Okay, put on these gloves and don't touch the handles.'

They watched Sam's methodical examination of the drawer's contents. 'I had a pair of new black running shorts in here,' he said. 'They were on sale in town last week. I left most of my stuff in Colorado, so I've bought some new things since we got here. It had a matching black and red long-sleeved top, which I thought may come in useful because it can get chilly here. Both are definitely gone.'

Heikkinen straightened up and took another look around the room. 'Could Anna have put them in the laundry already?'

'Doubt it. Feel free to check. She's trained me to put whatever needs washing in that basket over there,' Sam said. His smile faded and he frowned at Heikkinen. 'Seriously though, did that bastard escape in my running kit?'

'We'll think *how* later, for now we try to work out *why*,' Heikkinen replied. 'Listen man, you need to get back to the hospital. Why not come back tomorrow; the house will be sealed off for a couple of days. First impressions don't suggest robbery as the primary motive.'

'Or, if it was, Anna's presence unnerved them.' Masters checked his watch and pointed to the doorway. 'Give the kids' rooms a quick once-over and if all's in order I'll drive you back to Barton. But first...' He pointed at the bloodstains on Sam's shorts, now a rich shade of carmine through their exposure to the air. 'Didn't you say you wanted to get changed?'

****

8.34pm – PDT
Mattole Road, near South Lake Tahoe, Nevada

'We interrupt this bulletin with some local breaking news...'

Anticipation prickled his skin, the sensation comparable to the night he'd seduced that uptight little virgin from next door. Images of a forest community in disarray filled the small television's screen; the narrow road a chaotic mess of law enforcement personnel and cop cars, providing a dramatic backdrop for a blonde-haired woman whose foundation-encrusted face now filled the screen.

'Earlier this evening, the Douglas County Sheriff's Office was called to this quiet community a short distance from Kingsbury Grade Road, from where an emergency ambulance rushed a resident to South Lake Tahoe's Barton Memorial Hospital. An official statement has yet to be made, although recent reports suggest a brutal attack on a young woman in her own home occurred right here. Ever vigilant, we'll be sure to bring you more updates as we receive them. This is Emma Rigby reporting for Stateline News Channel.'

The warm glow from an old-fashioned wood burner seeped into the small living room and soothed his aching muscles. Tomorrow, he'd scatter its cold ashes deep in the forest, where no trace of the recently incinerated running gear he'd taken from the Bury's cabin would ever be discovered. He picked up the remote control and surfed the channels for a couple of minutes, the saturation of reality TV shows and crime dramas enough to send him to the kitchen where he pulled the fridge door open and contemplated the bottom shelf.

A second bottle top clattered against the countertop in recognition of the first bottle of locally brewed beer failing to neutralise the unfamiliar and confusing gamut of emotions he'd ridden since fleeing Kingsbury. In the attack's immediate aftermath, Konrad berated his uncharacteristic impulsivity. An unexpected revelation soon followed – assuming his split-second decision to kill Sam's wife had been successful.

Try explaining that to your kids, dickhead. That you got their mother killed because you didn't let things lie.

Konrad squinted past the window into the darkness and swallowed another mouthful of ice-cold beer. Despite the stretches he'd performed since his return, the discomfort in his calves and thighs increased as he hobbled back to the living room and collapsed onto the sofa, then pushed up his sweatshirt's sleeves to examine the full extent of the scratches she'd inflicted. Long red gouges screamed against the tanned skin on his left forearm, criss-crossing where she'd repelled him for a second and final time. *Quite the little honey badger*, he thought with a mirthless smile.

He raised the bottle to his lips again and contemplated the dilemma presented by his need to escape – whether to make a run for it and possibly generate suspicion, or lay low for another week and stick to his original plan. The news report contained no mention of roadblocks, and its scant images of cars, cops and chaos revealed a lot by revealing very little. They seemed at a loss to identify a motive, let alone a suspect.

The alcohol that had begun to replace the day's adrenaline seeped through his body and Konrad's drooping eyelids lost their battle. Maybe he'd have a short snooze and then put the TV back on in an hour or so – hoping to hear confirmation that the bitch was now laid out on a slab in the morgue, her toe tagged and a cork rammed firmly up her ass.

****

11.01pm – PDT
Barton Memorial Hospital, South Lake Tahoe, California

Like many others before him, Jed Masters never understood why hospitals insisted on an insipid green colour scheme for communal areas. At best, it reminded him of nasal mucus, the shade no doubt decided upon by a committee of overpaid men in suits – who'd then pontificate about the haven of tranquillity their hospital provided. Someone once told him how decades-old research loaned evidence to this logic but, in Masters' opinion, the only thing to render a hospital waiting room a calming environment would be a large shot of Propofol with a swift Fentanyl chaser.

In the adjacent seat, Sam leaned forward and laced rigid fingers behind his head. The polished linoleum below blurred in and out of focus as an indistinct intercom announcement and the mixed aroma of hand sanitiser and pine-scented disinfectant assaulted his senses, painfully fragmenting the evening into shards of disjointed images.

Masters lifted his arms in an attempt to stretch out his stiffening shoulders, the movement curtailed by his companion's deep sigh.

'What's taking them so long?' Sam said, the words muffled by his unchanged posture.

'They'll be doing everything they can for Anna; you need to trust them.'

'If I'd got to her sooner, she might not be so ill. I should've left the pancake house the second you phoned.' Sam turned to face Masters and detected a hint of discomfort when the older man broke eye contact. 'You told me they traced Konrad Kratz to Reno six years ago. What's to say he's not come back to the area? It's a long shot, but perhaps he's closer than we think and he's waiting to finish off my family? It's bad enough he–'

Masters braced himself and took a deep breath. 'We think he recently returned to Reno.'

'You what?' Sam sat bolt upright and glared at Masters. 'How do you know?'

'The Rolex he bought in Phoenix this summer was sold in Reno a few days ago.'

Sam's stare hardened. 'You didn't think to tell me?' he spat, momentarily drawing the attention of an older couple on the other side of the waiting room who were, up until that time, apparently oblivious to their companions during their own personal vigil.

'We didn't want to worry you in case it proved unfounded,' Masters said. He felt relieved to see the couple return to their bubble. 'It was a difficult call, surely you understand that?'

Sam massaged his pounding temples. 'Could it be a coincidence?' he asked. 'He sold it to some unsuspecting sucker who then sold it in Reno to fund a trip to the casinos.'

'That's what the team at Reno's resident agency first thought. However, because this is such a serious and high-profile case, they decided to send a pair of agents to local banks and casinos to inquire whether anyone recently tried to withdraw or win a bunch of cash.'

'Did they?'

'One bank worker recalled a guy who accessed his safe deposit box and left it one hell of a lot lighter than when he went in,' Masters replied, relieved Sam's previous anxiety had lessened, if only outwardly. 'The agents obtained surveillance footage and a warrant to access this guy's account and the deposit box. Does the name James Haigh mean anything to you?'

Sam shook his head. 'Never heard of him.'

'They found the box empty and he left two thousand bucks in his checking account. They think he didn't withdraw it so he could cover the box rental for the foreseeable future.'

'Is it Kratz?'

'They don't know for sure, yet,' Masters replied, feeling no less guilty now he was being entirely honest. 'Do you remember that Rick Jones guy in Cyber Crimes at Reno?' Sam considered the name and shook his head. 'No? Guy's a little nerdy, but he sure knows his stuff. They only got the footage and other information through mid-afternoon, so he didn't have a whole lot of time to get started on it. Grainger said he'll be running it through facial recognition and more complex height analysis software first thing.'

Sam snorted in derision. 'Can't they work a bit of overtime and do it tonight?'

'Jones needs to obtain previously verified data from LAPD, which should be through by morning. He's done a preliminary analysis and it looks promising.'

Sam eyeballed a large clock high up on the opposite wall. 'It's been nearly two hours since that nurse spoke to me. What if something's really wrong?'

'Didn't they tell you anything?' Masters asked, his six-minute absence when he'd left the room to take a phone call from Heikkinen coinciding a second contradictory update on Anna's condition.

Sam angled a Venetian blind covering the door's glass inlay until it no longer obstructed his view of the corridor beyond. 'Only what I've already told you.'

'Do you want me to go ask someone?'

'What's the point?' Sam replayed the one-sided conversations of earlier: the first with the surgeon who performed Anna's emergency surgery, who'd calmly explained how he'd stopped the internal bleeding and repaired two perforations in her bowel. Sam's gratitude had been short-lived when, minutes later, a nurse shattered any relief by informing him of Anna's hurried return to the operating room.

'Perhaps they need to operate to find what's causing this bleeding?' Masters suggested.

Sam reclaimed his seat and clenched his jaw, his speech slowed by tension in the surrounding musculature. 'I just want an update. Is that too much to ask, for Christ's sake?'

'It's not the largest hospital,' Masters said. 'I'd guess they scale back the staffing at night.'

'Just one poxy update wouldn't hurt, would it? I mean, I'm only her bloody–'

The blind rattled against the door, causing the words to die in his throat and dryness to spread where they'd previously been. He recognised the nurse, her mid-blue scrubs a shade darker than those worn by the nurses in the Emergency Department.

'Dr Bury.' She lowered herself onto the chair beside Sam and waited for his reply. 'Do you remember me?' she continued, uncomfortably aware of the plastic's coldness seeping through the thin material she wore. 'My name's Anita. I'm here to give you an update.'

Sam swallowed twice and clenched his fists until the knuckles glowed white. 'How's Anna?' he asked, his parched mouth barely able to articulate the question.

'She's back in Recovery and making good progress. However, I'm afraid I have some unfortunate news.' She watched Sam's guarded expression change into one of panic and exchanged an uncomfortable glance with Masters. 'While your wife was in surgery the first time, a number of diagnostic blood tests were carried out in our labs. In addition to confirming her blood group, we also learned that your wife was pregnant–'

'Was.'

She stopped mid-way through pushing a lock of thick black curly hair away from her forehead. 'Pardon me?'

'You said *was*. Past tense. Which means she isn't any more, right?'

'You knew?'

'No, I didn't,' he snapped. 'Is she still pregnant?'

Anita sighed and looked Sam straight in the eye. 'I'm sorry to tell you that Anna began to bleed minutes after arriving in Recovery. At the time we didn't know if another injury from the assault had caused this, so we took her straight back to the OR where the bleeding intensified and she miscarried the pregnancy.'

'How far along was she?'

'Five or six weeks,' she replied and winced at the sight of all colour draining from Sam's cheeks. 'I'm sorry if this is a personal question, but was this a planned pregnancy?'

He shook his head. 'Our son is only seven months old and we're not sure how long we're going to be living in this area.' He noticed her puzzled expression. 'It's a long story. Does Anna know about the baby?'

'For now, it'd be better not to tell her. She underwent major surgery and lost a lot of blood prior to that, so she needs as little upset as possible.' Only a year into her long-awaited career change, Anita unconsciously straightened a faint crease near the hem of her loose blue top and wondered if the act of breaking bad news to patients' relatives might become marginally easier one day. 'We hope to take Anna to the Medical-Surgical floor within the next hour, so you're welcome to wait here until she's ready for you to see her.'

'You want me to lie to her?'

'You can tell her when she's stronger.' She watched him slump against the wall beside his chair, worried a single wrong word could make the situation far worse than necessary. 'I'm so sorry for your loss, sir. Do you need anything?'

Sam shook his head. 'Just for my wife to be okay.'

'We're doing our best. I'll come get you when she's been transferred to a room.' Anita paused in the doorway and acknowledged Masters' mouthed vote of thanks. 'Dr Bury? I don't know if this is significant. On both occasions Anna was taken to Recovery, she said the exact same thing. It's probably nothing; the meds given to surgical patients are pretty strong.'

Sam rubbed his hands over his eyes in the hope he'd remove the gritty sensation which had become impossible to ignore. 'What did she say?' he asked, not trusting himself to remain composed.

'He's back.'

Chapter 9 – Saturday 5th September 2009

7.23am – PDT
Barton Memorial Hospital, South Lake Tahoe, California

Unlike on previous mornings, the brilliant sunlight forcing its way through the window and past a kink in the blinds did not promise new beginnings: that today things would revert to how they'd previously been, that Konrad Kratz would be located and apprehended, that the Bury family could return to living a normal life in Colorado.

Sam was unsure how long he'd maintained his vigil at Anna's bedside, where a night of harsh artificial lighting and suppressed emotion coated everything in a translucent glaze no amount of eye-rubbing was able to disperse. He'd drifted in and out of a state he doubted could actually be classified as sleep, one in which scenes from their joint past ebbed and flowed. A chance meeting during the hostage situation that took him to Boulder, a series of dates that cemented their feelings, the day they'd spent in the Lake District three months after their worlds collided. It had always been one of his favourite parts of rural England; the perfect backdrop for his future wife to accept his proposal of marriage.

'Steve and Charlotte put on quite the wedding shindig,' Sam commented to Anna. He checked the moorings of the rowing boat they'd hired for the afternoon and then carefully lowered a large rattan picnic hamper onto its floor. 'And now it's nice to get some time just to ourselves, isn't it? A bit of rest and relaxation before we have to fly back on Thursday.'

Anna nodded and used his outstretched hand to help her balance as she gingerly climbed into the small wooden vessel and eased herself onto one of its slatted seats. Sam joined her seconds later, watching her inhale deeply and cast a wondrous gaze across Lake Windermere to where distant mountains lay beyond.

'Smell that air,' she said. 'How did you find such a cute spot? Did you know it already?'

'We used to come up here for days out when I was a kid,' he replied, ready to row out onto the lake from their location five miles south of Windermere's quaint town centre. 'Dad always hired a boat and me and him would come out onto the water, although my sisters usually preferred staying on dry land with Mum. We'd get back and they'd have stuffed themselves silly with ice cream. We always said it must be a girl thing.'

'Your family has been so welcoming,' Anna said. She observed the jetty gradually decreasing in size and turned to stare at the opposite shoreline. 'It's so kind of them to offer us a place to stay over these two weeks, and to allow us to use their car for the weekend.'

'Yeah, they've always been really supportive of whatever I've wanted to do or wherever I've wanted to go,' Sam replied, feeling slightly breathless due to the unfamiliar nature of the exertion brought on by rowing. 'I think they're happy to see me happy.'

Anna flicked a few drops of cold lake water at him and stretched out a foot so it pressed against his. 'What's making you happy these days?' she asked.

Sam paused for a couple of strokes and twitched his shoulders in the faintest of shrugs. 'Oh, just little things like catching up with my family and seeing the lads at the wedding.'

'Anything else?' she pressed, unable to hide the enjoyment she gained by teasing him.

'Well, there's this lady called Anna,' he said, his tone nonchalant now he'd started to row again. 'She's been a big part of my life for the past three months, ever since I met her on a case in Granola Town, Colorado'. He chuckled at her mock-disapproving stare. 'We've been on some lovely dates, and seem to be spending more and more time at each other's places. She's pretty, funny and makes a mean cup of coffee. She also understands the demands of my job, and makes sure I get to unwind regularly.'

'I've never heard us call it that before!' She leaned forward to squeeze his knee. 'Anyway, all this fresh air makes a girl hungry. What do you say we make a dent in the picnic?'

He smiled nervously. 'Why don't you dig in if you're feeling a bit peckish?'

Anna pulled back the basket's lid and spotted the small bottle almost hidden between a selection of sandwiches and a punnet of strawberries. 'Champagne?' she queried. 'Should we really be drinking on a boat in the middle of a lake?'

'We're nowhere near the middle, and I thought you'd enjoy it,' Sam replied. 'Anyway, it's only a tiny bottle and definitely not enough to get us pissed. There's a pair of flutes in that case near the bottom. Why don't you pour the drinks while I finish securing the oars?'

'Okay,' she replied. 'Do you mean the green case?' She saw him nod. Her slim fingers coaxed it out of the hamper and opened the lid to reveal its cream satin interior. 'What's this?' she asked, her voice hitching.

Sam reached over to take the small burgundy jeweller's box from her shaking hand and, trying not to wobble, lowered himself into a kneeling position. 'Anna,' he whispered, opening the box to reveal a simple gold ring inset with a solitary diamond. 'I meant everything I said before, and there's still a lifetime of things I haven't had the chance to say to you yet.' She noticed a slight tremor in his right hand as he removed the ring from its velvet inlay and slid it onto the fourth finger of her left hand. 'Will you make me the happiest man alive and become my wife?'

He thought he detected a nod before she flung her arms around his neck. Sam felt her shoulders begin to shake, suddenly scared to realise that he couldn't tell whether she was laughing or crying.

'Anna?'

She pulled back and, still giggling, admired how easily the sparkling diamond reflected unusually bright Cumbrian sunlight.

'Yes.'

Beyond the doorway, the hospital's Medical-Surgical Unit bustled with early-morning activity, a vague whiff of coffee failing to evoke any interest from a man who claimed he couldn't function properly in the morning prior to the consumption of at least two cups of Columbian roast. A faint squeak drew his attention to the door and Sam lifted his weary head to see a shadowy figure lurking behind the partially open blind. The door handle turned slowly, instigating unexpected feelings of panic until an unfamiliar nurse came into view.

'Dr Bury?' she asked, anxious at the prospect of her first encounter with the FBI since she'd commenced her nursing career.

He replied with a solitary nod and eased his cramping arms off the bed. 'Was I asleep?'

'I think so,' she replied. 'My name is Mary and I'll be taking care of Anna today. I need to run some routine post-surgical observations, then you'll be able to stay with her.'

Sam stretched half-heartedly and slowly pushed himself out of his seat. 'I could do with taking a bathroom break,' he said, the residual stiffness in his left ankle responsible for a detectable limp. He ignored the uniformed police officer seated outside the room and let an information board point the way to the nearest restrooms, that failsafe place of refuge whenever things became too much to comprehend, let alone deal with. On his way to the stairway he passed a dozen more inpatient rooms and imagined what lay beyond the row of doors, each cell a clone of its neighbour aside from the personal effects brought by visitors to neutralise their loved one's clinical surroundings.

The thought of bringing some of Anna's books and photographs lost its impetus faster than it had appeared. Their temporary home continued to be processed as a crime scene, hindering access to Anna's possessions – not that she'd packed much from Colorado in the first place. Now uncomfortably close to the emergency department he pushed open the restroom door and was relieved to see its promise of solitude remained unbroken. Here, the cloying scent of antiseptic merged with synthetic lemon. It surreptitiously coated the back of Sam's throat and confirmed that repeatedly swallowing could never replace the astringent qualities of vending machine coffee.

He zipped his fly and approached a row of pristine white porcelain hand basins. The mirror spanning their length told a sad tale of little sleep and probably the most traumatic night of his life, or at least the one he could actually remember. Dark circles infiltrated the skin around his eyes to form an unfortunate alliance with the fine stubble coating his cheeks; one which put years on his age and hinted at a possible liking for the bottle, or maybe something worse. Although this definitely wasn't the time to get hung up on his appearance, he'd noticed changes over the past months: faint lines emerging around his eyes to match those on his forehead, and his first grey hair – which resolutely returned each time it met its demise with the aid of Anna's eyebrow tweezers when he was sure she wasn't looking.

The door swung open and a silent sympathetic nod provided sufficient acknowledgement between Sam and the similarly aged man who'd entered.

Smart attire and a spritely demeanour suggested he may be a member of staff rather than a visitor, a hunch confirmed by the ID badge clipped to his shirt. Sam wondered whether he should ask for more information on the likely path Anna's recovery would follow. He almost instantly decided against it, quietly left the restroom and wondered whether the nurse had completed her morning evaluation of Anna's condition. His wife had remained asleep all night; a combination of residual anaesthetic and morphine rendering her oblivious to the events that brought her within a pint of fatal blood loss.

Not to mention the death of what would have been their third child.

Sam paused outside her room to slowly and deliberately rub the sanitiser he'd ejected from a nearby wall-mounted dispenser over his hands and between his fingers. The chill produced by it evaporating made him shudder, a movement spotted by another visitor on her way to a more distant room.

'Are you okay?' she asked. Obvious concern filled her chocolate-coloured eyes as they roamed his face.

He contemplated what type of terrible situation also allowed her to visit out-of-hours and nodded slowly, unable to convince neither himself nor the elderly woman now standing beside him. 'Yeah, thanks. You?'

'As much as you can be in these places, I guess,' she replied through a sad smile. She left Sam alone and hobbled down the wide corridor, a sturdy cane supporting her arthritic gait. He shook his head and closed his eyes for a moment. Yet again, the favoured pale green colour scheme failed in its quest to put both visitors and patients at ease.

Do the staff actually notice?

Sam's hand hovered inches from the door's handle. Should he go back in or wait for the nurse – Mary, if he'd recalled her name correctly – to emerge? He took a deep breath and gripped the cold metal, a light downwards pressure sufficient to open the door.

'She's doing good,' Mary said with a cautious smile. 'The incision is draining well, her vital signs are stable and it looks like she'll be awake soon. Depending on how her recovery progresses, we may let her try eating something light later today.'

Sam lowered himself into the seat where he'd already spent an uncomfortable night. 'Does she know anything yet?'

'About... no, no; she's been asleep all night.'

'Should I tell her?' he asked, unsure how to break it to Anna that a baby neither of them knew existed would never meet nor play with Angela and John.

'It's not my place to tell you what to do, but I'd strongly advise leaving it a day or two. Let Anna start to get her strength back.'

'She's so pale,' Sam murmured. He reached for her hand and carefully avoided an IV taped to the back of it. A faint, evenly timed bleep sounded in the background, a beacon of reassurance whilst Anna's eyes remained closed.

'She lost a lot of blood, so we've transfused enough to allow her body to replace any extra she needs within a few days.' Mary pointed to a series of brightly coloured digits on Anna's bedside monitor. 'You can see her heart rate and blood pressure are within normal limits.'

He watched her chest rise and fall in a steady rhythm, aided by the cannula positioned beneath her nose delivering a welcome supply of extra oxygen. 'How long does she need to stay here for?'

'Assuming there's no complications...' Mary recalled her shift-change conversation with a co-worker. 'The doctor said usually around a week in this type of case. We need to closely monitor the bowel and, uh...' she fell quiet for a couple of seconds and nodded pointedly at Sam, 'for potential infection.'

'She's a tough cookie, you know,' Sam said with a faltering smile. 'Keeps me in line. People see her and think because she's *petite* – God, she hates that word – she'll be a walkover. They soon learn otherwise.'

Mary hung a fresh IV bag from the same pole as an almost complete blood transfusion and nodded in return. 'How long have you been married?' she asked.

'A little over four years,' Sam replied, his smile genuine this time. 'We met just over a year earlier on a case in her hometown, and then the kids soon came along.'

'How many do you have?'

'A girl and a boy.' Sam flipped open his credentials and pulled out a usually hidden photo of a family picnic beside a patch of snow nearly four months ago in Rocky Mountain National Park, the quartet's ruddy cheeks and wide smiles captured forever by the camera's timer. Mary drank in the happy image and the smooth skin around her eyes crinkled as she imagined the family she planned to have in the future. 'Anna's often talked about having a third, or even a fourth. I usually say my sanity and wallet wouldn't be able to cope, but now I'd give anything to take those words back.'

Mary handed the photo back to Sam. 'You have a beautiful family,' she said, then returned her attention to Anna. 'I think she's waking up,' she added in a whisper when Anna's eyelids fluttered and her fists clenched. 'Go ahead, say something to her.'

'Anna?' he said, unable to hide his apprehension. 'It's time to wake up, sweetheart.'

'I'll come back in around a half hour, see how you're both doing,' Mary whispered and backed towards the door. Sam cautiously stroked Anna's cheek, prompting her to turn her head closer to the sound of his voice.

She licked her dry lips. 'Sam?'

'I'm here, Anna,' he said between the deep breaths he hoped would halt the cascade of questions he wanted to ask. 'I'm so glad you're awake. Can you hear me?'

Her dulled eyes, usually a sharp shade of blue he'd always found so captivating, slowly focussed on his face. 'Where am I?' She lifted her head a couple of inches off the pillow. The movement caused her to gasp and flop back against the smooth cotton, breathing heavily.

Sam scanned her bedside for the call button he knew to be situated nearby. 'Do you need me to get a nurse?' He saw her frown and shake her head. 'Can you remember anything?'

The pain in her abdomen dissipated and Anna stared at the white tiles directly above her. 'Am I in the hospital?' she asked.

'Yeah, you're in Barton in Tahoe,' Sam replied. He lowered himself back into his seat without loosening the light yet firm grip around her cool hand. 'You've had surgery and you need to rest up and get well again so you can come home.'

'My stomach hurts.' She moved her free hand until it rested on the blanket. 'It's like I've been hit by a truck. Are the kids here?'

Sam shook his head. 'They're being cared for by one of the other agents.'

'At the cabin?'

'They're in a hotel,' he replied, unexpectedly relieved when her eyes lost their battle to remain open. 'And they're fine.' He fervently wished she wouldn't recall the previous evening for now, or maybe forever. 'You get some rest now; it'll make you feel better.'

'Did they catch him?' Sleep swallowed her thoughts and her slurred voice faded. 'He...'

Sam's pulse quickened at the prospect of explaining the aftermath of what happened at the cabin. He knew the Sheriff's Office wanted to interview Anna as soon as her condition permitted, but all he wanted for her was a few more hours of undisturbed sleep. He stroked a fan of stray hairs away from Anna's forehead and continued the motion when her eyes remained closed and her breathing slowed into a regular rhythm. 'That's right, you go back to sleep,' he said, the words almost inaudible. 'I'll be here when you wake up.'

Minutes later and finally reassured by the steady patterns on the monitor, Sam gently eased his hand from Anna's. His fists balled and a line of bitten nails pinched against his skin, pushing thoughts of destroying whoever did this to his wife to centre stage. The first rumble of hunger sounded and reminded him how long ago yesterday's lunch had been. No wonder the room spun every time he got up from the chair.

You shouldn't leave her.

A second rumble commanded he locate a vending machine and, after one last glance at Anna, he slipped out of the door.

Perhaps she wasn't really the target.

The thought crept up on him from nowhere, an insidious notion absorbing its strength from Sam's inability to discard it into the oblivion it deserved. He'd never forgotten Angelo Garcia's death on I-70 back in 2001. The punctured brake lines identified during forensic analysis of their government-issued SUV left Sam wondering whether his tendency to take the wheel meant he'd been the intended target, rather than the agent assigned to mentor him during his first year with Denver's Metro Gang Task Force. Coupled with Sam's own near-fatal crash in almost identical circumstances seven years later and the linkage of both acts of sabotage to Kratz, a normally preposterous idea had firmly taken root by the time he reached the elevator. His mind in overdrive during the short descent, Sam pulled out his Blackberry and discovered three missed texts, the last sent by Jed Masters fifteen minutes ago:

In the waiting room. Need to see you. Don't leave the hospital. Coffee on me.

Had they caught Kratz, or was it purely a matter of Masters not trusting him? He'd go out and find his own clues, head straight to Reno and track down the sick son of a–

'Sam? You okay?'

163

He pushed the phone back into his pocket. 'Me? Yeah. Just picked up your text.'

Masters narrowed one eye and simultaneously raised the opposite eyebrow 'Man, you look like shit,' he said. 'Come with me and I'll buy you that coffee I mentioned.'

'Thanks.'

'How's Anna?'

'Sleeping,' Sam replied as he followed Masters. 'She woke for a couple of minutes, then went back to sleep. They've got her tanked up on all these drugs and I'm not sure how much she remembers. I really don't want her having to think about any of that stuff yet.'

'The café's through here.' Masters pointed to a relatively narrow corridor linking the larger part of the hospital to its original building. They walked in silence, both mulling their own thoughts until they reached a sign for cardiology. 'Make a left along there and I'll go get us that coffee. What do you want to eat?'

Sam shook his head. 'I'm not hungry.'

'You're eating something, man,' Masters said from the doorway. 'The last thing I need is you passing out on me.' He inhaled the room's savoury aroma and gestured towards a small table nearby. 'That one will be okay. Last chance to put in an order or I'll choose for you.'

Sam shrugged and turned his attention to the nearest window, beyond which another warm and sun-filled day brightened the hospital's neatly tended grounds. He noticed the parking lot was already half full, over an hour before standard visiting time commenced. Did the place really get that busy or did people arrive early, intending to first grab breakfast in the café or speak with a member of the medical team caring for their loved one?

He watched Masters get in line behind a woman he guessed to be in her early forties, her neat twinset and linen trousers the polar opposite of the teenage boy slouched against a pillar. A shock of dyed black hair covered most of his face, matching the colour of the cut-off denim shorts and obscure European death metal band t-shirt he'd thrown on that morning. Sam assumed the boy to be around fifteen, the relaxed way he conversed with his mother and the way she smiled adoringly at her son producing a small jab of guilt deep inside Sam's chest. Would the baby he didn't know existed less than twelve hours ago have become a child like this, secure in their chosen identity rather than following the herd, all because of the love and support of their parents?

Boy or girl?

He knew Anna would still be as much in the dark as he'd been. They'd known about John almost from day one, after a pair of pregnancy tests confirmed the happy news on one of the Friday nights he'd returned from a stint in New York. Angela came first and was a surprise, albeit a welcome one, for the newly married couple. He wondered if Anna had detected any signs recently, besides the occasional grumble her cycle hadn't returned to normal since John's birth. She'd also complained of tiredness and been a little weepy during a couple of movies they'd viewed since their relocation to Tahoe, but the stress of this unexpected move and their uncertainty surrounding Kratz's whereabouts sufficed to explain those away.

Until now.

'Two extra-large coffees, each with an extra espresso shot, and a couple of big-ass muffins,' Masters grinned and set down the laden tray. 'Better than nothing, I guess.'

'I see why you don't work in the restaurant trade,' Sam commented and reached for the nearest disposable coffee cup now the smell seeping from it proved difficult to ignore. 'What time are the cops coming to interview Anna?'

'Whenever the doc gives the green light,' Masters replied, eyeing the muffins. 'I didn't know what flavour you'd prefer, so I went with one chocolate and one blueberry. I'm easy on either; you know anything loaded with carbs rings my bell. You choose.'

Sam looked at the cakes, mindful not to throw Masters' act of kindness back in his face. 'I quite like the chocolate ones these days. Angela's developed quite a taste for them recently but can't manage a whole one, so it's usually my job to hoover up the crumbs.'

A tanned hand placed the sticky dark brown muffin on Sam's plate. 'I'm serious when I say you need to keep your strength up. Did you eat dinner last night?'

Sam shook his head, grudgingly picked up the cake and forced himself to take a small bite. 'I can't spread myself this thin,' he said after he'd swallowed two more mouthfuls. 'I can't be in two places at once and it's not like we've got anybody here to babysit.' He broke off another piece of cake. 'Fuck this witness protection that isn't witness protection shit. We'll have to move away from here once Anna's recovered if there's the slightest chance Kratz is behind this.' A man at a nearby table glanced across at them and Sam lowered his voice. 'Anna and my kids need familiar people around them. Her mother should be here, at the very least.'

Masters set down his coffee. 'What about you? Would that take some of the pressure off?'

Sam shrugged and pulled his cell phone closer. 'Anna's mom could get a flight out here,' he said. The phone connected to the café's Wi-Fi and soon gave access to a flight comparison website. 'She's miss today's direct flights. There's one from Denver this evening with a short layover in Salt Lake City, or she can fly direct tomorrow.'

'Under the circumstances, that should be okay.' Masters made a mental note to square it with Grainger immediately after they'd finished breakfast. 'Milne's put me in touch with one of your New York teammates, a guy by the name of Joe.'

'Studdert? You think this'll need his level of expertise?'

Masters observed Sam's scrutiny of a chocolate chunk he'd balanced on his thumb. 'Based on Kratz's connection to the region and what just happened to your wife, we need to see if anything links the cases.'

'You think he did this to Anna?'

'It's far-fetched, I buy that. But we all know experience says don't rule out the wackier ideas straight away.'

'What happens if it is Kratz?'

'We'll know either way sometime tomorrow. Skin collected from beneath Anna's fingernails has gone to a lab in Sacramento for urgent DNA testing.'

Sam's eyes narrowed. 'Do you really think he attacked Anna?'

'We can't discount it,' Masters replied. He leaned forward to grab a handful of napkins in which to wrap the remaining half of his muffin. 'Listen, man; Anna's going to be asleep for a few hours, then the cops will want to interview her if she's up to it. Go to the hotel, play with your kids, get some proper sleep and come back later. I need to drop in at the office, so I'll give you a ride.'

Sam followed Masters' lead, pushed his chair closer to the table and discarded his empty coffee cup in a recycling container. The glass doors slid open and they exited across the parking lot, where a cool breeze sliced through the sun's delicate warmth seconds after the doors closed behind them.

****

Detective Martin Boothroyd departed from Hutton nearly an hour earlier than required to cover the forty-minute journey to his coastal counterparts. Never one to take the absence of weekday commuter traffic for granted, he knew all too well the magnetic pull the Illuminations' first Saturday night display of the year would have on every good-time Charlie within miles, and intended to be in and out of Blackpool faster than a rat up a drainpipe.

Boothroyd had yet to comprehend the run-down seaside town's appeal. He'd spent his first quarter of a century never more than three miles from Huddersfield's fine Victorian architecture and the town's seedy underbelly, the latter of which kept him in a job once he'd completed his police training. From being a young boy, his family's apparent obsession with making an annual trip to the Fylde coast for a day or, if cash was plentiful, a weekend of cold chips, grumpy seafront donkeys and the obligatory inebriated Glaswegians remained a mystery. He'd gone along with it, even going so far as to enjoy the occasional seaside stag weekend with the boys in his early twenties. Thankfully, after his transfer to Preston he'd soon learned his new wife shared a similar outlook, meaning west-bound trips along the M55 rarely occurred unless they were work-related.

Now he seemed to spend more time here than at home with the family.

Later that afternoon, Boothroyd would revel in describing how negotiating his unmarked vehicle through the town's crowded streets was akin to being in the midst of a battlefield, with him starring in a solitary good guy role amongst enemy legions. He regaled his wife with tales of hordes of people constantly wandering into the road; their sole focus the polystyrene trays of fat-sodden chips in their sovereign-clad fingers, oblivious to both the future coronary they shovelled into their mouths – and his car. At the time, he'd debated whether to activate the blue lights hidden inside the Ford's front grill and add a complimentary blast of the siren but, knowing his luck, one of the bastards would already be pissed-up, topple over and do themselves a minor injury, for which they'd then claim a nice bit of compo.

Two more left turns brought him to Bonny Street's car park, a cramped concrete-flanked arena where a pair of empty spaces close to the police station's nondescript entrance caught his eye. That these were probably designated for a couple of detectives based in the building further aggravated his shredded nerves.

Fuck it.

He swung the Mondeo into the closest parking spot and turned off its engine without bothering to straighten the car's wheels. A stash of one pound coins in the ashtray had dwindled to almost nothing, the result of his monotonously regular visits to this neck of the woods. At least he could claim it all back on expenses if he remembered to keep the tickets together in a safe place.

So much for only meeting in Preston these days.

Satisfied he'd bought enough time to discuss the case's latest developments with Harry Irwin, Boothroyd slapped the ticket's sticky side to the inside of the windscreen and gave the door a hearty slam. His long strides took him through a glass door and into a small reception area, where two perpendicular wooden benches provided a less-than-comfortable place for a quartet of young men to wait. Boothroyd barely cast them a second glance, certain they'd be there to either sign the bail book or report some tit-for-tat pettiness that would generate far more paperwork than it deserved.

'Is Irwin in residence yet?' he asked the support officer as he slid his ID beneath the Plexiglas screen for her to inspect. 'I got here sooner than I expected.'

Her greying ponytail bobbed in confirmation. 'He arrived back ten minutes ago. You go on up and I'll phone through to tell him you're here.'

'Cheers,' Boothroyd replied. He hoped he and Irwin would indulge in the usual strong cup of coffee before knuckling down to business. He ignored a nearby lift Irwin regularly swore couldn't get any slower, took the stairs two at a time to the fourth floor and then proceeded down a windowless corridor that led to CID's small suite of offices.

'Yeah, I remember,' Irwin shouted seconds before the footfalls revealed their identity. 'Milk, two sugars and there's a half-eaten packet of chocolate Rich Tea in the brew room.'

'You'd better get your arse into gear and fetch me the bloody things!' Boothroyd shouted back. He sunk into the nearest chair and eyeballed a neatly colour-coded pile of paper on Irwin's desk. 'What's all this then? You auditioning for a job on *Blue Peter*?'

'Caffeine and then Kratz, how does that sound?' Irwin asked, his voice muffled now he'd stepped into the nearby kitchenette. 'Got a bit more through today. Nothing earth-shattering, but it all lends fuel to the fire we're going to roast our friend on when he gets caught.'

Boothroyd squinted at the sheet on top of the pile. 'Sounds good,' he replied, distracted by the first lines of what appeared to be Roger Mortimer's phone bill, until Irwin's annoyingly cheerful whistle increased in volume.

'Having a nosey, are we?'

'Too right I am,' Boothroyd said. He smiled and reached out to accept a chipped blue mug sporting a faded police emblem. 'Cheers, big ears. Looks like Mortimer's phone records.'

Irwin threw the packet of biscuits at Boothroyd and watched him untwist the wrapper. 'Finally came through today after I got the higher-ups to give BT a rocket. Doesn't tell us much more, apart from in the days leading up to his death there were a significant number of calls to and from a previously undialled mobile number'

'Any idea who it belongs to?'

Boothroyd shook his head. 'Not yet. The number's on Orange's network if my research is correct, so I sorted a warrant and said if it's one of theirs we want everything – and I mean *everything* – on it. Full incoming and outgoing call records, where the calls were made from, where the owner purchased the phone, how long it's been in use for. I'm not expecting a real name, let alone an address. Saying that, I'm hopeful we'll get *something* from this.'

Boothroyd swallowed and helped himself to another two biscuits. 'Do you reckon it'll be much help?'

'Who knows?' Irwin replied. He reached across the desk to grab the packet, the tightness of his waistband a stern reprimand for leaving a large bag of apples at home yet again. 'If Kratz has been keeping a lair over here and we find it, there might be stuff to tell us where he's hiding out in the States.'

'Stuff?'

'I dunno... some kind of documentation, plane ticket stubs, bank statements.'

'They're pretty sure he's been back to that Reno place in the past week or so,' Boothroyd said. He narrowed his eyes and willed his biscuit to remain intact as it emerged from his coffee. 'Isn't that the investigation's focal point?'

'Just because he conducts some of his business there, it doesn't mean that's where he's hiding.' Irwin gave his email's inbox another quick once-over. 'You know what they say: don't shit in your own bed.'

Boothroyd grinned, a trace of sodden biscuit still visible on an upper incisor. 'Then let's hope Kratz gets caught short.'

****

2.04pm – PDT
Barton Memorial Hospital, South Lake Tahoe, California

Anna couldn't pinpoint the exact point at which she became aware of someone else's presence. Whether it was their slow, even breaths or the slight squeak whenever they shifted position on the faux leather chairs, she had no idea. Perhaps Sam had returned? She'd found herself alone when, for a matter of seconds, she'd fought her way out of a chemically-induced slumber, unable to prevent the return descent into nothingness before she'd been given a chance to think about where he'd gone.

This time the fight ended in her favour and she'd triumphed over the lure of deep, empty sleep. The ache around her waist remained, too vague to accurately locate yet sufficient to induce pain if she tensed the underlying muscles. A regular bleeping matched the faint pulse deep inside her abdomen, masking any further sounds from whoever was nearby.

What if it wasn't Sam?

A sudden chill spread throughout her chest and she heard the bleep take on a different pitch: higher, faster, a representation of her need to escape the sights and sounds crowding her memory. A face loomed over her, both familiar and alien...

'Anna?'

What if it's HIM?

'You're okay, Anna.'

170

Anna's eyes snapped open and her surroundings blurred for a split-second. She distinguished the outlines of three people: one beside her bed, the other two further away and possibly leaning against the wall.

'You're okay,' the voice she'd recognised as Sam's repeated. 'Take some nice deep breaths and try to relax.'

Anna felt his hand grip hers and the panic begin to subside, as if he'd absorbed it directly from her. She blinked repeatedly and cleared her vision enough to reveal his concerned face.

'How are you feeling?'

'Tired,' she replied in a flat tone and looked past Sam to Jed Masters, whom she recognised from a short conversation when she'd woken for a second time late that morning, and an unknown tall blond-haired man beside him. 'I thought you were him, Sam.' She saw him meet the other man's eye and his expression harden. 'That he'd come back for me and–'

'Anna, listen carefully to me,' Sam interrupted when Heikkinen stepped forward. 'I can't be with you for this. I need you to answer this detective's questions about… last night.'

She tightened her grasp on Sam's hand and pulled him against the side rail. 'Don't go,' she begged, an audible quiver in her voice. 'Why can't you stay here?'

'Sweetheart, you know the rules for police interviews,' Sam said, feeling sick at the thought of leaving her. 'We can't risk me being here influencing what you say. I'll be down the hall and I'll come straight back when you're done.'

'You promise?'

He stretched a tepid smile across his face. 'Absolutely. You know I will.'

Anna took a couple of seconds to look the newcomer up and down and reluctantly let go of Sam's hand. 'I thought you were a doctor.'

'No chance of that with my appalling high school science grades,' Heikkinen replied. 'But, she did say I'm allowed to come see you and we can have a little talk.'

She frowned and tried to make sense of this transparent ploy to put her at ease. 'I don't understand.'

'My name's Jonno,' he added after Sam carefully closed the door behind him. 'I'm with the Douglas County Sheriff's Office. We need–'

'Did you catch him?'

'Not yet. That's why we need your help today, Anna.' Heikkinen manoeuvred his chair closest to Anna, ready to lead the questioning like he'd previously agreed. 'I'd like us to start at the beginning, if you feel up to it. Is that okay with you?'

She released a heavy sigh and twitched her shoulders in the slightest of shrugs. 'It's all kind of blurry.'

'That's no problem; we'll take our time and try to refocus things,' he suggested with what he hoped to be an encouraging smile. 'Take some deep breaths and think back to what you did after Sam took the children out for the afternoon.'

'Please could I get some water?' She stared at the plastic jug and trio of matching cups on the nightstand. 'I'm a little thirsty.'

Masters grabbed a cup and poured a generous amount of the iced liquid into it. 'They even left a couple of bendy straws for you.' He placed the drink into her trembling hands. 'Are you sure you're up to this, Anna? You don't have to, you know that. We can come back later today, or tomorrow morning.'

'I'm good,' she replied, her grip on the plastic so tight it threatened to buckle. 'Sam went out with the kids shortly before four. The house was real quiet, almost too quiet. If you have kids you'll understand.' They nodded. 'I poured a glass of wine, took a shower, set out our clothes for later and made a start on dinner.'

Heikkinen leaned back against the chair. 'What did you prepare?'

'There's this British dish named shepherd's pie. Some restaurants over here make it with beef and it drives Sam nuts because apparently that's *cottage* pie.' She shifted position, the effort required quickening her breathing, and offered them another weak smile. 'It has to be made with ground lamb, or *minced* lamb as he'd say, because shepherds look after their sheep, right? I got it ready for the oven and then made a start on dessert.'

Heikkinen watched a single tear trickle over a pallid cheek. 'What was that?'

'Something named Eton Mess.' She glanced at the door and wondered if Sam knew she'd intended to serve two of his favourites. 'I was a little lazy and bought ready-made meringues from Trader Joe's this time. You crush them and then mix them with whipped cream and chopped strawberries.'

'Sounds delicious,' Masters said from his seat on the other side of Heikkinen. 'Is that a British thing too?'

'Yeah. Sam's stomach sometimes gets homesick, even if the rest of him doesn't. It only takes around ten minutes to make and then you can chill it for later.'

Heikkinen smiled and shifted closer. 'What did you do after preparing dinner?' he asked, ready to steer the conversation closer to the event that put Anna in the hospital.

'Poured myself another glass of wine and went downstairs to fix my hair and make-up.'

'You didn't get changed into your new clothes?'

She shook her head. 'I wanted to surprise him once the kids were in bed.'

'What time was it by now?'

'Probably around five, I guess.' She looked at a small bedside clock as if it would supply a more precise answer.

'Did you go back upstairs?'

'Yeah, I finished the wine and picked up some toys Angela had left lying around.'

'What happened next?' Heikkinen asked. He noticed her jaw clenched whenever he asked a question and quickly reassessed his approach. 'I realise this is hard, Anna. What you tell us will make a real difference to our investigation, I promise you.'

Masters left his seat and gripped the bed's footrest. 'I've worked with Sam for less than a month and all that time he's constantly told me what a great detective you are.' He saw fat tears welled up in her reddened eyes and ignored a momentary pang of guilt. 'I can't imagine what it's like to be put in the opposite situation and be questioned like you've questioned so many others over the years. Sam's taking this a good deal harder than he's letting on, you know what us guys are like. All he wants to do is make this all go away for you and he can't, and that's making him so mad right now. We all put on this hard-ass front, but you know that underneath we feel things just as bad as other folk, if not worse.'

'You can do this, Anna,' Heikkinen added. 'Take your time and remember it doesn't matter if it seems totally trivial; you of all people know the smallest things can be the most important. You said you tidied up your daughter's toys?'

She nodded and used the heel of her hand to smear a fresh round of tears across her cheeks. 'She's a good girl, and usually pretty compliant at putting away her toys after playing with them. She'd only left some books and a couple of dolls out. The kids don't have many toys since we moved; if we're still living here at Christmas we'll have to change that.'

'You finished the tidying, and…'

'I went back to the kitchen to get everything for setting the table. Then–' She shook her head and released a deep shuddering breath. 'I'll be okay, just give me a minute.'

Both men relaxed their posture and sensed she'd soon reveal whatever happened in the cabin nearly twenty-four hours earlier. Anna continued to evade eye contact and her gaze fell to her hands, the left hooked up to an IV she'd been told would probably be removed in a couple of days, once the chance of sepsis passed.

'I don't remember if I heard or sensed something,' she said, her voice shaky. 'That sounds totally nuts. My back was to the stairs, I turned around and there's this guy standing there. At first I thought I was seeing things, like I'd had too much to drink on an empty stomach. I'm quite the lightweight these days.' She took another deep breath and halted the cascade of words for a split second.

'I was standing there for what seemed like forever, and he walks toward me, like it was… Christ, I don't know. I didn't know what to do. What do you say when some stranger comes into your house? I said *Who the hell are you?*' and he said nothing, he just kept on walking. He stopped and asked where Sam was and that's when I realised this wasn't some random breaking and entering, so I said my husband would be home any minute and to get the fuck out of my house.'

Heikkinen and Masters exchanged a sideways look. 'What did he say or do next?' Heikkinen asked.

'He laughed. Can you believe that?' she spat, surprising them with her anger. 'He laughed at me, said even if it was true Sam wouldn't be able to help me as he's a pussy and it's a shame he wasn't home instead of me. He started closing the gap so I grabbed a knife from the block on the countertop and told him if he didn't go I'd stick it in him.'

Masters' warm hazel eyes never left her tear-streaked face. He cleared his throat. 'Do you need to take a short break?'

She shook her head and accepted a handful of tissues. 'He rushed at me and took me by surprise. The knife fell from my hand and the sound of it hitting the floor was so loud, almost like a gunshot. I really tried so hard to fight him off and he was trying to grab my wrists so I tried to scratch at his eyes or face, silly as it sounds I thought if he did kill me at least he wouldn't be able to hide those marks and somebody would know he'd done something bad. All I managed to scratch was his arm.' She stared at her fingers, where a trio of ragged nails corroborated her account.

'We obtained skin from beneath your nails and it's being DNA tested as we speak,' Heikkinen said, his words enough to curl Anna's lips into a fragile smile. 'You did good on that score, detective. Do you remember what happened next?'

She moistened her lips and returned to looking through the window. 'I don't recall how we ended up on the kitchen floor. He pinned one of my wrists against the tiles and was trying to grab the other. I managed to twist onto my back and bring a knee hard up into his balls. I thought it would incapacitate him but he barely noticed, then I saw this flash of something in his free hand and then this pressure here.' Anna's hand moved to her waist and prodded harder than she'd intended. She took a sharp intake of breath. Heikkinen's mouth opened, but she pressed on before he could speak. 'It was weird. I didn't feel anything for what seemed like ages and then it was like I was on fire. He did it again and I couldn't move, I must have been in shock. He said something and I didn't hear any words, just this ringing in my ears. I closed my eyes like it would block out everything, and then he grabbed my hair and smashed my head against the floor.'

'Perhaps we should stop?' Masters muttered, more to himself than to Anna.

'No!' she snapped, her voice raised.

'Anna...' Heikkinen loosened his tie and looped a finger beneath his collar. 'Let's leave it for today. Your doctor won't be happy if she hears you've gotten all worked up.'

'My doctor isn't here, so let's get this over with.' She ignored the sharp ache in her abdomen reproaching her for the outburst.

'He smashed your head against the floor,' he reluctantly continued. 'Do you remember anything after that?'

'I played dead. I could feel him kneeling over me so I kept my eyes closed and held my breath then I finally heard him move away. There was this burning heat, I guess where the knife went in. The rest of me was so cold and by the time I was sure he'd gone I couldn't move. My cell phone was on the countertop and I tried to call for Sam, but he didn't come. I really did think my time was up and I'd never see my kids again. I guess I then passed out.'

'You're doing great, Anna. Can you describe the guy for me?'

She squeezed her eyes tightly shut and confronted her attacker for a second time. 'White guy, kind of tall and athletic. He wore running gear and was around my age, I'd guess.'

'Hair colour? Eye colour?' Heikkinen pressed. 'What was he wearing?'

'He wore a baseball cap and sunglasses. His accent was kind of weird.'

Masters frowned and remembered how more than one police report he'd seen stated Kratz had recently varied his accent depending on his location. 'In what way?' he asked.

'It kind of drifted. Sometimes he sounded American, other times… something else, maybe Australian or British. Even after five years with Sam, I can't always tell the difference.'

'Did you see him anywhere before?' Masters added. 'Maybe in the neighbourhood or around town, or at the grocery store?'

'He seemed kind of familiar. I can't say he reminded me of anyone specific.'

'Do you think you'd recognise the guy if you saw him again?' Masters asked. He caught Heikkinen's eye and discretely pointed at the leather folder he'd placed on a nearby chair.

'I don't know; it all happened so fast.' She stared at the door and her eyes widened in terror. 'Do you know who he is?'

'No, but…' Heikkinen took a deep breath. 'We have some photos we'd like to show you, if you feel up to it.' He nodded once at Masters, who picked up the folder and unzipped it. 'It's your choice, Anna. We can always do this tomorrow. You know that, right?'

'I'm ready.' She steeled herself with a deep breath and accepted the sheets of paper.

Masters watched her eyes rove over each image. 'Is he there?' he eventually asked.

'This guy, I've seen him before.' Anna pointed to a CCTV still from the footage obtained at JFK airport. 'I can't say where. He looks… I don't know, like I've seen him somewhere… although there's something different about him here. I'm not sure what though.'

'That's awesome, Anna. Good job!' Heikkinen felt his own adrenaline begin to flow. 'Think hard, where did you see him?' He saw her gaze travel to the white ceiling tiles again, as if she wanted them to bleach away all memories of the previous evening. 'Take a look at the others, see if there's anyone else you recognise.'

She lowered her head and manipulated the images in her clammy palms. Heikkinen and Masters watched, their tension evident for the entire time she stared at the second array of photographs.

'I don't know,' she whispered. 'I'm sorry.'

'That's okay.' Masters' neutral tone masked his disappointment.

Anna yawned, unable to fight the exhaustion sweeping through her body. 'Can Sam come back in now? Please.'

'Sure he can,' Heikkinen replied. 'I'll go find him while Jed here stays with you. Is that okay with you, Anna?'

She nodded, turned her face to the window and stared at the thin blue lines peeking between the slatted blinds. It was almost like yesterday afternoon's sunshine had occurred years ago, a lifetime in which crime skirted around them – usually at work, sometimes a little closer to home – but was never permitted to wrap its spindly fingers around their family unit for more than a short while.

The barely detectable squeak of the door's hinges preceded a whispered exchange, the content of which she barely registered. Her focus remained beyond the window and she pictured herself beneath the rich cobalt Tahoe sky, her exposed skin warmed by the late summer sun. The hinges squeaked for a second time to announce Heikkinen and Masters' exit, shattering the protective spell she'd created for the shortest of times.

The room darkened, a solitary cloud able to cast shadows around the figure in the doorway. She blinked repeatedly and wondered whether her head's sharp contact with the kitchen floor was responsible for this intermittent blurriness. For the first time she noticed Sam's dishevelled appearance and how the creases in yesterday's clothes mimicked the worry lines carved into his face.

'The guys said you gave them a lot of useful information,' Sam said, unable to keep the fragile timbre from his voice. 'I'm so proud of you.'

At that point something collapsed inside Anna. The strength she'd maintained for over a year dissolved as the room blurred again and her tears fell thick and fast. She felt the warmth of Sam's strong arms pull her into a gentle embrace and she clung to him like she'd never let go, his whispered words obliterated by the loud sobs she suddenly realised came from deep within herself.

****

4.46pm – PDT
FBI Resident Agency, Kietzke Lane, Reno, Nevada

Heikkinen pulled into the resident agency's almost empty parking lot and cursed a set of roadworks and the aftermath of a fender bender; their ready alliance extending his journey time by an extra thirty minutes. He adjusted his tie whilst covering the short distance to the building's main doors and, for a moment, wondered exactly how forgiving the team of agents he'd scheduled a meeting with might be at this hour on a sunny Saturday afternoon.

From behind her office's reflective glass, Denise Grainger registered the unmarked vehicle's arrival and, once they'd exchanged pleasantries in the lobby, Heikkinen followed her up a polished metal stairway to the FBI's suite of leased offices. She directed him to a partially open conference room door, beyond which two women and one man were seated at a large oval table. He was relieved to see a half-consumed plate of chocolate chip cookies that looked to have neutralised any hint of displeasure caused by his late arrival.

'Detective Jonno Heikkinen from Douglas County Sheriff's Office,' he said, and shook each agent's hand in turn during their introductions. 'Sorry I'm running behind schedule, the traffic had other plans.'

'That's okay,' Anahid Avakian replied. 'Agent Jones here made coffee for everyone.' She nudged Rick Jones' shoulder and pointed to a three-quarters full glass jug resting on a hotplate. 'He lost, so he's on serving duty today,' she added with a wry smirk.

'What's this penance for?' Heikkinen asked, mirroring her expression.

'Apparently working computer magic in my office is less strenuous than trailing around downtown looking for disgraced movie icons,' Jones replied as he grabbed a clean cup from the sideboard. 'I'm repaying my debt by saving their delicate little feet from additional wear and tear. We have sugar and creamer, or I can go get some real milk if you prefer?'

'Black with one sugar is great, thanks.'

Raquel Vasquez pushed the plate across the desk. 'Help yourself before he scarfs down what's left,' she said, enjoying the humour after an intense couple of days. 'Don't know how he isn't the size of a house.'

Jones set down Heikkinen's drink and reclaimed his seat. 'They're just jealous of my metabolism,' he commented. 'I guess it's now over to you, ma'am.'

Grainger cleared her throat and opened a brown case file folder containing a summary of the investigation's key points to date. 'I'd like to thank everyone for being here today and, unless we have any significant developments between now and Monday morning, enjoy your Sunday away from this place,' she said. 'I'll personally be working with Jed Masters over at Stateline tomorrow but, until then, let's bring ourselves up to speed on the Kratz case.'

Grainger took five minutes to recap over events surrounding the transatlantic bank transfer organised by moonlighting computer-whizz Joel Nattrass, and his mysterious disappearance days later. She followed this by explaining how Jones' Microsoft-based college buddy called in a couple of favours of his own, both confirming that the IP addresses for Stamford's and Nattrass' emails had originated in Reno and Sparks respectively.

Heikkinen listened intently to the remainder of Grainger's update, impressed by what her small team had achieved in a surprisingly short space of time. Avakian's feet silently squirmed against the oatmeal-coloured carpet and a gleam in her dark eyes hinted of more to come; his theory confirmed when Grainger pushed her seat back and turned to the youngest agent on her team.

'Annie, perhaps you'd like to bring Jonno up to speed with what else we've learned in the past twenty-four hours.' Grainger's serious expression melted as she spoke. 'You both did an amazing job yesterday; I really feel we're getting closer to taking down this son of a bitch.'

'Yeah, persistence sure paid off in the end.' Avakian allowed herself to bask in the approval of her mentor. 'Raquel and I made inquiries at several banks in the downtown area, and showed them recent photos of Kratz taken from security footage. A service operative at the Sierra Nevada bank was pretty damn sure she recognised a guy she'd taken down to his safe deposit box earlier this week, so we rushed a warrant through and gained access to what's now an empty box. We also obtained the bank's security footage of this guy for Jones to work his magic on.'

Jones nodded and sensed his turn to update Heikkinen had arrived. 'This morning I received footage from the Los Angeles Field Office showing Kratz at LAX Airport. Using the photogrammetric data verified by LAPD and measurements taken inside the bank this morning, I matched our suspect's height and build to Kratz. He did a mighty fine job of not looking at the cameras, so my guess is he'd checked out their locations on previous visits. He wasn't so careful when he left the bank and bumped into a passer-by, meaning I managed to isolate and enhance a three-quarters facial shot showing a strong match to our elusive friend.'

'Therefore, we can say with a high level of confidence this James Haigh guy is Konrad Kratz,' Grainger said. 'Members of Sacramento's Evidence Response Team collected the safe deposit box for processing and with any luck they'll get fingerprints and maybe some DNA to compare to the reference samples.'

'It'll take another day or two for the DNA results to come back on the skin scrapings from under Anna Bury's fingernails,' Vasquez said. 'Our problem is even if both profiles match, by the time we get confirmation he'll probably be long gone.'

Grainger set down her cup. 'Jed Masters said over the phone that your interview with Anna revealed more than we expected at this stage?'

'She sure is one tough lady,' Heikkinen replied. 'Her doctor allowed us to speak to her once she was awake and she handled it pretty well. Once it all hits home is when it'll get harder for her to deal with.'

'I understand she miscarried the baby she was carrying?' Grainger's question produced a collective sigh and downcast expressions from the other three agents.

'That's correct. She hasn't been told, yet. Her husband, Sam, plans to break it to her tomorrow if she's still improving. I don't know, ma'am; it's like she's holding something back from us, whether she realises it or not.'

Grainger raised her eyebrows. 'What do you mean?'

'Masters mentioned that during Anna's time in the recovery room after surgery, she said *'He's back'*. It could be the anaesthesia talking so she can't recall it now, but you have to ask what triggered those two words. Who's the *he*? She described her attacker as tall and having a weird accent which varied between American and possibly British or Australian, and she said one of the photos of Kratz in disguise looked familiar, although she was unable to place exactly where she may have encountered the guy, if at all.'

'Repressed memories.' Avakian thought back to a college tutorial she'd attended. 'The person blocks a memory they find too traumatic to confront and deal with. They continue to be affected by what happened, although they can't specifically recall the event or events.'

'Do we pursue this?' Jones asked, his uncertainty growing now he'd departed from his computer-based comfort zone.

Avakian gazed at a small scratch on the table's otherwise smooth surface. 'This is sure to stir up a real emotional shit-storm for her.'

'We could wait for the DNA results,' Jones continued. 'If it matches Kratz's, we don't need to put her through what would surely be a seriously traumatic interview.'

'And if it doesn't match?'

Grainger crossed her arms and turned to Avakian. 'We deal with it.'

****

5.19pm – PDT
Mattole Road, near South Lake Tahoe, California

The rhythmic thud of his feet on the wooden floors resonated with the blood thumping against his eardrums. Since the story had broken, all the local news channels brimmed with reports of a savage attack on an unnamed local woman in her own home, their sparse images and lack of specific detail feeding the public's hungry imagination.

Konrad scowled, recalling the moment he heard the bitch had survived. Why the fuck hadn't he gone for the jugular and finished her off once and for all? It wasn't like him to lose his cool at these moments. Death was nothing for his victims to fear: a momentary transition from life to nothingness. He contemplated the possible reason why he'd neglected to confirm her demise. Christ! He didn't even know the name of Sam's wife; the news channels assumedly gagged from releasing too many details.

Don't say you're scared of that pussy.

Sam Bury: the wimpy kid he'd tormented all those years ago. He'd underestimated the man's resilience, his ability to bounce back from situations which would have tipped most people over the edge – if they'd actually managed to survive in the first place. What would have happened if Sam had arrived at the cabin just has he was delivering the fatal blow? He

181

was obviously stronger than Konrad first realised – did that also extend to his physical prowess? Who knew what repercussions might have been if Sam had found him standing over his dead wife, her body still warm despite bleeding out all over the kitchen floor?

Perhaps it's not Sam who's the pussy.

The cabin's solitude felt suffocating and, even though he appeared to be safe within his wooden cocoon, he'd soon need to emerge, head into town and replace the dwindling reserves he'd worked his way through since his arrival. It was strange to think the future held such positivity before the unexpected presence of Sam and his apparently perfect little family shattered all plans to lie low. Why they were in Tahoe, Konrad could only speculate, and he remained highly doubtful that Sam would be given the task of smoking him out. Surely it would be a conflict of interests and, in the unlikely event of this being the case, why did his wife and kids accompany him on a potentially dangerous mission?

You fucked up; she should be dead, and you didn't check on her. Schoolboy error.

At first he'd assumed the family were on vacation in the area, a *freak* coincidence he'd ride out until they returned to Colorado. Sam's departure from the cabin at the same time each morning like the good little worker bee in the Federal Hive he'd always been, and his other observations of their day-to-day routine, swiftly disproved this theory. Either the family had chosen to relocate to Tahoe, or the choice was taken out of their hands. The latter scenario suggested the FBI knew Sam and his family could be in danger, although placing them in the same area as Public Enemy Number One seemed a giant balls-up – or a crystal clear sign the G-men remained ignorant of the tiny cabin he'd secretly owned for years.

Konrad's thoughts returned to his latest dilemma: whether to leave suddenly under the cover of a dark Tahoe night, or wait another week and claim he'd been called back to his fictitious San Francisco workplace for a meeting, never to return. The latter was tempting, but would focus the attention of his neighbours firmly upon his unexpected departure; a juicy morsel ready to be fed to the cops if they released a long-overdue appeal for information.

What if Sam finds you first?

He slumped into the nearest of two armchairs and pointed the remote control at the room's opposite corner. The cabin filled with the sights and sounds of local media speculation, baying for the latest scoop to edge their channel into pole position. It took less than a minute to confirm his freedom; the lack of new information evident when the same footage, claiming to be exclusive at lunchtime, played out for the umpteenth time.

Konrad decided the likelihood of discovery was negligible, unless the police released more specific information. He'd stick to his original plan and allow the dust to settle, then gather his cash and possessions and, by the middle of next week, vanish into the northern wilderness to begin his new life.

****

5.55pm – PDT
FBI Resident Agency, Stateline, Nevada

Joe Studdert's early arrival and check-in at JFK Airport that morning left him with plenty of time for breakfast, before commencing the first leg of a cross-country journey west through three time zones. It had certainly been a while since he'd found himself in this neck of the woods, Studdert now mused. He steered through a left turn off Kingsbury Grade Road and gently accelerated along an anonymous street which, according to the satellite navigation system he'd thought to pack, led to the FBI's Tahoe base and his journey's end.

A long-time behavioural analyst and current member of the New York-based CRSU, Studdert had been surprised to receive a phone call from Denver's field office the previous afternoon. In under five minutes, Colin Milne revealed the whereabouts of CSRU co-ordinator Sam Bury and the latest developments in the hunt for Konrad Kratz, before requesting that Studdert join the multi-agency investigation high in the Sierra Nevada.

He slammed the Nissan's door and inhaled the rich pine carried on a light breeze from the nearby forest; a scent that never failed to instantly remind him of childhood vacations in the area. Every other summer his parents had borrowed his uncle's RV and made the long drive north to his mom's favourite destination, ready for two blissful weeks away from the relentless Sonoran heat. After a customary one-night stopover near Pahrump, they'd spend the next day meandering through Death Valley on their way to the mountains, a detour Studdert never quite understood if the main objective of their vacation was to head for cooler climes. Ten days of hiking, fishing and water sports followed, and the absence of school's pressures provided a chance to refocus his attention on his younger twin brothers, whose admiration he'd always been conscious of. Patrick and Craig soon followed in his footsteps and joined the Bureau: the former a language specialist at the Portland Field Office, the latter a member of El Paso's Violent Crime Task Force.

Studdert cast another look around the almost empty parking lot's landscaped borders and neatly-mown grass that, to his eye, appeared out of sync with the rugged Ponderosas surrounding the apartment blocks immediately opposite. The whole set-up was the antithesis of his usual workplace; that huge government building buried deep within New York's concrete jungle. Sure, he enjoyed city living – he'd admit that to anyone. Nevertheless, the lure of retiring to a place like this had started to wrap itself around the part of his brain that all too often reminded him he wasn't getting any younger. At first, Studdert questioned Sam's reluctance to uproot his family from Colorado and move to New York on a permanent basis. The younger man's insistence on airborne commutes and obscenely long working hours every other week had seemed the not-so-perfect compromise, but Studdert now understood.

A flicker of movement in his peripheral vision returned his attention to the wooden building and he saw a familiar figure emerge into the setting sun's mellow light. Studdert rapidly closed the distance between them and spread his arms wide, unable to properly scrutinise Sam as he drew him into a bear hug.

'Long time, no see,' Studdert said. He placed his hands on Sam's shoulders and looked him up and down, conscious of the man's tense demeanour. 'I can't lie, Sam. I've seen you looking better than this.'

'It's been a rough couple of days,' Sam replied, aware the constriction in his throat had eased. He'd noticed Studdert's same calming effect in the past, and always attributed it to an undetectable aura radiating from the man's shrewd blue eyes and tanned face. 'How much do you know about what's happened?'

Studdert squeezed Sam's shoulders one last time. 'I phoned Masters from Phoenix for another update.'

'Phoenix in Arizona?'

'Layover.' He grinned at Sam. 'Don't tell my Aunt Judy I was in town for an hour and didn't swing by to see her.'

Sam's head bobbed back and forth to satisfy himself that the lot remained devoid of prying eyes and ears since the press had grown weary of their unproductive wait and departed. 'Masters and a local detective interviewed her this afternoon. She remembered a fair bit of what happened.'

'Did she make a positive ID?'

'Kind of.'

'Kind of?'

'She said the photo of him at JFK looked familiar, but she was unable to provide a positive identification. Looks like we'll have to wait for the DNA results to come back.'

'This mountain air always makes me ravenous,' Studdert said, the truth of his words serving his intentions well. 'What about we go get us some dinner and you can update me?'

Sam glanced at the Saab parked a couple of empty rows away from where they were standing. 'I wanted to go back to the hotel and see the kids.'

'That's okay. A burger and a beer first will do you good.' Studdert pressed the remote key and observed the amber lights dancing around his smaller vehicle. 'I'll bet my ass you haven't eaten much since yesterday,' he added, 'let alone slept properly.'

'Bloody profilers.'

'Common sense, not profiling.' Studdert eased himself behind the wheel and leaned across to open the passenger door. 'So get your ass in the car.'

****

7.54pm – PDT
Hotel Sierra Nevada, South Lake Tahoe, California

Angela Bury stifled a yawn and clambered onto the bed. 'I want to see Mommy.'

Sam found the innocence in her tone far more unsettling than a face-off with any gang member or associated criminal. He stroked the last stray strands of fine blonde hair away from his daughter's face and forced a smile.

'Soon, sweetheart. I promise.'

Don't say you're feeling guilty?

'Before bedtime?' Angela replied, the blue eyes so similar to her mother's wide and accusatory.

'You're already way past your bedtime, Angela.' He adjusted a large pink leopard print fleece blanket until it covered her chest, thankful he'd relented when she pleaded for it during yesterday's impromptu stop-off at Tahoe's factory outlets. 'Maybe you can go to see her tomorrow, or the next day.'

Her feet thumped against the mattress. 'I want to see Mommy *now*!'

Sam sighed and shook his head. 'Mommy's not feeling too good. She had a little accident and the nice doctors and nurses want to make sure she's better before she has lots of visitors.'

'Not fair, Daddy.'

'Perhaps Grandma will be able to take you to see Mommy.'

'Gran-ma?' she echoed.

'I'm meeting her at the airport tomorrow.'

'Will she see John too?'

'Of course she will.' Sam stole a sideways look at the sleeping baby, his plump cheeks moving in and out with each breath. 'She's coming to see you both, and to see Mommy.'

She looked past the open doorway through drooping eyelids. 'Who's that man in there?'

'That's Uncle Joe, he's a good friend of Daddy's and he's going to help look after you because Aunty Colleen's gone home.'

Angela's small fingers looped around his thumb. 'Are you staying here tonight?'

'That's right,' Sam replied, 'so you need to go to sleep.' He watched her eyelashes meet, defeated in the battle to stay awake now an unpredictable procession of unfamiliar adults had ended. From what Masters had told him, a Tahoe PD family liaison officer called in a favour to secure the suite after a recent bachelor party got out of hand. The hotel manager had hastily manipulated her reservations in a grateful acknowledgement of the swift and low-key end to the type of disturbance not usually associated with her establishment.

Their suite was comprised of two adjacent bedrooms and a bathroom that all opened out onto a communal living area. Opposite the main doorway a modest kitchenette occupied one corner, where gulping down a couple of early morning cups of strong coffee in the privacy of his own room appealed to Sam. He listened to the little girl's breathing take on a slow regular pattern and his attention shifted from her serene features to the bedroom's warm pine walls.

Sam eased his thumb from her relaxed grip and edged away from the sleeping children. He tiptoed through to the living area, grinning at how Studdert casually reclined against an overstuffed chenille couch. The deck shoes he favoured for travelling lay haphazardly to one side and he flicked through the television's cable channels whilst waiting for Sam to emerge.

'Are they both asleep?'

The screen darkened and fell silent as Sam snorted and flopped down on the couch. 'I've barely seen them all day, and then I go out of my way to make sure they go to sleep and stay asleep,' he said. 'Dad of the Year Award goes to me.'

Studdert nodded and stretched out his aching legs. 'How much does Angela know?'

'I've told her Mommy had an accident at the house and the doctors and nurses at the hospital are making her better. John was oblivious in the car, but Angela saw the paramedics put her mommy in the ambulance and I left them both with an officer to go with Anna.'

'Are you going to the hospital tonight?'

'I'll give it twenty minutes, then when Angela's definitely asleep I'll go and see Anna for half an hour or so.' Sam checked his watch and stared through a nearby window to where an irregular ring of lights traced the darkened lake's circumference. 'They'll prove if he's behind it either tomorrow or Monday, assuming the DNA from beneath her nails comes back.'

'You mean Kratz?'

'I suppose, or whoever the murdering piece of shit is.' Sam lifted both hands to his forehead and caught Studdert's flicker of confusion. 'She was pregnant,' he announced. 'We didn't know until it was too late. She was probably around six weeks gone, but we'll probably never know for sure.' Sam stared down at the carpet. 'He killed our baby.'

'How did Anna take the news?'

'She doesn't know. I agreed with the doctor not to tell her for a couple of days. We'll wait for her to get her strength back, and then I'll have to break the news to her.'

Studdert exhaled slowly and edged closer to Sam. 'This wasn't a planned pregnancy?'

Sam shook his head. 'Even if we'd been thinking about it, the timing wasn't right. Who knows how long we'll be looking over our shoulders?'

'Did you tell Anna we suspect Kratz could be behind this?'

Sam shook his head again.

'Keep it that way, for now.'

Chapter 10 – Sunday 6th September 2009

Martin Boothroyd had never been particularly enthusiastic about sometimes having to work on the Sabbath. Although not a religious man, he retained the belief some things should be held sacred – even if this only extended to the consumption of a large roast dinner and then sleeping it off in front of the drivel that passed for Sunday afternoon television.

The faint spots of rain on his windscreen abated by the time he pulled into one of the parking places across from half a dozen two-storey buildings, their drab grey exteriors a relic of the concrete architecture prevalent in the sixties. A fresh breeze picked up the first autumnal leaves as he crossed the narrow road to the closest building, where the Cold Case Unit's base of the past four years occupied the middle of three floors. He took the stairs two at a time, conscious he'd twice ignored his alarm clock, and broke into a grin when a smug-faced Irwin appeared in the office doorway.

'At least *you're* early for once, I see,' Boothroyd said. 'And, before you complain, we've done you a massive favour by asking you over to this neck of the woods.'

Irwin snorted and pulled the nearest empty chair from beneath a desk. 'It's Sunday morning, a time our Good Lord decreed should be spent in bed sleeping off last night's ale.'

'At this time of year?' Boothroyd laughed and shook his head. 'You'd be wrestling scroates on the Prom all afternoon. Hair of the dog that bit them and a tray of salmonella – it's the fuel of champions, I tell you.'

'I can certainly see why Roger Mortimer preferred to conduct business over this way,' Phelan added. She gathered up the accumulated mugs on her desk and placed them in the sink. 'Does anyone fancy a coffee while I'm making one?'

Boothroyd flashed her a thumbs-up. 'Yeah, thanks.'

'Whatever you Preston types need to say to convince yourselves...' Irwin replied. 'So, what have you found since we last spoke?'

'A lot of it's purely speculative, based on the limited evidence,' Sanderson said. 'Nothing points to how or where Mortimer and Kratz crossed paths back in 2003, even though it led to a sizeable investment from the latter.'

Irwin frowned. 'Why not stash some cash back in the States?'

'He'll probably have done that too,' Sanderson replied. 'We've theorised this is his English nest egg in case he ever got rumbled over there and managed to flee the country. Once here he'd call in his investment and use it to either fund a new life over in the UK or do another moonlit flit overseas.'

Irwin considered the idea. 'So, what went wrong?'

'The calling in his investment part. Roger obviously agreed to go along with it because he served notice on his tenants, then something happened.'

'Roger recognised him,' Boothroyd said. 'I'm guessing they had a business meeting and then, possibly round the time that media shitstorm blew up earlier this summer, Roger realised who he was dealing with. Next we caught that exchange between them on the Edward II's CCTV, so did they have some kind of altercation prior to that? Roger may have said he'd keep his trap shut if he could keep the houses, or the money tied up in them. Kratz couldn't risk being rumbled, so he decided to silence him once and for all.'

Sanderson plucked a sheet of paper from his desk. 'I'm still waiting for Orange to get back to me with details of the unregistered mobile used to phone the Mortimer house shortly before his death, for what it's worth.'

'So what do we do in the meantime?' Irwin asked. 'I'm happy to muck in if it means we get this turd once and for all, but without any fresh leads...'

'Go over the tracking from the GPS on his Cockney hire car again and see if there's anything indicating the possible location of a hideout,' Boothroyd said. He fell silent and tapped briskly on his laptop's keyboard. 'And, even if he's now back in the US, it doesn't mean he's going to stay there forever. I'd guess it'd be easy enough to slip into Canada.'

Phelan set down a pair of hot drinks. 'I put an extra sugar in it. Reckon you need sweetening up,' she said, moving her fingers to allow Boothroyd to grasp the handle.

'You're a cheeky bugger!' he replied between sips. 'From what you've said Kratz pretty much came straight here and then buggered off back down south. No detours between Lancashire and the Big Smoke.'

Phelan reappeared carrying two more coffees. 'Which means if he's got a place in the area, it's either here or Blackpool or somewhere between,' she commented.

'Blackpool's more likely,' Irwin said. He noticed the others' eyebrows unite in a collective raise. 'It's always had a transient population. Someone coming and going over the years, or maybe renting a place for that length of time wouldn't particularly stand out, even if he's not there much. It wouldn't matter whether he sounded local or foreign, there's that many people passing through the town he'd just be one of thousands. Failing that, there's plenty of B&Bs to doss down in. They're used to a rapid turnover these days.'

Sanderson pondered Irwin's idea. 'What about doing door-to-door inquiries?'

'At the hotels and B&Bs?'

'Yeah.'

Irwin chuckled and set down his mug. 'Have you got any idea how many there are here?'

'Not really,' Sanderson replied, conscious that in the two decades since he'd moved away from London he'd rarely encountered the nitty-gritty of Blackpool's underbelly.

'For us four, it'd be well over two hundred each.'

Phelan groaned and shot a sideways glance at Boothroyd. 'Sack that!'

'And if checking his satnav doesn't work?' Irwin asked.

'*Crimewatch*.' Boothroyd caught Phelan's eye and clapped his hands together in delight.

'*Crimewatch*?' Irwin echoed. 'As in on the telly?'

Boothroyd cast his mind back three years to their successful request that the BBC's monthly crime reconstruction programme include a particularly chilling unsolved triple murder case that had rocked Accrington in the early eighties. 'Ask our budding actress here,' he said, pointing at Phelan. 'She'll tell you *everything* about her starring role.'

****

191

Studdert listened to the echo rebounding off the mountainside seconds after Sam slammed the rental car's passenger door. His sharp eyes tracked through the forest opposite the cabin and registered how the density of the trees increased with their distance away from the road. The sky's intense blue, a prominent feature of these altitudes, formed a striking backdrop for their surroundings; its perfection marred by a quartet of growing dark grey clouds.

'Quite a contrast from Federal Plaza, right?' He saw Sam wrap rigid arms around his chest and stare at a stationary patrol car nearby. 'Are you sure you're up to doing this, Sam?'

Sam nodded and swallowed down the golf ball-sized lump that had lodged itself in his throat. 'I'd like to go in alone first, if that's okay? Check it's all ready for the kids.'

'No bother, man. I'll stay in the car with this cheeky pair.' Studdert leaned into the rear of the vehicle to exchange faint words with Angela and then twisted back to grin at Sam. 'Looks like I'm going to be an expert in all things cat by the time you're done.'

Sam nodded again, aware of the lump's return to its original position. From the outside, the cabin he and Anna had tried so hard to view as a family home appeared exactly the same as on the day they'd moved in. A pair of carved pine bears stood guard to one side of the entrance and the moose to the other. Their sightless eyes watched him raise the key and insert it into the lock on his second attempt, the tremor in his hand almost enough to knock the key to the ground.

A gentle push opened the door and Sam stepped into the entryway. Coats and shoes left there by the family were now jumbled haphazardly wherever the forensic examiners or clean-up team thought to place them. He remained motionless and surveyed the disarray, at first oblivious to the key he now clutched biting into his skin.

Sam pushed it into his back pocket, walked through a second doorway and entered the upper floor's living area. Bright mountain sunlight streamed through the windows and cast rectangular pools onto the polished wooden floor. The sight reminded him of the day his family arrived to commence what he and Anna assumed would be a short break from normality, rather than a new life. Since then, they'd dotted some personal possessions around the place, a feeble effort to counteract its sterility. The crime scene clean-up company brought in by the sheriff's office had really done a number on the place, and a combination of bleach and pine instantly transported him back to every hospital he'd ever been unfortunate enough to visit over his thirty-three years.

Content to see John's playpen remained untampered with, Sam descended to the cabin's lower floor and tightened a clammy hand around his gun when he reached the bottom of the stairway. All five doors leading off the corridor were a couple of inches ajar, permitting narrow bands of light to print patterns on its plain carpet. One by one, he checked the spare room and family bathroom to ensure all windows were securely locked, and then partially closed the blinds in the children's bedrooms.

Sam retraced his steps and hesitated outside the master bedroom. A slicked hand grasped its handle and he took a moment to regulate his breathing before entering the room. Intense sunlight flooded in through the balcony doors that opened onto the lake view Anna adored, as if its energy was sufficient to drive away the clouds previously obscuring it.

Pathetic fallacy at its best... Mrs Willis would've loved that one.

He recalled his English teacher, one of many who'd strived to ensure he fulfilled the academic promise he'd shown from a young age. Life seemed so much simpler during his schooldays, until Peter Umpleby's influence cut short this new phase of his life and turned Crettington High School into Sam's own private hell. The relentless bullying by a pair of boys two years his senior eventually culminated in a showdown between his livid parents and a less-than-contrite headmaster, and Sam found himself at Rockhirst days later. He'd been unable to deny his relief at being away from Umpleby, even if he did miss the small circle of friends he then only saw at weekends.

The group maintained their strong friendship over the next two decades, although they were now split between two continents. Sam later learned that Umpleby, or Konrad Kratz as he became known worldwide, had instigated the campaign of intimidation marring his short time at Crettington High – another example of how the man appeared dead set on ruining Sam's life by taking away anything or anyone he valued or loved. He sat on the bed, nestled his face against the pillow he'd picked up and inhaled. A faint hint of vanilla filled his nostrils; a scent he'd associated with his wife since their first dates. The subtle combination of Anna's shampoo and perfume never failed to remind him of those heady weeks after their chance meeting at Boulder's police station, during which he'd fallen harder for her than anyone else he'd ever met.

The shrill ringtone from his pocket jolted Sam back to the present and he pulled out the Blackberry, not surprised to see the name flashing on its screen. 'It's all fine,' he said. 'I'm on my way up.'

Angela stared at Sam when he reappeared, oblivious to her father's trepidation about letting them re-enter the cabin where her mother had come close to losing her life. A familiar light breeze stirred the wispy hair around her face and reminded Sam he'd need to either find some hair clips in her room or buy new ones if he went into town later.

'Let's get the kids in.' Studdert shifted John from one arm to the other. 'I swear this one's getting heavier by the second.'

'Sounds like a plan,' Sam agreed. 'If we sit Mr Greedy in there with a couple of toys, he can amuse himself while I sort lunch.' He watched Angela run into the lounge area and gaze longingly at the staircase. 'Do you want to go and play in your room?'

Studdert lowered John into the playpen and shook out the ache in his wrist. 'I think that smile means *yes*.'

'Remember to be careful on the stairs.' Sam listened to her footfalls fade to nothing and the house lapse into a short silence. John's squeal refocussed the men's attention and Sam leaned over to ruffle the baby's light brown hair. 'And, this one's always hungry,' he said. 'I'd swear he has hollow legs, but carrying him for too long knocks that theory on the head. I'll grab the groceries from the car and give him a bottle and some yogurt. That should keep him going for half an hour or so.'

Studdert nodded and crouched beside the playpen. 'Hey, buddy,' he said, his tone cheerful. Wide blue-grey eyes scrutinised him in return and helped the baby form thoughts he'd never be able to articulate. 'What you got there? Is that your little bunny?' The plush blue rabbit, a favourite toy since before the move, remained clasped between John's plump fingers whilst he scanned the room. 'Are you looking for Daddy? He's at the car finding you something good to eat. Bet you like the sound of that? Daddy says you sure love your food.'

John lifted his arms and cooed in delight, the rabbit forgotten before it hit the floor. 'You want to see what's going on, right? Let's see what you're getting for lunch.' Studdert lifted John from the playpen and pointed at the front door. 'That's where Daddy's gone.' They approached the doors to the upper balcony, a five-foot wide structure running the full length of the cabin's rear. 'We need to make sure Daddy eats something too, don't we? He loses his appetite if he gets worried, and that's not going to help anyone catch the worthless piece of... dirt who hurt your mommy.' The rustle of polythene alerted Studdert and John to Sam's return and both fell silent to watch him cover the short distance to the kitchen.

'I just hope they didn't rearrange the stuff they didn't need for evidence.' Sam set down two carrier bags on the countertop and opened the nearest wall cupboard. 'Bottles in here...' he continued and reached for one, 'and scissors in there.' He pushed the drawer closed and snipped off the corner of a ready-prepared baby milk carton. 'Have you tried this stuff?'

Studdert failed to hide his surprise. 'Can't say I have.'

'Don't bother, it's bloody disgusting. Angela was content enough to drink it, but this little guy goes mad for it.'

'So you decided to see what all the fuss is about, right?'

'Seemed like a good idea after a couple of beers,' Sam replied. He lifted the half-full bottle to his maximum reach and swooped it into John's outstretched hands. 'There you go, Buster – and don't gulp it, or else we know what happens.'

John tilted the clear plastic and lifted it to his mouth. 'He has a real good grip,' Studdert commented. 'My kids were lazy and preferred me or their mom to hold it for them.'

'Yeah, that's something else he learnt to do over in England,' Sam said. The anger in his tone caused John to lower the bottle. 'Another thing that piece of shit took from me. Do you want a drink, Joe?'

'Coffee, please. The usual.' He watched Sam press the kettle's *on* switch harder than required. 'They change pretty fast, don't they?'

'Especially at that age,' Sam said. He lifted four plates down from a different wall cupboard and was pleased to see John return his attention to the drink. 'I'd better take something down to Angela.'

'She'll be okay for a few minutes. What time do you want to go to the hospital?'

'In a couple of hours," Sam replied. "You're sure you don't mind watching the kids?'

'It'll give me some practise for becoming a grandfather next year. I did say I'd go by the resident agency later this afternoon, but only if Anna's okay with you coming back here.' Studdert frowned when Sam broke off from his search of the fridge. 'You've been granted leave and your wife and kids need you. It's not up for debate.'

'I can help'

'My best offer is keeping you in the loop. How do you think Anna will react?'

Sam shrugged. 'What she says and how she feels could be totally different.'

'And what about you?'

'What about me?'

'How do *you* feel?'

'I don't know,' Sam replied. 'Maybe with things so up in the air it's for the best. Well, that's what I'm trying to tell myself.'

Studdert glanced at the plate closest to him. 'You want me to take the cheese and crackers down to the little lady?'

'Yeah, please.'

'And this little guy?' He used his finger to remove the globule of saliva sliding a leisurely path down John's chin.

'Bread and butter is his current favourite,' Sam replied. He wiped the knife clean of cream cheese and scraped it across the tub of pale yellow butter. 'And so's yogurt. Actually, he wants to eat whatever we're eating. He got really upset when Anna made a curry and we wouldn't let him have any. It was stupid of us, really. She made it mild so Angela could try some, and what do you think they feed babies in India? Bland mush like mac and cheese?'

'You don't need to internalise things.'

Sam scowled and continued to cut the buttered bread into fingers. 'Pardon?'

'If you need to talk, I'm here for you. If you don't, I'm still here for you. You need to promise you'll tell me if it all starts getting too much.'

'What do you think I'm going to do?'

Studdert's silence endured until the two men made eye contact. 'Keep that promise.'

****

2.13pm – PDT
Barton Memorial Hospital, South Lake Tahoe, California

The tick of the SUV's cooling engine pecked its way into Sam's consciousness and drowned the nearby excited chatter of a young girl walking beside her father. Her beaming smile complimented the balloon she brandished, a blue helium-filled bear broadcasting to the world how she'd recently become big sister to a new baby brother. Sam sighed at the memory of Angela choosing a similar balloon for her own baby brother, nearly seven months ago.

What colour would the balloon have been this time?

John's birth had offered both a slender ray of hope and brief respite from the despair engulfing Sam since Kratz's second attempt to kill him – and the week he spent *drugged up to the eyeballs* in a New York hospital's neurological ICU. From there he'd been flown to Denver to continue his recovery, where a serious bout of pneumonia and the deterioration of his mental state twice delayed his discharge from the hospital's prison-like walls to the preferable anonymity of home.

His dislike for hospitals magnified with each subsequent visit, and merely being in proximity to one sufficed to send his sympathetic nervous system into overdrive. The reason for his visit didn't matter, the thought of inhaling the smell of antiseptic and, on occasion, death was always enough for the clamminess to start creeping across his skin.

Six weeks maximum. Another thirty-four or so to go. His mind calculated how far into the future this would have taken his family…

May: early May.

By then John would be fifteen months old and Angela would be getting ready to start Kindergarten later that summer. To balance the demands of a new baby and a toddler without neglecting the needs of their eldest would no doubt have posed challenges, even if plenty of people had managed it in the past – his parents being a prime example.

I guess I'll never find out.

His children possessed the ability to make him run the emotional gauntlet. Now he'd live alongside the perpetual sadness associated with the knowledge any future baby would be labelled at the couple's third when, in reality, it would be their fourth: the missing member of their family consigned to obscurity by well-meaning people unaware of the truth.

A crisp image of Anna cradling their newly-born daughter faded into one of a baby they'd never meet wrapped tightly in white blankets, their tiny face a blur. Sam exhaled, relaxed his hold on the steering wheel and felt the tension caused by his arrival also loosen its grip. He took another deep breath and found the will to leave the car's warm confines and follow the building's perimeter to its main entrance.

The glass doors slid back to reveal a wide lobby. Sam paused to control his breathing, his grip on the polythene bag tight despite the sweat coating his palms. To his left, a freckle-faced man was seated behind an information desk opposite a gift shop, its cheerful window carrying the suggestion to brighten a patient's day with a varied selection of treats and essentials. Sam entered the shop, conscious nothing was capable of diminishing the impact of the news he needed to break.

Arms laden, Sam left the shop minutes later and proceeded along a grey corridor, where two left turns in quick succession took him to the elevators. The middle of the three opened and he returned the smile of the teenage girl who alighted, the twenty-dollar bill she clutched likely to be destined for where he'd just left.

The doors slid closed and gave Sam barely enough time to go over the lines he'd rehearsed for much of that morning. Whatever he thought of saying seemingly trivialised the ordeal Anna was yet to learn she'd gone through; a life-changing event neither of them would ever be able to forget. The doors on the elevator's opposite side opened onto the Medical-Surgical floor and he cast a glance at an adjacent seating area, where he and Jed Masters awaited news of Anna's surgery two nights ago. Chairs lined three sides of the room, their dark green upholstery toning with the lighter green hue of the walls. He looked from side to side in the hope he'd see a member of staff to either update him on Anna's recovery, or page someone who could.

Sam sunk into the nearest chair and rested Anna's gifts on his lap. His tired eyes settled on a panoramic view of Emerald Bay and Lake Tahoe's tranquillity immediately beyond. Angela's fascination with Fannette Island's isolation within the bay showed no sign of relenting and she'd begged Sam to take her there for a picnic on an almost daily basis. Maybe he'd research whether it was possible, a welcome treat for both of them to cushion the upheaval of the past couple of days. He'd have a word with Jed Masters, if anyone–

'Can I help you, sir?'

The voice nudged Sam from his thoughts. He blinked and struggled to organise his reply through the sleep-deprived fog which had thickened considerably throughout the morning.

'My wife, uh, Anna Bury?' Sam swallowed to moisten his dry throat. 'I'd like to speak to her doctor before going in, if she's available to talk.'

A tall nurse in his mid-thirties ran a tanned finger down the clipboard he carried. 'Doctor Solis? Sure thing! You take a seat and I'll put a call through to her.' He eyed the bouquet Sam cradled. 'Those sure are beautiful.'

'I picked them up downstairs,' Sam replied. 'Your gift shop has some lovely presents. Anna never admits it, but she's quite fond of flowers. And wine, which I suppose is out of the question for a while.' He stopped and shrugged his shoulders, unsure what else to add.

'Sounds like a sensible lady,' the nurse replied. He smiled and cast another look at the flowers. 'If you don't mind waiting a couple of minutes, I'll go page Dr Solis for you. Try to relax and I won't be too long.'

Sam returned his attention to the photo inside its sleek black frame and peered at the picturesque bay and the island Angela was so keen to visit, cut off from the mainland's rocky shoreline by a deep blue stretch of water. He'd have to make enquiries into renting a boat. The kayaks he'd seen other people enjoying were definitely too risky for a three-year-old who was, at best, nervous during her weekly swimming lessons.

'Dr Bury? I'm glad you asked to see me–'

'Is she okay?' Sam interrupted. The bag of treats shifted to occupy a precarious position against the chair's arm and he automatically grabbed its handles.

Dr Solis, an athletic woman who appeared considerably younger than her forty-two years, offered Sam a friendly smile. 'She's making good progress. Let's go somewhere a little more private.' She watched him juggle the flowers and carrier bag, then cautiously rise to his feet. They walked along the corridor to a pair of offices he hadn't previously noticed. The closest door opened into a small room decorated in the hospital's favoured colour scheme, where three identical armchairs in a shade darker occupied its furthest corner.

'Anna's been making a steady recovery since being admitted to the unit,' she said, after Sam sunk into the nearest chair. 'Her blood pressure is within normal limits, the oxygen saturation of her blood is good and she's eating a soft diet with no adverse effects, which we're delighted with so soon after major surgery. Your wife is one tough lady.'

'Don't I know it,' Sam replied. His face softened and he lowered the bag to rest on the carpet. 'You've said her physical recovery is progressing well; what about the psychological aspects? She's been through one hell of an ordeal in the past couple of days.'

Solis nodded. 'She's certainly giving the impression of bearing up okay. Earlier she became a little tearful when she asked if the police knew anything more, and she told me she's looking forward to seeing you and the children.'

Sam rustled the glittery paper enclosing roses, chrysanthemums and other unfamiliar varieties of flower. 'Am I okay to take these in?'

'Sure, go ahead.' she replied. 'I'll be in to make some observations in around forty minutes.' Dr Solis didn't miss the immediate concern crossing his face. 'It's purely routine, there's nothing for you to worry about.'

Sam thanked her and retraced his steps along the corridor until he reached Anna's room. Only partially fortified by a couple of deep breaths, he nodded to the latest uniformed police officer seated nearby, looped the bag's handles around his wrist and opened the door. 'Hey, sweetheart. Do you want a visitor?'

Anna's face lit up at the sight of the large bouquet and her eyes moved to the bag. 'Only if he comes bearing chocolate,' she replied.

'I could only find that horrible American stuff.'

She puffed out her cheeks and sighed. 'I'm past being discerning. If my next two sets of obs are fine I'm allowed a little this evening.'

'How are you feeling?' Sam asked, his mouth already parched.

Anna shrugged and stared at the thin blanket tucked across her chest. 'Been better, been worse, still sore. How are the kids?'

'John's completely unfazed by it all. Angela... she's doing well.'

'What did you tell her?'

'I said you had a small accident at the cabin when we were out, the doctors are now making you feel better and you'll be coming home soon.'

'Are *you* okay?'

'I should be asking you that.' Sam swallowed to clear the all-too-familiar lump. 'But I think a hug will help me.' He placed the flowers on a chair and cautiously leaned over the bed to ensure he avoided contact with anywhere below Anna's ribs. 'That's better,' he whispered when she pressed a gentle kiss against his cheek.

'Not to sound like a total mercenary, but what's in the bag?'

Sam reached for the Safeway bag and placed it on the mattress beside her. 'Just a couple of trashy celebrity gossip magazines, a brand new copy of *The Stand,* some fresh fruit and enough chocolate to sink a battleship.'

'I remember the first time I read that novel,' she said. 'Chrissie Palinkas loaned it to me one weekend, I think it was sometime in eighth grade as we were still at middle school. I'd read it cover to cover by the time Monday morning rolled around. We were all so impressed he set part of it in Boulder.'

'Does that mean your hometown's a magnet for crazy people?'

'I guess so. Delusional hostage-takers, trust fund hippies, granola heads, federal agents making a mess of my neatly-organised evidence...'

'I suppose I must like crazy.'

'Seriously?' Anna muttered, trying not to smile as she reached into the bag. 'You bought grapes again?'

'You're in hospital. It's tradition.'

'Yeah, I remember. And don't think you're continuing the part of your so-called tradition of eating them all before the patient gets a chance.' She held the large bunch of deep red seedless grapes aloft and shook her head. 'You English people are too weird. Couldn't they have been part of a fruit basket?'

'It's why you love me,' Sam replied. He swallowed again and forced a smile. 'I'm so glad you're feeling okay.'

'Yeah, though my period chose a real bad time to arrive.' Anna frowned at his immediate flinch. 'Hey, it's not like you to be squeamish. I told you they've been all over the place since John arrived; light one month, heavy the next. I'm really not sure this IUD is agreeing with me. The last one arrived in England, so I guess I'm a little late – probably because of the travelling and all the other recent upheaval. It's so undignified having others deal with it, and I've suffered from some nasty cramps this time. I know they've seen it all before and much worse, but you don't have to lie there while they–'

'Anna.'

Her frown deepened. 'What?'

'There's something I need to tell you.'

'They've caught him?' she exclaimed, and her expression instantly changed to one combining hope and delight. 'I knew they'd get him in the end. Didn't I always say he'd do something stupid and it'll lead to his downfall?' She saw his head shake and her face and shoulders fell. 'He's still out there?'

'There's something else.' Sam lowered himself into the chair closest to the bed and clasped his hands around hers. 'Anna, when you were admitted the doctors took you straight through to surgery to stop the internal bleeding and repair your bowel.'

'I know all of this.'

'Whenever someone is admitted, even as an emergency, the doctors have to do all these tests to get some background on your general health.'

She nodded impatiently. 'Like an HIV test?'

'Amongst other things. All women of childbearing age are given a pregnancy test and–'

'I'm pregnant?' She watched him give the tiniest shake of his head. 'What the hell are you trying to say, Sam?'

He licked his bottom lip and took a deep breath. 'The test came back positive. Soon after they'd taken you back to Recovery you started to bleed. They tried really hard, but there was nothing they could do to stop it.'

Anna pulled her hand from Sam's and stared at the door. 'I *was* pregnant?'

'I'm so sorry.'

'It would have been your baby too,' she whispered, her eyes downcast. 'I really didn't know.'

He reached for her hand again and stroked the smooth skin beside her thumb. 'It's not like we'd planned to have another so soon.'

'You're saying you're glad?' She snatched her hand back for a second time.

'Of-of course not,' Sam replied. An uncomfortable warmth spread throughout his chest. 'I meant we didn't think to look out for the signs. With John, it was different. We knew.'

Anna fell silent for what seemed like an eternity and closed her eyes. 'How far along was I?' she eventually asked, unaware her hand now rested a couple of inches below her waist.

'Five weeks, maybe six, give or take. We must have conceived around the time you came back from England. I suppose we thought the IUD was enough for it not to happen.'

'It should have been enough. I've been drinking wine and not really watching my diet.'

'You did both those things right up to us learning Angela was on the way, and she's turned out just fine.'

She stared directly at Sam and her steely gaze unnerved him. 'What if there's something else I should have done?'

'This isn't your fault,' Sam said, surprised by how calm he sounded. He noticed Anna roll her eyes and shake her head. 'You could've died, Anna. Perhaps your body just didn't have the reserves to save you both?'

'Which means I'd still be pregnant if this hadn't happened.'

'We don't know that for certain.'

'You really are dumb if you believe that.' She folded her arms and continued to stare him squarely in the eye. 'That son of a bitch killed our baby, and I couldn't do anything to stop it.'

'Anna...' he pleaded, realising he needed her support as much as she needed his.

She turned to face the opposite wall. Dense silence filled the room, penetrating everything other than the faint whir-click sound emitted by her IV pump.

Sam cautiously rested his hand on her tense arm. 'Anna?' he whispered, aware whatever he said must surely exacerbate her feelings of loss. 'We really need to talk about this.'

'I need some time alone to process this; I think you should leave,' she replied, the words barely audible, her voice thickened by emotion.

'But–'

'Now!'

****

5.26pm – PDT
FBI Resident Agency, Stateline, Nevada

Joe Studdert checked his watch with a quick flick of his wrist and smiled at the woman standing beside him. 'Four minutes to go,' he announced, nodding at the recently emptied section of the parking lot closest to the building. 'I always say give them enough to whet the appetite, but always leave them begging for more.'

'You don't think we're giving away too much information?' Denise Grainger asked. 'We're never usually this free and easy with the details, it gives the whackjobs more stuff to bullshit us with later.'

'We need to throw the public a bone and give them something to chew over,' Studdert replied. 'This guy's profile and Kratz's has many parallels. We pick out the common threads and let the public do their work. Humans are a naturally curious species; that's what my old Dad always used to say. It's how we are. Someone out there will recognise this guy.'

She raised a slender eyebrow. 'And no mention of Kratz?'

'Hell no!' he replied, watching the local news channel's TV crew finalise each position of the two cameras and three microphones they'd be using. 'Every media outlet in the western hemisphere would descend like a plague of goddamn locusts. We need Kratz to think we don't have a clue where he is. We lull him into a false sense of security so he stays where he is long enough for the tip line to start ringing red hot.'

Grainger turned away from where the crew intended to record her latest television appearance. 'How's Sam doing?'

'I've seen him better,' Masters admitted. 'He broke the news about the baby to Anna this afternoon. She didn't take it too well.'

'Can you blame her?'

'Absolutely not,' he agreed. 'But the last thing they need to do is shut each other out.'

She scanned the authorised personnel gathered nearby. 'I assumed he'd be here.'

'Colleen Dexter said she'd mind their kids this evening for however long it takes Sam to drive back from Reno.' Masters caught the unspoken question in Grainger's stare. 'The mother-in-law's flight arrives in a couple of hours.'

Grainger winced and checked her watch. 'I wouldn't like to be in that car.'

'Sam said they usually get along okay.' He spotted the twenty-something female reporter he'd seen near Sam's cabin on the night Anna was rushed to the local hospital. 'Looks like they're about ready to go on air. Are you ready to get miked-up?'

'As I'll ever be,' Grainger replied. She tucked her hair behind each ear. 'It's not something you ever get used to. I guess I have a better face for radio.'

'I didn't like to mention it,' Masters said. He gave her shoulder a fleeting squeeze of support. 'Go on, ma'am – knock 'em dead.'

'Not the best choice of words, Joe,' she said as she approached the podium and its array of additional microphones. 'I hope they tell me when we're rolling this time.'

Masters and Studdert watched a camera swing through ninety degrees and zoom in on an over-coiffured young woman nearby. Emma Rigby's trademark twinset picked out the piping around her immaculately pressed knee-length skirt which, coupled with her hairstyle and make-up, gave her the appearance of a Barbie doll seconds after being removed from its packaging. Rigby's career goals lay firmly on bigger and brighter things than small-town reporting and she'd soon cultivated a reputation for doing whatever it took to guarantee her place on the screen, even if some of her previous attempts could have jeopardised ongoing investigations had she'd been successful.

Studdert stifled a smile at the two uniformed members of Douglas County Sheriff's Office glaring daggers in Rigby's direction when she began her report. He'd learned of the woman's modus operandi from both Masters and Grainger, the agents vitriolic in their dislike for her. At first they'd been cynical regarding his suggestions for the content of Grainger's live statement on the early evening news bulletin, until he'd convinced them that an apparently unlinked case had the potential to smoke Kratz out of his lair.

Rigby flashed the fakest of gleaming smiles at Grainger and begrudgingly relinquished her place in the limelight, a move made solely on the understanding the agent revealed sufficient details to increase local interest in the case and therefore guarantee higher viewing figures for Rigby's follow-up reports. Grainger bit her lip and fixed her gaze on the camera, relieved she'd chosen to change into trousers now the breeze had strengthened.

'Approximately forty-eight hours ago, a thirty-five-year-old woman was brutally attacked in her Kingsbury home and left for dead. Her husband, who has since been ruled out as a suspect, discovered his wife upon his return with their two young children and immediately raised the alarm. I am presently unable to divulge specific details, but we do not believe this to be a random attack.

'Based on the description provided by the victim and our investigation alongside Douglas County Sheriff's Office, I am able to provide a description of our suspect. The Caucasian male we wish to question is aged in his late

twenties to late thirties, tall and of an athletic build. He has a fair complexion and evidence suggests he works out regularly, be it at a gym or by running. We do not believe he is native to the Tahoe area, although he may have resided here for some time.

'In addition to this horrific crime, from which the victim is slowly recovering, the FBI wishes to take this opportunity to request local assistance on another crime in the area, in conjunction with the DEA's District Offices in Reno and Sacramento, and the Douglas County Sheriff's Office. In recent months, a new type of methamphetamine has been seized in the Tahoe area. Our intelligence suggests it is being imported into the region, most likely from one of the larger cities within a four-hour radius.

'Therefore we ask all Tahoe area residents to think carefully. Do you know someone, or a group of people, who visits Tahoe on a regular basis from the city? Consider how much you actually know about this person or their group. Do they keep you at arm's length, always having a ready and feasible explanation for their lifestyle and reason for visiting? Does their appearance change from visit to visit, again always with a convenient explanation? Their choice of accommodations, be it hotel-based or an owned or rented property, will not match their alleged background. They sound plausible, almost too plausible, yet when you try to recall anything of depth about them, you will realise just how little you actually know about the individual in question.

'If you have any information on either case, no matter how insignificant it may seem, we urge you to call any of the telephone numbers scrolling across your screen at the end of this news broadcast. These numbers are also available on the FBI's Las Vegas and Sacramento Division's webpages, in addition to those belonging to Douglas County Sheriff's Office and the DEA's Los Angeles and San Francisco Divisions.

'I will end by posing this question: Do you have a stranger next door?'

Grainger cautiously alighted from the podium and re-joined Masters and Studdert. They watched Rigby hurriedly reclaim the camera, her glossy platinum blonde hair radiating the sun's rays as she revelled in her return to centre stage.

Masters offered her a grin. 'Nice job, ma'am. Do you really think this is going to work?'

'We've given people two things to think about,' Grainger replied. 'There's potentially a madman going around stabbing people in their homes, and a new type of drug flooding the area. Sure, the meth story isn't true but, by linking a similar perpetrator to both, anyone who knows someone who fits either or both of descriptions is going to be suspicious. We then hope they'll find it pretty damn difficult to ignore that little *ding-ding-ding* in their head.'

The deepened lines on Masters' tanned face gave away the residual doubts he clung on to. 'Even if that's the case, what if they're too scared to phone?'

Studdert chuckled and listened to the last part of Rigby's half-baked speculation. 'Would *you* want a murderous meth overlord living next door?'

****

7.34pm – PDT
Mattole Road, near South Lake Tahoe, California

A perpetual televised loop of national news interspersed with inane local stories had filled the cabin for much of the day. Between updates, Konrad transferred blocks of cash and a minimal selection of clothing to a large backpack – ready to make an immediate hasty getaway if circumstances demanded it. The recent live broadcast allayed his concerns and suggested the cops and their little friends remained confused about what actually went down in the Bury's cabin. Despite the woman surviving what should have been fatal injuries, he'd been reassured by the certainty that if the Feds had the slightest inkling he was responsible for the attack they'd have already kicked his door clean off its hinges.

He rolled up another sweatshirt and placed it on the bed. Just another backpacker wending his way through the Northwestern states, he thought with a chuckle, albeit a backpacker boasting over a million bucks stuffed in his bag. Set up for a life under the radar, so long as–

Stan's frantic barking and a sharp *rap-rap* on the door echoed throughout the cabin, creating an adrenaline surge unlike any other Konrad had ever experienced. *Shit.* Probably another goddamn asshat who'd gone to the wrong address. He'd learned the three cabins further along the road were vacation lets which had a tendency to attract people who were apparently unable to read, let alone follow simple directions. He'd smile sweetly, open the door and point them on their way, all whilst inwardly cursing their stupidity.

'Hi Dale! How ya doing this evening? And, is this my waggy-tailed four-legged friend come to greet us? How ya doing, boy? Did you miss Mommy and Daddy? I'll bet you did!'

When the fuck did you get back?

Mike Saunders raised a bushy eyebrow in response to his wife's exuberant greeting and Konrad's surprised expression. 'Who else did you expect at this time of night, Dale?' he drawled. 'Don't tell me you've finally gotten yourself a nice little lady to take care of you?'

His wife Irena, her shock of blonde hair barely level with her husband's shoulder, issued a hearty nudge to his ribs. 'That ain't none of your business, buddy.' She turned her attention to Konrad and patted him on the arm. 'You just ignore him; he needs to learn to butt out of things that don't concern him. We're just swinging by to collect our baby boy and thank you for looking after him, and we're inviting you to the barbecue we're having Friday evening. My brother and his wife are flying in from Florida and we don't want you to go making other plans between now and then. Plenty of good food for you; put some meat on those bones.'

'That'll be awesome!' Konrad replied, unable to stop looking back to the television across the room. 'Name the time and I'm there with a case of beer. How's your mom?'

'On the mend, thank the Lord. It was in His hands for a while, but He answered our prayers,' Irena replied. 'That's why Randy and Lori are visiting for a few days.'

'That'll be nice for her.'

'Horrible business, ain't it?' Irena pointed a red-tipped finger at the screen. 'That poor young woman almost stabbed to death in her own home.'

Konrad pursed his lips and shook his head. 'Yeah. Horrible, right?'

'Apparently she has children and everything,' Mike said. He squinted at the screen. 'I hope those poor little kiddies didn't see nothing of what happened to their mommy.'

'Did you see the cops put out that statement earlier?' Irena continued when Mike paused for breath. 'An attempted murder and drugs on the doorstep? Jeez, I thought this was a safe neighbourhood to see out or retirement. Maybe we'll have to rethink–'

An unexpected gust of wind whipped through the trees and silenced her onslaught. 'Kind of,' Konrad said before she resumed. 'I was doing the dishes and only heard a snippet of it.'

'They've got the FBI in. That means they must be taking it real serious to get those guys involved.' Dale's tone sounded earnest, his trust in the American judicial system never having any reason to falter. 'Perhaps there's more to it than they're saying.'

'That's obvious,' Irena replied. She gave an exasperated shake of her head. 'They never tell you everything until after they've caught their man. What do *you* think, Dale?'

Konrad shook his head for a second time. 'Like you said, it's horrible. Let's hope they catch whoever's responsible soon, then we can stop worrying.'

'So, we'll see you Friday evening, Dale?' Mike reached a clenched fist towards the cabin. It bumped with Konrad's, a signal all was good in the world.

'Sounds totally awesome, man. Thanks. Can't wait.'

Irena checked her slim gold watch. 'Seven o'clock do you?'

He nodded. 'Seven's sweet.'

****

9.56pm – PDT
Kingsbury, Nevada

'How was it?' Studdert called, the jangle of keys in the entryway confirming the faint slam of a car door had indeed been Sam's return from Reno airport.

Sam pushed the door open and. kicked off his shoes. 'Surprisingly civilised' he replied and walked across to the kitchen. 'Did the kids behave themselves for Uncle Joe?'

'They sure did,' Studdert said. He leaned over the back of the couch and caught Sam's eye. 'I thought you said you and her got along okay.'

'We do,' Sam replied. He lifted the kettle and flipped open the lid. 'Carolyn and the rest of Anna's family have always been great; I've been very fortunate in that respect. Let's face it though, her daughter's lucky to be alive and, if we're correct, it's my fault.'

Studdert's expression hardened. 'I'm not getting into that again,' he said. 'The usual, please. Is she at the hospital?'

'Yeah, I dropped her off. Because she's flown in from out of state, they've waived normal visiting hours for tonight. I said I'd go back at eleven to pick her up.'

'How much does she know?'

'Everything,' Sam replied. 'Including this afternoon's disaster. I'm not going to hide stuff from her. It would sound worse if I let her find out from Anna.'

Studdert swung his legs off the couch and kneaded the occasional reminder of a long-ago college football injury in his lower back. 'Have you seen Anna since you told her?'

'No, I thought it best to give her some space,' Sam said. He pulled the fridge door open and grabbed a carton of milk. 'Though I did ask Carolyn to tell Anna I'll be there tomorrow.'

'How did Carolyn react to everything that's happened?'

Sam shrugged. 'She's been quite rational about it all. I'd say she's more upset we weren't allowed to tell her any details about exactly why we had to move and where we were going.' He poured a generous slug of milk into the extra-strong coffee he'd made for himself and took a hesitant sip. 'She wants to take the kids out in the morning so Anna and I can have time alone to talk.'

'That must be a relief?' Joe said. He placed his drink on the countertop and narrowed one eye. 'You need somewhere proper to sleep tonight, Sam. You must be exhausted.'

'The sofa's fine, honestly.' Sam eyed its thick seat cushions and the newly purchased deep red throw draped over the back. 'The kids need their own rooms, the guest room's got your stuff in it and Carolyn's in the main bedroom.'

Studdert stared at Sam's hip, knowing he'd have at least one weapon concealed beneath his polo shirt. 'We've got an armed cop outside. You don't need to protect us.'

'I'm not. A couple of whiskeys when I get in and I'll be well away all night.'

'If you say so.'

'Don't be going all profiler on me, Joe!' Sam replied. 'Has there been any response to the appeal yet?'

Studdert shook his head and stared into nothing through a nearby window. 'Just a couple of tweakers falling out over whose turn it is to buy the next fix.' He picked up his half-finished black coffee. 'It's a big decision to drop a dime, especially if you're not totally sure. Unless someone's life's in immediate danger, they're not going to rush into anything. He grinned at the audible rumble from Sam's stomach. 'Don't tell me you're hungry?'

Sam rubbed circles above his waist, doubting this would suffice as an apology for not eating since breakfast. 'I suppose I've just been so preoccupied with things today...' He forced a grin. 'This is one of those times I wish there was a proper chippy on the corner.'

'As in fish and chips?'

Sam remembered Studdert telling him that his biennial journeys across the Atlantic were a convenient excuse to combine an overseas vacation and a visit to his paternal relatives. 'Is that what got you into the Bureau? Being bilingual?' he asked, enjoying the kind of banter they'd regularly shared until last summer.

'Worked for you, didn't it?' he replied with a light-hearted punch to Sam's upper arm. 'Mom's parents were also from the UK, so I guess that makes me as much a Limey as you.'

'You poor bastard!' Sam smiled and searched the half-empty cupboards for something quick and easy to prepare. 'I really appreciate all this, Joe. I owe you big time.'

Studdert nodded and pushed his empty cup back to Sam. 'Don't you worry, I'll be the first to call in a favour when we catch him.'

Chapter 11 – Monday 7th September 2009

Masters ignored the ping of a newly-arrived email and reached for a Danish pastry. A full evidence board in the conference room's furthest corner slipped in and out of focus as he chewed, barely tasting the cinnamon swirl's sweetness. Special Agent Matt Jessop, Sacramento-based up until July, selected the largest of the last pair and thanked Masters with a weary smile. Three days of frantic activity meant exhaustion's grasp continued to tighten around both men, irrespective of the night's sleep they'd managed to grab in a downtown motel. Stateline's resident agency was usually deemed too small to be staffed overnight, meaning that three agents were drafted in from Sacramento and Reno on a daily basis to cover the communities surrounding Lake Tahoe.

Jessop swallowed the last of his coffee. 'Did you get another tip?' He set down the cup and watched Masters shake his head. 'Never fails to surprise me how many folks nearer home think law enforcement in this neck of the woods is a cinch. I love seeing their faces when I tell them beauty's only skin deep.'

'It's like that in most tourist towns,' Masters replied. 'We've gotten ourselves a couple of murders and the usual assaults and drug-related crimes over the years. Considering the number of folk passing through, it could be one hell of a lot worse.' He tapped the computer's mouse on the desk. 'C'mon, you useless piece of crap; let's solve this case so I can go home and get some more shut-eye.'

Jessop picked out a plump raisin from his Danish pastry and rolled it between his fingers. 'That phone call from Zephyr Cove sounded interesting, though I don't think it's Kratz.'

'The weird guy and the even weirder guy next door?'

Jessop nodded, dropped the dried fruit into his mouth and pondered their latest tip, left by a male caller from the small lakeside community three miles to the north. In a lengthy message, the man disputed his neighbours' claim to run a construction firm from the adjacent sprawling property. An almost total absence of diurnal activity apparently formed a stark contrast to the couple's nocturnal habits, which by all accounts involved keeping the lights on until daybreak and regular strange noises emanating from the garage. The informant concluded by sharing his wife's theory that the neighbour could only afford to reside there because his non-existent construction business provided cover for a money-laundering scam, probably due to the manufacture and sale of *illegal drugs*.

Masters raised a dubious eyebrow. 'We can't rule anything out of this investigation. I'd guess there's been some kind of dispute and he's trying to drop this guy in the shit. I need you to check out his tax and employment records, and I'll also send a pair of uniforms – minus their uniforms – to walk the area.'

Jessop topped up their coffee from an almost empty carafe. 'They'll be suitably attired?'

'Yeah, the last thing we want is the phone ringing off the hook with reports of two creepers flashing their junk around the neighbourhood.' Masters picked up a plaited pecan twist and took a large bite. 'Damn, that's another awesome way to start the day.'

Jessop chuckled. 'The idea of a couple of perverts on the loose?'

'Carbs can solve a whole lot of problems,' Masters replied. He grabbed the mouse again and moved the cursor across the page, relieved to see it regain its function. 'Looks like we've gotten ourselves a new lead here.'

'More drug kingpins in the 'burbs rearing their ugly heads already?'

The words on the screen succeed where caffeine had failed. 'It's from the DNA lab. The skin under Anna Bury's fingernails yielded a positive identification.' Masters paused for effect. 'It's the same profile as the one already identified as Konrad Kratz's!'

Jessop left his seat faster than he'd returned to it and stared at the computer. 'Is it watertight?' he asked, unsure whether to believe that a case that had consumed so many days and nights may possibly be solved in days or, if the last pieces of the puzzle fell into place, maybe a matter of hours.

'This profile totally matched the one obtained from both his homes, which in turn was an exact fifty-fifty match to the baby girl he fathered *and* a partial match to his paternal uncle,' Masters replied. He took another bite of the twist and scrolled through four more emails he'd received overnight. 'We've gotten some weak possible leads, *if* he's still in the area. People coming and going from a house at weird hours, flashy cars way beyond the owners' earning capacity and yet another place keeping their lights on at all hours of the night.'

'Is there anything that points directly to Kratz?'

'Nothing specific.' Masters turned to the map pinned next to the evidence board and his gaze flitted around Lake Tahoe's shoreline, wishing the answer to their fugitive's whereabouts would magically appear. 'We need a guy who disappears for weeks on end and the dates fit with his filming schedule, and maybe a recent change of car.'

Jessop frowned. 'Why the car?'

'He usually drove a BMW, and the detectives in Glendale also found an older Honda sedan at his home. They think that's what he used if he wanted to go somewhere and stay under the radar. Would you be driving either of those now if you were Konrad Kratz?'

'There's the plates,' Jessop said. 'Surely any random police check will lead back to him?'

'Let's say it's likely he's gotten some new plates made up to match an identical car in this area. If we traced the vehicle to Sacramento or San Francisco, it's not unreasonable to assume the owner is here on vacation. He–'

Jessop frowned again when the office door swung inwards.

****

10.46am – PDT
Barton Memorial Hospital, South Lake Tahoe, California

Sam felt vindicated by Masters' revelation, confirming Kratz's long-term vendetta was neither a figment of his imagination nor a product of last summer's head injury. The temperature inside the parked Saab increased, swelling beads of sweat on his forehead until they merged into a watery pearl which veered past the top of his nose and spread across his cheek. No wonder there were regular appeals not to leave your dog, or child for that matter...

Who the hell would do such a fucking stupid thing?

...unattended in a vehicle during the sunny summer months. He cracked open the driver's door, inviting cooler air from outside to envelop his clammy skin. The vehicle's leather seats moulded around Sam's tired body and he closed his eyes, determined not to enter the hospital until a zen-like calm descended. It wouldn't do Anna any good to see him riled, he thought; better to think nice thoughts and try to relax. If he'd been this embittered five years ago he doubted their relationship would have got off the ground, let alone lasted.

A wailing ambulance siren jolted Sam from his memories of the night they'd finally got together and the following carefree months, and he forced his eyes to open. There was no point in delaying the inevitable and he swung his legs through ninety degrees to rest his feet on the asphalt. A line of parked vehicles separated him from the hospital's rear entrance and he registered shadows moving behind the double doors seconds before they slid open with a faint *whoosh* to reveal a young couple. The woman stopped and smiled when the man lifted a carrier closer to their faces and blew air kisses to the newest member of their family. A white blanket offered Sam no indication of the baby's gender – another faceless, nameless child.

The new parents checked carefully for oncoming traffic and scuttled across the parking lot to a grey Ford Focus beneath a large shady conifer. Sam tore his gaze away, conscious they'd mistake his attention for something considerably more sinister if they saw him. The prickling sensation he'd experienced yesterday returned at the prospect of entering the hospital – and the additional revelation he was the reason he'd found Anna less than a pint of blood away from death three days earlier.

Only partially fortified by a succession of deep breaths, Sam slipped through the doors and passed the café's animated chatter without a second look. The mingled aromas of coffee and an indeterminable savoury dish faded by the time he reached a waiting area, where two men from opposite ends of the age spectrum were seated across from each other, their noses buried in the free newspapers someone had left on the table. Sam took the stairs two at a time, his pulse quickening at the sight of the deserted Medical-Surgical floor's waiting area. He silently lowered himself into the nearest seat and glanced up at the panoramic photo of Lake Tahoe, his attention once again drawn to Fannette Island.

'Sam Bury?'

'Pardon?'

'I'm sorry, I didn't mean to make you jump. I'm Jeannie, by the way.' The unfamiliar nurse pointed at the adjacent seat. 'May I?'

'Yeah, of course.' Sam forced himself to mirror her smile. 'If you don't mind me asking, how did you know who I am?'

The middle-aged woman laughed and brushed a strawberry-blonde ringlet away from her forehead. 'Anna and I got talking during some routine observations and she did a great job of describing you.' She saw Sam's smile freeze and laughed again. 'I know, right? There's nothing worse for a guy than hearing his wife's been talking about him to another woman. Don't worry, she played nice.'

Sam nodded, suddenly aware the colourful selection of pre-packaged dried fruit he'd purchased from a local delicatessen still sat in the Saab's passenger footwell. 'How is she today? You know, after yesterday.'

'She's okay,' Jeannie replied. She tried not to stare at the dark circles beneath his eyes. 'Bearing up, I guess. She asked if you were coming to see her this morning.'

Sam rubbed a hand over his aching forehead and sighed. 'I didn't think she'd want me to visit.' He noticed the surprise on Jeannie's freckled face. 'She was upset yesterday afternoon, and I mean *really* upset. She told me to leave. The last thing I want to do is make things worse for her, if that's possible.'

'We talked a little at breakfast; I think she feels bad for what she said to you.'

He frowned. 'She wants to see me?'

'We all say things in the heat of the moment.' The skin around her Jeannie's eyes creased when she detected Sam's relief. 'I'll leave you for a couple of minutes, then you go right on in. Don't leave it too long – you hear me?' she added, already halfway along the corridor.

'Thanks,' he whispered seconds after she'd disappeared around a corner. The familiar hospital scent followed in her wake, a reaffirmation of his hatred for their prison-like interiors that seemed intent on trapping people, at least until their condition changed enough to let them leave one way or another. An ever-present rotation of uniformed police officers stationed outside Anna's room certainly reinforced *that* analogy.

You've spent enough time in hospital over the past year or so. You of all people should know how shit, not to mention isolated, Anna feels right now.

Self-pity changed into an equally uncomfortable feeling of guilt. He'd left it as late as possible to face his own fears and come to the hospital. Didn't he think Anna was battling fears of her own? That whoever tried to kill her would return, or that she may never be able to carry another baby. His hang-ups surrounding green paint and a whiff of bleach were nothing in comparison.

The blinds at the closed door were positioned so nobody could see in or out of the room unless they crouched to find a gap. Sam watched Anna flicking through a magazine he'd brought in the day before, her eyes seeing the page, but not its words. He reached for the door handle, ignored the tremor in his hand and entered the room.

'Hey,' he said softly, unsure whether to close the distance between them. Anna set down the magazine and looked him up and down, her face unnerving in its indifference.

'Hey yourself,' she replied. 'You okay?'

He nodded and took the gradual softening of her features as an invitation to pull up a chair beside her bed. 'You?'

Her fragile smile caused the hairs on his exposed arms to rise. 'Been better, I guess.'

'Anna–'

'Let me go first,' she interrupted. 'Yesterday... God, it was like it wasn't happening to me and the words you said were being spoken about someone else, not me. I mean, this time yesterday I wasn't pregnant.' Her words tripped over themselves in her desperation to offload. 'What I mean is I didn't know and then by the time I found out I had been it was all too late to do anything to stop it from happening.'

Sam clasped his hands around hers. 'It's not your fault,' he said. 'I should've told you in a more sensitive way.'

'I'm sorry.' She continued to stare at the rumpled green blanket.

Sam frowned and shook his head. 'Whatever for?' he spluttered, incredulous Anna believed herself responsible. 'You were upset about something you feel you should've been able to stop, but you need to accept it was way beyond your control.'

'Maybe, but that doesn't make it right to take it out on you.' Anna resumed eye contact. 'There was a lot of time for me to think last night.'

'Did it help?' He clasped her hands more tightly so she couldn't draw away.

'A little,' she replied. 'I realise we didn't plan to have a third child, especially so soon after John. But, something good could have come out of this shitty situation: that life goes on, irrespective of what happens to you.'

Sam tentatively stroked her arm and failed to swallow down the lump in his throat. 'You're right,' he said, unsure how to comfort her without adding to her pain.

'Except life got taken away before it really began. I didn't know it had begun and then it ended, and our kids will never meet their little brother or sister. I was never given the chance to know this baby and whisper to her that although she hadn't been planned it didn't mean she was any the less loved or wanted.' Anna extricated the hand still connected to the IV she hoped to be freed from later that day. 'I so wish we'd met her,' she added, her voice choking on the final word. "She'd have been so beautiful.'

'We'll never forget her and who she might have become.' Sam wondered if it would ever be the right time to share his premonition the child would have been a little brother for John and Angela. He'd keep those thoughts to himself, determined Anna should take the smallest degree of comfort from anything. 'When we're back home, and I mean in Golden, we'll do something; maybe plant a tree in the back yard in her memory? There must be something that flowers in late spring.'

'Gramps grew crab apple trees in their back yard,' Anna said. She thought back to childhood visits to her grandparents' home on Boulder's western edge. 'They flowered around April or May. Dolgo, I think the variety was called. Mom used to take us up there and we'd pick some of the flowers, then later in the year we'd help Grandma collect the fruit and she'd cook up huge vats of crab apple jelly. The whole family was eating it for weeks, and even the folk in *our* neighbourhood got where they'd politely decline another couple of jars.'

Her words faded and they lapsed into silence, the air heavy with suppressed emotion as a faint ticking sound seeped through the room, the slow passage of time unable to instigate the healing process. Through lowered eyes Sam caught glimpses of Anna picking non-existent fragments of lint from the blankets, her fingers robotic in their quest to distract her.

'What's wrong?' she asked.

Sam took a deep breath. 'There's something else I need to tell you.'

'About the attack?' She saw him nod slowly. 'They caught him?'

'You fought back, just like I'd expect you to. They found skin under your fingernails,' he said, catching a glimpse of the previously ragged nails that had since been trimmed into a neat curve. 'The police sent it for urgent DNA processing.'

'They know who it belongs to?' she asked. Sam nodded again, once this time. 'Tell me.'

The fluttering in his stomach increased to a crescendo. 'The Bureau did all the checks and more before relocating us here, you do realise that?'

Anna's brows creased in a frown deeper than he'd ever seen. 'Who the hell tried to kill me, Sam?'

'Konrad Kratz,' Sam admitted, the words next to inaudible. He saw tears well up in Anna's already swollen eyes. 'Anna, they'll catch him.'

'Like they've managed to do for the past fifteen or more years?' she shouted, grief contorting her face. 'How many more people are going to lose their lives because of some piece of shit, who for some reason seems to have an unhealthy fixation on you and anyone connected to you. Why does he have such a vendetta against you, Sam? What the hell did you do to make him so pissed he'd want to leave our kids without a mother?' She watched him deflate, his shoulders slumped and head bowed by the shameful realisation he'd failed to protect her. 'What *did* you do?'

'Nothing,' he retorted through clenched teeth. 'Joe said people are phoning in with leads all the time.'

Anna snorted and folded her arms across her chest. 'Some leads. He could be anywhere. Again.' She glared at Sam and struggled to stop the floodgates breaching. 'How did the goddamn FBI seriously not know he's here?'

'They checked out where he had connections.' Sam wondered how readily he'd accept this explanation if the situation was reversed. 'Kratz never mentioned Tahoe, or Reno, or anywhere closer than San Francisco, where he filmed that movie. There's no paper trail, and he'd never been here on any kind of promotional visit or vacation. Absolutely nothing points to him coming here, and it didn't fit the geographic profile which suggested any hideout was likely to be inside a ten to twelve-hour drive of *both* Glendale and Paradise Hills.' He paused and pre-empted her next question. 'There's very little overlap, and it's in Utah. It was passed to local law enforcement as a BOLO, but the few leads generated proved to be dead ends.'

Anna's upper lip twitched in derision. 'I wonder why that is?'

'You know any kind of profiling isn't an exact science.'

'Did Joe tell you to say that?'

Sam jumped to his feet. 'How long are you going to keep this up?' he yelled, shocked by the conversation's venomous turn. 'You can't keep pinning the sole blame on me! All I've ever done is love you and try to do my best for our family. I'm sorry if you don't think I've managed and I'm sorry I've never been good enough for you.' It was his turn to see her cave, for massive shuddering sobs to swamp her narrow shoulders.

He watched the strength Anna had maintained since her frantic dash to New York a little over twelve months ago flood from her body, the trickle of tears now a relentless torrent. A wail of despair filled the room and her hands pressed against the two stab wounds that had almost left him a widower; whether to lessen the physical pain or as a response to medical guidance, Sam could only speculate. He cautiously wrapped his arms around her and she immediately fell against him, dampening his polo shirt until exhaustion took over.

Sam lifted a hand and rhythmically stroked Anna's tangled hair, the couple remaining in the same position long after her sobs subsided. A deep intake of breath eventually gave her the strength to raise her head and place the lightest of kisses on his chin. 'I keep forgetting this is just as difficult for you,' she said, every other word punctuated by a sniff. 'Sorry.'

'Perhaps I should be the one to apologise.' He smiled at her genuine confusion. 'About last year. I treated you like shit for months.'

Anna reached for his hand and laid a thumb over the ragged scar where he'd torn out a stitched arterial line. 'That's not your fault either.'

'Like *this* isn't your fault,' Sam replied. Anna's mouth opened to commence a counter-argument and he pressed a finger over her lips to silence her. 'We'll come through this stronger than we went in.'

'Like we did last year?' she said when he resumed eye contact.

Sam nodded. 'Yeah. I guess this makes us even.'

She squeezed his hand. 'I guess it does.'

****

Konrad crossed the cabin's small bedroom and stopped to peer through the solitary window, its bright blue blind swaying in the light breeze that crept through a narrow opening. He hoped the sky beyond matched the blind; even though the stuffed backpack beside the bed had declared itself waterproof he didn't want to learn whether or not its claim was true, if recent weather forecasts delivered their promise of rain further north over the next week.

Hopefully, the worst of the weather would pass before he reached Oregon. The first leg of his convoluted escape plan was to dump the car at the first truck stop he found and hitch an overnight ride from Sacramento to Portland. If the cops discovered the car they'd never definitely link it back to him. For years he'd hidden a different set of fake plates at the cabin, ready for if tomorrow ever came.

Tomorrow had almost arrived: the first day of the rest of his life. The second to last fake driver's licence of a previously impressive collection waited inside one of the backpack's pockets, ready to ease him into a new identity as Oregon merged into Washington and then into Idaho. Maybe he'd put down roots in Montana, or perhaps the nomadic lifestyle would suit him? Maybe he'd change? Settle down and raise a little family of his own. It wouldn't be the first time someone on the lam morphed into a respectable family man. Could *he* do it?

The loud, throaty purr of an engine catapulted him from these thoughts, his senses heightened. A door slammed and a peal of laughter he recognised as Irena's floated across the rough ground between their cabins. The pounding in his chest echoed around his head and drowned any conversation Irena and her husband shared on the short distance between the Jeep and their little forest sanctuary.

Today was the last day he'd be able to call them his neighbours.

Tomorrow couldn't come soon enough.

****

Carolyn Bouvier, a lithe, grey-haired woman regularly mistaken for being at least a decade younger than her sixty-five years, twirled her granddaughter around the middle of the room and smiled at her son-in-law. 'John's going to be napping for a while; do you want me to take Angela for a walk in the fresh air while you guys discuss whatever it is you need to?'

'If you don't mind, that would be nice for her,' Sam replied, his stilted voice conveying the emotional toll of that morning's visit to the hospital. 'Don't go too far, Angela.' He watched the little girl sway across the room to where she'd left her shoes.

'Honey, all we're going to do is collect pine cones to build a fort. There's thousands of them, so we won't be going out of sight.' Carolyn squeezed his arm and surveyed the limited view beyond the front window. 'He won't come back here, trust me. There's way too many cops out front for a start.'

Joe Studdert and local detective Jonno Heikkinen feigned outrage from across the room. Since Sam's family were granted permission to return to the cabin, he'd laid out everything he recalled about the case on the dining table and partially ignored Studdert's suggestion to focus on his family whilst law enforcement took care of business. Contrary to this advice, the men gravitated towards the table and refreshed themselves with a quick once-over of Sam's notes, always aware that the smallest snippet of previously overlooked information could solve the case. Perhaps if he said it enough, it would become reality, Sam thought.

Carolyn's warm smile conveyed the immense gratitude towards those trying to apprehend her daughter's attacker, something she'd articulated the moment they'd walked through the door. 'Come on, sweetie pie! Let's go get some fresh air and collect those cones,' she called. 'Be careful you're not feeling dizzy.'

'Okay, Gran-ma!' Angela looked through the window and clapped her hands. 'Can we go see Monty-cat?'

Carolyn nodded and rooted in her pocket for the spare key Sam had given to her. 'Sure, if he's around.'

Sam rolled his eyes. 'He's always hanging around, because he's greedy. It's not like Mal doesn't feed him regularly though.'

'It's called being a cat,' Heikkinen added, unable to forget his resentment over how his ex-wife pandered to her spoilt Siamese boy for the majority of their five-year marriage.

Angela waved from the doorway. 'Bye, Daddy!'

'You be a good girl,' Studdert said, his stern tone and exaggerated wink causing the three-year-old to erupt into a fit of giggles. 'Or Daddy won't get you that cute fluffy kitty-cat he told me you want.'

'Can I get a Kit-Kat later, Gran-ma?' Angela's words faded as she ran up the driveway.

'My dad introduced her to those things in England this summer,' Sam said. He reached into a stoneware jar he knew contained a selection of chocolate-coated treats and slid a pair of the four-fingered chocolate bars across the table. Sam ignored his now almost-constant dull nausea, snapped his own bar in half lengthways and peeled back the foil wrapping. 'Try dunking it in your coffee,' he said, inviting them to do so by example.

Studdert laughed and readily copied Sam. 'That's another gross habit my old man got us kids doing,' he explained when Heikkinen appeared unconvinced.

'It's good though,' Sam said, his voice muffled, 'and don't deny it.'

For the next five minutes they relaxed and Heikkinen chuckled over Sam's tale of Studdert's reaction to the smoke that had started billowing from the incident room's two-week-old printer, minutes after he'd first set foot in the resident agency. The conversation soon shifted, settling on tales of strange meals consumed on distant travels, and sometimes closer to home. Sam shared the story of the first time his Denver-based team took him out, and their unanimous choice to initiate their newest member into Colorado life with a taste of the Rockies at Denver's oldest restaurant.

'Don't tell me...' Heikkinen said, the victim of a similar prank by his Canadian ex-wife and her family.

'They weren't seafood,' Sam confirmed. 'The thing is though, they were actually pretty tasty.'

Studdert shifted position, pulled a pen from behind his ear and flipped open a reporter's notebook. 'I hate to curtail a rare opportunity to cut loose, but we need to start looking over places you may have crossed paths with Kratz.'

'Do you want me to focus on the California side of the state line?' Sam asked, fully aware of Studdert's enduring conviction that Kratz's hideout was almost certainly in California, and probably only a short distance from the Nevada state line.

'We have to start somewhere, and the Cali side is more likely based on how we think he used to drive here from Glendale,' Studdert said. 'Californian plates in California won't arouse suspicion. Has Kratz ever met Anna?'

Sam stared at a recent family photo he'd pinned to the fridge with a quartet of magnetic letters. 'No,' he replied. 'I suppose there's always a chance he saw a photo on my desk when we liaised for *H.O.S.T.A.G.E.* back in New York, although we tended to meet at the studios more often than not. I've always tried to keep work and family separate, but that seems to have gone tits up over the past year or so.'

'So, either as a family or just yourself, where have you visited on the Californian side?' Heikkinen asked. He pushed a street map of South Lake Tahoe closer to Sam, followed by a red whiteboard marker. 'Mark anywhere you remember, either with or without the family.'

Sam gripped the thick cylindrical plastic hard enough for his knuckles to whiten and pictured the places he'd visited over the past four weeks. Scattered deep red dots appeared, reminiscent of the blood-spattered aftermath of the violent crimes he'd long since become numbed to. Sam set down the pen and nodded at Studdert. 'It's pretty hard to remember every place. Actually...' He swiped the pen from the table and brought it to where he'd placed his left index finger on the map. 'I've just remembered I went into CVS a couple of weeks ago to get more teething gel for John, and there's likely to be other places too.'

'Let's start at Safeway,' Heikkinen suggested. 'Do you visit as a family?'

Sam narrowed one eye and scanned the streets leading away from the shoreline, the momentary blankness a manifestation of his occasional difficulties remembering events since the accident. 'I think we've only been in two or three times as a family, and nobody stood out. Same at Greta's – I've taken the kids for pancakes a couple of times without Anna.'

'Gas stations?' Studdert prompted.

'Same again,' Sam said, I suppose if he's working at one he could've made a note of the car's number and followed us home if he spotted us at a later date.'

Studdert's pen scratched across the pad. 'Have you ever been aware of or suspected somebody's been following you?'

'Only once, just after we got here.' Sam chuckled at his companions' startled faces. 'That was me being paranoid though, and a completely false short-lived alarm. Honestly.'

Studdert pointed to an isolated circle five miles west of town. 'What's this?'

'Kiva Beach. We soon learnt it's quieter than the other beaches closer to town and the kids love going there, I suppose it's the novelty value. We often take a snack or a full picnic and make a morning or afternoon of it. It's one of those dog friendly beaches, but it's extremely clean and has the bonus of a free parking lot – those nearer town make you pay.'

Studdert's tongue darted back and forth over his bottom lip and his pen sped up. 'Do you see the same people there regularly?'

'There's an older couple who walk their two Labradors there quite often. Anna said she'd spoken to them a couple of times after Angela made friends with the dogs.'

'Did you ever speak with anyone there you didn't know?' Heikkinen asked. 'Someone may have engineered a conversation and asked you about the local area, or maybe trying to glean more information about you or your family?'

'Let me think...' Sam laced his fingers behind his head, furrowed his forehead and thought back over their most recent visits. 'There was this one guy last weekend, I think.'

Heikkinen glanced from Studdert to Sam. 'What happened?'

Sam stared past them to the lake beyond the balcony and allowed it to blur into a deep blue puddle. 'Angela wandered away from us,' he said, worried they'd think he and Anna were irresponsible parents. 'She was still in sight though. The man had a greyhound, or something similar. My mum always says what sweet little faces they have, so I can see why Angela approached the dog. I went over, more to tell her to stop annoying people, but the man seemed quite happy to talk to her while she fussed his dog.'

Studdert sensed Sam's discomfort and leaned back to resume his questions. 'Describe this guy to me.'

'White guy, quite tanned, around my age give or take,' Sam replied, surprised he immediately remembered the man in detail. 'Quite sporty, wore a running kit. Similar height and build to me, and looked like he spends considerably more time down the gym than I do. He wore sunglasses and a baseball cap, so I can't really comment on his hair or eye colour.'

'Accent?'

'Definitely American. I think he had some slight southern twang going on, but I couldn't place where.' Sam wondered if unshared information from a recent tip-off fuelled their sudden interest in the man. 'Mind you, that's easy enough to fake for some people.'

Studdert mirrored Sam's posture. 'Did you see him again, like in the parking lot?'

'No, but then I wasn't really looking.'

'Do you object to me asking Angela a couple of questions when she comes back?'

Sam considered the request, reluctant to involve his daughter if she didn't have anything relevant to add. 'Only if she doesn't realise what's going on. I don't want her to know there's a guy out there that tried to kill her mommy; she thinks Anna fell and hurt herself when I'd taken her and the baby out that afternoon.' He gave a hollow laugh and walked over to the window overlooking the driveway. 'Jesus, it's like the Spanish Inquisition!'

Studdert smiled at another memory of his late father. 'Bet you didn't expect that?'

'Nobody does,' Sam said. He turned back and pointed at the kettle, satisfied Angela was engrossed in her mission to rid the road of pine cones. 'Do you guys want another coffee?'

The expected unanimous affirmative saw Sam return to the kitchen whilst the other men stayed seated at the table and silently contemplated what had occurred at Kiva Beach. Conscious that in his tired state he'd again served supermarket instant coffee to two hardened caffeine connoisseurs, Sam apologised when he set down the mugs. The good-natured disapproval he received in lieu of thanks lasted for mere seconds, all-too-suddenly interrupted by the front door swinging open and the rapid patter of small feet.

'I found millions!' Angela announced. She brushed her hands until they were free from dust. 'I put them by the front step.'

'That's so neat.' Heikkinen left his seat to crouch beside her. 'Do you want to help Daddy and Uncle Joe and Uncle Jonno catch a bad guy?'

She met his eye and inquisitively scanned the rest of his face. 'Is there a bad guy in here?'

'Not in here, sweetheart,' Sam said. He kneeled beside Heikkinen and gave his daughter a hug. 'We think you met a man who's friends with the bad guy, and if you can help us find this man he can help us find the bad guy.' He watched Angela consider his words, her growing pout a sure sign of reluctance. 'Will a Kit-Kat help?' he added, shooting a sideways glance in Studdert's direction.

'A big one?' she exclaimed. Large blue eyes widened when Studdert reached into the jar.

'Only if you wash your hands first.' Sam noted Studdert's covert wink and helped Angela clean and dry her hands before he let her unwrap the treat. She chewed happily amidst its shredded wrapper, her thoughts consumed by the chocolate's sweetness.

Sam returned to the table and slid onto the seat beside Angela's. Studdert and Heikkinen leisurely reclined against the nearest kitchen countertop, from where they could observe and listen to the conversation. 'Do you remember when you went to the beach with Mommy, Daddy and John last weekend?' he asked after she swallowed her last bite of the first finger. 'You met a man and his cute dog.'

Angela picked up the pen Sam had used earlier and twirled it in her fingers. 'It had a waggy tail. It wanted to be my friend.'

'Did the man tell you his name?' he asked. Angela chewed thoughtfully on a new piece of chocolate and shook her head. 'Have you ever seen him away from the beach?'

'This is real important, Angela,' Studdert said. 'Did you ever see him someplace else?'

She nodded and swallowed. 'At the big store.'

'Big store?' Heikkinen echoed.

'I think she means Safeway. Did you see lots of pretty bunches of flowers by the front door?' Sam asked. She responded with another nod and then put down the pen. 'Yeah, she means Safeway. We stopped there on the way back to pick up some groceries. Did you see the dog at the big store?'

'No, Daddy.'

'Was the man near us?'

Angela scrutinised the melted chocolate on her fingertips and carefully licked one clean. 'He was giving money to a lady,' she eventually replied.

'He was paying for his food?'

She nodded earnestly. 'Yes, Daddy.'

'And then he went outside to the parking lot?' Sam asked. He managed to hide his disappointment when she shrugged her reply. 'You're such a clever girl, Angela. I think you should show Grandma how you make pictures out of all those pine cones you collect.'

She jumped down from the chair, grabbed the remaining pieces of KitKat and hopped across the room to the sofa. 'Come on, Gran-ma!' she shouted, then grabbed Carolyn's hand and dragged her to the door.

'Seriously?' Heikkinen whispered. 'The chances of it being him are slender at best.'

'It's a start,' Sam replied, keeping his tone neutral to mask an embryonic idea that had implanted itself during the conversation with his daughter. 'Perhaps you guys should visit Kiva Beach tomorrow morning to see if he's there?'

Studdert couldn't help raising his eyebrows at Sam. 'I thought that's what you'd be doing, even if you aren't supposed to be anywhere near this case,' he said, surprised by Sam's sudden willingness to distance himself from the investigation. 'You do realise it's to ensure no evidence ends up being inadmissible in court?'

'Yeah,' Sam replied. He gathered up the three empty mugs and deposited them in the kitchen sink. 'I can't say it's easy to step back, but sometimes you just have it to do.'

****

10.48pm – PDT
Mattole Road, near South Lake Tahoe, California

'Do you have a stranger next door?'
Mike Saunders fired the remote control at their ageing television and emitted a hearty chuckle. 'Goddamn TV networks scaremongering again,' he said now the screen had faded to black. 'What they trying to do to folk? Scare the living crap outta someone so they don't sleep tonight? Stranger next door, my ass!'

'Well, there's always those vacation homes a couple of doors down,' Irena replied. She frowned when Mike heaved himself off the sofa and grabbed an empty beer bottle from its resting place on the floor. 'You turning in already?'

He shrugged in a non-committal manner. 'They're all strangers, those staying there. You can't really call them neighbours. I figure the cops just want to know if anyone has a regular neighbour they think is kind of hinky.'

'Lots of people don't interact with their neighbours these days.' She raised her voice so he'd hear her in the small kitchen. 'I'll bet that tip line is ringing off the hook.'

The bottle joined a number of others in a recycling box and the sharp clatter made her jump. 'I understand what they're trying to say,' Mike called back. 'You think you know someone, but just how much do you really *know* about them? If you're unlucky, you may have the next Charles Manson living next door.'

'They've got a point, Mike.'

He reappeared in the doorway and rubbed a nerve dancing below his right eye. 'You think Dale's set up some murderous racist hippie commune here in Tahoe? For real?'

'Of course not, dumbass!' Irena said. She eased past him and plucked a small glass from the drainer.

'He does come and go one hell of a lot, don't he?' A grin spread across Mike's tanned face. 'Quite the little hideaway he's gotten himself.'

'It's a vacation home, for Christ's sake.' She paused beside the sink with glass in hand, already exasperated he'd indirectly find humour in a young woman's misfortune. 'Quit being an asshole. Would you want a daily commute to and from San Francisco? Saying that, I'd sure visit more regularly than he does.'

'What the hell's gotten into you?' Mike's attention drifted to a framed photo, taken in his first year working for a San Diego construction company in the late Seventies. 'He's a young guy and he has friends in the city. You can't tell me he don't spend most weekends partying.'

Irena stopped the faucet when her glass was almost full. 'It's interesting he suddenly changed his job so he can work up here in the mountains.'

'Perhaps he's playing it the other way? Live here instead and keep a crash pad back there.'

'It's sure possible,' she replied. 'Have you noticed how different he looks? Short hair, glasses – I've never seen him wear a baseball cap quite so often as he does these days.'

Mike grabbed a couple of cookies from a barrel on the countertop, flicked the light switch and plunged the kitchen into darkness. He followed Irena through the lounge and into the larger of their two bedrooms, crunching contentedly. 'He said his hair was thinning. You know how self-conscious men can get if we think we're losing our hair,' he said through a mouthful of crumbs. 'He's getting older and his priorities have changed. Look how long it took for me to feel ready to settle down.'

'How much do we *really* know about the guy?' She turned back the bed's comforter, her tone serious. 'The FBI asked the people of Tahoe and nearby to think about who their neighbours are. He turns up from time to time; the cops think there's someone bringing meth into the area. Then there was that poor dear woman who was attacked in her own home.'

'You think he's a psychotic, misogynistic meth cook?'

'I don't think they're connected,' Irena said. She pulled her nightshirt from beneath a pair of flattened pillows and shook it out as Mike gave her an incredulous look. 'Why did they combine an appeal for two such important cases? Either they know there's a link, or the drugs part is a lie to make people think more deeply about the attack.'

Mike chuckled and pulled off his socks. 'Well, it's sure doing that.'

'I think they've gotten themselves a suspect already and they know enough about his movements, but don't know enough to track him down to his exact location. One tip-off from a concerned member of the community could blow their case out of the water. Seriously, who wants a meth lab next door?'

He got up from where he'd perched at the edge of the bed and rubbed a hand over the coarse stubble coating his cheeks. 'So why the sudden fixation on Dale?'

'It sounds real weird, Mike...' she fell quiet and shook her head. 'But, he does fit some of their suggestions, don't he?'

He turned away from her blushing face and lifted the curtain. 'So what do you suggest we do? Call it in?' A small gap framed the glow emitted by the smaller cabin a short distance from theirs. 'You really think he's cooking meth in there?'

Irena joined him and rested her head against his shoulder. She spotted a shadow moving behind the blind and wondered about the thirty-something guy next door, the guy she knew next to nothing about, the stranger next door. 'Let's sleep on it and discuss it again in the morning,' she conceded. 'It's not like he's gonna come murder us in the middle of the night.'

'Now you're talking sense,' Mike said. He planted a kiss on her cheek and whistled loudly. 'You get settled and I'll let Stan out for one last call of nature.'

****

11.56pm – PDT
Kingsbury, Nevada

The sofa had surpassed Sam's expectations in the comfort stakes. He stretched out against its plump yet firm cushions, wishing for deep sleep to blanket him. In reality, he knew it would likely elude him for the rest of the night. The new idea from that afternoon had taken root, an idea so simple he was surprised it hadn't come to him much sooner. It grew rapidly, engulfing all plans to empty his mind and claw back the countless hours of empty sleep he craved. His eyes remained open, staring at the darkened ceiling whilst he unscrambled the puzzle's final pieces.

Sleep all but forgotten, Sam threw off the fleece blanket and pushed himself into a seated position. The day's warmth had long-dissipated from the cabin, replaced by a light chill that taunted his bare arms and legs as he padded to the kitchen. Thick floor tiles leached the heat away from his bare feet when they made contact, the faint sheen on the floor's surface able to obscure the events of three days ago. A pair of tall glasses beside the sink reflected the pallid moonlight oozing through the window and added a bluish tinge to the room. He filled one of the glasses, lifted it to his dry lips and swallowed.

The water carved a cold path down to Sam's stomach and further sharpened his senses. He left the empty glass on the countertop, glanced across to the stairway and listened. The moon disappeared behind a passing cloud and he blinked rapidly, now certain a few short steps and one word would end all these years of looking over his shoulder. Maybe Kratz would have settled for just killing him, but what if he did the unthinkable and turned his murderous intentions to Anna, Angela and John; leaving Sam to endure a lifetime of grief? Neither scenario was a risk he'd be prepared to take. Not now. Not ever.

Sam silently descended into the sleeping heart of a place he'd never be able to call home, surrounded by the stillness that had already lulled the other cabin's other occupants into a deep sleep. He slipped into John's room and took a minute to gaze at his seven-month-old son sleeping soundly in his cot. Sam's guilt reared its ugly head again: guilt for how he envied the child's obliviousness to his mother's ordeal, guilt for the way he'd distanced himself for the first weeks of John's life, guilt for leading his family into *this* situation.

He backed out of the nursey and crept along the corridor until he reached the last room, relieved to see a slither of Angela's creamy nightlight peeking through a narrow gap between the door and its frame. Should he do it? Ask that one tiny question, the answer to which could enable his family to return to Colorado and live with a normalcy they'd never previously experienced.

Cautiously, he pushed open the door.

Chapter 12 – Tuesday 8th September 2009

10.28am – PDT
Barton Memorial Hospital, South Lake Tahoe, California

Sam knelt until he met his daughter's eyeline, conscious she hadn't uttered a single word for the duration of their walk to the unit where her mother continued to make a steady recovery. He took her small hands in his and his features softened as he drank in the image of a miniature blonde-haired version of Anna, wondering if he'd shared too much information during their drive from the cabin.

'Do you remember what we talked about in the car, Angela?'

The little girl's downcast stare reached the floor and she sighed heavily. 'Mommy's hurt, so no shouting and no jumping.'

'That's my girl!' Sam ruffled her hair and pointed at Anna's room. 'Go on, sweetheart. You first.' He nodded again when Angela turned back, unsure whether to push the door open. 'Looks heavy, doesn't it? Let's push it together so Mommy can see who's come to visit.'

Anna's face broke into the widest smile Sam had seen since she'd been admitted to the Medical-Surgical Unit. 'Hey! Is that my gorgeous girl?' she called, surprised to see Angela hesitate halfway across the room.

'Hi Mommy,' she whispered.

'No hug?' Anna's smile faded. 'Mommy really needs a big hug from her girl.'

Angela turned to Sam for her next instruction. 'Daddy said you got hurt.'

Anna held her arms out wide. 'Okay, a *little* hug won't hurt. Come on, Sam; lift her up.' She ignored his dubious expression and patted the mattress. 'I missed you so much,' Anna continued, hiding the discomfort produced by Angela immediately cuddling into her side. She closed her eyes and inhaled the scent of their daughter's favourite apple shampoo. 'Are you being a good girl for Daddy and Grandma?'

Sam nodded. 'There's been no arguments about bedtime and she's played with the baby. Yeah, she's been a really good girl.'

'Where's the little guy?'

'Screaming at Gran-ma,' Angela said disapprovingly. 'He's a naughty boy.'

Sam noticed how quickly the worry returned to Anna's face. 'He's cutting another tooth and is beyond grumpy this morning, so I decided to leave him at the cabin. He didn't even fancy eating his breakfast,' he replied. 'Your mom said she'd manage.'

Her eyes widened. 'Is it safe up there?'

'There's a uniformed officer out front, and the Sheriff's Office has stepped up patrols in the area until… developments happen.'

Angela lifted the thin, green blanket and pointed at her mother's hospital robe. 'Who hurt you, Mommy?'

'I slipped and fell in the kitchen,' Anna replied. She paused to swallow away the dryness coating the inside of her cheeks. 'But, I'm doing real good now.'

'Pinky promise?'

'Sure,' she said, and locked her little finger around Angela's. 'I'll be out of here in no time, just you watch me.' She swallowed again, entranced by the difference in size between the two digits. 'Is that your new colouring book?'

Angela nodded and pointed at the bag Sam had placed at Anna's feet. 'Can I draw you a picture, Mommy?'

'That would make me feel so much better.'

Sam lowered the bag to the floor. 'If you can sit down there, sweetheart, then you'll have a nice, private place to draw a nice picture.' He helped Angela down and opened the bag. 'You take your time and do a *really* good job while Mommy and Daddy have a talk, okay?'

Her attention diverted to the assortment of felt tips and crayons Sam had packed as an afterthought. He pulled the nearest chair up to the bedside and stroked Anna's hand, his concerned eyes circling her face before they settled on the bilious shadows across her left cheekbone. One doctor thought the bruise a likely result of Anna colliding against the granite countertop during her attack, whilst another suggested a punch to the face may be responsible. Either way, Konrad Kratz was accountable for the blemish; another thing he'd have to face the consequences for.

'How are you feeling this morning?' Sam asked. 'You're definitely looking better than you did yesterday. Got some colour back in those cheeks, I see.'

She squeezed his hand in return and focussed on the ceiling, reassured by the unidentifiable faint mark directly above her. What had caused it, she could only speculate, but it was a constant presence – something permanent in this time of uncertainty.

Sam listened patiently to her repeat the doctor's opinion that she would probably be allowed to leave that upcoming weekend, and how a lack of infection suggested the powerful antibiotics coursing through her system had fulfilled their purpose. She gingerly prodded her lower abdomen and reassured Sam things were less tender than the previous day, rueing that the effort her body now put into repairing itself left her exhausted and able to fall into a deep sleep at a moment's notice. He gently brushed a lank lock of hair away from her forehead. It appeared darker than usual, a combined product of the room's sallow lighting and her pallor since the attack.

'Did you sleep well last night?' he asked, certain of her answer, but unsure what else to ask at that time.

'I guess.'

Sam narrowed his eyes. 'Which means you didn't.'

Anna shifted against the pillows and sighed. 'Have they caught him?'

'There's a couple of leads. Nothing definite,' Sam replied, aware of a prickle on the back of his neck. He averted his gaze and watched Angela's drawing of the family take shape. 'That's amazing, sweetheart. Make sure you put lots of colour and detail on it.'

'Leads?' Anna echoed. 'What leads?'

'They're going to run background checks on all current and recent employees at the gas stations we use, and at Safeway and Greta's.'

She pursed her lips and shook her head. 'That's going to take ages.'

'There's a team at Reno working on it. They're really good, trust me.'

Now it was Anna's turn to look at Sam. 'You're too relaxed this morning and you haven't shaved.' She narrowed her eyes. 'What's going on, Sam?'

He held his hands up, palms facing outwards. 'Hey, they won't let me anywhere near this case. You've got to let the right people do their jobs. Joe's right, I need to focus on you and the kids, and trust justice will prevail.'

'I'm not buying it,' Anna replied, her suspicions confirmed by a faint pink blush spreading across Sam's face. 'Do you have any plans for this afternoon? Will you be seeing Joe?'

His shoulders rose and fell in what most would take to be casual indifference. 'Chilling with the kids and giving your mom a well-earned break. I'll be back to see you after dinner. You want me to bring anything?'

'Some good news,' she shot back.

'I'll see what I can do.'

****

12.56pm – PDT
El Dorado Veterinary Center, South Lake Tahoe, California

Intermittent howls and growls reverberated through a treatment room door, their volume sufficient to elicit nervous glances from nearby owners and their pets. In the waiting area's most crowded corner, an elderly woman poked her fingers into the basket balanced on her lap and whispered softly to placate a fluffy black and white kitten cowering at the back. The young man beside her smiled an apology for his spaniel puppy peering through the basket's wicker sides, only for the dog to swiftly recoil as the tiny cat lunged forward with a surprisingly loud hiss.

Sam clenched his teeth and inhaled deeply, the intention to calm his mind scuppered by a residual aroma of something unpleasant. A teenage boy at the counter stooped to pick up a wire cage and Sam wondered how much longer he'd take to pay for the rabbit's treatment. The information he needed must be here: there was no other animal hospital in town, besides the place he'd just come from. The chance the mutt's owner took it out of town for treatment was an unlikely scenario, although possible if they'd recently moved to Tahoe from another town in the area.

The receptionist, a sour-faced young woman who appeared barely out of high school, pressed the service bell twice in quick succession, struggling not to roll her eyes when the casually dressed man in his own little dream world appeared intent on ignoring her again.

'Can I help you, sir?' she repeated.

It took Sam a couple more seconds to process her question, let alone realise she'd directed it at him. He blinked rapidly, forced a stilted greeting and pulled his credentials from his wallet. 'I urgently need information pertaining to a particular dog,' he continued in a low voice, not caring that

236

her face immediately drained of colour. 'Perhaps there's someone I can speak to in private.'

She nodded and tapped three digits into a cordless phone. 'Hi, Julie? Yeah, fine. We have a... I wouldn't quite say a situation. Can you swing by the front desk? Yeah, that's great.' She repositioned the phone in its cradle and tucked a couple of strands of light brown hair behind each ear. 'The manager will be right with you, sir. Please take a seat if you wish.'

'I'll stand, it's pretty busy in here,' Sam replied, surprised by how much satisfaction he'd gained from her discomfort. He continued to ignore the woman whose name he'd neglected to make a mental note of and returned to his thoughts, this time keeping half an ear open for the manager's arrival. Did the dog actually belong to the guy he'd seen at the beach, or perhaps he was walking it for a neighbour? The latter seemed more likely, especially if Kratz intended to move from place to place in his bid to evade capture. A dog would draw attention from others and make him more memorable to those he encountered. Perhaps he–

A squeal of hinges announced the presence of another person behind the counter. 'Is this the guy?' an older woman asked, her voice deepened by years of heavy cigarette smoking. She disdainfully looked Sam up and down after the receptionist nodded. 'Julie Petersen,' she said, holding out an over-bronzed hand. 'How can I help?'

Sam retrieved his credentials for a second time and gestured to the door she'd come through. 'Can we go somewhere a little quieter and more private?' he asked, relishing how her skin blanched in exactly the same manner her co-worker's had done – quite an achievement considering the amount of make-up she'd plastered on that morning.

She nodded and reached for the door handle. 'Sure, my office is upstairs. Can I get you a coffee, or maybe something chilled?'

'Water's great, thanks.' Sam fell into step behind the woman and maintained his silence during their climb. After breaking halfway up, the upper flight opened onto a landing devoid of natural light, from where four doorways led. Julie pushed open the closest door and entered her recently refurbished office.

'Take a seat, please.' She pointed at two chairs on the nearest side of her desk. 'Sorry it's a little stuffy in here, the air conditioner's been a real pain in the you-know-what for the past couple of days. I planned to bring a fan from home but it's always such a crazy rush in the mornings, the kids being the age they are.'

Sam half-listened to her nervous chatter and absent-mindedly rubbed the centre of his chest as he watched her fill his cup from a large water cooler in the furthest corner. His gaze settled on the photo of two teenage boys in an ornate frame beside her computer and he coughed twice in an attempt to dislodge the now-familiar burning behind his sternum. 'I appreciate your assistance,' he said when the discomfort subsided. 'Please understand that this matter has no connection to your business.'

'No problem at all,' she replied whilst filling a second cup for herself. 'It's not every day we get a visit from the FBI. This has to be the first time. Is it a staff or customer concern?'

'I need you to look up details of a dog whose owners may be able to assist in an ongoing investigation.' Sam paused to thank her when she placed his drink on the desk. 'I've already been to Emerald Veterinary Center and they were unable to help.

Julie nodded and lowered herself into the plush leather swivel chair behind the desk. 'They're crooks?' she asked, inwardly amazed by the lack of emotion on his face.

'They may know our person of interest.'

She shook the mouse back and forth until Sam saw a tiny computer screen reflecting in each eye. 'Okay, shoot.'

'The dog's a greyhound, or maybe a greyhound-cross or similar breed. Probably quite young and goes by the name of Stan or Stanley.'

'Sure thing, if this thing ever wakes up.' She moved closer to the screen and waited for the machine to consider her search parameters. 'Yeah, we have a Stanley and a Stan. Stanley is a ten-year-old Yorkshire Terrier...' she said, chuckling when Sam cringed, 'and Stan is a fifteen-month-old greyhound. I can print the owner's details for you, if that helps?'

A chill seeped across his shoulders and down his arms. 'Please, and I'd also like the details for the Yorkie while I'm here.'

'You betcha,' she replied, almost too cheerfully. The printer released a second sheet of paper and she cautiously passed it to him. 'There you go, sir.'

Sam leaned forward and rested his hands on the desk, causing Julie to glance at the door and lean away from him. 'These people are not directly connected to our investigation,' he said, his voice barely audible. 'It goes without saying this matter isn't mentioned outside this office.' She nodded once and her jaw slackened now he'd got to his feet. 'That includes your employees, your family and the owners of each of these dogs. If anyone asks, you were unable to provide anything pertinent to the investigation. Got that?'

She visibly exhaled and cleared her throat. 'Can I, uh... help you with anything else?'

Sam looked down and took in the full extent of her fear. Finally, he understood why a minority of agents he'd encountered over the years bragged about the power afforded by a small photo ID card. He'd always discounted them as dicks; the kind of guys who suffered inadequacy in some other aspect of their past or present life. He swept the sheets off the desk's polished surface and flashed a smile. 'Not at the moment. If I think of anything else I'll come back.'

The veins in Julie's neck pulsed so hard she was sure they would rupture any second 'Anytime, sir,' she eventually said. 'We're always happy to help keep crime off the streets.'

'Much appreciated.' Sam swallowed the last of his water and dropped the plastic cup in a trash can. 'I'll see myself out.'

****

1.36pm – PDT
Stateline FBI Resident Agency, Nevada

Less than a quarter of the way through her two year probationary period, Seattle native Rita Sykes had settled into her new role at Reno's Cyber Crimes Task Force, proving herself to be a competent and versatile team member. In recognition of her diligence and keen to provide opportunities for new agents to widen their skills, Grainger assigned the tall, athletic redhead to the Stateline office for an indefinite period, where she coordinated incoming tips and passed details to the more experienced agents working on the Kratz case. Sykes accepted the longer days and additional commuting distance from her Sparks home without question, grateful to be involved such a high-profile case.

She leaned against the front desk and cast a sharp eye over yesterday's edition of the *Tahoe Daily Tribune*, its front page filled by images of a weekend parade celebrating the safe return of a young girl kidnapped eighteen years ago. Happy faces and pink balloons showed a community united in delight that one of theirs had come back to them. Sykes unconsciously copied their smiles and wondered whether she'd ever be able to comprehend the magnitude of the woman's ordeal.

The printer at the front desk's furthest end clicked twice and Sykes returned her attention to the last couple of paragraphs, keen to finish the article before she analysed the next tip. A flicker of movement registered in her peripheral vision and she startled at the sight of a man standing only a matter of feet away, not entirely sure if this was the agent she'd been introduced to around the time of the recent media circus in the parking lot. He'd looked different then; his smart suit and clean-shaven face radiating the professionalism of a man fully in control. Now his rumpled shorts and creased polo shirt told her a different tale. Perhaps she read too much into these things, although that Joe Studdert guy had been plenty impressed by how she'd interpreted some of the phone calls resulting from their live appeal. She smiled hesitantly and pushed the newspaper to one side.

'Sam?'

'Hi there, Rita,' he replied in a tone to match the smile plastered across his unshaven cheeks. 'Is Joe Studdert around? I really, really need to speak to him.'

She shook her head. 'He left already. Said he's going to check out some tip at Lakeridge and should return by three. Can I help?'

'In that case, I just wondered if there'd been any developments before I head on over to the hospital to see my wife. I'd love to be able to share some good news with her.'

Sykes swallowed hard and recalled Masters and Studdert insist that Sam be kept away from the case: partly not to compromise the investigation's integrity and partly on compassionate grounds. 'I don't know if I can help,' she eventually replied.

'What do you mean, *I don't know if I can help*, for Christ's sake?' He loomed across the counter until his face was less than a foot from hers. 'It's fucking easy. Has anything new and relevant come in since I was last here?'

She gripped the counter's edge tightly enough to whiten her knuckles. 'I can ask Jed if he'll come speak to you instead, if that's okay?'

His instant change in disposition threw her off guard and the silence continued as his cold blue eyes bored into her slate grey ones. 'I'm just going out back to see Jed,' she added, her gaze never leaving his during her slow, steady retreat to the office.

The mumble of voices behind the thick wooden door faded. Sam eyed the computer and immediately realised how stupid it would be to attempt to gain access during the limited time he'd be alone. Nearby, a red light flashed on the printer, demanding it be restocked with paper. He glanced at it for a second time, surprised to see a number of sheets in the output tray. The voices in the next room increased in volume as Sam grabbed the sheets and cast a momentary glance at the first one. Unable to stop his hands from shaking, he folded them into rectangles small enough to shove into his pocket. He'd seen more than enough.

'He says he'll be out in–'

Sam ran to the exit and pulled the main door closed. 'Forget it!' he yelled, the words barely able to penetrate its tempered glass. Sykes stood rooted to the spot, her mouth agape when she saw the blue Saab screech out of the parking lot and speed towards the main road.

****

1.46pm – PDT
Safeway, South Lake Tahoe, California

The Saab squealed into the supermarket parking lot's deserted far end, hurriedly reversed and came to a halt across two parking spaces. Oblivious to the stares of disapproval from customers nearer the store, Sam left the engine running and yanked his Blackberry from the glove box. A quick check of its screen told him he'd received a voicemail message from Studdert and he jabbed the phone and held it to his ear.

'Sam? I'm coming back to the office right now. Call me back immediately.'

He heard his own laughter fill the car.

'Fuck you!'

Sam switched off the phone and flung it back into the glove box, where it came to rest between a pristine map of the region and a half-eaten packet of gummy bears. He reached into his pocket to retrieve the sleek iPhone he'd received as a wedding anniversary gift from Anna. Despite his initial scepticism it was yet another gimmick from Apple, the device's appeal had

241

grown on him and its ability to access the internet away from hotspots regularly proved useful, especially since they'd moved to the area.

He pulled the folded sheets of paper from his other pocket, memorised each address and screwed each sheet into a tiny ball. A swift sweep of the parking lot and confirmation that Studdert was on the Nevadan side of the state line reassured Sam he had free reign to continue his plan. He returned his attention to the iPhone, taking only a few seconds to bring up a map of the area and enter the address he'd already recognised from his earlier visit to the veterinary clinic.

There's no way it's just a coincidence.

Sam slammed the Saab into drive, roared through a left turn onto the main road and accelerated west.

****

1.59pm – PDT
Lake Tahoe Boulevard, South Lake Tahoe, California

The dark blue Dodge Charger weaved in and out of slower-moving traffic, an angry horn fading into the background after it missed a station wagon making a right turn by a couple of inches. The speedometer's needle edged past fifty and blurred the hotels, restaurants and shops along South Lake Tahoe's main drag for its two passengers.

Masters' head ducked from side to side. 'Where the fuck is he?'

A pick-up truck moved into their lane without signalling and Studdert's usual calmness deserted him. 'Either slow down or put the siren on! Even if two of us are looking, you're going way too fast to see every car.' He watched Masters activate the hidden blue and red lights at the top of the windshield and then turned to an ashen-faced Sykes behind him. 'You okay back there?'

She grimaced and replied with a quick nod. 'I think so,' she said. 'I haven't seen his vehicle. Everything's happening too quickly to take a proper look around.'

'Blue Saab SUV, right?' Studdert noticed Sykes use both hands to grip the door handle. She nodded again. 'And he's wearing shorts and a t-shirt?'

'Khaki shorts, the kind that end above the knee. His top is kind of an off-white or cream colour, and maybe there's some red on the sleeves. More like a polo shirt, I guess.'

242

'He took the info I sent through to test the new printer before I left, so let's try the addresses on them.' Studdert turned to Masters and wished he'd checked the machine's outgoing tray on his way out. 'Mattole Road and Glorene Avenue: which is closer?'

'Glorene,' Masters replied, absolutely certain after visiting the area to interview a bank robbery witness last winter. 'Head straight down here, across the intersection and make a right turn.'

Sykes caught a glimpse of a group of carefree vacationers strolling along a sidewalk, separated from the cobalt blue lake by a waist-high wooden fence. 'What if he's gone to Mattole first?' she asked, captivated by the blue-grey mountains directly opposite and their small patches of last winter's snow clinging on in sheltered spots.

'Calculated risk,' Studdert replied. 'We could request Tahoe PD send any available units in the area?'

Masters shook his head. 'Let's keep it in house unless we really have to.'

'He's putting innocent members of the public at risk,' Sykes said.

'Mattole's a single track road and barely paved.' Masters glanced into the side mirror and pulled out to overtake a Jeep. 'The only folk likely to be in the area are those who live there.'

Studdert snorted his derision. 'Yeah, exactly.'

'And don't forget there's the matter of a federal agent taking the law into his own hands. How's that going to look? We get to Sam and stop him from doing anything dumb, find this douchebag who might be Kratz and the whole thing's neatly wrapped up.'

Studdert adjusted his seat and, like Sykes, stared through the window to his right. The motels at this end of town were generally oriented to the cheaper end of the market, and he was sure a couple of the least salubrious could make Norman Bates think twice before planning a low-cost Tahoe vacation. Numerous fast food outlets, budget stores and gas stations dotted the highway, yielding to open space on each side for a short stretch before reverting to their previous concentration for the approach to where Emerald Bay Road intersected Lake Tahoe Boulevard.

'For fuck's sake, man!' Masters muttered when the lights ahead flipped to red, realising there was no way he could floor it and get across seven lanes without putting everyone's life at risk.

'You'll have to use the siren.' Studdert maintained a steady gaze ahead. 'Who's going to do the honours?'

A harsh wail filled the air and startled Sykes to their rear, even though she'd pre-empted the sound. She reached for the gun above her hip and wondered if those extra sessions she'd put in at the firing range on many of her days off would reap dividends today. The car slowed to enter the intersection, where a familiar screech of brakes to her rear announced a near miss with a soft-top Mercedes carrying four young women deep in conversation, the quartet rendered oblivious to the Charger's attempt to cross the highway by a juicy morsel of workplace gossip. Sykes' seatbelt pressed against her ribs when Masters swerved to regain his course and then pressed hard on the accelerator.

Fewer cars shared the road here, and only a trio of other drivers dotted the short stretch between them and the spot at which the road disappeared beyond a gentle bend. The deactivated siren continued to ring in her ears and she saw Masters point at an auto repair shop and pull the steering wheel to the right. 'Glorene's down there!' he announced, barely easing up on his speed.

The Charger spun onto the narrower spruce-lined road and revved loudly. A teenage boy seated on a large rock outside an apartment complex watched it zoom past, responding to the unexpected disturbance with a bemused frown and a one-fingered salute. Masters' eyes remained fixed to his left and noted the odd numbers decrease in magnitude, then pulled up on a dusty verge and yanked the keys from the ignition.

'Should be a couple of houses after this one.' He turned to the others. 'I don't see that car of his anywhere.'

Sykes flexed her neck and peered through the windshield. 'We should check it out to be sure, see if he hasn't been and gone already.'

Studdert nodded, opened his door and took care not to hit a nearby snow pole. 'You stay here in case we need you to radio for assistance; me and Jed will check out the house.' He swung himself out of the car with an agility defying his years and strode up to a single storey cabin, its wooden exterior festooned with biker memorabilia. Masters exited the car in a similar manner and broke into a jog to catch him up in seconds. Both men shared a look and moved their hands to the guns concealed beneath their shirts now they knew they'd reached the correct dwelling.

'I'll do the talking, you observe his body language and all that profiler shit you guys do,' Masters whispered. They slowed to a walking pace on the rough ground used as the cabin's driveway. He saw Studdert grin and shake his head. 'Hey, I've seen all the movies. You people can read their minds, right?'

'If only it was that easy,' Studdert replied. A shadow moved behind the nearest window and he nudged Masters. 'I guess the doorbell is surplus to requirements around here.'

The weathered front door opened before they reached the top step, followed by a heavy aroma of stale cigarette smoke. Studdert sniffed a couple of times, not sure whether he detected a little something else mixed into the tobacco.

'Mr Lehman?'

A tattooed hand lowered a pair of dark glasses. 'Who's asking?' the short, muscular man said, his voice low and gravelly. 'I paid that goddamn 'lectric bill, if that's what you pair of jackasses came for.'

Masters raised an eyebrow and his credentials. 'Agents Masters and Studdert, FBI.'

'FBI?'

'You sound surprised.'

Lehman pulled out an almost empty packet of Marlboro. 'It's not every day the Feds rock up on your doorstep.'

Masters eyed the mixed-breed pacing behind a chain-link fence to the property's furthest side. 'That your dog, sir?'

'Rocky? Yeah, had that mutt since he was a pup. Going on eight now. Used to be a vicious little bastard, then we got his balls cut off and it sure chilled him out.' He chuckled, placed an already half-smoked cigarette between his lips and relit it. 'My buddy Hank says you guys should try doing that to some of the douchebags you catch. Calm the bastards down all right.'

Masters cleared his throat and nodded an acknowledgement to the similarly-aged woman who'd joined Lehman in the doorway. 'Have you received any other visits from law enforcement?'

'Well, the neighbours don't like it when Rocky barks too late, and there's the time I clipped some guy's mirror avoiding a speeding delivery truck. Didn't know I'd done it and then the cops turned up right where you are now.'

'I mean recently.'

'That was a little over a week ago. They were–'

'We mean today, like in the past half hour,' Studdert interrupted, his terse tone a reminder to Masters that they didn't have time to waste.

Lehman reached an arm around the woman's narrow shoulders and his Adam's apple bobbed up and down. 'No, sir.'

'Who else resides at this property?' Masters asked. He stepped forward and halved the distance between them.

'Just my wife here, and our two kids.' He noticed Masters shake his head at Studdert. 'We ain't perfect, but we try to get along with folks.'

'So you've had issues with your neighbours?'

'Just that half-dead asshole across the street. He thinks I'm up to all kinds of crazy shit.'

'Are you?'

'No way, man. Just trying to keep a roof over our heads and keep my kids on the straight and narrow. It ain't easy these days.'

Studdert smiled politely and nodded at the Charger. 'Thank you for your time, Mr Lehman.'

The two men jogged back to the sleek muscle car, their shirt tails flapping in the gentle breeze. 'Is that all?' Lehman called after them, unsure whether to feel relief or indignation.

'We appreciate your help, sir,' Masters replied and opened the driver's door. 'Don't go leaving town this afternoon but, in the meantime, you have a nice day.'

Studdert looked over his shoulder and winked at Sykes. 'You okay back there, kid?'

She shrugged and re-buckled her seatbelt. 'I guess so. Has Sam been here?'

Masters turned up the air conditioning. 'Doesn't sound like it and that dude definitely isn't Kratz.' He gunned the engine and pulled away from the kerb. 'Even if he *is* up to no good we can always check him out at a later date.'

'How long to Mattole Road?' Studdert asked. He drummed his fingers on the door handle and checked his watch.

'Using lights and sirens?' Masters eased the car through a U-turn and considered his reply. 'At least seven or eight minutes.'

Studdert frowned and decided to keep his increasing concern unvoiced. 'Pedal to the metal,' he said, wondering whether they'd be too late.

****

Until recently, Sam rarely neglected the need to appreciate all life offered, especially since his move across the Atlantic fifteen summers earlier delivered all the opportunities he'd dreamed of during his childhood in Preston. Sure, he could have carved out a successful career in the police, or maybe at the British Secret Service, but the parallel life he'd never know held little interest. Infrequent return visits across the Atlantic always reminded him of the person he used to be: a nerdy little guy with his nose perpetually buried in a schoolbook, trying to avoid Peter Umpleby – or getting his head flushed down the crapper by those who'd pissed off Peter Umpleby.

And here was life, doing its funny little trick of going full circle with the same person trying to ruin (or end) his life, although neither of them was really the same person they'd been nearly half a lifetime ago. Peter Umpleby had reinvented himself as Konrad Kratz, full-time global movie sensation and part-time serial killer. Sam Bury had reinvented himself as... Sam Bury, full-time federal agent and full-time family man. Both roles complemented each other; his rise through the FBI's ranks a product of his need to prove his capabilities matched those of his American-born comrades, supported by the wife he'd met purely by chance after an especially fraught case back in 2004. They'd built a comfortable and contented life together in his adopted hometown of Golden, where the small city provided a safe haven in which to raise his family; nestled in a comfortable spot between Denver's big city lights and the imposing Rocky Mountains.

Tahoe's own breath-taking mountain scenery beyond the richly-scented forest's feathery tips now failed to register. He drove along the single track road, drawn deeper into the woods by the decreasing numbers on the cabins. A film reel played through his mind; its scenes comprised of images and memories from his life, changing from happy to mocking and back again with each blink. From his beleaguered yet successful schooldays to the elation of his wedding day, the latter only surpassed by the births of his daughter and son. They faded in and out of view; his recollection of bringing his wife and new baby daughter back from the hospital replaced by a blurred image of someone leaning over him, their face obliterated by masked indifference to the indescribable pain ripping through his shattered body.

Sam reversed the Saab into a gap between two mature Ponderosas and turned off the engine. A light breeze whistled through the trees, carrying loose pine needles in a feeble vortex across the thin strip of blacktop. He cautiously alighted from the vehicle that had served his family so well in recent weeks and slowly spun around, his eyes and ears straining to detect any other human presence. The chatter of birdsong echoed over a constant hum from the highway and competed against the overhead power lines' frantic buzz. There was no crack of twigs or babble of voices; nothing to suggest he shared his immediate surroundings with anyone other than the local wildlife as the soles of his running shoes fell silently against the road's faded surface.

He passed a cosy wood-built home and noted the number on its mailbox matched the address provided by the couple who'd raised concerns about their neighbour and, according to veterinary records, also owned a greyhound named Stan. The limited information on the print-out he'd taken suggested *Dale Hargreaves* – the guy who came and went, and who'd recently changed his appearance – lived within sight of their modest cabin.

Sam stopped close to where a thicket of younger fir obscured what lay beyond and, heart pounding, tucked himself into the underbrush and steeled himself to peer through the gap framing a smaller cabin. Its compact exterior suggested only one bedroom, or that another part of the living space had been compromised to enable a second.

The slightest of movements immediately caught Sam's attention, the breath hitching in his throat when the cabin's front door swung open and a man carrying a gym bag emerged onto the front porch. The athletic figure descended a couple of steps to the forest floor and pointed something beyond the cabin. A loud bleep revealed the presence of a car out of view from his current vantage point and the man then placed the bag on the ground and turned around, enabling Sam to take a proper look at his face.

Gotcha, you sick son of a bitch!

The baggy jeans and a 49ers tank top were a far cry from Kratz's usual apparel, especially because he'd always declared himself to be such a vociferous Broncos fan, but there was no mistaking the man's identity. Sam had no internalised nagging doubts – the face from his nightmares loomed little more than a gunshot away. His hand crept to the fully loaded pistol holstered on his belt, hidden by the kind of loose-fitting polo shirt so many FBI agents favoured for casual summer attire. The larger cabin behind lay dormant and added weight to his theory nobody was home to witness the most likely outcome – or to call 911.

Sam wondered whether the couple ever previously suspected their part-time neighbour might be one of the country's most wanted men. The tale of the tiny cabin being a bolt-hole from the grind of San Francisco life was perfectly feasible; why he'd been walking their dog was something Sam could only speculate. He watched the man deposit a second bag, this one bigger and – by the way Kratz grappled with it – significantly heavier than the first, and tensed at the sight of him lose his footing on the last step. Muttered curses crossed the clearing as the backpack slid out of his arms and hit the rough ground, causing a taut seam to instantly rupture.

Years of training and cases blended flawlessly. Sam regained his composure, whipped the weapon from its holster and silently approached, mindful to watch every step and avoid the thicker twigs littering the ground. With his back turned and attention solely focussed on the retrieval of his scattered stacks of cash, Kratz remained blissfully unaware of the advancing barrel.

'Peter Umpleby!' Sam shouted now he'd closed the distance between them to a car length, 'Put your hands behind your head, turn round and stay on your knees. Do it now!'

'Congratulations.'

Sam cocked the gun and took a deep breath. 'I said put your hands behind your head and turn round!'

'Well, ain't you just the big bad FBI man,' Konrad drawled, amusement evident in his tone. 'What's it going to be, Sammy? Talk me to death or just take me out with that little toy you're holding in those sweaty palms of yours.'

'Do it now!'

'Okay, okay,' Konrad muttered. Still on his knees, he shuffled through 180 degrees and tilted his head to one side. 'Jeez, keep your knickers on, man! You're a bit wound up there, aren't you?'

Sam's grip on the firearm caused his knuckles to blanch. 'Put your hands behind your head, or I'll shoot.'

Konrad focussed on a large pine cone and shook his head. 'No you won't. If you were going to shoot me, you'd have done it already.'

'Look at me!'

'Quite the professional, aren't you?' he said, chuckled loudly and then followed the instruction. 'Did they teach you to talk like that at the Academy?'

Sam swallowed and narrowed his eyes. 'They taught me how to protect decent people from pieces of shit like you.'

'I bet that's the kind of talk you used to reel in that little wife of yours, or maybe it was the Rohypnol that made things easier?' Konrad spotted Sam's jaw clench and allowed a languid smile to spread across his face. 'Just how did someone like *you* get a pretty girl like that in the sack? She's quite a looker, isn't she? Well, she is when she's not bleeding out on your kitchen floor.'

'Shut the fuck up!'

'Touched a nerve, have I?' Konrad re-established eye contact between them. 'Perhaps I should have stuck the knife in again and finished her off. I could have saved her from having to put up with you and your shit for another fifty years.'

Sam took another deep breath and maintained the stare. 'So you recognise our relationship is strong enough to last? That makes you wonder what's wrong with you, doesn't it?' He noticed the first blink of confusion and pressed on. 'Why someone who's got your looks and your money can't get more than a one-nighter, except the teenage girl you knocked up?' Sam took a step back and winked at Konrad. 'Yeah, that baby helped us conclusively identify you through your DNA profile. Her gift to the so-called father she'll thankfully never know – her mother will see to that.'

'How did you track me down?'

'Followed the clues, used my brain...' Sam replied nonchalantly. He closed one eye and repeatedly raised and lowered the gun between Konrad's head and torso. 'In the past I'd have said that's where we differ but actually, Peter, we're not so different in that respect. We're actually quite similar in a lot of ways.'

The sneer quickly returned. 'What the fuck are you going on about now?'

'You see, Peter, I never previously realised you're not as thick as you look. Far from it. But, while I channelled my abilities into doing good, you used yours to manipulate people and destroy lives.'

Konrad puffed out his chest. 'I did well for myself.'

Sam shook his head and grinned. 'No, you didn't. Everything you've done has been built on a lie. You failed.'

'Says the kid who couldn't hack it at the local comp.' Konrad quivered his bottom lip in an exaggerated manner. 'Who went home crying to Mummy so she'd send him to posh school instead? Not me.'

'Answer me one question. Do me the honour, humour me, whatever you want to call it,' Sam paused when an unexpected gust of wind rattled through the trees and chilled the sheen of perspiration on his neck. 'What did I ever do to you? I mean, I must have done something really bad to piss you off this much; I'm assuming round the time we started primary school. I've always wondered what I did. Please, put me out of my misery.'

Konrad scowled and shifted enough for the discomfort in his knees to subside. 'You don't half talk some shit!' he retorted. 'Anyway, who says I needed a reason? Perhaps I just didn't like that snivelling little face of yours.'

'There's a reason for everything.' Sam's thumb stroked the gun's grip with a tenderness he'd usually reserve for Anna. 'The reason I worked so hard, won a place to study over here and was accepted into the Bureau was *you*, Peter. You drove me to be the man I am today, to prove that whatever anyone said about me, I can and will always be the best that I can be. Are *you* that kind of man?'

Konrad hawked loudly and spat on the ground. 'Yeah, I am.'

'Are you really sure?' Sam continued, the words falling like desert rain. 'Can you say you really deserve your admittedly now fucked-up career, the string of failed relationships that never were, a kid who'll grow up without a dad? I mean, I built my career all by my own efforts, my wife loves me in spite of everything you've put us through, our kids are happy and healthy and will always know their father's love. Can you say that for yourself, Peter?'

'Fuck you!'

Sam chuckled and lifted the gun again. 'That's the best you can do?'

'Do you have any idea what it was like for me growing up in Preston?'

'Jesus Christ, it's not that bad a place. Plenty of people live there and don't turn into a fucking serial killer.' Sam stared Konrad directly in the eye and felt his top lip curl. 'You'll have to do better than that, *Peter.*'

'Everyone hated me, no matter what I did. Kids, teachers, my parents...'

'So you killed them? For some unfathomable reason your parents actually loved you. We've spoken to members of your extended family. One of the reasons your dad took that job in Denver was to give you a fresh start, yet you still managed to balls that up, didn't you? That's why you pissed off to California and changed your name after you turned eighteen. Showed everyone just what a good actor you really *were*.'

'They hated me!' Konrad shouted, his twisted face whitened by rage.

'Not true, even if you did give them justifiable cause.' Sam laughed and shook his head. 'Because whatever you do, Peter, you just can't empathise with anyone else. It's all about you and fuck whoever gets in your way.'

'I could've been like you.'

'You really reckon something as stupid as that?' Sam's shoulders tensed as he trained the gun's barrel directly between his quarry's ice-blue eyes. 'And, I'm still waiting for you to answer my question. What did I do that was so bad you ended up trying to kill me?'

'You always knew who I really was. Who I really am.'

Sam frowned, incredulous. 'Did I?'

'I overheard you on the phone once, telling your wife there was something bad about me. At that point I knew it was only a matter of time before you realised.'

'You've almost fooled me into thinking you actually feel some kind of regret for all those innocent people you killed.'

'Perhaps I do,' Konrad whispered. 'If only I could turn the clock back–'

'Bullshit!' Sam opened his mouth to continue, to tell this piece of crap what he thought of him. The faint yet distinct sound of a car engine caused him to fall silent and his ears strained to ascertain its direction.

Konrad stole a quick glance at Sam and seized his chance. 'I'd have given everything to make a life like yours. Wife, family…' his voice rose an octave. 'Have you got any idea what it's like to go through life knowing there's something wrong with you?'

'You actually expect me to buy into this shit?' The engine's volume continued to increase, but to Sam's surprise he no longer cared. 'Boo-bloody-hoo! You think I'm going to believe you and then let you escape out of pity, don't you?'

Konrad held out his upturned hands and crossed his arms at the wrist. 'I surrender, no word of a lie,' he replied, now he realised the approaching vehicle had ceased to purr.

Sam shook his head and laughed, a hollow sound that echoed around the clearing. 'If that's really true, you'd have already put your hands behind your back and let me cuff you.'

Konrad nodded. 'I will if you don't shoot me.'

His gun still trained on his nemesis, Sam reached into his left pocket. 'If we're really that similar, Peter, you'll know I'm a man of my word.'

****

2.25pm – PDT
Mattole Road, near Lake Tahoe, California

Masters spun around in the middle of the road, swirling the surrounding trees into a tornado of greens and browns. 'Where the fuck is he?' he snapped, the words rigid with anger now he'd failed to isolate any sight or sound to indicate Sam's presence nearby.

'His car's there, so he can't be too far away.' Studdert fell silent and ran up to the Saab. 'Hood's still warm!' he called.

'Should we spread out?' Sykes asked, unsure which direction to take. 'If Kratz isn't home Sam's probably lying in wait. And, what if he thinks Kratz is one of us?'

Masters unholstered his gun and turned to Studdert. 'Based on the previous house number, that's the neighbours' place through those trees. Kratz's can't be much further if they saw enough to arouse their suspicions.'

Studdert and Sykes drew their weapons and broke into a jog to match Masters' pace. They watched him gesticulate wildly to the thicket Sam had used for cover minutes earlier, the determination on their faces replaced by horror seconds later when Masters gasped and stumbled to the ground.

'What's wrong?' Studdert asked, his concern divided between Masters' welfare and the group's vulnerability whilst they remained exposed.

Masters gripped his left ankle and groaned. 'Fucking thing's given way again! I've been delaying surgery on it for months.'

Sykes grabbed his arm and attempted to hoist him up. 'Can you make it over there?' She nodded at the underbrush only feet away from them.

'Jesus Christ!' Masters hissed, 'this really ain't the–'

A pair of razor-sharp cracks shattered the air and stole the rest of his sentence. The sound reflected off the closely packed trees and reverberated throughout the forest, immediately followed by a silent roar that engulfed the three agents and froze them into stunned silence. Time became fluid, until Studdert grabbed his gun and pointed to where the sound originated.

'Through there, Rita,' he said, waving them forward. 'Come on, let's go!'

Sykes and Studdert ran along the sun-dappled road surface, each footfall sounding like its own mini gunshot. Beyond the young conifers, a man leaned over another lying prostrate between the dozens of fallen pine cones decorating the forest floor. A gun hung from his fingertips, as motionless as the leaden air.

Studdert dropped to one knee and pointed his own weapon at the gunman. 'Drop the gun, turn around and put your hands in the air.'

The man didn't respond. 'Do it!' Masters hollered from behind them. He laboured across the clearing, limping heavily. 'Right now, else I shoot you in the leg.'

The Glock fell and the figure wrapped his arms around his torso. He falteringly turned towards them, his ashen face haunted by images only he would ever be able to see.

'Sam?' Sykes placed her hand on her own weapon and commenced a cautious approach. 'Are you okay? Tell me what happened.' She noticed a sinister fine red mist on his cream-coloured polo shirt. 'Are you hurt?'

Sam sunk to the ground and scrunched his eyes shut. 'He reached for his pocket, I had to,' he mumbled. 'He needed to be stopped.'

Masters, his gun still raised, slowly approached the prone figure. He crouched beside it and pressed two fingers to the man's neck, beneath which a crimson halo had already begun to spread.

The others stared at him, their silence screaming one question.

Masters shook his head.

Epilogue – Friday 6th February 2015

Strengthening winter sunlight cast an unexpected burst of warmth across the parking lot's expanse of newly-laid asphalt. To those employed at the nearby facility, the light giving its pale brickwork an almost blanched appearance was a constant part of everyday life in this area of the Golden State, although its intensity was unusual for the time of year.

A gentle breeze stirred and muffled I-80's constant hum nearly a mile to the north. From behind a small dust cloud roused by the wind, a pair of blue eyes drank in their surroundings; narrowed after being deprived of undiluted natural light for over five years. The sun's rays continued to seep into an emotionless face; a blank canvas now paler than at any time since incarceration commenced.

An involuntary shiver passed through the figure's bony frame. Too many months of minimal exercise and, in their opinion, a diet barely worth eating had decimated their previously toned physique beyond recognition. A thin, grey sweater offered little protection from a harsh wind cutting through the feeble warmth, reinforcing the notion it would be prudent to obtain a substantially thicker coat by nightfall.

It seemed unwise to remain in the area for too long, a decision based upon a sudden fear of being dragged back into the building where their confinement had felt eternal. The authorities now appeared convinced by the apparent remorse shown over the past eighteen months, knowing that the life-long consequences of that one split-second decision would never diminish.

Going it alone was the sole option, after family, friends and former employers hadn't hesitated in turning their collective backs on the predicament now faced by this once highly regarded member of society. As things currently stood, any attempt to reclaim their former life would be futile – but maybe there was *one* way to remedy the situation?

The time to repay their debt to society and repent for past wrongdoings had arrived.

43633847R00153

Printed in Poland
by Amazon Fulfillment
Poland Sp. z o.o., Wrocław